Tales of
King Cambrinus

Charles Deulin

Tales of
King Cambrinus

Tales of
A Beer-Drinker

translated, annotated and introduced by
Ruth Berman

A Black Coat Press Book

English adaptation and introduction Copyright © 2023 by Ruth Berman.
Cover illustration Copyright © 2023 by Michel Borderie.

Acknowledgement: "The Devil's Stewpot" previously appeared in *Space and Time*, 1995.

Visit our website at www.blackcoatpress.com

ISBN 978-1-64932-258-6. First Printing. November 2023. Published by Black Coat Press, an imprint of Hollywood Comics.com, LLC, 18321 Ventura Blvd., Suite 915, Tarzana, CA 91356. All rights reserved. Except for review purposes, no part of this book may be reproduced or transmitted in any form or by any means, electronic or mechanical, including photocopying, recording, or by any information storage and retrieval system, without permission in writing from the publisher. The stories and characters depicted in this novel are entirely fictional. Printed in the United States of America.

TABLE OF CONTENTS

Part I of this book is dedicated with love to my nieces:
Sharon Appelbaum Hoffmann, Margit Berman McDonald,
Harriet Sogin Avery, Meghan Berman,
and to the memory of Lisa Berman.

Part II is dedicated with love to my nephews:
James Appelbaum, Joseph Berman, Peter Berman,
Mark Berman, Michael Berman, Samuel Sogin,
and to the memory of Daniel and Jonathan Berman.

R.B.

Introduction

Charles Deulin (1827-1877) was a folklorist and an author of original fairytales. His work has been largely forgotten, in spite of its humor, sense of wonder, and love for the culture of eastern France/western Belgium. He published two collections of fairytales, *Contes d'un buveur de bière* (*Tales of a Beer-Drinker*, 1868) and *Contes du roi Cambrinus* (*Tales of King Cambrinus*, 1874). A third collection of his short fiction, *Contes de la petite ville* (*Tales of the Little Town*, 1875), contained mostly realistic fiction, but one fairy tale, "Pipette's Paradise" is included here with the *Tales of King Cambrinus*. He also prepared *Les contes de ma Mère l'Oye avant Perrault* (*Mother Goose Tales before Perrault*, published posthumously, 1879) an annotated anthology of the Italian stories that influenced Charles Perrault (1628-1703), the most famous of French fairytale writers.

For folklorists, the problem with Deulin's work is a lack of authenticity. Although he claimed (in the introduction to *Tales of King Cambrinus*) that he was simply writing down the tales he heard told in his hometown of Condé-sur-l'Escaut—and in some cases may have been doing just that—the plot parallels and long stretches of verbal parallels make it obvious that in many cases he was taking fairytales recorded in the Grimm Brothers' *Märchen* and asking himself how they would come out if told by French-speakers on the Belgian border. For the scholars of more original, literary fairytales, the problem is too much authenticity. His stories have the simplicity of tone of the oral tales. He did not aim at the artistic flourishes of style characteristic of, for example, Hans Christian Andersen (whose work he knew and loved).

In spite of this neglect, at least two of his stories are well known—but not usually remembered as Deulin's. "The Twelve Dancing Princesses" tends to be thought of as a Grimm Brothers story. And so it is—but their title is "The Shoes That Were Danced to Pieces." Deulin's catchier title is usually attached to English translations of the story, and in some cases, even when what follows is identified as a Grimm story, the version actually given is Deulin's. (Deulin's hero is a day-dreaming cow-herder instead of a forthright soldier home from the wars, and he worries about whether the princess wants to marry him, instead of taking it for granted that she is willing.) Another of Deulin's stories, "Misery's Pear Tree," although some of its incidents have cognates in folktales, is largely original with Deulin and this story has escaped into folklore, having been collected many years later, by twentieth-century folklorists, told orally in places as distant as Greece and Puerto Rico.

Deulin's home-town of Condé, on the banks of what French speakers call the Escaut, and Flemish speakers the Scheldt, is politically in France, but the cultures of eastern France and western Belgium are very close, and Deulin always seems to have felt himself imaginatively as much a native of the one as the other, sometimes even referring to his townsmen as Flamands, or to nearby French towns (such as Douai, in "Bold Gayant") as being in Flanders.

Although the territory of Belgium as a culture is as old as its neighbors, politically it was much younger—barely older than Deulin was himself. And it was a surprising choice for nationhood, combining French-speaking Walloons, and Flamands, whose Flemish language was close enough to Dutch for the two to be mutually comprehensible. It might have been expected that the two groups would split apart, joining their linguistic counterparts. But they were divided by religion (the Walloons and the Dutch mostly Protestant, and the French and the Flamands mostly Catholic). And each objected to being probably dominated by the larger and politically older nations they bordered, and each resented the centuries of battles in which their territories had been passed back and forth from one distant overlord to another. When the re-drawing of maps at the end of the Napoleonic wars gave the Flamands and the Walloons the opportunity to join together to make a nation that was large enough to resist being taken over—although still a much smaller nation than those of their neighbors—they took their chance and joined in a sometimes uneasy but so far lasting union. Deulin admired their bravery and their stubbornness.

Culturally, Deulin felt closer to his Belgian neighbors across the river than he did to his compatriots in western France, dominated by the capital city of Paris. Pipette in "Pipette's Paradise" is a resident of Condé, but the Paradise he gets to is a "Paradise for true Flamands"—a replica of Condé. And Condé in "Death's Godson" is described as part of "west Flanders." Characters like Cambrinus, King of Beer, or Green-Jeans, or Walnut-John may start out on the Condé side of the river, but they skip over it with ease, and end up located in Belgian towns. The Little Soldier, starting out in Belgium, travels to another territory hoping to win the hand of a princess, but he heads east to woo the daughter of the King of the Low Countries, not west into France, and his story ends with him at home in Belgium, with a bride who is a commoner, not a princess, and taking pride in belonging, after all, to the little-but-brave Belgian country.

Deulin's plots often depend on Belgian traits and provide origins for Belgian festivals, such as the annual slaying of the Lumçon, in Mons, or Wheat Marie's former festival in Valenciennes (in Deulin's time, on the French side of the border, but in the olden times of his story, serving as the capital city of the "Count of Flanders"). Belgian landmarks, such as the prominent hill of rock in "Caillou qui Biques!" or the titular tree of "The Wolf-Oak," serve as settings, and the stories provide origins for such Belgian landmarks as the fountain with the statue of the Pissing Boy in Brussels ("Mannekin-Pis"), or the figures of the lovers on the clock-tower in Cambrai ("Martin and Martine"). Belgian enthusiasms, such as the love for pancakes, waffles, and pipe-smoking, figure in several stories. "Misery's Pear Tree" stays in France, but the news of the terror of Death's absence is heard first in the towns of eastern France, then in "all of Flanders," and only after that in Western France and the rest of the world. He provided an origin-myth for King Cambrinus, a popular visual figure advertising beer who had no story of his own, giving him a history and plausible final location in the town of Cambrai.

For his humor, his love of his home territory and of the little-but-brave, new nation just across the border he identified with imaginatively, and for his love of the folktales he adapted to his home settings, Deulin's variations on the plots he found in folktales deserve to be better known.

With a Flemish expletive to emphasize his patriotic pride in his imaginative homeland, he closed his version of "The White Sparrow" with a claim which is comically both boastful and modest, all in one:

"The Belgians gladly retell this story. It teaches us not to scorn anyone. There's no friend or enemy so small that he can't be stirred by courage to defeat the strong, and even if Belgium is about as big as a fly next to an ox, the Belgians are not any less to be admired or feared, you know. It was the Belgians who took the town of Anvers, godverdom!"

In *Tales of King Cambrinus*, Deulin continued to celebrate as a culturally unified territory both his home-town of Condé, with the towns around it, in eastern France, and the new country across the river, Belgium. As a counterpart to the story from his first collection of Culotte Verte and his festival in Mons, the second collection supplied an origin-story for Gayant and his annual festival in Douai. He continued to use "Flanders" as a term that included towns like Douai, Autreppe ("Caillou qui Biques!"). Avesnes ("Love's Desire"), or Valenciennes ("The Maids of Wheat-Marie") that in Deulin's time were on the French side of the border, and he continued to use a mixture of stories set largely in France, stories set largely in Belgium, and stories with heroes (as in "La Ramée's Tale" and "The Champion Crosse-Player") who travel back and forth across the border.

A third collection of Deulin's stories, *Contes de la petite ville* (*Tales of the Little Town*, 1875) was published, and, as the title indicates, these stories are set in Deulin's hometown, the "little town" of Condé. Most of the stories he included in this collection are realistic, but one of them, "Pipette's Paradise," is a charming fairy tale and is included here as a fitting example by way of closing of Deulin's love of his home territory: Pipette's Paradise, which he finds located in the Moon, turns out to be a replica of Condé. Going the furthest afield for its setting, it is thus also the one that stays closest to home.

"Pipette's Paradise" also allowed Deulin to make a final exploration of a theme that amused and interested him—the attempts of a rogue to get into Paradise, or of ordinary people to escape dying at all. In "The Guerliche's Nutmeg-Balls," "The Tailor's Flag," "La Ramée's Tale," and "The Champion Crosse-Player," as compared to their equivalents in folklore, Deulin was more interested in the psychology of his rogues and how they felt about what they were doing. In both "The Guerliche's Nutmeg-Balls" and "Pipette's Paradise," he drew on local characteristics to resolve the plot—the Guerliche gets into Heaven through his love of waffles, and the unlucky Pipette loses Paradise through his addiction to smoking. (In his earlier stories such as "The Little Soldier" and "The Champion Crosse-Player," Deulin had portrayed pipe-smoking as an essentially positive, lovable trait, but by the time of "Pipette's Paradise," he was worrying more about the effects of tobacco on health.) Those who seek to escape Death entirely, such as Death's Godson, and old Misery, are not rogues, as Deulin sees them, but their attempts do not add much to their happiness. The Godson's partial escape gives him long life, but not much happiness, while Misery's success becomes a horror to the world and of no particular value to her.

For both those who see Deulin as not folkloristic enough and as not literary enough, it is a common criticism to complain that his work is not actually based on records he made of local oral folktales and/or not

10

original with Deulin, but rather that his stories are simply imitations of stories he found in the Brothers Grimm. And certainly many of his stories follow closely the stories he found in the Grimms. But even when that is the case, he made significant alterations. He might combine two stories, as "The Lady of the Lights" combines "Rapunzel" and "The Nixie of the Millpond," following the straightforward happy-ever-after of "Rapunzel" into a trial belonging to married life. Or he might split one story into two, as he did with "Death's Godson," making the Godson's own father something of a rogue in his attempts to cheat Death, and having him wind up with the dramatic punishment fitting his roguery that the Grimms assigned to the Godson, while the Godson himself, as Deulin sees it, gets an ironically quieter, happier-but-not-entirely-happy ending fitting his rather more honest dealings. Deulin might spend more time exploring the psychology of the characters, as he did with the concern over actually winning the princess's love (instead of simply winning the princess and taking her willingness for granted) in both "The Twelve Dancing Princesses" and "Caillou qui Biques!," or looking at the rogue's vacillations between defiant roguery and occasional attempts at honesty, as he did in "The Tailor's Flag" and "La Ramée's Sack."

And the Grimms were not his only source. From French fairytales he drew the popular figures of fairies and ogres—excluded from the Grimms' stories, as they evidently felt that supernatural beings with names that were French-derived-from-Latin did not belong in German stories. Like Charles Perrault, Deulin studied the famous Italian fairytale writers, and in "Love's Desire" he drew on both the story of "The Three Lemons" (by Giambattista Basile), and the play, *The Love for Three Oranges* (by Carlo Gozzi). Touches of Hans Christian Andersen appear in the use of nettles in "The Nettle Spinners" and the royal delicacy of a princess who could feel a pea even through the thickness of the mattress in "The Twelve Dancing Princesses." Occasionally he used medieval literary sources, as he did for the portrait of the Seven Deadly Sins in "The Inn of the Seven Deadly Sins" or the statue that comes to life to fulfill a promise in "The Viol d'Amore." And through it all, in the second collection of his fairytales as in the first, runs his humor, his love of his home territory, and his delight in imagining wonders.

Like Pipette, who climbed his magic beanstalk to the Moon and, finding Paradise there, recognized it at once as his hometown, by the pear carved on the belfry spire, Deulin delighted in his own provinciality,

11

laughing at the provinciality but at the same time seeing wisdom in finding Paradise in his own backyard:

"What good luck!" Pipette cries. "This is just what I always dreamed Paradise would be!

Ruth Bermnan

TALES OF A BEER-DRINKER

In olden times, in Condé-sur-l'Escaut, these tales were told by moonlight, on street-corners and at cellar-doors. They are dedicated to Augustus Deulin, a true friend and pleasant beer-drinker, by his brother and companion

C. D.

Cambrinus, King of Beer

I

In olden times, there was a glassmaker's assistant in the village of Fresnes-on-the-Escaut. His name was Cambrinus, or as some said, Gambrinus. With his fresh, rosy face, his golden beard and curls, he was one of the handsomest fellows you'd see anywhere.

More than one of the glassmakers' girls, bringing their fathers' dinners in, glanced teasingly at the handsome boy, but he had eyes only for Flandrine, the glassblower's daughter.

Flandrine, for her part, was a superb girl, with gold hair and red cheeks. The curate couldn't have given his blessing to a couple so well-matched, if only there hadn't been an unbreakable barrier between them.

Cambrinus didn't come from a glassmaking family and could not hope to master the art. For the rest of his life, all he'd be able to do was hand the unfinished bottle-shapes to the glassblower, without ever hoping for the honor of completing one himself.

In fact, as everyone knows, glassmakers are all gentlefolk by birth, and they teach their noble trade of glassblowing only to their own sons. Anyway, Flandrine was too proud to lower her eyes to look at a simple servant, as a glassmaker would put it.

13

And so it happened that the unhappy boy, consumed by a fire ten times hotter than the fire in the furnace, lost his fresh complexion and became thin as a heron.

One day, when he could stand it no longer, finding himself alone with Flandrine, he took his courage in both hands and told her what he felt. The haughty girl heard him out with such scorn that, in despair, he set his unfinished work down and never came back to the glassworks again.

As he loved music, he bought a violin to charm him out of his sorrow and tried to play it, even though he'd never been taught how.

Next, he took it into his head to become a musician. "I'd become a great artist," he said, "and maybe then Flandrine would have me. Surely a good musician is as worthy as a gentleman glassblower."

He went in search of Josquin, the old canon in the church-college at Condé, who had a marvelous genius in music. He told him all his troubles, and begged him to teach him his art. Josquin took pity on his grief and showed him the rules for fiddle-playing.

Cambrinus soon learned enough for girls to dance to in the meadow. He was ten times better than the other strolling fiddlers—but, sad to say, no one is taken for a prophet in his own country.

The people of Fresnes couldn't believe that a glassmaker's assistant could become a good musician that fast. So it was under a fire of non-stop jeers, one fine Sunday, armed with his viol, that he mounted the stage (if I can call his barrel a stage).

Although he felt their jeers keenly, he drew the first strokes of his bow with a sure hand, and led the dance with a strength and spirit that silenced their laughter. It was all going beautifully, when Flandrine appeared.

At sight of her, the unhappy boy lost his head, came in late with the tune, and wandered so far off key that the dancers, thinking he was making fun of them, pulled him down off his barrel, broke his viol over his shoulders, and, hooting and booing, sent him on his way with a pair of black eyes.

The worst of all was that it so happened that at that time there was a judge in Condé who handed out verdicts with all the precision of a grocer weighing out candles to sell—and making the weights on the balance lean to whichever side he might choose. He had a stammer, spoke almost entirely in Latin, mumbling prayers from morning to evening, and looked so much like a monkey that everyone called him Jocko.

Jocko understood the matter and had the troublemakers called up before his tribunal. The Fresnians hurried to the trial, each one carrying a couple of chickens to offer to the judge. He found the chickens were so nice and fat, and Cambrinus so clearly guilty that, even though the unlucky lad had already been given a beating in broad daylight, he condemned him to a month in jail, on a charge of assault and battery and raising a ruckus by night.

This was heart-breaking for the poor boy. He was so ashamed and overcome with sorrow that when he got out of prison he was determined to put an end to his life. He unhooked the nice new rope from his well and headed for the wood of Odomez.

When he came to the darkest part of the way, he climbed up an oaktree, sat down on the first branch, tied the rope tight around it, and wound the other end around his neck. With that done, he lifted up his head and was just going to fling himself off, when all at once he stopped short.

There before his eyes stood a tall man, dressed in a green coat with copper buttons, with a plumed hat on his head. He was armed with a hunting knife and carrying a silver horn on top of his game-bag. He and Cambrinus looked at each other for some time in silence.

"Don't let me disturb you, sir!" said the stranger at last.

"Oh, I'm not in a hurry," said Cambrinus, feeling a little less determined in the presence of a stranger.

"You may not be, but I am, my good Cambrinus."

"Hey! How do you know my name?"

"I also know that you're about to dance your final jig, my lad, because you were thrown in jail, and sweet Flandrine refused to enroll you in the great brotherhood of glassmakers." And, having said that, the stranger took off his hat.

"What! So it's you, Mynheer van Beelzebub! Well, well! Considering your two horns, I would have thought you'd be uglier.

"Thank you!"

"What good wind blows you here?"

"It's Saturday, isn't it? My wife is cleaning the house, and as I can't stand all that mopping up—"

"You cleared out. I can see why. Anyhow—have you had good hunting?"

"Pooh! All I got was the soul of the judge in Condé."

"Really! So Jocko's dead! And you're carrying off his soul! Oh, but you don't want to lose any time, Mynheer. Why are you waiting here?"

"I'm waiting for yours."

"Mine, my God!"

"Anyone who's hanged goes into Hell's gamebag."

"What if I don't hang myself?"

"That would be a living hell."

"That's hardly any better. That's really not fair, it isn't, godverdom! Look, Sir Devil, be a good devil and save me from that!"

"But how?"

"Make Flandrine want to marry me."

"Pooh!—that's impossible. What a woman wants—"

"God wants, too. Yes, I know. But suppose it's something she doesn't want—"

"When she really doesn't want something, the devil himself could lose his horns trying."

"Well, then, make me stop loving her."

"I agree—on one condition, that you give me your soul in exchange."

"Right now?"

"No. In thirty years."

"Done and done. I'm so miserable—but if you'll help me out, to top off the bargain, I'll get even with the Fresnians."

"Let's think first about getting you well, and the rest can wait. One nail drives out another. There's no passion so strong that it won't yield to a stronger passion. Try gambling night and day, and the love of gaming will replace the game of love."

"I'll try it," said Cambrinus. "Thank you, Mynheer."

He untied the rope, bowed, and took his leave.

II

The following Sunday, there was a great archery contest at Condé. Cambrinus went to see it, and so did the rest of the townsfolk.

The brotherhood of the archers of Saint Sebastian had put up, as a prize, five dishes and three tin coffeepots, as well as six silver spoons for hitting the bird. Cambrinus all by himself won four dishes, two coffeepots, and the six silver spoons. People had never heard of such skill.

Then, a week later, they were going to play tennis on Green Square in Condé, and in Fresnes they put together a team of players. Before that time, the Fresnians had hardly ever shone in the game, but even so, they felt no fear at competing against the teams from Valenciennes and Quaregnon, the two strongest teams in the country. The Valenciennes and Quaregnon teams were beaten by the Fresnians. They were angry, and fist-fights broke out in all the streets.

Cambrinus then bought a blind finch and carried it around with him everywhere, as the custom was among the Walloons. When he heard tell that there was going to be a great finch show at Saint Amand, he took his little travelling companion and set out.

As he drew near the town, he met up at Croisette with some finch owners, about three hundred of them, all going to the contest, two by two, each one carrying in his hand a little wooden cage, decorated with iron wire. The procession was headed by a drum-major, flourishing his baton, and two drums and six hams decked with flowers and ribbons, which were going to be a prize worth winning in the competition.

Cambrinus fell into step with them, and when the cages were set up in lines ready to compete, all the length of the abbey grounds, a lovely concert began. Each bird called out its cheerful notes as loud as it could, and its master, monitored by the judges, took a slate and a piece of chalk and conscientiously wrote down the notes coming from the bird's throat. The noise was so loud that you couldn't even hear the big bell in the clock-tower ring.

The Fresnians had laid a bet of three thousand florins that Cambrinus's virtuoso of a bird wouldn't get mixed up with the *p'tee-p'tee-p'tee recapio-placapio* that the second-rate artists were singing, and that Cambrinus's bird would repeat nine hundred times in an hour its rat-a-plan-plan-plan-biscuity-baskety, the true solo, the only one that counted.

The bird kept singing nine hundred times right through, and its master took first place and the three thousand florins, after which the Saint-Amandians triumphantly paraded their man and his bird, the one carrying the other.

Cambrinus set about traveling all over Flanders, beating even the most famous finch-trainers with his bird. And that's why ever since then the Flemish are as devoted to finch-fights, as the English are to cock-fights.

From Flanders, he went into Germany, and traveled from town to town playing in every game of chance or skill. Everywhere he went, the luck was with him. He was admired by all, but he wasn't healed of his love the least bit.

His never-failing luck at first enchanted him. Later, it only amused him. Then it left him feeling cold, and soon it bored him. In the end, he was so tired of this perpetual winning that he would have given the world to lose just once—but his good luck pursued him relentlessly.

He was beginning to feel himself just as unhappy as before, when, one morning, he woke up with a brilliant idea: "Good luck is a good thing," he said to himself, "and perhaps Flandrine will consent to marry me, now that I'm rolling in riches."

He went to offer his treasure at the feel of his cruel beloved, but Flandrine—an incredible result that would astonish maidens nowadays—refused him.

"Are you a gentleman?" she said.

"No."

"Well, then! Take your treasure away. I'm not going to marry anyone but a gentleman."

Cambrinus was in such despair that one fine day, as the light was failing, he returned to the wood of Odomez, climbed an oak, sat himself down on the first bough, and tied his rope tightly around it. He had already put the noose around his neck, when the green huntsman appeared.

"Humpf!" Beelzebub exclaimed. "I'd forgotten the old proverb: unlucky in love, lucky at cards. Do you want me to tell you a way to deal with love?"

Cambrinus pricked up his ears.

"Yes, you can lose, and you can do even better than losing your gold. You can lose your memory, and, along with that, the torments of remembering."

"But how?"

"Drink. Wine is the father of forgetting. Pour out floods of joy for yourself. There's nothing better than a bottle of wine to drown your human sorrow.

"You might well be right, Mynheer."

And Cambrinus rolled up his rope and went back to Fresnes.

III

Without delay, he had a wine-cellar built, made of big stones from Tournai. It was forty feet high and six hundred feet long. He stocked it with the finest wines.

He had casks set against the walls in parallel rows and he put into them to age hot burgundy, sweet Bordeaux, sparkling champagne, cheerful malmsey, bubbly marsala, ardent sherry, generous tokay and the tender johannisberg that opens the golden doors of dream to thick-headed Germans.

Night and day, Cambrinus drank he fruit of the vine in glasses from Bohemia. The unfortunate young man thought he was drinking to forget, but he was drinking nothing but love. How could this be? Alas! That's how good Flemish-folk, more than people in other lands, are defeated.

Among us, when the fumes of wine rise inside the brain, when the divine liquid fills the skull, like the lava in the volcano's crater, then the imagination catches fire.

At the sixth glass—it never fails—a Flamand would see before his eyes a crowd of dancers at his side, myriads of Flandrines jeering at him as they dance wildly, in endless farandoles.

So Cambrinus next tried to forget his sorrow in Norman cider, perry from Le Mans, Gallic hydromel, French cognac, Dutch gin, English gin, Scottish whiskey, and found that drink only fed the fire. The more he drank, the more it roused him—and enraged him.

One evening, he could no longer resist it. He ran without stopping to the wood of Odomez, climbed the oak, tied the rope, and, without looking at the world around him—to make sure he wouldn't change his mind—he flung the rope around his neck. But the rope snapped, and the hanged man fell into the arms of the green huntsman.

"Let go of me, you cursed imposter!" cried Cambrinus hoarsely. "What! Can't a fellow hang himself in comfort?"

Beelzebub burst out laughing. "I wanted to see," he said, "just how far a good Flamand's strength of will would take him. But now, after all your trouble, I'm going to cure you. Come, now—look here!"

All at once the trees drew apart, some to the right and some to the left, leaving an empty square, and Cambrinus saw tall poles of chestnut wood line up in long rows, encircled by delicate plants bearing green, sweet bell-flowers. A bunch of stakes lay on the ground, and three or four hundred women, squatting down, seemed to be picking the makings of an immense salad. This strange forest was shut in by a neat wall of bricks.

"What's that, myn God!" said Cambrinus.

"That, my fine fellow, is a field of hops, and the house you see down there is the brewery. The hop-flowers are going to cure your love-sickness. Follow me."

Beelzebub led him down to the building. Inside were giant vats, furnaces, casks, and boilers full of a golden liquor that gave off a tart perfume. Some men in blue aprons were engaged in an odd task.

"With hops and barley," Beelzebub explained, "following the example of these men, you are going to brew the Flemish wine—otherwise known as beer. The hop-flowers will give their scent and flavor to the barley-wine. Thanks to this sacred plant, beer, like the fruit of the vine, will age in the casks. It will come out as golden as a topaz, or as dark as onyx, and turn the good Flamands into gods on earth. Come, drink!"

And Beelzebub dipped a big pitcher into one of the casks and drew it out foaming with beer. Cambrinus obeyed him, and made a face.

"Drink some more, more!"

He took another swallow and another, and felt a sort of calmness descending little by little on his nerves.

"Aren't you as happy as a god, now?"

"Very much so, my lord, except that the supreme pleasure of the gods is missing."

"Which one?"

"Vengeance! The Fresnians weren't willing to dance to my fiddle before. Give me an instrument that will make them jump when I tell them"

"In that case—listen!"

At that moment, the clock of Odomez struck nine.

"What of it?" said Cambrinus.

"Quiet! Listen again."

The bell of Fresnes rang again, followed by the bell of Condé, and then the bell of Bruille.

"What of it?" Cambrinus said again.

"You're asking me for an instrument that forces people to dance. Here it is, ready-made. Have you noticed that each of these bells has its own particular sound? Put them together, put them in tune with each other, get their chimes ringing from two boards, one the keyboard and one the pedalboard, and you'll have a fine carillon."

"A carillon! I'll baptize this marvelous instrument with that name!" cried Cambrinus. "Thanks, Beelzebub, my friend, and—goodbye!"

"No, not goodbye, not forever—just till we meet again. In thirty years. Also, as I like to have affairs all in order, be so kind as to sign this paper with a drop of your blood."

He handed him a pen and a piece of parchment covered with cabalistic marks. Cambrinus pricked his finger and signed. At once, the hopfield, the brewery, and Beelzebub all disappeared.

IV

On his way back to Fresnes, Cambrinus noticed a deep, fertile stretch of land, out of the wind. He bought it and planted hops there. He also had built, in the village nearby, an immense brewery, just like the one Beelzebub had showed him. He crowned it with a belfry in the shape of a gigantic beer bottle, with a pint-pot and a quart-measure turned upside-down for a spire and finished it off with a golden cock at the top.

If a foreigner had come into the neighborhood to carry out the bizarre construction, people would have refrained from laughing at him, but the builder was born in Fresne, so they thought—reasonably enough—that it was crazy, and went back to making fun of him.

He didn't care, but called in some mechanics and clock-makers and had a carillon set up at the front beside the brewery.

When it was all completed, he constructed two big vats, one for light beer and one for dark, and sent out an invitation, for next Sunday, when the Mass was beginning, for everyone to drink a cup.

"Ugh! It's so bitter!" said one.

"It's terrible!" said another.

"Detestable!" a third added.

"Abominable!" the fourth concluded.

Cambrinus smiled in his beard.

That afternoon, he had some long tables set out all around the square. On these tables, he had mugs and glasses of dark beer set out, waiting for the drinkers. When the Fresnians left the church after vespers, the brewer urged them again to refresh themselves with a drink. They refused.

"So you don't want to drink, my lads," thought Cambrinus. "Fine!—then you can dance!" And he climbed into his bell-tower.

"Ding dong, ding dong," went the carillon.

Suddenly—oh, wonderful! At the first strokes of the bells, men, women, and children—they all stopped moving away and got in position to dance.

"Ding, dong, dong."

Everyone put a leg out, and the Mayor himself shook the ashes out of his pipe and stood up.

"Ding, dong, dong, ding dong."

They all jumped to the rhythm, and the Mayor and the constable jumped higher than all the rest.

Cambrinus paused, and then struck up the tune. Young and old, fat and thin, tall and small, straight-legged and crooked, lame, or limping, they began to dance beautifully—even the dogs reared up on their hind legs and danced, too. A chariot drove by—the driver, the horse, and the chariot all joined in the dance. They danced in the square, in the main-streets, and the side-streets—everywhere they could hear the chimes of the carillon. On the highway, the Condéens on their way to Fresnes danced without knowing how or why. Everyone indoors was dancing: people, pets, and furniture.

The old folks danced by the fireside, the invalids danced in their beds, the horses danced in their stalls, and the cows in the barn, the chickens in the coop—even the tables danced, and the chairs, and the wardrobes, and the dressers. The very houses were astonished to find themselves dancing, and the brewery danced, and the church. The town where Cambrinus was playing the carillon bowed to the steeple, and they joined in gladly. Never, since the world began, had anyone seen such joyous swinging!

After an hour of this exercise, the Fresnians were drenched in sweat. Panting, worn out, they cried to the carillon-player, "Stop! Stop! We can't keep it up anymore!"

"No, no. Dance!" he said, and the more he played the carillon, the more they jumped. Their heads were banging into each other, and the crowd began to wail piteously.

"We need something to drink! Anything!" they cried at last.

The carillon-player stopped playing, and the men, women, children, animals and houses stopped dancing. The dancers, one and all, grabbed for the mugs, which, surprisingly enough, had been jigging with the ta-bles without spilling a single drop of beer.

And so the Fresnians, getting a taste for it, stopped finding the new liquor detestable—quite the contrary!

After each of them had emptied three or four pints, they asked Cambrinus to start playing his music again, and they went on dancing the whole evening and half the night.

The next day and in the days that followed, the news spread, and people from all over came to Fresnes to drink beer and dance to the carillon.

A crowd of carillons, musical clocks, breweries, taverns, inns, and saloons were soon being built in Fresnes, Condé, Valenciennes, Lille, Dunkirk, Mons, Tournai, Bruges, Louvain, and Brussels.

The carillon, like a Spanish dance, shook a silver apron full of sparkling notes into the wind, and the barley-wine poured out in waves of gold over the Low Countries, and out to Holland, Germany, England, and Scotland.

People were drinking dark beer, light beer, double beer, strong Belgian beer and Brussels beer, pale ale, scotch ale, porter, and stout, every kind of beer there was. And all the time, the carillon in Fresnes was the only enchanted carillon, the beer in Fresnes was the best beer, and the Fresnians were the finest drinkers in the world.

Assemblies of drinkers would be held, just like the assemblies of finches, in all the Low Countries. But only in Fresnes would you find the really proper drinkers, able to take in a hundred pints or so in one day at a fair, or a dozen tankards while the church-clock was striking.

In order to give fair reward to the inventor, the King of the Low Countries had him made the Duke of Brabant, Count of Flanders, and Lord of Fresnes. It was at that time that the new Duke founded the city of Cambrai; but the title he preferred above all the others was "the King of Beer," the title that his country-folk honored him with.

As for the rest, he was not slow to test the generous effects of the dark liquor himself. For a while, every evening he emptied two bottles. At the end of six months on that system, his mad passion for Flandrine was cooling. The image of Flandrine seemed to him less distinct and less mocking.

By the time he could swallow down his twenty pints, all he felt was a vague, indefinable dream. Soon after that, his rosy face rivaled the full moon: he became very fat and perfectly happy.

When Flandrine saw that the Lord of Fresnes had no intention of laying claim to her hand, she started hanging around him. But he was nodding off, his eyes half closed, and he didn't even recognize her. He only offered her a pint.

The King of Beer, however, was a fine figure of a king. He found his happiness in smoking his pipe and drinking his tankard, sitting around the table with his subjects. His subjects all followed his example, and ever since then, the good Flamands have been meditative smokers, with prominent bellies and noses, passing their lives in drinking tankards, thinking ill of no one, and having nothing to wish for.

V

Meanwhile, the thirty years had rolled around, and Beelzebub expected to lay claim to Cambrinus's soul. The devil doesn't always go in person to collect on his debts. Like creditors in the world above, sometimes he sends a bailiff.

Then, too, seeing that the world was getting older, and growing more and more wicked and giving more trouble to those from down below, Beelzebub, in order to keep up with things, had to gather recruits, from time to time. To keep the organization fully staffed, he chose, from among the newcomers, fine fellows who on earth had been particularly like him.

So the judge who in former days had condemned Cambrinus won the glory of passing for a devil, and, in memory of his former role in life, Beelzebub decided to raise him to the rank of Infernal Bailiff.

"Come here, Monkey-Face," he told him one day. "The time has come for you to win attention with new deeds. You're going to go the village of Fresnes, and there you're going to seize the soul of Cambrinus, the King of Beer, in my name. Here's the warrant."

"Th-that's g-good enough p-proof, m-my lord," said Jocko. And he set out at once on the road to Fresnes. He got there the following Sunday, the feast-day of their patron saint.

The King of Beer had just then climbed to the top of his tower. He saw far off the arrival of Beelzebub's emissary, recognized him, and guessed what brought him there.

VI

It was about six o'clock, and people had left the table. They had been eating and drinking since noon. Some of them had spread out into the taverns to smoke a pipe while they were digesting their food. Others had gone to play at skittles or the raven-game or, better still, at bricoliau.

24

Beelzebub's messenger spoke to a circle of drinkers seated in front of the door of a pub called Great Saint Laurence, after the patron saint of the glassmakers.

"C-could you tell me where C-Cambrinus is?"

"Well, well! So it's you, M-Mister Judge," said a glassmaker named Cobiotte, mimicking his stammer. "I-I-I thought you were d-dead."

Just then, ding-ding-dong! a shower of notes burst through the air like a rocket, and the carillon began to play:

Good day to you, Vincent my friend,
And are you in good health today?

Immediately, the judge began jumping about like a gigantic jumping-jack.

"Wh-wh-what's happening to me?" he said. There was nothing funnier than the furious face he was making as he capered about.

All the Fresnians gathered around, splitting their sides with laughter.

Oh! what a nose that kid has got! was the tune the carillon started to play, and two hundred voices sang in chorus, *Oh! what a nose that kid has got!* for so long that the dancer fell to the ground, exhausted and out of breath. The carillon fell silent.

As Jocko was complaining of a horrible thirst, they brought him a tankard of beer. He emptied it in one gulp.

And he'd always been one who liked to bend his elbow, so he raised his arm to drink a second, then a third, then a whole series more, with his good friends of Fresnes.

With all that drinking, he completely forgot his mission, and, along about the fifth tankard, when heads were getting over-heated, and the hop-poles began, as the saying is, to be carrying too much to support, all of a sudden a rush of mad glee overcame him.

He stood up, seized the jugs, the bottles, and the glasses, pushed them all to the floor, over-turned the table, and the footwarmer on top of it, then began to dance all by himself, calling for music as loud as he could.

The Fresnians all ran up behind him in one long line. He danced around the square several times to the tune of "The Codaqui" and led the line out of town half a mile.

Then he fell down in the road, exhausted, and completely out of action. They put him to bed in a haystack, and here he slept for three days and three nights non-stop.

When he woke up, he was so ashamed that he didn't dare return either to Fresnes or to Hell. He had no idea where to go, when he noticed an empty begging-bag that a pauper was holding out to passers-by. He jumped into it and hid himself there so well that he's there still.

And from that comes the common proverb that says that a man without so much as a penny has the devil lodging in his bag.

VII

The lord of Fresnes went on playing the carillon and drinking beer for almost a hundred years, and heard no further news from Hell. But everyone knows that the devil never loses in a deal, and Beelzebub hoped to snap up the Duke of Brabant's soul on the day of his death. But when it came to the very last moment, instead of his debtor, all Beelzebub found was a keg of beer. He'd been tricked.

Was it a result of the drink of forgetfulness, or did Beelzebub prefer to avenge himself for the trick that Cambrinus had played on him? The memory of the King of Beer was soon forgotten in Fresnes and throughout the Low Countries.

The people of Douai to this day celebrate the feast of their old Gayant, but at Cambrai it's been a long time since they've paraded through town with a giant made of willow-wood to represent Cambrinus, the royal founder of the town.

So it's the Prussians who have preserved the memory of the Bacchus of hops. There, in every tavern, you will see hung up in the place of honor a magnificent painting which shows a gallant knight, sitting on a keg, and wearing a cloak lined with ermine. His left hand rests on a crown and a sword; his right hand triumphantly lifts up a mug of foaming beer.

That's Cambrinus himself, the King of Beer, just as he looked in life, with his handsome, ruddy face, his long golden curls, and his long golden beard.

The students each year elect a bierkoenig, a King of Beer, the best drinker among them, and he alone has the right to that badge of honor and takes the seat under that foaming monarch.

The Fresnians will be astonished when they read this true history. Just as they never believed, long ago, in Cambrinus's genius, so nowadays they do not believe in his glory, and when the writer who penned these lines goes to drink a pint on the feast-day of the Fresnians' patron saint, they won't hold back from treating me as an impostor. It's so true—no one is a prophet in his own country!

Death's Godson

I

In olden times, there was a big farmer named John-Phillip who lived in the village of Chêne-Raoult, four bow-shots' distance from Condé-sur-l'Escaut.

Don't confuse Chêne-Raoult with Queue-de-l'Agache. Both of them are next to Macou, but the one goes to the left and the other to the right off the highway to Ghent.

John-Phillip had a wife and twelve sons, as strong as so many ropes on the mill. John-Phillip himself was going grey, although he still stood as straight as a poplar.

Well, it happened that his wife gave him a new year's gift—a thirteenth boy, who did not look at all like his brothers.

"You're as skinny as a cat in May, my poor little lad," said John-Phillip. "And what's more, you're number thirteen, which is an unlucky number. You'll never have much luck, but I know a good way to change your fate. What you need is a godfather who's a just man. It shouldn't be hard to find one among the neighbors."

John-Phillip considered them all in turn. Unfortunately, one of them had once tried to steal some twenty yards of ground from John-Phillip, another had killed his chickens, and a third had cheated when they played cards last Sunday, after the evensong service, in the Bold-Cock Inn.

"Bah! No doubt, I'll shake one out of the tree in Macou," John-Phillip said to himself. He weighed in the balance all the people in Macou, and then in Condé, and he rejected them all, each one for one reason or another. Even those gentlemen the Justice of the Peace and the Curate of Condé found no favor in his eyes.

At that time, the Justice of the Peace, to get through the trials faster, had taken to delivering his judgments to the hearers ready-made in advance; and the Curate was always putting the Burgomaster's son in the first place at the catechism, even though the boy was, with all due respect, an ass.

The big farmer scratched his head. "It's really not as easy as I thought," he said. "Let's get some advice."

He called in his wife and sons and put the case to them.

After mature deliberation, they decided that since they couldn't find a just man in West Flanders, they'd go look further east, in Belgium.

The Belgians, who were all businessmen, talked all the time about honesty and justice, so surely they'd have plenty of them.

So the next day, early in the morning, John-Phillip put on his spats, took his cross, and started off. He walked for three days and three nights, asking around everywhere; but nowhere could he find justice—all he saw was the claim to it.

Even the most scrupulous Belgians all had some peccadillo on their conscience. And perhaps John-Phillip was being too demanding.

At last he came to the city of Brussels, in Brabant. As he strolled through the streets, he noticed a large, beautiful house, with these words written over the door: *Palace of Justice*. John-Phillip gave thanks to heaven that he knew how to read and felt easier at heart.

"My journey wasn't a waste of time," he said. "I don't even need to wonder if the master inside there is a just man. Let's go on in."

He went in, and saw everybody gathered together in a vast hall.

At the far end of the hall a semi-circle of several grave gentlemen were sitting, looking very solemn. They all wore long black robes, and had caps on their heads. Opposite them, an old man with a long beard was pacing back and forth, like a bear in a cage.

All at once, the one who seemed to be presiding, judging by the silver stripe on his hat, said in a loud voice: "This hearing is open. Officers, make the accused sit down, can't you!"

The officers wanted to obey, but the man, as if impelled by a superior force, shoved them to the ground and kept on pacing. The officers prudently stepped aside and formed a square around him.

"Your name?" said the president.

The accused, in a quavering voice, replied with a well-known song:
"I'm Isaac Laquedem.
That's the name to fit me.
I'm from Jerusalem,
A famed and noble city.
Come bid me how d'ye do,
For I'm the Wandering Jew."
"Your age?"

"Eighteen hundred years
I've seen, or maybe more.
Time just disappears,
But I don't age a score.
The tortured might entreat,
But I left God to be killed.
I wander every street,
My days still unfulfilled."
"How do you earn your living?"
"I have no goods, no home,
Just five sous in my purse
Wherever I may roam —
Just five sous and the curse
I find in every place
Where I may show my face."

"You were arrested last night for being a vagabond. What do you have to say in your defense?"

"Gentlemen, I say
I know enough of sorrow.
Nowhere can I stay —
Not now, and not tomorrow,
Forever lost and knowing
That still I must be going."

"Is that all you have to say?—Officers, lock him up, can't you!"

The eternal wanderer followed the officers, smiling in his long beard.

John-Phillip drew back, thinking hard. "So that's how they do justice in its palace!" he said to himself. "God has condemned this man to go on walking until Judgment Day, and here they try to arrest him. They're putting their human laws over the divine law. No, it's not at the Palace of Justice in Brussels that I'm going to find my man."

He left the city. Night fell. John-Phillip heard steps behind him. He looked around, and, by the speed of the steps, he recognized the Wandering Jew. He went to him and said, "Sir—you who have been walking for eighteen hundred years—haven't you ever seen a just man?"

"Never but once," said Isaac, "and they crucified him. Yet that man was a God!"

So there'd never been a just man under the heavens! John-Phillip was in despair. He started back toward Chêne-Raoult.

Toward midnight, at the edge of the Forest of Baudour, he felt the need to smoke a pipe. He looked for his tobacco-case: it had disappeared. It was a nice case, made of brass, and he'd been using it for more than thirty years.

The farmer remembered that at the Palace of Justice, he thought he'd felt someone reach stealthily into his pocket. He understood then why Justice had such a big house: they had plenty to do and needed plenty of room.

Fortunately, he saw a man coming toward him, and it seemed to him in the starlight that he was as tall as a hop-pole. This man carried a scythe as long as he was himself. John-Phillip stopped him.

"Whoever you are, child of God," he said to him, "Could you be so kind as to let me have enough tobacco to fill my pipe? Someone stole my tobacco-case in the Palace of Justice in Brussels."

The reaper, without saying a word, drew out his tobacco-pouch and handed it to John-Phillip. The big farmer filled his pipe and struck a light with his tinder-box. While he was doing that, he had time to examine the stranger.

His skull was bald and gleaming, his eyes small and sunk deeply in his head, his nose was flat, his mouth enormously wide with only a few yellow teeth to be seen, his cheeks hollow, and his skin dry. You'd have thought he was a skeleton escaped from the graveyard. The stranger looked even older than the Wandering Jew. Every time he moved, his limbs made a dry noise, like the clacking of the wooden slats the wind tosses around over grocery-shop windows.

"Thank you, Grandfather," said John-Phillip, handing him back the pouch. "You know, it seems to me, reapers don't get much good around here."

"Why do you say that?"

"Because by the looks of you, anyone would think that the reapers around here never get to eat their fill. You're as thin as a capon that might get offered to pay the rent. You need to take care of yourself, believe me, or you'll never live to have old bones."

"Don't worry, my lad—my bones will see yours into the grave."
And the old man's little eyes sparkled like a pinch of salt thrown on the
fire. Then he said, "What are doing here so late?"

"My wife presented me with our thirteenth boy, and the poor thing
is about as big as a minnow. I wanted to keep misfortune away from him,
and I got the idea of looking for a just man to be his godfather. But now
I've been walking for three days and three nights—"

"And you haven't found one?"

"Not one. I would never have believed that a good man was so hard
to find."

The stranger made a face that seemed to be meant for a smile.
"What about me?"

"You!—You're a just man, are you?—Well, you're lean enough for
it. What's your name?"

"I'm called Death."

"Death!—The devil you are!—But then you're really the one
who..."

"Yes, my lad, I'm the one who—"

"Oh!—Well, well, you're right!—Death is just. His scythe harvests
rich and poor alike. It's a bargain, Partner, and let's go drink a bottle. I
can promise you we'll have a baptism worthy of the godfather."

"When is the baptism?"

"On Sunday, at Chêne-Raoult, four shots' distance from Condé. Just
ask for John-Phillip, the big farmer."

"Then that's settled. Good night, Partner."

"Good night, Death."

And the new friends went their ways.

III

John-Phillip went home, feeling light of foot and light of heart, to
Chêne-Raoult.

"Wife," he said, "I've found a famous godfather, and he'll protect
our little lad—the kid won't die while he's still a nurseling." As women
worry about everything, he didn't explain further.

On the day named, so they'd have a celebration fit for his colleague,
John-Phillip put on his bottle-green velvet pants, his shoes with the silver
buckles, and his sturdy jacket. His wife, his sons, and the godmother, too,
all came dressed in their party clothes.

The godfather arrived wearing a big cloak that floated around him like a sail on a mast, when the wind happens to fall. He was generally considered to be too thin, but they had to admit he looked like someone who was well-to-do.

They held the baptism in Condé—for at that time there was as yet no chapel in Macou—and Old Jacob played the tune of "King Dagobert" on the church carillon.

The dinner that Mrs. John-Phillip served was so splendid that people still remember it around here. She had killed the pig in honor of the occasion.

First, she put on the table a soup, lightly salted, and so thick that the spoon stood up in it; then, as an appetizer, she brought in some hot sausage, some cold, a black pudding, and chitterlings. The first course was pork cutlets, breaded pig's-feet, and kidney with fried pork. For the second course, some pork-back, and roast goose—I mean, roast goslings from Hergnies—stuffed with sausage-meat, and served between two ducks; then came a dish of larded brussel-sprouts, and mashed beans in bacon grease. In the middle of the table lay a superb suckling pig.

The meal was washed down with innumerable pints of dark beer, well aged. With the dessert, for a change, they drank a tub of light beer. The dessert was splendid to see—an enormous cheese pastry and an apple pie as big as the moon. Both were accompanied by plates of little sweets, sugar-cookies, and bar-cookies from Lille.

It was Epiphany Sunday, and the night before, in the Condé market, Mrs. John-Phillip had gone to Rousseli's and bought a sou's worth of cards for the Three Kings, and that way you get two hits with one stone, because after the benediction, you mix the cards in the godfather's bowl, and draw for the Kings.

It was Death who got the King, and John-Phillip got the Fool. They all cried "The King drinks" each time Death emptied his glass.

The cry went up, when they'd finished counting, a hundred-ninety-nine times.

It was fun to see Death eating. He ate enough all by himself for fifteen guests, even if they were all Flemish. John-Phillip rubbed his hands together happily, and thought privately to himself that it was true what people said—Death swallows all. He couldn't help but wish he had a little of that healthy appetite.

When it came time for coffee, his gaiety was at its height, and, in a voice as loud as an ox, he sang "Mathurin's Flock," remarkably out of tune. He would gladly have given his partner a friendly poke in the belly, but unfortunately, his partner didn't have a belly.

Even the finest feast comes at last to an end, at ten o'clock, when they sound the curfew in Condé. Then they all drank a parting glass, and Death, after kissing his partner the godmother and managing a smile for his godson, took his leave of the family. John-Phillip wanted to walk him out and see him to the end of the street. They left arm in arm, singing.

At times they stopped to recite a prayer in the chapels along the way, as we say around here—that's to say, to drink a pint and light a pipe in the inns that were still showing a light.

These chapels shone in the night, as numerous as the stars, for everyone wanted to take a turn trying to draw a King, as the village constables well knew.

"Well, now, my dear sir," said the big farmer, as they chatted about this and that, "you must have a difficult job, all the same, and your work is harder than a farmer's. I don't wonder at it any more that you're so skinny, even though you ate so much. How many heads do you mow down each day, on average?"

"On average, sixty thousand."

"And how many did you reap this morning?"

"Not one."

"Really! So that's sixty thousand Christian souls in debt to me for a good candle's worth."

"Oh, no, my lad, I didn't have any work today! I get three or four days off each year."

"How do you know when the hour has rung for each mortal?"

"Come visit me at our place, and you can see for yourself."

"At your place!—oh, that's too far."

"No farther than three flights of an arrow."

They were getting near the Forest of Baudour, in fact. From chapel to chapel, John-Phillip had been walking for six hours without knowing it. But he noticed that he was a little unsteady on his legs, when they reached the godfather's house.

IV

The godfather's house was a poor hut, and the only ornament that could be seen there was the great scythe that gleamed in the moonlight like a scythe of silver.

"For a master workman like you," said the big farmer, "you have to admit you don't have much of a house."

"Bah!—it isn't the habit that makes the monk, nor the pitcher that makes the beer!" said Death. "And anyhow I'm just a servant. Let's go down."

He took his scythe, his hammer, and his whetstone, and lifted up a trap-door. John-Phillip followed him. They went down, down, down, so far that it seemed to the big farmer he must have come to the center of the world.

The staircase was very steep and very dark, and John-Phillip ran out of breath more than once, but curiosity kept him going.

They stopped at last before an iron door. Death unfastened a big key from his belt and opened it. Suddenly, they were flooded with light. John-Phillip, dazzled, shut his eyes. When he opened them again, he saw before him a long series of immense galleries, lit by thousands of lamps.

There were lamps of gold, lamps of silver-gilt, lamps of silver, lamps of copper, lamps of brass, lamps of tin-plate; in short, lamps of every sort of metal, from the finest to the basest.

They were hung from the vault, or hooked to the walls, or displayed on shelves of porphyry, and—strange to say—their lights didn't run together. The rays from each lamp could easily be told from one another.

"What are those, myn-God-Jesus!" said John-Phillip.

"Those are the lamps of all mortals. This is the great row of the lamps of life. When one of these lights happens to die, it means that the corresponding life up above must go out, too,"

"Oh! How curious! And the lamps of gold?—"

"Those are the lamps of kings; the silver-gilt the princes, the silver the dukes, the copper the counts, and so on in order to the lamps of iron, which are the lamps of ordinary folk."

The big farmer walked on for some time, fascinated. He noticed that the lamps of several high and mighty lords that you would have thought were still full of oil gave out a light that was dimming to red. In general, it was the rich whose lamps gave out the light that was least clear.

The one that, undeniably, shone out with the brightest and liveliest light of them all was a miserable old oil-lamp with an antique shape. John-Phillip realized it was the lamp of Isaac Laquedem.

When his eyes had feasted enough on this spectacle, he said: "Partner, I would very much like to see the lamps of the people of Chêne-Raoult."

"First gallery, third section, left-hand side."

And Death started to lower his scythe.

The hammer blows kept sounding, all together, and from time to time an exclamation of surprise or a burst of laughter echoed in the first gallery. That was because of the discoveries John-Phillip was making. Suddenly he stopped short, frightened.

"Partner," he said, mysteriously, "I should warn you that my lamp is very low."

"Yes, I know, my lad," said Death serenely

"Oh!" said the big farmer, surprised that he took it so calmly. "And is that a sign that soon I'm going to—?"

"Yes, by God!"

"But surely it isn't for me that you're going to?—"

"Yes, it is, my lad."

And Death lowered his scythe still further.

"Devil take it!" said John-Philip. He nudged the reaper with his elbow and giving him a wink of his eye, he whispered these words into his ear: "Well, tell me, Partner, couldn't we, between us, put a little more oil in? It would be doing me a great favor."

"Put more oil in! Do you know what you're asking?"

"Bah! We're all by ourselves, and the good Lord won't see anything but the fire."

"What do you take me for? Say your prayers, my lad."

"Just between friends!"

"Friends as much as you like, but say your prayers anyway."

"Just the least little bit!"

"Come on now, enough talking!"

"All I'm asking is to get to Ash-Wednesday—we have a history of going together to the carnival. Let me invite you to join us for the Mardi-Gras. You'll see such merry-making!—we drink more than two hundred mugs apiece. We masquerade as hunchbacks, and then we go to knock things over in Condé."

"Look, I'm warning you, I'm all set."

"Only just a little!—You could take some from that big lamp that belongs to the curate of Condé that's overflowing and shines so badly."

"I'm very sorry, my friend, but it's impossible. I can't."

"What's stopping you? The curate is a saintly man, and it'll only mean that he'll get into Paradise a little sooner!"

"No, my lad, no, it's time for you to take the plunge. When you were looking for a just man, no one—not even the Justice of the Peace in Condé—had a clear enough conscience, as you saw it. And you've no sooner found your man than you try to bribe him with mugs of beer. You're a funny kind of Christian, I must say!"

John-Philip was going to reply, but suddenly a rattling sound could be heard in the first gallery.

His lamp had gone out.

The Inn of the Seven Deadly Sins

In olden times, it happened once that the Seven Deadly Sins traveled together to pay their respects to Milord Satanas, their colleague. On the road, the pilgrims had such a pleasant time that it occurred to them that they did not want it to stop.

By chance, they were going by the Lille town-square in Flanders, so they turned into the tavern of the Grand Pint, to think the matter over at their ease, and they sat down together around a pitcher of dark beer.

"My daughters," said Pride, filling his pipe, "—for I am your father, just as Sloth is your mother—I'd be happy to condescend to have us set up a household to stay together. But if we do that, we need to decide now where it should be. In the first place, it seems to me that people of our high rank should not take lodgings in an inn like a troupe of acrobats.

"Besides, it would cost money," said Avarice judiciously.

"Well, then, let's make a choice," said Pride, "some nice house where they could put us up for free, and give us all the consideration due to persons of our station."

"By the strong beer of the Low Countries!" cried Gluttony, "here comes the Burgomaster to digest his dinner and smoke a pipe. Suppose we ask him for hospitality? In my opinion, we would be royally lodged with him, judging by the size of his paunch."

"Speak for yourself, my sweet," hissed Envy. "What contentment do you think I'd find staying with a mynherr who's the biggest big shot around, and who sees all the world groveling at his feet? Instead, let's follow that good peasant over there whose bones jingle beneath his jacket and is squinting to get a sidelong look at us."

"That's a nice host, on my word!" yelled Wrath, "a wretch whose soul has been worn down by misery to the bare threads, and who hardly dares to stir when something squashes him! But all hail to the handsome captain over there with his terrible eye and handlebar mustache! He's a fine fellow, who won't leave us behind and forced to go on foot!"

"A fine fellow!" Sloth yawned, "a man who, in peacetime, gets up at cockcrow to do his exercises, and who, in the battlefield, gets laid out there and can never rise again. You won't catch me going around with any saber-rattler."

"I foresee, my children," said Pride, "that finding a place to stay in is going to be harder than we thought. Dear, dear! I would never have believed that the good sons of Adam would give us so much trouble."

"Skies above!" cried Lust, "here we are looking among people who lead ordered lives. What would you expect them to be able to do for us, all wrapped up as they are in their duties? Tell me about madcaps and joyous hearts, rejected by all the world, following only the rules of their whims! Do you see that pretty actress coming toward us? She's a woman, a flirt, and a comedian—sometimes she gets excommunicated—that's the kind for us. She's vain, amorous, jealous, gluttonous, wrathful, and lazy, and there's nothing to stop her from being avaricious, too. That's obvious. When I tell you that the damsel is a very nest of sins—"

"—too many eggs in that nest for me to hatch out, you can be sure," said Sloth. "If you think that I'm going to cudgel my brains learning a lot of nonsense every blessed day just to make a lot of gawkers laugh every night, and not get to bed until time for morning prayers!—Thanks a lot! Don't forget, my daughters, that it's not for nothing that Milord Satanas made me your mother, and no one's going to give you as much as a blackbird to eat, unless your mother gets some roast thrushes."

"—From which it follows," said Pride, "that it's absolutely necessary that we find a host with nothing in particular to do. Well, then, let's go look for one."

These good folk looked, and looked, for a long time, but every time and everywhere they found some obstacle that closed the door to them.

They very nearly tried asking a rich nobleman, who lived on the income of his rents, to put them up, but the nobleman gave himself so little trouble when it came to keeping an eye on his steward, that there was nothing left for the steward to steal.

Avarice proposed that they should really take up lodgings with the steward, who'd hoarded away a lot of money for himself. But Pride flatly refused to go live with a servant, even if the servant did have a nice house.

At last, Pride grew weary of the dispute, and said, "My dear children, I must admit I'm ready to give up. Look how late it's getting! Let's drink a stirrup-cup, and, no matter how it grieves our hearts, go on our separate ways."

They had already kissed each other goodbye on the front doorstep, when Sloth cried out, all of a sudden, "Eureka!" That's a Greek word. It means: I have found it!

"I've found that phoenix among mortals who does nothing and has nothing to do. Girls, do you see that good monk going with his eyes cast down? There's our host."

"A capuchin monk? Oh!" said Lust, scandalized. "But this good father took a vow of chastity, surely?"

"And poverty," said Greed.

"And obedience," added Pride.

"And for just that reason, he's going to welcome us with open arms. Nothing encourages a body to violate a vow like the fact of having taken it."

"Your line of reasoning's not dumb," Pride remarked.

"No, it isn't. Think about it: someone who takes a vow voluntarily undertakes to deprive himself of something; once you've said you can't have it, that means you don't have it, and, without it, the consequence is a violent need to have it."

"Your words, my wife, are golden," said Pride. "Let's follow the reverend father."

And they followed him. The good monk looked back at the noise of their footsteps, and at once turned into a narrow street where no echoes sounded. The reverend father then slowed his steps, and the pilgrims caught up with him.

They started to make their request to him, humbly, when he himself spoke these words to them, gently: "My dear little ladies, I wonder what you can want with me. I caught a glimpse of you, although I wasn't staring. Unfortunately, I don't have anything to put at your service. It's hard enough to refuse to receive your noble father and Madame your mother, who are not so compromising—Ah! I regret it very much," he added, chucking Lust under the chin, "because, by my beard!—it's a fact that you're all of you very nice."

"If you think we're so nice, my fat father," she said, with a flirtatious look, "what's to stop you from giving us a place to stay?"

"What stops me, my darling, is my mortal enemy, who always comes right behind you."

"Who's that?"

"Scandal!"

"Oh, well! The door will be slammed in his face."

"Who's there, myn God!"

"Me!" said an unfamiliar voice.

In that moment, a light happened to gleam from a window, lighting up the whole street, and that allowed the pilgrims to see the person who had just spoken. Her face was covered with a mask, and her arms were crossed on her breast.

"It's Hypocrisy!" said all six women in chorus.

"Yes, my ladies, it's Hypocrisy, your sister, whom our holy mother the Church—no one knows why!—forgot to recognize as a member of our family. Milord Satanas, who appreciates me more, has sent me to you to save this good father from embarrassment. Don't be afraid, reverend monk—I can explain anything, and woe be to anyone who tries to unmask me!"

"Amen," said the father, and he conducted his guests to his convent's guest-rooms, where, ever since, they have lived a joyous life, protected by Hypocrisy.

Green-Jeans, The Conqueror of the Lumçon

I

In olden times, in Condé-sur-l'Escaut, there was a boy about 14 or 15 years old who was really the naughtiest scamp who ever ran around barefoot on the cobbles of the streets. He lived on Neuve Street. Now, everyone knows that Neuve Street is the poorest street in Condé, and, consequently, the one where you see the most crooks, or so we say in these parts.

His mother sold candy-bars; his older brother was a ropemaker's apprentice, but, as for the younger, he was nothing at all, because he thought work was a bore and unworthy of someone of his quality.

His godfather had named him Gilles, but the townsfolk of Condé generally called him Green-Jeans, because he almost always went around wearing a shirt over an old pair of green pants held up by a bit of string. But his gang-leader had baptized him the Fearless, because he wasn't afraid of wind, or storm, or God, or the Devil, or the town-officials.

Strong as a bull and bold as a cock, he scorned anybody who was weak or timid especially women. Women seemed to him a species inferior to men: "I'll never get married," he often used to say, "until the day when I learn how to be afraid," which was, so he thought, as much as to say, "I'll never get married."

Meanwhile, he spent his days infuriating the neighbors. When the feast-day of the town's patron-saint came round, he was always the one who knocked over the gingerbread sellers' displays. On Saint Nicholas's day, he was the one who deafened you with holiday hullabaloo. At the midnight mass, he tied together the gentlemen and ladies whose chairs were too close together. On the feast of the Holy Innocents, he was the one, likewise, who led a troop of explorers through people's houses to steal the hams and tarts. At the feast of the Three Kings, he threw broken pots and bottles against the shutters. On Saint John's Day, Green-Jeans led his good-for-nothing friends banging their sticks on people's doorsteps, while singing the old song:

Wood is what we're looking for,
Pretty Lady, at your door.
Give me just a stick the more
To light the fire down low I've got.
Poor Saint John, he tripped and fell.
Saint Peter pulled him from the well.
Give me wood to get him hot.

Thanks to Green-Jeans, Neuve Street always had the best bonfires, because the Fearless, at the head of his band, carried off wood from other neighborhoods, and lit such a big fire that the folk from Fresnes and Macou came running as fast as they could, thinking that Condé was in flames.

Every Sunday and Monday, he spent the evening at Mother Boucaud's place playing cards for pancakes, the kind we call ouliettes. He drank his cup of small beer, smoked his pipe, and pounded his fist on the table, just like a man.

The other days of the week, Green-Jeans amused himself with belling cats, breaking street-lamps, and pulling them down, and, in winter, throwing snowballs at the passers-by to knock them down. In short, he was the terror of all decent folk, the joy of the naughty little scamps, and the despair of his mother, a good, God-fearing woman.

"If Gilles doesn't learn to behave," she would say sometimes to her older son, "you'll see, the rascal will end up like a mole caught between heaven and earth."

"Mother, I've often heard our priest say that fear is the beginning of wisdom," Green-Jeans' brother replied one day. "If Gilles once had a really good scare, perhaps he'd change his ways. Send him tonight to get a jug of water from the Fountain of Saint Callistus, and just you leave the rest to me."

II

The Fountain of Saint Callistus rose up a league outside Condé, and its water had the property of bringing down the fevers that cause so much sickness around about the country every autumn, because of the damp marshes.

That evening, when Gilles came home to go to bed, his mother said to him: "Gilles, go and get me a jug of water from the Fountain of Saint

43

Callistus. I can feel a shiver of death running down my spine, and I'm afraid I'm coming down with a fever."

So Gilles went out. The road that led to the fountain passed by a cemetery. The night was so dark you couldn't see a thing, and all there was to be heard was the leaves that fell from the poplars now and then. The Fearless kept going calmly, whistling the tune of the Codaqui, when all of a sudden, a ray of moonlight came and showed him, two steps ahead, a big white ghost.

"Huh!" Gilles said to himself, "Here's something escaped from Laguernade's garden!"

Laguernade was the Condé grave-digge.

"I'm not sorry to meet it—I'll be able to say I've seen a ghost."

He continued on his way, but the phantom wouldn't budge to make room for him to pass.

"Hey, you, out of the way, or I'll break you in two!"

The phantom did not move.

Green-Jeans flung himself on him and struck him on his head with the jug so furiously that the jug broke in a thousand pieces. The ghost fell flat, letting out a groan.

"Huh! That's a man," said Gilles. "And I've killed him. So much the worse for him! That'll teach him how to live."

He considered, however, that the result of such a fine blow might be to teach him—Gilles himself!—the same lesson. He wasn't afraid of the town officials at all, but he didn't care for the society of policemen, especially policemen who go riding on horseback and leading someone between them on foot and in handcuffs. He made up his mind that he mustn't go back to Condé, but should just skip over the border, only an hour away.

Fortunately, it was Monday, and Green-Jeans had a little money he'd won playing cards with Mother Boucaud. With just a little money, he could follow the example of the Belgians and take up trading. With necessity spurring him on, he surely had enough to buy a jackass and set himself up as a junkman, or, if you prefer, a peddler.

He traveled from village to village, calling out, "White sand for sale!" or, better, "Any old iron!—I'll give cherries for old iron!" And youngsters would give him all the scrap-iron there was in the house in exchange for a pound of cherries.

He journeyed around for three years. He could have made money that way, but he didn't know how to keep from gambling. Because of this accursed passion, he often found that he had only the devil lodging in his purse, and, as for himself, all the lodging he and his jackass had was the Starlight Inn.

One evening, he came to a village in the Low Countries. He asked for lodging at several inns, but as he didn't have one red cent on him, everywhere he went they said they had no room.

"The only place you'll find for that price is Bellringer Castle," he was told; "but who would dare to spend the night at Bellringer Castle?"

"Me!"

"You don't know what haunts the Red Room there, do you? That's why the castle was abandoned."

"Oh, ghosts! I'm not afraid of ghosts, not me! I'm not afraid of anything. Comes the day when I am, I'll get married. Just give me a good staff."

Bellringer Castle had such a reputation in those parts, that everyone was astonished to find someone who dared to risk it. They told him how every time an apparition was due to show up there, the moment midnight sounded on the village clock, the spirits would repeat the twelve strokes on an invisible clock.

They found him a hawthorn-wood staff—but Gilles snapped it like a match.

"That stick isn't strong enough," he said.

They found him an oak-wood staff. He broke that like the hawthorn.

"Hold on," said the blacksmith, "I'll give him one he can't break."

He forged a bar of iron as thick as his little finger. Gilles took it and broke it. So the smith forged one as thick as his thumb. Crack! It met the same fate. Finally he made one as thick as the fist of a three-year old child.

"That'll do all right," said Green-Jeans, once he'd tried bending it over his knee. "If the ghosts don't behave themselves, this'll teach them a lesson. Now I'm all set. If we're going to go bothering these folks, we have to give them a little something in return. Now give me some wood, some coal, a candle, a pitcher of beer and some glasses, some flour, yeast, salt, milk, brown sugar, butter and eggs, a stove, a pan, a ladle, some napkins, a table, and two chairs. It's carnival week, so I'll cook them some rats."

"Rats," in our part of the country, is the name of a kind of pancake even better than the ordinary kind.

Everything Gilles had asked for was brought to him.

45

"And don't forget," he added, "a deck of cards and a plug of tobacco. I don't know anything as good after supper as a good pipe and a game of Marrying Cards."

Green-Jeans loaded his jackass with his provisions, and then set out on the road to Bellringer Castle. The castle was in the woods, ten minutes away.

It was an old manor-house with four turrets, and walls that were ten feet thick, just exactly like the one that you can see in Condé, in Green Square, where Nanasse Moucheron, the dentist, lives.

The doors were wide open, but no one dared to go near there. And, anyhow, there was nothing there to steal.

Once under the vaulted ceiling, Green-Jeans struck a light, lit his candle, unloaded the jackass, put him in the stable, and bravely set about locating the Red Room.

It was not hard to spot. It was a cold, damp room, with tapestries hanging in tatters on the walls.

Gilles began by building a fire in the big, tall chimney, not a little fire an old widow might light, but a big, bright fire to cheer up the room with its sparkle.

Then he broke the eggs, beat them, added the flour, the salt, and the yeast, poured in the milk, and mixed it all together.

While the batter was rising, he lit his pipe, drank a glass of beer, and laid out the cards to tell fortunes.

When he thought it was ready, he put the butter in the pan, and the pan on the stove, and as soon as the butter began to sizzle, he poured in a spoonful of batter.

Just when he was going to flip his rat over, he heard midnight strike on the village clock.

"Good!" said Green-Jeans, "the first one to come will get the first off the stove."

He waited a minute, but nothing happened. The invisible bell was silent.

"What a nuisance," said the Fearless One. "And the rat looks so tasty! Well, too bad—I'll get the best part of it."

The words were hardly out of his mouth when he heard a frightening voice, like a man shouting from inside a hollow tank. This voice seemed to be coming from the top of the chimney.

"Am I going to fall? Or not?" the voice was saying.

"Wait until I take the stove off," said Gilles. "There, that'll do. Now go ahead and fall." And he stretched out his hands to the chimney.

A leg dropped out of it.

Green-Jeans caught it as it fell and threw it in a corner, where it landed standing up. Then he put the stove back on the fire.

"Am I going to fall? Or not?"

"Wait—all right—go ahead."

A second leg dropped, and Gilles threw it in the corner, as he had the first, and, like the first, it landed standing straight up on its foot.

"Am I going to fall? Or not?"

"Go ahead and fall— don't just hang there."

An arm fell, and then another.

"That makes four," said Gilles. "Soon I'll have enough for a game of skittles,"

"Am I going to fall? Or not?"

"Fine!—That one can be the middle pin."

Down fell a torso. Gilles tossed it into the middle of the game, and it landed standing on end, like the legs and the arms.

"Now all I need is the ball."

"Am I going to fall? Or not?"

"Oh, here's the ball," said Gilles, catching the head. "I bet I can bowl over three at a time."

He threw the head in with the other pieces. Suddenly they joined themselves together, and a man stood up.

"You have an odd way of showing up in society," said Green-Jeans. "But that's all right—I invited you in."

He sprinkled brown sugar on the rat and cut it in two.

"Thank you, but I'm not hungry," said the man.

"Oh! Well, then have a drink. You must have a dry throat after traveling here in pieces."

"I'm not thirsty."

"Huh! Well, it's just the opposite for me. I'm always hungry and thirsty. Here's to your good health, holy man!"

And Gilles drank a glass of beer and began eating his share of the rat.

"Follow me," said the ghost, all of a sudden.

"Where?"

"To the cellars of the castle."

"Thanks, but forget it! I don't want to catch cold."

Gilles lit his pipe.

"You're going to follow me," said the phantom.

And he stretched out his long, bony arm.

"Hang on!" said Gilles.

He grabbed his iron bar and struck a blow on the arm. It seemed to him that the blow fell on empty space, and yet the spirit pulled back his arm with a cry of pain.

"You are the first one to resist me," he said. "You're the one who's going to redeem me."

"Only if I want to!"

"Tell me your terms."

"Let's play a hand of Marrying Cards first. I boasted that I was going to play a game of cards with you, and I don't want to make myself a liar."

"If I win, will you follow me?"

"I will!"

Gilles dealt eight cards to his opponent, kept as many for himself, and led a club. He glanced at his hand and was not unhappy with it: he had four trumps in the major suits.

"I'm not worried," he said.

And he declared Marriage.

"The cards make a fine Marriage—just look!" And the phantom showed his hand, with the cards married in spades.

"But I led clubs!"

The ghost smiled and pointed a finger at the card. Gilles, astonished, could not explain how the club had turned itself into a spade.

"I'm all at sea," he said. He threw down his cards, adding, "I'm ready to follow you."

"Take the candle and lead the way."

"Lead the way yourself!" said Gilles. "I'm not your servant."

He was brave, but, after all, you never want to turn your back on a phantom—he might throttle you.

The ghost took the candle and set off, with Gilles following.

They went down into the castle cellars and, after they had walked for some time, they came to a big stone—it looked like a gravestone.

"Lift the stone," said the ghost.

"Lift it yourself."

The ghost obeyed, and Gilles saw some big pots full of gold coins.

"There," said the phantom, "behold the cause of my torment. Long ago I stole this gold from the Count of Hainaut, and my soul was condemned to haunt the castle until it was paid back. So take two of these pots to him, and keep the third for yourself, and try not to waste it."

Gilles scratched his ear, thinking this over. He was thinking about the false ghost he'd hurried into the next world.

"Could you tell me," he asked, "what happens to a soul in Hell who has murder on his conscience?"

"If he hasn't atoned in life, he is condemned to wander through all eternity with his head tucked under his arm."

"The devil you say! Is there a way to make payment while you're still alive?"

"Yes, just one way."

"And that is—?"

"To save someone from inevitable death."

"Thank you, sir," said Gilles. "You're a brave man, and I'll undertake this errand for you. Let's go back upstairs."

But suddenly he heard "Cock-a-doodle-doo!" Chanticleer the rooster was announcing the break of day, and the phantom disappeared. Gilles found himself alone with the three pots of gold. He took them, went upstairs, led his jackass out of the stable, and started right off for the city of Mons, where the valiant Count of Hainault had his court.

III

He got there a week later, and went down to the Great Saint Druon Inn.

The whole city was in chaos. The streets were full of people weeping and lamenting. Green-Jeans asked what was the cause of all this grief.

He was told that a league and a half away, in the swamps of Wasmes, there was a dragon—the kind we call a lumçon—ravaging the country. Every year they had to give a girl to the monster to appease his anger.

This year, the lottery had named Fair Ida, the daughter of the Count of Hainault. The Count had sent out trumpeters to announce that he would give her in marriage to the man who would kill the monster; but no one had dared offer to try, and the victim had left, that very morning, for Wasmes, escorted there in a procession. That's why they were all weeping and lamenting.

"Good! I'm making this my business," said Gilles. "I'll kill the monster and save the lady; and the result of that in the Next World is that I won't have to carry my head around under my arm."

"And will you marry the pretty girl?"

"Oh, as for that—no! I call myself the Fearless. I just laugh at pretty girls, and I'm not going to get married until I've felt fear."

The people shrugged their shoulders, but he didn't pay any attention, and left, brandishing his iron bar.

Green-Jeans got to Wasmes at dusk. He didn't find anyone there. They had all run a league away from there, being so afraid of the dragon. Guided by frightful bellows, he went straight to the monster. The monster was just getting ready to devour the maiden.

"Hey, my boy, just come a little closer!" cried Gilles.

The monster left his prey and came to the entrance of his lair. He had a head like a horse, a tongue like a snake, teeth like a crocodile, wings like a vulture, and a tail like a shark.

He leaped on Gilles, but Gilles hit him with his iron bar and knocked off one of his wings.

"You just wait! I'm going to carve you up, you big turkey!" he cried.

With a second blow he struck off the other wing, then the tail, and finally he cut off the head.

That done, he led the girl out. "Don't cry, Fair Ida," he told her. "I'm going to take you back to your father."

"And you're going to marry me for your reward."

"But have I felt fear?"

"No."

"Oh, well! I call myself the Fearless, and I'm not going to get married until I've felt fear. It's a vow that I made."

Fair Ida made no reply, but she thought quietly to herself that it was a strange sort of a vow, for Gilles was a handsome lad, even though his pants were so shabby.

They walked on together without saying anything, each on one side of the path, as lovers do in Fresnes, when they are going to serve Our Lady of Mercy. Suddenly, when they reached Jemmapes, Gilles heard a voice that shouted: "Hey! It's Green-Jeans."

He turned around and recognized Mimile Becanne. Mimile Becanne was, after Green-Jeans, the most famous robber in Condé. When children played at being thieves, it was always Gilles who was the captain and Mimile who was his lieutenant.

"How nice to see you! I thought you were dead! Let's go drink a mug," said Mimile Bicanne.

When you've just killed a monster, you really deserve a cup of something. And anyhow, you won't find anyone who can boast of having two Flamands meet up without emptying a mug, and besides that, Mimile and Green-Jeans were such good friends.

Even so, Green-Jeans hesitated. If the Fair Ida had been a simple peasant girl, he would have suggested straightforwardly that she come and have some refreshment with them, but how do you escort the daughter of the Count of Hainault into a tavern!

Fair Ida removed the difficulty.

"Go with your friend," she told him. "I'll have no problem getting home on my own. The way is easy from here."

"It's straight ahead as far as Jemappes, and after that you take a left, my lady," Green-Jeans said, finding her charming now. "Please bid my lord your father good-day for me, and tell him that I'll come to see him shortly. I'm on an errand to him."

And he followed Mimile Bicanne inside.

Mimile Bicanne told Green-Jeans that all Condé had grieved at his departure. No one was having fun hanging bells on the cats, or knocking over the signboards, or baying like werewolves so people couldn't sleep in peace. In short, they were in a sad state.

"No one's found a corpse on the pathway, about three years ago, near Laguernade's yard?"

"Your brother was found there—you'd almost knocked his brains out. He'd been there pretending to be a ghost."

"What—my brother?"

"Yes, but he's well again now."

"Thank God!" said the Fearless. Then, after thinking it over, he said, "So I didn't have to go to the bother of saving the daughter of—Bah! it doesn't matter. The nuisance of having killed someone could still happen!"

So they sat gossiping, Green-Jeans and Mimile, and drank thirty mugs or so, and Green-Jeans was reeling a bit, when, around ten, he returned to the Great Saint Druon Inn.

IV

"What errand could he possibly have with my father?" Fair Ida wondered.

Turning this idea over and over in her mind, the poor girl took the wrong road and lost her way. She realized her mistake when she found herself in front of about twenty coke furnaces. She heard a man's footsteps and stopped short. It was a coal-worker, or, if you prefer, a miner, coming home from work,

"What are you doing here, pretty lady?" he said.

"I'm looking for the road to Mons, my fine fellow. If you'd like to escort me, you'll get a reward."

"Who saved you from the monster?"

"No one much—and he doesn't want to marry me."

"Where is he?"

"He left me at the edge of Jemmapes."

"What a pity he didn't want to marry such a nice girl," said the miner, thinking it over.

This miner had a soul as black as his face. His pal the Devil had put an infernal idea into his head. "You see those coke furnaces?" he said to Fair Ida.

"Yes,"

"Well, now! You're going to swear to me, on your soul's salvation, that you'll tell your father that I was the one who saved you, and if you refuse I'm going to roast you alive!"

He put his large hand on her shoulder.

The poor girl was frightened, and swore that she'd do all that the wicked coal-worker wanted.

The Count of Hainault was delighted to see his daughter safe and sound, and held a feast for her pretended rescuer, even though he wasn't much to look at, and seemed like a very bad match for a young lady.

A few days later, he called his court together for an engagement dinner. It was such a grand celebration that the folk in Mons had never seen one to match it. Five oxen, ten pigs, and twenty sheep were killed for it, and a hundred casks of beer and five barrels of brandywine were opened. Honestly, they were even drinking wine, although they didn't grow grapes around there. As the dining hall wasn't vast enough to hold all the guests, a big table was put up in the main courtyard.

Everybody was rejoicing, all but Fair Ida, who was pale and sorrowful. She didn't dare tell anybody the cause of her grief, for fear of going at her death to burn in hell, where the fire, so people said, was seventeen times fiercer than the flames in a coke furnace.

When the dessert was served, a guard came in and announced to the Count that there was a young man, a stranger, asking to speak to him.

"Bring him in!" said the Count.

And in came Green-Jeans, all dressed in velvet silk embroidered in gold. Besides his cape, his doublet, and his short cloak swept proudly over his shoulder, he had the most charming face ever seen. In each hand he held a pot full of gold coins.

"Welcome, welcome, Sir," said the Count, and told the servants to set another place.

Fair Ida turned her eyes toward the newcomer and gave a little cry of surprise, or maybe joy. This cry drew Green-Jeans' attention, and he bowed to her.

The coal-worker saw all this. "What does that popinjay want with you?" he said in a loud voice to Fair Idea, for he was as surly and rude as a boatman.

"The popinjay wants to pluck you like a goose!" said Green-Jeans, and he threw his plate at the coal-worker's head.

The coal-worker looked as if he would jump over the table and attack Green-Jeans, but the people caught hold of him and kept him back, so he had to limit himself to heaping insults on him.

"My lord Count," said Green-Jeans, "I must inform you that it wasn't this fine jackdaw who saved your daughter."

"Who is this?" said the Count.

"You'll learn that later."

"You're a liar, you screeching magpie!" roared the coal-worker.

"The jousting field can settle this," said the Count.

"Yes, right now!" said Green-Jeans, and he threw off his cap and his cloak.

V

The two champions got ready for the combat, which would take place in the courtyard. The coal-worker entered armed all in iron—helmet, mailcoat, breastplate, wrist-braces, and boots, on a horse also in iron gear. It has to be mentioned that the rider didn't look comfortable in the saddle.

Green-Jeans thought it would be useless to mount a horse, and didn't even send for his good bar of iron. He contented himself with turning up his sleeves so as not to spoil the quilted jacket embroidered with gold.

The coal-worker lowered his visor and, holding his lance at rest, galloped at him. Green-Jeans jumped to the side, caught hold of his foot, and tipped him up and off the horse (which kept on going), letting him fall into his arms. Then he wrung him out like a washcloth, the way a servant wrings out his rag after washing the floor-tiles, and flung him into a corner, where the traitor went rolling over with a clanging like a load of scrap-iron.

"He's dead," said the Count, "so he must have been in the wrong."

"And I won't have to carry my head under one arm in the next world," said Green-Jeans, "because I really was the one who saved your daughter from inevitable death."

"So you're the one who's going to marry her?"

"But I haven't felt fear yet, have I?"

"No."

"Well! I call myself the Fearless, and I'm not going to get married until I've felt fear. It's a vow that I made—just ask the lady."

Fair Ida said nothing, because she'd fainted away, understandably.

"When you save a girl, you're supposed to marry her. That's the custom," said the Count, much annoyed. "And you're going to marry her, or else!"

"I won't!"

"You will!"

"If you can make me feel fear, I will," said Green-Jeans, unruffled.

The Count reflected that killing Green-Jeans would not be a good way to force him to marry her. "All right—I'm still going to manage it," he thought, and whispered a few words to a captain, who went out straightaway. Then the Count said to Green-Jeans, "Just as you like."

"Well, well! you're a fine fellow, my lord," replied Green-Jeans. He stood up, his glass in his hand. The others did the same. "I drink," he said, "to the health of this il…"

At these words—boom!—a horrible explosion went off. You'd have thought the castle was collapsing. Everyone jumped.

"…lustrious company," Green-Jeans finished. And he emptied his glass in one gulp. "Tell your guns to shut up when I'm talking," he added, setting down his glass.

"The rascal doesn't fear twenty cannons, not a bit. What's to be done?" murmured the Count.

The noise of the cannons had awakened Fair Ida from her faint. Someone told her what the Count had tried.

"Wait here!" she said in a low voice. She went out for a moment and came back, followed by two bold squires, one holding a tart made with plums as big as cartwheels, and the other a superb mince pie. "I'm going to slice the tart, and meantime, you can cut into the pie, my lord," she told Green-Jeans.

Green-Jeans, like someone well brought up, took a knife, bent down over the pie, and set about the task of lifting off the crust.

Suddenly something jumped out of it and landed on the slicer's nose.

It was fair Ida's canary.

Green-Jeans, who was not expecting anything of the sort, jerked back a step, frightened.

"He's afraid of it!" the people there all cried with one voice. "He's going to marry Fair Ida!"

"I will marry her, gentlemen," said Green-Jeans, "because she's a girl with spirit, and it seems to me that a girl with spirit is stronger than a man without fear."

VI

The Count dubbed him a knight of Saint George, on the spot, in honor of his victory over the monster, and a week later the new knight married Fair Ida at Sainte-Vaudrue.

There was a celebration even finer than the one before. Green-Jeans' mother and brother were there, as well as Mimile Bicanne and Mother Bocaud. But they didn't serve any pancakes.

During the dessert, Antoine Classe, the singer from Mons, struck up a song, accompanied by Roland Delattre on the theorbo. And a famous astrologer from Bernissart came, and predicted that the young couple would live long and happily together and have many children. Strange to say, they did live happily together, which mainly means that the wife of the Fearless would always lead her husband around by the nose.

It's in memory of these curious events that every year, in the duchy of Mons, they hold a magnificent tourney that people call the Lumçon. A charcoal-brick-maker, armed head to foot, represents the knight of Saint George. With a shot from his pistol, he kills a frightful monster made out of willow-branches, and that night in all the bars of Mons they fill their glasses and sing songs of Green-Jeans' fame.

The Little Soldier

In olden times, there was a little soldier, who was on his way home from the war. He was a fine little soldier, not missing a hand or an eye, and not lame, or old and worn out. He had no need to count up his limbs to make sure they were all there. But the war was ended, and the army had been disbanded.

His name was John from the Basse-Deûle, the son of a boatman and his wife, who lived in the Basse-Deûle, near Lille, in Flanders. In a lucky hour, he'd been nicknamed Rôtelot, which around here is the word for "Wren," but means "little king," because the wren is called the King of the Birds.

Was he called that because he was so short, a rarity among the Flemish, or because one day he ought to become a king, or was it rather because he was a wren in temperament?—wrens are trusting sorts, and easy to tame. I don't know, and even he himself would not have been sorry to find out just why.

While they waited for him, the stove in their house had collapsed, and the result was that his father, his mother, his brothers, his sisters—nobody was still alive to welcome him home. Although he had a long way to go, he was taking his time going back, not trying to hurry.

But he stepped out proudly: one, two, one, two! Sack on his back, sword at his side, one, two! One evening, while he was passing through an unfamiliar forest, he found himself wanting to smoke a pipe. He looked for his tinder box so that he could strike a light, but was much annoyed to find that he'd lost it.

He kept on going, about as far as a crossbow shoots, and at that point he spotted a light among the trees. He turned toward it, and soon found himself in front of an old castle. The door was open.

He went into the courtyard and saw through one of the windows a big fire in one of the lower rooms. He filled his pipe and knocked gently, calling out, "Could someone give me a light?" in the usual way. But no one answered.

John knocked more loudly. Nothing moved. He lifted the latch and went in. The room was empty.

The little soldier went right to the chimney, took hold of the tongs, and reached down to pick up an ember, when all of a sudden, click! He heard the noise of a spring snapping open, and an enormous serpent sprang at his face from the middle of the flames.

What a strange thing!—the serpent had a woman's head.

I know more than one fellow who'd have taken to his heels, but the little soldier was a true soldier. He only took one step back, and put his hand on the hilt of his sword.

"Don't draw your sword," said the serpent. "I've been waiting for you—you're the one who's going to free me."

"Who are you, my lady?"

"I'm called Ludovine, and I'm the daughter of the King of the Low Countries. Take me away from here, and I'll marry you and make you happy."

If a serpent with a woman's head proposed to make me happy, I'd ask for time to think it over; but Wren did not know that distrust is the mother of safety. Besides, Ludovine was looking at him with eyes that fascinated him, as if he'd been a lark.

They were very beautiful green eyes, not round like a cat's, but almond-shaped, and opened wide. Her gaze shown out of them with a strange brilliance. They gleamed like lights reflected in the Vicq Marsh, and they lit up a ravishing face, framed in long golden curls. You'd have thought it was an angel's head on the serpent's body.

"What must I do?" said Wren.

"Open this door. You'll see a hallway there, and at the end of it a room just like this one. Go to the back of the room, and take out my blouse, which is in the wardrobe there, and bring it to me."

The little soldier set out boldly. He went through the hallway without any trouble, but, when he came to the room, he saw, by the light of the stars, eight hands holding themselves up in mid-air, at about the height of his face. No matter how hard he stared, he couldn't see what was holding them up.

He attacked them bravely, head lowered under a hail of blows, which he paid back by striking out with his fists. Reaching the wardrobe, he opened it, took out the blouse, and carried it back to the first room.

"Here it is!" said John, a little out of breath.

Click! Ludovine burst into flame. This time she was a woman down to her hips. She took the blouse and put it on.

It was a magnificent blouse of orange velvet, all embroidered with pearls—but never mind that. What was important for Ludovine was that now she was so much a woman that she had her white shoulders back, even if you couldn't see them.

"But that isn't all," she said. "Go down the hall, take the stairway on the left, go up to the next floor, and in the second room you'll find another wardrobe. This has my skirt. Bring it to me."

The Wren obeyed. When he got to the room, instead of hands, he saw eight arms holding enormous rods. He didn't turn pale, but drew his saber and attacked them, as he had done the first time. Swinging his saber round and round, he held them off, and was only just grazed by a couple blows, no more.

He took the skirt, a skirt of silk as blue as the sky in Spain.

"Here's the skirt!" said John, and the serpent appeared. Now it was a woman down to the knees.

"Now all I need is my shoes and stockings," it said. "Go and find them for me in the wardrobe two floors up."

The little soldier went there, and found himself in the presence of eight goblins, armed with hammers, their eyes flaming.

At sight of them, he stopped short, on the threshold.

"My saber can't keep me safe from these," he said. "These things are going to smash me like glass, and I'm a dead man, if I can't come up with some other way."

He looked at the door and saw that it was made of oak, thick and heavy. He put his arms around it, lifted it off the hinges, and held it on his head. He went straight to the goblins, threw the door on them, ran to the wardrobe, and took out the shoes and stockings. He brought them to Ludovine, who this time became a woman, head to foot.

If there was still anything of the serpent about her, Wren could not see it, and, as for the rest, he had never seen anything finer.

Ludovine, while putting on her pretty stockings of white silk embroidered at the tops, and her darling blue shoes, decorated with garnets, said to her deliverer: "You can't rest here for long, and, no matter what happens, you must not set foot here again. Here is a purse with two hundred ducats. Go take a room for the night at the Inn of the Three Lime-trees, at the edge of the forest, and be ready tomorrow morning. I will drive past the door at nine o'clock and take you into my coach.

"Why don't we both leave right now?" suggested the little soldier.

"The time hasn't come yet."

And the princess accompanied these words with a look of royal command that bewitched the Wren.

She was tall and proud, her figure as thin and swaying as a birch-tree. In her every move there was something yielding like a wave and yet regal.

John had already half turned to leave, when the princess seemed to change her mind.

"Wait," she said, "You've surely earned a little glass of something to drink."

A soldier, especially a Flemish soldier, never turns down a parting cup.

The Wren turned back, and Ludovine took from an old sideboard a crystal flask. A liquid sparkled inside it and seemed to bubble with flecks of gold. She poured a little glass of it and handed it to John.

"Here's to your good health, my beautiful princess," said the Wren, "and to our happy marriage!"

And he drank off the glass in one draft, without noticing that Ludovine's lip had quirked on the left side in a slight smile, like the tail of a lizard curled up on itself.

"Make sure you're on time tomorrow," the princess advised him.

"Don't worry—I will."

And John, after lighting his pipe, made her a military salute and left.

"Anyone would think," he said to himself, "that when I was nick-named for the King Wren, it must certainly have been because they thought I'd be a king someday."

He didn't stop to think that there was one point he'd forgotten. He hadn't asked what could have made three-fourths of such a beautiful princess into a serpent.

II

When he got to the Inn of the Three Limetrees, John of the Basse-Deûle called for a grand supper. Unfortunately, when he was sitting down at the table, he felt so sleepy that, even though he was very hungry, he started to fall asleep on his plate.

"That's what comes of such hard work," thought John.

He left word that they should wake him at eight o'clock, and went up to his room.

The little soldier slept like a log all through the night. The next morning, at eight o'clock, when he heard a knock at his door, he cried, "I'm here!" and fell back into a sleep as heavy as lead. At half past eight, at quarter to nine, they knocked again, but every time John fell back to sleep. They decided to let him be.

Noon had struck when the sleeper awoke. He jumped out of bed, got dressed in no time, and went in search of the landlady to ask if anyone had come to ask for him.

"Yes," said the landlady, "a beautiful princess in a coach all trimmed with gold was here. She said she would come by again tomorrow at eight o'clock precisely, and she left this bouquet to be given to you."

The little soldier was in despair over this mishap, and cursed his sleepiness a hundred times. He even considered going to the castle to apologize, but he remembered that Ludovine had forbidden him to come back, and he was afraid he would displease her. He consoled himself with looking at the bouquet. It was a bouquet of immortelles—dried flowers that could not fade.

"Immortelles are flowers for remembrance," he thought. It did not occur to him that they're also the flowers for the tomb.

When night came, he slept hardly a wink, and kept waking up twenty times in the hour. When he heard the birds bidding good-day to the dawn, he jumped out of bed, left the inn through the window, and climbed up the tallest of the three lime-trees that shaded the door.

He perched himself astride the biggest branch, and sat contemplating his bouquet. It shone in the shadowy dawning like a sheaf of stars.

He looked at it so hard and so often that at last he fell asleep over it. Nothing could wake him up, not the bright sunbeam, nor the twittering of the birds, nor the clatter of Ludovine's gold coach, nor the landlady's cries, who was looking all through the inn for him.

Again, this time, he woke at noon, and looked very sheepish when he saw through the window that they were setting the table ready for dining.

"Was the princess here?" he asked.

"Yes, indeed. She left this flame-colored scarf for you and said that she would come by tomorrow at seven o'clock, but that will be the last time.

"Someone must have cast a spell over me," thought the little soldier. He took the scarf, which was made of silk embroidered with the princess's initial in gold. It gave off a sweet, strong smell of perfume. He tied it around his left arm, closest to his heart. It occurred to him that the best way to be awake at the hour named was not to go to bed at all. So he paid his bill, bought a lively horse with the money he had left, and when evening came, he mounted into the saddle, and waited there in front of the inn-door, having made up his mind to spend the night there.

From time to time he bent his head down toward his arm to smell the scarf's sweet scent. He bent over it so hard and so often that in the end he fell asleep on the horse's neck, and very soon both horse and rider were snoring together.

When the princess arrived, it was in vain for anyone to call them, or shake them, or hit them. Nothing worked. Man and beast did not wake until after she had left, at the moment when the coach disappeared around a bend in the road.

John galloped his horse at full speed, calling at the top of his voice, "Stop! Stop!"

The horse was an excellent animal and went like the wind, but the coach, for its part, went rolling along like lightning, so they rode for a day and a night, always the same distance apart. The horse could not gain on the coach by even the length of one turn of the wheel.

In this way they crossed through an infernal round of cities, towns, and villages, and all the people came out and stood on their doorsteps to see them pass.

At last, they came to the edge of the sea. John hoped that the coach would stop there, but—a wonderful thing!—it rolled out into the waves and glided over the liquid plain as if it were still rolling over solid ground.

The brave horse, exhausted, fell, and could not get up again, and the little soldier sat down on the shore, looking sadly at the coach as it vanished over the horizon.

III

Nevertheless, he did not lose heart. After resting long enough to catch his breath, he started walking along the beach to see if he might find any kind of a boat, so that he could follow the princess. He didn't find any boats, big or small, and he was almost worn out when he came across a fisherman's cottage.

No one was there except a girl mending a net. She stood up quickly, and seeing the little soldier ready to collapse, she offered him her stool. Then she helped him to a pitcher of water, some fried fish, and a hunk of brown bread, spreading them out on a table of white wood. John ate and drank, and, recovering his strength, he told his story to the pretty fisher-girl.

She was very pretty. In spite of living in the fierce winds at the sea-shore, her skin was as white as the wings of seagulls seen against a storm-black sky. Indeed, Seagull was what everyone called her.

But John did not notice the whiteness of her skin, nor the infinite sweetness of her eyes, like a pair of violets in milk; he thought only of the princess's green eyes.

When he had finished his story, she seemed touched with pity for him, and she said, "Last week, fishing at low tide, I could feel from the weight of my shrimping net that it held more than just shrimp. I drew it in carefully, and I saw through the mesh a big vase made of copper and sealed with lead. I carried it here and set it on the fire. When the lead began to melt, I was able to pry it off with my knife and open the vase. Inside I found a cloak of red cloth and a little purse with about fifty florins. Here's the cloak on my bed, and you can see the vase there, on the chimney, and here's the purse."

And with that, she opened the drawer in the table. "I keep the fifty florins to be my dowry, because I don't meant to live alone all my life…"

"Alone?" John interrupted. "You don't have a father or mother?"

"My mother died in bringing me into the world. My father, and my two brothers, sank with our boat to the bottom of the sea a year ago."

"Poor child! Indeed, you'd do well to get yourself married as soon as possible."

"Oh! there's no hurry. And as I'm hardly likely to find a husband to my liking all that soon, here, take the purse. When you've had a rest, go to the port nearby. It's only half an hour away. You can get a boat there, and when you become the King of the Low Countries you can repay me the fifty florins. I'll wait for you to return."

After saying this much, the poor little thing could not keep from sighing.

The sigh meant: "Why does he have to go running after princesses who, it seems to me, are making fun of him? He'd do better to stay here with me. He seems to have such a brave heart, that if only he'd ask me to be his wife, I couldn't ask for any other husband."

But the Wren didn't hear her sigh, and even if he had, he wouldn't have understood why, because the Seagull hadn't explained it to him.

"When I am the King of the Low Countries," he said, "I'll make you the queen's maid of honor, because you are as good as you are beautiful."

The girl smiled weakly and said: "It's time for me to see what I've netted. If I don't see you again here, I wish you well and happy."

"Goodbye for the moment!" said John, and while the Seagull was gathering in her net, he wrapped himself in the cloak and stretched out on a heap of dried grass.

He went over in his mind all that had happened to him since he had looked for his tinder-box, and he couldn't keep from exclaiming to himself: "Oh! how I wish I were at the capital city in the kingdom of the Low Countries!"

IV

All at once, the little soldier found himself standing in a big court-yard in front of a superb palace. He opened his eyes wide, he rubbed them, he pinched himself, and when he was quite sure that he wasn't dreaming, he went over to a merchant who was smoking a pipe on his doorstep. "Where am I?" he asked him.

"Good heavens!—you can see, can't you, you're in front of the king's palace?"

"Which king?"

"The King of the Low Countries," said the merchant, trying not to laugh at him, for he took him for a madman.

You can just imagine how astonished John was. Being an honest man, he considered that the Seagull must be thinking him a thief, and he grew sad at the idea. He promised himself that he would surely bring the cloak and the purse back to her.

It occurred to him that there might be a power attached to this cloak and that it might have been enough to have transported him in an instant to the end of his journey. Wanting to find out for sure, he wished himself in the best hotel in the city, and there he was, in the same moment.

Enchanted by this discovery, he ordered a good supper to be served him, drank two bottles of Louvain beer, and, as it was too late to pay a visit to the King, he went to bed. He certainly felt ready for it!

The next morning, pressing his nose against the window, he saw that the houses were hung with flags, decked with leafy green branches, and garlanded with festoons of flowers that bridged the street, running from each attic window to the one opposite. Carillons were playing in all the town's bell towers, and, in the middle of that noise, he could also make out the jingling of drops of glass hanging from the wreaths.

The little soldier asked if they were expecting a prince to arrive, or if it was a festival to consecrate the street.

"We're expecting the king's daughter, the beautiful Ludovine," was the reply. "She's been found, and she's going to make a triumphal entrance. Listen!—do you hear the trumpets? Here's the procession coming."

"That's wonderfully convenient," thought the Wren. "I'll go stand at the door, and let's just see if my princess will recognize me."

He got dressed lickety-split, and, going down the stairs in two jumps, he was there just at the moment when Ludovine's gilded coach passed in front of the door. She was dressed in a gown of brocade, with a gold diadem on her head, and her blonde curls falling down to her shoulders.

The King and the Queen were seated beside her, and the courtiers, dressed in silk and velvet, were jumping for joy alongside the door of the coach. Ludovine's imperious gaze fell by chance on the little soldier. She turned a little pale and looked away.

"Can it be that she isn't going to recognize me?" asked the Wren, "or is she angry because I wasn't on time to meet her before?"

He paid the landlord and followed the crowd. When the procession had gone into the palace, he asked to speak to the King, but it was all in vain for him to swear that he was the one who had saved the princess. The guards thought he was touched in the head and stubbornly barred the way against him.

The little soldier was furious. He felt that he needed to smoke a pipe. He went to a tavern nearby and drank a pint of beer.

"It's this miserable military uniform," he told himself. "They're hardly likely to let me get near the King unless I glitter like all those fine lords, and I can't manage that on fifty florins—besides, I've already spent some of them."

He pulled out his purse and remembered that he hadn't counted to see how much was in it. He found fifty florins there.

"The Seagull must have miscounted," John thought, and paid for his pint. Then he counted what was left, and found it was still fifty florins! He put five aside and counted the rest a third time. It still came out fifty florins. He emptied the purse completely and closed it. Opening it up again, he found fifty florins inside.

"Good heavens!" said John, "here I am richer than rich, when I've never had more than five fine sous at once before. I'm beginning to hope that the people at the palace won't treat me next time like a dog in a ball-game at Condé.

He came up with an idea then, and carried it out without delay. He went straight to the court tailor and coachmaker.

At the tailor's, he had made a jerkin and a cloak of blue velvet, all embroidered with pearls. He chose blue because the princess had seemed to prefer it. At the coachmaker's, he ordered a gilded coach just like the one the beautiful Ludovine had. He paid double the price to have it ready as soon as possible.

A few days later, the little soldier rode through the city streets in his coach, drawn by six white horses richly caparisoned, and driven by a fat coachman with a great beard. Standing on the back of the coach he had four poor devils for lackeys, all tall and decked out in fancy clothes.

Dressed in his fine clothes, looking too high-born for anyone to challenge him, John carried in his hand the bouquet of immortelles, and wore over his left arm the princess's scarf. He rode twice through the town and passed the windows of the palace twice.

On the third time round, he drew out his purse and flung fistfuls of florins right and left, as the godfathers and godmothers in our country fling small coins when they come out after the baptism. All the little scamps in town followed after the coach, crying, "Hey! Hey!" at the tops of their voices. There were more than a thousand of them when the coach, for the third time, reached the front of the palace. The Wren saw Ludovine, glued to the window, lift up a corner of the curtains and peep out at him from behind it.

V

The next day, all they talked about in town was the stranger-lord who kept pulling fistfuls of florins out of his purse, which never ran out.

People even talked about it at the court, and the queen was so full of curiosity that she had a fierce longing to see the marvelous purse.

"There's a way to take care of that," said the King. "Have someone run and invite this lord in my name to come here this evening to play cards."

You can imagine how careful the Wren was to come without fail. The King, the Queen, and the Princess were waiting for him in the little red room. The Queen and the Princess were spinning, and the King was smoking his pipe. The cat was turning around in a circle in a corner of the chimney, and the pot was bubbling over the fire.

The King called for some cards and invited John to sit at the table. John lost one, two, three, ten hands. He thought he could see that the King was cheating a little, but that didn't matter. John had come on purpose to lose.

The game was for fifty florins, and each time he emptied his purse, it always filled up again.

At the tenth hand, the King said: "That's astonishing!"

The Queen said: "It's startling!"

The Princess said: "It's astounding!"

"Not as astounding," said the little soldier, "as your transformation into a serpent!"

"Shush," the King interrupted, for he did not care for this subject of conversation.

"If I can allow myself to put it this way," John went on, "it's just that you see before you the one who had the happiness of drawing your young lady out of the goblins' hands, as witness the fact that she promised to marry me for my pains."

"Is that true?" the King asked the Princess.

"It's true," replied the beautiful Ludovine, "but I had instructed my deliverer to be ready at the time when I would drive by in my coach. I came by three times, and every time he was sleeping so soundly that no one could wake him."

"It wasn't for lack of trying to fight against that cursed slumber," the little soldier sighed, "but if it was the result of your generosity in giving—"

"What's your name?" asked the King.

"I'm John of the Basse-Deûle, but people call me the Wren."

"Are you a king, or the son of a king?"

"I'm a soldier, and the son of boat-folk."

"You wouldn't be the right sort of husband for my daughter. Even so, if you'd like to give me your purse, the Princess is yours."

"The purse isn't my property, and I can't give it away."

"But you could let me borrow it until our wedding day," said the Princess, passing a cup of coffee to him with her fair hand, and gazing at him so intently that John did not know how to refuse her anything.

"When shall we be married?"

"At Easter," said the King.

"Or at Trinity Sunday," the Princess said softly.

The Wren didn't hear that, and he let Ludovine take the purse.

The King went to fetch a bottle of old Schiedam whiskey to drink to the bargain, and they chatted together over the bottle so long that John left the palace two hours after the clock in the belfry had sounded the curfew. He walked in zigzags, and although it was black night—for in those days the street-lamps were put out at nine o'clock—to his eyes everything was rose-colored.

The next evening he presented himself at the palace to play piquet with the King and court the Princess; but he was told that the King had gone to the countryside to collect the rents on his farms.

He came the next evening and got the same answer. He asked to see the Queen; the Queen had a migraine. He returned three, four, six times, and they always shut the door in his face. He realized that they were making fun of him.

"For a king, he's being very unfair," said John to himself. "I won't be surprised anymore if he cheats. What a crook!"

While he was feeling so hurt, he happened to remember his red cloak.

"By my patron saint, Saint John," he cried, "I'm a fool to get in a temper. I can get into that shack of theirs whenever I like."

And that evening he went to walk in front of the palace, wearing his red cloak.

There was only one window lit on the upper floor. A shadow passed behind the curtains. John, who had the eye of a falcon, recognized the Princess's shadow.

"I wish," he said, "to be transported into Princss Ludovine's room." And there he was.

The King's daughter was sitting at a table, busy counting the florins she was taking out of the inexhaustible purse: "Eight hundred fifty, nine hundred, nine hundred fifty—"

68

"—a thousand!" said John. "Good evening to all here."

The Princess turned around and gave a little cry. "You here! What do you mean to do? What do you want? Go away! go away, I tell you, or I'll call—"

"I came, said the Wren "to hold you to your promise. The day after tomorrow is Easter, and it's time for us to think about our marriage."

Ludovine burst out laughing. "Our marriage! Are you fool enough to think that the daughter of the King of the Low Countries would marry the son of a boat-man?"

"In that case, give me back my purse," said John.

"Never!" said the Princess, and reaching out quickly she grabbed it and put it in her pocket.

"Oh, is that how it is!" said the little soldier. "He laughs best who laughs last." He took the Princess in his arms and cried, "I wish to be at the ends of the earth."

And there he was, still holding the Princess in his arms.

"Oof!" said John, setting her down at the foot of a tree. "I've never made such a long trip. How about you, my lady?"

The Princess understood that it was no time for her to be laughing at him, and said nothing. Besides, she felt stunned by so swift a journey, and she could hardly pull her thoughts together.

VI

The King of the Low Countries was not a very scrupulous king, and his daughter was scarcely any better. Like comparing bread to pie, as we say around here. That's why Ludovine had been transformed into a serpent. She was fated to be saved by a little soldier, and, for his pains, she would have to marry her liberator, at least, unless he failed three times to show up for their appointed meeting. The tricky Princess had arranged matters accordingly.

The drink she had given John in the goblins' castle, the bouquet of immortelles, and the scarf she had given him, all had the power of inducing sleep. You couldn't drink the liquor, or stare at the flowers, or smell the scarf's perfume without falling into a deep sleep. And at this critical moment, Ludovine kept her wits about her.

"I thought you were simply a poor boatman from off the streets," she said in her sweetest voice, "but now I see that you are more powerful

69

than a king. Here's your purse. Do you still have my scarf and my bouquet?"

"Here they are," said Wren, charmed by her change of tone, and he pulled out the bouquet and the scarf.

Ludovine fastened the flowers in his buttonhole and tied the scarf around the little soldier's arm. "Now," she said, "you are my lord and master, and I will marry you whenever you like."

"You're better than I had thought," said John, touched by her humble submission, "and I promise you that you won't be unhappy in our household, because I love you."

"Really and truly?"

"Really and truly."

"Then, my little husband, tell me how you were able to carry me off and transport us so quickly to the ends of the earth."

The little soldier scratched his head. "Are you asking me that seriously," he said, "or are you going to fool me again?"

But Ludovine said, "Oh, do tell me, you can tell me," in a voice so coaxing, with such a tender look, that he didn't know how to resist.

"After all," he thought, "I can confide my secret to her, so long as I don't confide the cloak itself to her."

And he revealed to her the power of the cloak.

"I'm very tired," Ludovine sighed. "Suppose we go to sleep for a while? Then we can consider what we should do."

She lay down on the grass, and the Wren did the same. He pillowed his head on his left arm, and as that had him breathing the full perfume of the scarf, soon he was in a deep slumber.

Ludovine stayed alert, both with eye and ear, and as soon as she heard him snore, she unfastened the cloak, pulled it gently toward herself, wrapped it around her, took the purse from the sleeper's pocket, and said: "I want to be in my own room!" And there she was.

VII

Who was as sheepish as our Master John, when he woke up, twenty-four hours later, with no princess, no purse, and no cloak. He tore at his hair, he struck himself with his fists, he trampled the treacherous Princess's bouquet underfoot, and tore the scarf into a thousand pieces.

"I definitely think," he said, "that if I'm called the Wren, it's because I'm too trusting, and I follow like a little bird when I hear a birdcall."

But it was no time to sit around in despair, because he stil had to live, and John was so hungry he could have roasted larks in mid-air, just by looking at them. Was he in a wasteland, or was it somewhere people lived, and what would be on the menu for his dinner? That's what worried him at the moment.

Ever since he was a little boy, he had often heard his grandmother say that at the ends of the earth there were housewives who hung out their linen to dry on the lines of the rainbow. That would be a good way to see if the place was inhabited, at least, if they'd just done a washing.

On the other hand, the good woman had also told him that the moon was a big golden apple; that the dear Lord picked it when it was ripe and put it in a row with the other full moons, in a big closet at the ends of the earth, at the part where the end is boarded up. A quarter of the moon would make a meal that a man so famished wouldn't turn down. John felt he was even hungry enough to gulp down a whole moon.

Unfortunately, he had always suspected that his grandmother's wits were wandering a little, and anyhow he didn't see any boards closing off the end, or any closet, and, as it had stopped raining, the rainbow had faded away several minutes earlier.

The little soldier turned his nose up and realized that he'd been sleeping under a splendid plum tree, its branches loaded with plums as yellow as gold.

"Plums will do!" he said, "nice little Mirabelle plums! In wartime you have to take what you can get!"

He climbed the tree and perched on a branch as if sitting down at a table. But what an unbelievable wonder! He had hardly eaten two plums when it seemed to him that something was sprouting out of his forehead. He put up his hand to feel, and found he grown two horns.

Frightened, he jumped to the ground below the tree and ran to a brook that was babbling nearby. And there—alas!—he saw two charming horns that would have looked very nice on a goat, but looked very awkward on the little soldier.

He began to despair.

"It's not enough," he said, "that a woman tricked me without having the devil show up and lend me his horns! What a fine figure I'll make once I get back to civilization!"

But the poor fellow had nothing else to eat, and a famished belly won't listen to objections, even when there's a risk of growing horns; and anyway the damage was done, so he could scarcely make it worse, and besides John had nothing else to sink his teeth into, so he boldly climbed a second tree. This one bore beautiful green plums, like the greengages Queen Claudia grew.

He'd hardly swallowed two, when his horns disappeared. The little soldier was surprised, but delighted by this new marvel, and concluded that you should never be too hasty to complain of being utterly miserable. He ate enough to satisfy his hunger, and, at that point, he had an idea.

"These pretty little plums here," he thought, "might help me get my cloak, my purse, and my heart out of the hands of that rascally princess. She has eyes like a gazelle already—she might as well have the horns! If I manage to plant a pair on her it's a safe bet that I'll be too disgusted to want her for my wife. A horned girl—what a handsome beast!"

He bravely went on with the experiment to make sure of the plums' twin powers. He wove a basket more or less neatly out of willow twigs he picked from a tree growing beside a stream, put plums of both sorts into it, and then went exploring. He walked for several days, with nothing to eat but fruits and roots, before he came to a place where people lived. His only fear was that his plums might spoil on the way. But he saw, to his great joy, that in addition to their magical powers, they stayed fresh. He suffered hunger valiantly, and thirst, and heat, and cold, and fatigue. Several times he was almost eaten by wild animals, or cannibals, but nothing could discourage him. He was kept going by the thought of getting his revenge.

"I'll show them" he said, "that the Wren may be little and not distrustful by nature, but he's no more of a dumb beast than those fine friends of his, our royal masters."

At last he got to a civilized country, and by selling some jewels he had—for he'd bought them in preparing for his flight—he was able to take passage on a ship that was setting sail for the Low Countries. A year and a day later, he landed at the kingdom's capital city.

VIII

The day after his arrival, which was a Sunday, he bought a false beard, blackened one eye, and dressed himself like the date-merchants who come every year for the Kermess-fair at Valenciennes. Then he took a little table and set himself up at the church door.

He spread out his maribelle plums on a fine white cloth. They looked as if they had been freshly gathered, and at the moment when the Princess came out after attending Mass, he began to shout, in a disguised voice, "Plums for madame! Plums for madame!"

"I've heard of plums for the gentleman," said the Princess, 'but I've never heard of plums for madame. How much are they?"

"Fifty florins each."

"Fifty florins! What makes them so extraordinary? Do they make you smarter, or lovelier?"

"They can't make someone who is already perfect more so, divine Princess, but they can add unusual ornaments."

A rolling stone may not gather any moss, but it does take on a polish. John had not wasted his time while he traveled around the world. A compliment so neatly turned flattered Ludovine.

"What ornaments?" she said, smiling.

"You'll see, beautiful Princess, when you've tasted them. It has to be a surprise."

Ludovine's curiosity was roused. She took out the leather purse and poured on the table as many times fifty florins as there were plums in the basket. The little soldier was seized with a furious longing to grab the purse and shout "Thief!" but he managed to control himself.

Having sold the plums, he shut up shop and went to take off his disguise, changed clothes at an inn, and stayed there quietly, waiting to see what would happen, or, as we say around here, for the oats to grow.

The Princess returned to her room. "Now let's see," said the Princess, "what ornaments these lovely plums will add to my beauty." So, while she took off her hat, she took a couple of plums and ate them.

You can imagine the surprise mixed with horror that came over her as she felt her forehead sprouting! She looked at herself in her mirror and let out a shriek.

"Horns! Those are the beautiful ornaments! That miserable wretch! Send someone to find the plum merchant! Cut off his nose and his ears! Flog him! Burn him up, on a slow fire, and scatter the ashes on the wind! Oh! I'll die of shame and despair!"

Her waiting-women came running at her cries and, much astonished, tried to pull the horns off, but in vain. All it did was to give her a violent headache.

The King then sent out his trumpeters to announce that he would give his daughter's hand in marriage to anyone who succeeded in freeing her from her strange head-dress.

All the physicians and sorcerers and bone-setters in the Low Countries and the neighboring kingdoms came one after another to propose their remedies. Some tried soaking the appendages to soften them, or dissolving them by means of liquids, ointments, or pills. Others wanted to cut or saw them off. Nothing worked.

The number of people trying their prescriptions was so great, and the Princess suffered so much from their experiments, that the King had to declare, in a second proclamation, that anyone who proposed to cure the Princess and failed in the attempt would at once be hanged on high.

But the reward was too attractive for the likely result to quench the universal resolve.

So all the trees in the Low Countries bore strange fruit that year! Each of them held three or four hanged men. The crows, attracted by the smell, came flying in crowds from every point of the horizon. There were so many of them that they darkened the sky, and you couldn't see the end of your nose either by moonlight or sunlight.

Even though the air was infected by the gases given off by so many dead bodies, people noticed, as an extraordinary result, that the people roundabout had never been in such good health as they were after that immense hanging of physicians.

The Princess had to resign herself to keeping her horns.

To console her, the lords and ladies of the court assured her, shamelessly, that the horns were wonderfully becoming on her, and that, far from disfiguring her, they added an indefinably intriguing grace to her looks. They even pushed their flattery to the length of eating the rest of the plums in the basket themselves. There never was a court so well behorned as the court of the King of the Low Countries.

As there weren't enough plums to go around, the gentlemen and ladies who didn't succeed in getting any planted fake horns on themselves. In a little while, this head-dress was considered very beautiful, because they carried it off so well, and no doubt that is why, once the fashion had died away, that the phrase "a reason with horns" came to be used around here for reasons that were bizarre or extravagant.

IX

The King gave orders that the plum-merchant must be found, but, in spite of the most extreme diligence, no one could discover him.

When the little soldier believed that they had given up the search, he squeezed the juice of the Queen Claudia plums into a phial, bought a physician's robe at a second-hand clothing shop—you could get them for next to nothing—and put on a wig and spectacles, and then presented himself in this get-up at the door of the King of the Low Countries.

"Here's another madman who wants to be hanged," said the King. "Let him have what he likes. It's the custom not to refuse anything to those who are condemned to death."

As soon as the little soldier was in the presence of the Princess, he poured several drops from the phial into a glass. No sooner had the Princess drunk it than the tips of the horns disappeared.

"They would have gone away completely," said the fake physician, "if there hadn't been something counteracting the power of my elixir. It can only work a complete cure on patients whose souls are as clean as a new penny. Are you sure you don't happen to have some little sin? Think about it."

Ludovine did not have to examine her conscience for long, but she hesitated between a humiliating confession and her longing to be de-horned. The longing won out.

"I robbed a leather purse from a little soldier named John of the Basse-Deûle," she said, lowering her eyes.

"Give it to me. The remedy won't work until I have that purse in my hands."

It cost Ludovine a good deal to give up the purse, but she considered that it would be no use to her to be immensely rich, if she still had to have horns on her head.

Anyway, didn't her father have treasure enough?

She handed the purse over to the doctor, not without a sigh. He again poured out some drops from the phial, and, when the Princess had drunk it, the horns shrank, but only halfway.

"You must have some other little peccadillo on your conscience— didn't you take something more than his purse from this soldier?"

"I also took his cloak."

"Give it to me."

"Here it is."

Ludovine this time was reasoning that once her cure was complete, she would call her servants, and she would know very well how to force the doctor to give the things back.

She was laughing up her sleeve at this idea, when all at once the fake physician wrapped himself in the cloak, flung off the wig and spectacles, and revealed himself to the traitor as John of the Basse-Deûle.

She was silent with fright and astonishment.

"I could leave you with horns for the rest of your days," said John, "but I'm a good sort, and I remember how much I loved you, and, anyhow, to resemble the devil, you don't need his horns!"

He poured out the rest of the phial and disappeared. The Princess drank the glass down in one swallow, without leaving a single drop for the ladies of the court.

X

John had wished himself to the Seagull's house. The Seagull was sitting next to the window, and, while she went on mending her net, she looked out at the sea, from time to time, as if she was expecting someone. At the noise of the little soldier's arrival, she turned her head, and blushed.

"It's you," she said. "How did you get back?" Then she added, her voice trembling with emotion, "What about your Princess—have you married her?"

John told her his adventures, and, when he had finished, he gave her back the purse and the cloak.

"What do you want me to do with them?" she said. "Your example proves that happiness doesn't come from having treasures like these."

"It comes from work and the love of an honest woman," said the little soldier. And for the first time, he noticed that her eyes were the color of violets. "Dear Seagull, will you take me for a husband?" he said, and he held his hand out to her.

"I will indeed," said the fisher-girl, turning redder still, "but on one condition—that we put the purse and the cloak back in the copper vase and throw it all into the sea."

And they did.

The Seagull was a wise girl: she had figured out that a rhythm that comes so easy from the flute gets picked up just as easy by the drum. The only good that's going to stick around with you is the good you've earned yourself.

John of the Basse-Deûle married the Seagull, and they lived together as happily as people can be in this world down here, if they've learned how to limit their desires. It was John himself who told me his story, and he added at the end:

"I believe now that if I'm called the Wren, the little king, it's not because I'm more regal than you tall Flemish beanpoles—it's because I don't stand out."

The White Sparrow

I

In olden times, when the beasts could talk—I mean, when the humans, wiser than they are nowadays, understood the language of the animals—there was in the Forest of Amblise a misseron—or, if you like, a sparrow—as white as snow.

He was as different from the other sparrows in temperament as he was in his plumage. Even though he was as independent and free of a collar as the boldest of the band, no one could reproach him for being impudent, or thievish, or squawky, and that was why none of the others wanted to be friendly with him.

That grieved him, for he had an aspiring nature, and did not want to die as he had lived, without a friend. He resolved to go look for a friend from outside his own species.

He offered his friendship to the bear, but the bear told him rudely that he didn't need anyone. He offered it to the wolf, but the wolf growled and showed him his teeth. He offered it to the fox, and the fox accepted, but he seemed so false and sly that the sparrow decided right away that this companion was planning to have his new friend for breakfast.

So then, instead, he tried the horse, the ox, and the donkey. They shrugged their shoulders and said, "Why should it be any business of ours to take up with a companion so small and weak? You'd do better to go make friends with a gnat."

The poor sparrow became sadder and sadder, for he had thought that he deserved to have a friend, and would have been able to return favor for favor and protection for protection.

He would have tried asking a human; but humans are the wickedest and cruelest of all the animals. Indeed, if wolves eat sheep, they're only obeying the law of nature, in order to satisfy their hunger. A human, instead, does evil for the sake of evil, puts birds in cages, when he doesn't roast them on the spit, and butchers other humans for the honor of it, without the excuse of hunger.

II

One day in the month of May, the poor misseron had gone for a walk by himself out towards Quiévrechain, when he found on the road an old mastiff—lame, blind in one eye, half-starved, dragging himself painfully along. The misseron was touched with pity and said gently, "Where are you going, you poor old fellow?"

"Straight ahead, like any lost dog," said the mastiff. "I stood faithful guard at my house for a long time. Now here I am, almost crippled, and my master has given my job to a young dog, and he was going to kill me, so I ran away."

"What's his name, that scoundrel?"

"Tafarot, the Brewer."

"Is he the one who lives in that dreary big hovel, right on the edge of Quiévrechain, or just a little beyond?"

"The very same."

"I know him. He has a granary full of barley, with a hole in the wall. He's a brute. I've often seen him beat his wife. Well, so in short, you poor dog, you don't have anyone to love you and care for you in your old age?"

"No one."

"Would you like me to be your friend?"

"I'd like that a lot. But what good can you do me, gentle misseron?"

"Well, we can give it a try. While there's life there's hope. Meantime, is it a bargain?" And the friends shook on it.

III

The white misseron, flying ahead of his friend, led him to the farm of Vaucelle, which was the headquarters of the sparrows around there. On the way, they met a magpie who had a tongue that kept going like the clapper on a mill.

"Where are your wings taking you, flying along with that cripple?" cried Madame Goodbeak.

"That cripple is my friend," said the sparrow proudly.

"Behold!—a miracle! The white misseron has found a friend!" exclaimed the irritating magpie.

And she took off ahead of them to announce the news. "Come quick, everyone! Hurry!" she said.

79

In an instant the two companions were surrounded by more than a hundred misserons, who came flocking with an impudent air to look down on the dog. Soon the jeers began raining down as thick as hail.

"What a funny friend!"

"He's only got one eye!"

"He only has three paws!"

"He's all tattered and torn!"

"He's only an old shred of a friend!"

"Where the devil did you find him?"

"At Péruwelz, by heaven! Just yesterday they had their Rag Fair."

The white misseron took in the downpour and answered without getting upset: "Of course all of you are young, handsome, lovable, and, above all, strong-beaked—that's understood. Shut up, now, and let people love each other in peace."

IV

The dog whispered to his friend that he was very hungry.

"There's nothing to pick up here except for sparrows," was the reply, "but if you like to take a step toward Onnaing, I can invite you to dinner."

The mastiff accepted, and, a half hour later, the two companions made their entry into the village. As they came by the butcher's place, the misseron told the dog, "Wait right there."

He flew to perch on the attic window, over the butcher's stall, turned his tail to the street side, and let something drop out onto a big piece of neck-bone.

"You thief of a misseron!" cried the butcher.

He took the piece of meat and wiped it off on his apron, and he was just going to put it back in its place, when he saw the mayor's wife, who lived across the street, watching him from behind the curtain.

He thought it over, and, deciding that it wasn't much of a loss, he flung it to the dog, who was sitting back on his tail, with his nose in the air, expectantly. The mastiff jumped on it, and fled around a corner, where he soon gulped it down.

The two friends lived for some time in this way, the bird cleverly providing meals for the dog. From Onnaing to Quiévrechain, all through the forest of Amblise, nothing was talked about but the friendship of the mastiff and the white misseron.

Unfortunately, the poor old dog grew weaker and weaker, and sometimes when he fell asleep, he slept so deeply that it was hard to wake him.

One day, the misseron said to his friend: "Let's go a little way toward Onnaing and take a look to see if the chicory has come up." And they went there.

On the way, the sun was hot, and the air grew muggy, and the mastiff felt weary, and stretched himself out in the middle of the road to take a nap.

"Don't lie there!" cried his friend. "You could roast!" But the dog was already so sound asleep that he didn't hear him.

The sparrow perched at the top of an elm, and, while still keeping watch over his companion, he began to sing chirp... chirp... chirp to pass the time.

Ten minutes later, the look-out saw some distance away a bourlat, that's to say, a beer-cart, driven by Tafarot, the brewer from Quiévrechain, who used to be the mastiff's owner.

Tafarot was a very advanced brewer for those days. Ahead of all the other brewers, he had found a way to make beer without barley and without hops. But the drinkers of that time were a bunch of oafs, and didn't understand progress. They'd make faces at the taste, and generally refused to stock the product he'd invented at all.

He had just been to an inn in Onnaing, where he had to take back a barrel of new beer. It was in vain to scold. They just said, "Are you scolding?" and invited him to drink it himself.

He was murderously angry. Besides, he had already swallowed twenty pints or so, and the hops were starting to weigh down the perches—that's to say, from drinking toasts, as usually happened.

VI

At sight of the brewer, the misseron tried to wake up his friend. But it was no use to shout in his ear, "Quick, we've got to get out of here—

here comes your old master!" The dog, worn out by the long walk, woke only just enough to fall back into a leaden sleep. The sparrow took it on himself to go right up to the brewer.

"Would you, out of the goodness of your heart, sir," he asked politely, "not run over my old friend, who's asleep in the road?"

"Why don't you wake him up, and make him budge?" Tafarot replied savagely.

"I did my best. He's sleeping like a log, and I can't manage it."

"In that case, too bad for him!"

And the brewer kept coming along the road.

"Do you know that that's your faithful old dog, who served you for ten years!" cried the misseron.

"Oh! That's the old rogue who ran away, "said Tafarot. "I'm glad to find him."

He aimed his cart right at the sleeping dog.

"Stop, you wicked brewer, stop, or you'll be so sorry you'll be biting your thumbs!"

"Oh, yeah? What can you do to me?" said the brute scornfully. He flogged the cart-horse, and the wheel rolled over the body of the poor mastiff, squashing him flat. The misseron gave a cry, his feathers bristled, and his eyes shot fire.

"You wretch!" he cried, "you've killed my friend! You just listen to what I'm going to tell you: you'll pay for his death with everything you own!"

"Do what you like, you ugly magpie-pest!" said the brewer. "I don't care as much as a drop of small-beer."

VII

The white misseron flew off, his heart bleeding. He was cudgeling his brains for a way to avenge the poor dead dog, when he came across the gossipy magpie, who was chattering away, all by herself.

"Where's your friend? What've you done with him?" she asked.

"Alas, my good woman, Tafarot the brewer ran him over—and into the bargain, he called me an ugly magpie-pest!"

"An ugly magpie-pest! But then that's me he was insulting! Where is he?"

"That's him coming now."

"Oh, that's him coming, is it? Very good—stay there, pal, and you'll see something worth seeing."

The sparrow perched on a bush, and Tafarot drove up, cracking his whip.

"Hey there, my boy," Madame Van Goodbeak cried, "is it true that you called the white misseron an ugly magpie-pest?"

"So what?"

"You need to take your cap off and make me an apology. Now."

The brewer shrugged his shoulders. At that sight, quick as an arrow, the bird swooped down on him, grabbed his cap by the tuft, and flew away with it.

"My cap! my cap!" cried Tafarot.

And he chased after the magpie, aiming cracks of his whip at her. She perched herself at the top of a poplar.

The brewer climbed up the tree. He wasn't even halfway up when the thief, with the cap in her beak, was jeering at him from an ash-tree twenty steps away.

Tafarot climbed down and found at the bottom three men from Quaroube, who had taken their billhooks and gone to the woods to collect branches. The three Quarobins split their sides laughing at him. Tafarot, in a rage, pelted the tree with stones.

VIII

While he was thrashing about, the white misseron lost no time, He perched on the cart and, pounding at it with his beak, he pulled out the plug that held the bunghole shut.

The plug was so old and rotten that the beer, in fermenting, was already starting to push it out. So it was easy for the bird to open a gap, where the beer in the keg all ran out.

Tired from chasing the magpie, Tafarot came back to get hold of the reins again. He saw with astonishment that the barrel was drained and empty.

"I'm so unlucky!" he cried, with a groan.

"But not unlucky enough!" said the misseron. He perched on the cart-horse's head and began pecking at it. The horse began to kick and rear.

"Whoa, you miserable runt!" Tafarot yelled, in a fury.

He grabbed the billhook from one of the Quarobins and, hardly knowing what he was doing, struck at the bird. The sparrow hopped to the side, and the blow fell on the horse's head with such force that the horse fell dead.

"Oh! now I'm really unlucky!" wailed the brewer.

"But not unlucky enough!" said the misseron, flying away. "You'll find me when you get home."

IX

Meanwhile his wife was waiting for him and grilling some meat for his supper. She was a poor creature. He used to thrash her like wheat, and the force of the blows had left her almost an idiot. Her name was Clara, and from that she was nicknamed Clarette and then Raclette, because the scrapes and bruises she kept getting every blessed day made such a racket.

While the meat was grilling, she remembered that the beer was down below, and the keg needed to be tapped. If her brute of a husband came back and found no pitcher of beer on the table, she was sure to get a beating.

Raclette went down to the basement, tapped the keg, and put the pitcher under the opening. She had hardly turned the tap, when she heard a great noise, like a thousand birds swooping down on the roof.

Quickly, she went upstairs to see what it was. When she got to the attic, she almost fell over backward, seeing more than a hundred swallows devouring the grain with their beaks. The white misseron had led all the sparrows in the country there.

When he left Tafarot, he flew straight to the farm at Vaucelle, gathered all his fellows, and explained to them that he knew an attic full of barley, as tender as wheat, and the attic had a hole in the roof.

They took flight in a body, making a cloud so dense that as they passed the people down-below made the sign of the cross, thinking it was an eclipse, and a bad omen.

Raclette tried to chase them away, but they flew circles around her without leaving the place. She tried opening the attic window, but that didn't make them want to leave any the more—quite the contrary. The ones waiting outside came flashing in.

Raclette hurried downstairs as fast as she could to get a stick. And what should she find at the bottom of the stairs but the new guard-dog, who fled from her, the grilled meat in its mouth!

She set out in pursuit. Unfortunately, he got out into the open country, and she couldn't catch up with him.

The good woman then hurried back to close the tap on the keg, but, while she'd been running across the fields, the beer had run out all over the basement. The barrel was empty, and the basement flooded.

"Dear Lord!" said Raclette, "What am I going to do keep this mess out of sight?"

She went back up the stairs, very worried, and noticed a sack of flour that the miller had brought the evening before. In her simpleness, she thought that if she spread the flour over the beer, it would soak it up and clean the floor.

The sack was heavy. On the way down, Raclette tripped on the pitcher, and the beer inside it was spilled like the rest. It was the last pitcher of beer in the house, as the other barrels hadn't aged enough to be tapped.

X

Soon after, Tafarot showed up, drunk as a thrush and jolly as a rainy day. At the Faidherbe he had met two archers from Onnaing who had just come from the archery competition in the duchy of Mons. He had drunk more than thirty pints with them without being able to ease his anger.

Seeing him coming, his wife cried, "Hurry up to the attic, Husband. There are more than a thousand misserons eating up our grain."

The brewer rushed up the stairs, four at a time, armed with his club. But his arms dropped when he saw there really were a thousand sparrows, all drawn up around the heaps of barley. In the middle of them, the white misseron, like a general, seemed to be in command of the manoeuver.

"Blast it!" cried Tafarot, and he began lashing out right and left—bam! pow!—"If that's what you want—take that!"

Some sparrows paid for their greediness with their lives. The others were driven out, falling back all topsy-turvy. The brewer could then judge the extent of his disaster. Three-fourths of the barley had been gobbled up by the accursed pillagers.

"God almighty! Now I'm really unlucky!" he said, as he had before, and he tore his hair.

"But not unlucky enough!" said the misseron, flying out of the corner where he'd hidden himself. "Your cruelty will cost you your life!"

And he took his flight.

Tafarot flung his club after him, but it didn't hit him. It went and fell on the head of the dog, who was coming back inside, and was much surprised to find club-blows falling on him from the sky.

XI

The brewer and his wife went into the kitchen and sat down, opposite one another, their faces downcast, and their arms dangling. Tafarot told his wife all the misfortunes that had happened to him.

She didn't dare say so, but in the bottom of her heart, she didn't think that the white misseron was much in the wrong. Why had her husband run over the poor dog, which she, too, had loved, as a companion in suffering?

In heaving out some sighs, the brewer came to realize that even if he felt heavy-hearted, he didn't have to have a hollow belly.

Then it was his wife's turn to tell him the story of the grilled meat, the beerkeg, and the sack of flour, all destroyed by the misseron's ill-will,

In other circumstances, he would have beat Raclette black and blue. Overwhelmed by the implacable persecution, he could only cry, for the last time, "Oh, the devil! Now I'm really unlucky!"

"But not unlucky enough," a voice cried. "Your cruelty will cost you your life!"

It was the implacable misseron, who had been waiting outside, perched on the window. Tafarot leaped up like a furious cat, grabbed a stepstool, and threw it at the panes of glass, which flew into pieces.

The white misseron had the nerve to hop into the room. The brewer threw everything in reach at him—big saucepans and small, plates, napkins, chairs, and benches, but couldn't hit him.

But in the end he caught him.

"Wring his neck!" said his wife, who feared having to see the little animal suffer.

"No!" said Tafarot, foaming with rage. "That's too good for him. First, we're going to teach him to sing, by blinding him, as people do with larks. Then we'll tear his feathers out one by one, and his wings, and his feet. Put the poker in the fire."

Raclette obeyed. When the poker was red-hot, her husband ordered her to bring it over. With glee, he felt the poor bird quivering in his hands.

Suddenly the white misseron lifted up his head and cried with all his strength, "Brewer, this will cost you your life!"

Tafarot shivered. He was green with fury and gnashed his teeth. The sight frightened Raclette, and she accidentally burnt his hand.

Unable to control himself, he dropped the sparrow, and dealt his wife such a blow that she saw more than ten thousand stars.

He wanted to catch the misseron again. He could see him perched on the window, just out of reach. The bird eyed him with an exasperating air.

He grabbed a knife and struck Raclette with it. The luckless woman gave a cry and fainted. He thought he'd killed her, and, turning his rage against himself, he plunged the knife into his own heart.

Raclette was only slightly wounded, and she soon healed, but Tafarot was dead. The white misseron flew away to the farm at Vaucelle, prouder and happier than a God—he had avenged his friend.

XCII

This Adventure was soon famous all through the country. Opposite the brewery, an inn was built, and its signboard was: *At the White Misseron.*

People came to it in crowds: little by little a village grew up around that spot, and people called it by the signboard's name, which it has kept to this day.

The Belgians gladly retell this story. It teaches us not to scorn anyone. There's no friend or enemy so small that he can't be stirred by courage to defeat the strong, and even if Belgium is about as big as a fly next to an ox, the Belgians are not any less to be admired or feared, you know. It was the Belgians who took the town of Anvers, godverdom!

And as the song of the Borins says:
Wasmes, Pâturages, Framerie
And Bouveries,
Jemmapes, and Quaregnon,
These are townlets of renown!

They know how to open fire
On any who would start a war!

Manikin-Pis

I

In olden times, in a village called Boschfort in the forest of the Cambre, two leagues from Brussels, in Brabant, there was a sabotier—a maker of wooden shoes. With his three sons, he made a poor living by selling sabots. One morning, he saw an old man leaning on a staff who had stopped in front of his little hut.

The man had long white hair and a long beard, and wore a leather apron, He was tired out, and besides that, his shoes were so worn out that they looked ready to leave him on his way.

"Could you by chance," he asked the owner of the hut, "direct me to a shoe-shop?"

"We don't have any shoe dealers or leather-workers here," was the answer. "Father and sons, we are sabot-makers. Never in all our days have we dealt in shoes of leather."

The traveler looked disappointed.

"But you yourself," the sabotier added, looking at the leather apron, "aren't you a shoemaker by trade?"

"I have been," said the stranger, "and even though shoemakers ordinarily go around in worn-out shoes, yet I'm ashamed to be traveling in this state through the capital of the kingdom of the Low Countries. So I pray you, sell me a pair of sabots,"

He came into the hut, and, after finding a pair that fit him, he opened the wallet hanging from his belt. The sabotier noticed that there were only five sous inside, and, taking pity on the vagabond's poverty, he said, "Keep your money. You're a child of God, and God forbid that I should be the one to take the last few coins from a poor old fellow as worn with walking as you are."

"Since you have such a generous soul," replied the stranger, "I don't want to be behind you in courtesy. Let me tell you a story. Although it's not about recent doings, it's a true story, all the same.

"After the Tree of Life and the fatal apple tree that damned the human race, the most beautiful tree in the terrestrial paradise was a superb peach tree. It was also the only one that stayed on Earth when, through

Adam's sin, the Garden of Delight vanished from this world. Well, for the past eighteen hundred years, I've been condemned, for my lack of charity, to a journey which is nowhere near finished.

"One day, when I was going by the place where in olden days Paradise grew green, I saw the marvelous peach tree, and I gathered three peaches.

"I ate them, intending to strengthen my heart against the fatigues of such a long pilgrimage, and I kept the kernels, so that I could make a gift of them to those who practice sincerely the love of their neighbor that I had failed at so badly.

"In all the eighteen hundred years that I've been wandering about the world, I've only been able to give away two of them. I offered the first to Saint Martin, the patron of true drinkers, who divided his cloak in two to share it with a pretended sick man, who was none other than Beelzebub. I offered the second to King Robert of France, who, taking a poor devil of a robber by surprise in the act of cutting off the fringe of his mantle, good-naturedly begged him to leave it for the next fellow.

"Now, here's the third, Take it—for you, who have so little yourself, have given me the only treasure that is yours, the fruit of your work."

"Thank you, holy man," said the sabotier, and he took the kernel, while his sons opened their eyes wide as barn doors.

"But, good sir," said Little Peter, the tail-end of the family, "if you've been journeying for eighteen hundred years, you must be the one who—"

"Yes, that's me, my children. I am the Wandering Jew," Isaac Laquedem replied, singing the words to the tune of an old song. It really was him, and, having taken up his staff, he set out again on the road to Brussels, where, as everyone knows, he ran into some kindly townsfolk, who treated him to a pitcher of new beer, and begged him to tell them his story.

II

The sabotier and his sons never again saw the Wandering Jew, but they planted the kernel in their yard. The kernel sprouted and grew into an extraordinary tree.

It bore fruit four times a year, in spring as well as in summer, in winter as well as autumn, and the least good of the peaches were not those that ripened in the bise, the cold north wind.

I should explain that the throne of the Low Countries in those days had for its master a monarch who was a glutton, a worthy grandson of Adam, from whom we are all descended, kings and sabotiers alike.

This king passionately loved peaches, and as greenhouses hadn't been invented in those days to replace the sun, he felt miserable about not being able to get any, all winter long, from Christmas to Candlemas.

One Christmas, having a midnight supper after going to mass, an idea struck him—he would announce that he would gladly give his daughter in marriage to the first fine fellow who would bring him a basket of peaches for dessert. This decree came to the ears of the sabotier.

The marvelous peach tree was just then crowned with its fruit, and it was a rare and curious sight to see its boughs swaying, green under the sky grey with clouds, over the ground white with snow.

"Here," said the sabotier, "is an excellent chance to establish the oldest of my sons. He will marry the princess, and when his father-in-law dies, he will reign over the Low Countries, a job much less tiring than making wooden shoes."

He gathered the finest peaches, put them carefully into a little basket, and sent his son to the palace of the king. The young sabotier set off through the forest.

Passing near the city of Cambre, at the place called the Devil's Hole, he met a poor little old woman, who was gathering dead branches.

"What's that you've got in your basket, my lad?" she said.

"Some acorns, at your service, old woman," said the boy, who was not as well brought up as a budding prince should be.

"Oh, well, my lad!" said the old granny, "I wish you may have the most beautiful acorns ever seen."

The young man with his load presented himself at the palace-door, and, when he said he was bringing peaches for the royal dessert, he was taken before the monarch, who was in fact at the dinner-table.

He opened his basket—and imagine his surprise when instead of peaches he found it full of acorns as big as potatoes.

"Godverdom! Do you take me for some kind of a swine?" said the king, throwing down his napkin.

The boy had barely time to take to his heels, and returned at a run to his father's house.

"Well?" said the sabotier.

"They wouldn't let me in," said the scamp.

His father knew he was a liar and a glutton, and thought the boy must have eaten the peaches, instead of taking them to the palace. The next day he gathered another basketful, and sent them off with his middle son.

When he got to the Devil's Hole, the boy met a poor old woman, who said to him, "What's that you've got there, my little lad?"

"Some toads who saw you at the witches' Sabbath revels, you old witch," said the boy, who was even more foul-mouthed than his older brother.

"Oh well, my lad! I wish you may have the most beautiful toads ever seen."

Sure enough, when the basket was opened before the king, enormous toads jumped out of it and set themselves to hopping—black, sticky, and hideous—over the white tablecloth.

The king, the queen, and the princess leaped up with cries of horror. The monarch kicked the rude carrier with such force that he crashed against the head of one of the servants, who pushed him away, landing on another, who threw him off onto a third, and so, from one shove to the next, the rascal got to the door and was only too happy to leave on such easy terms.

The sovereign then declared in an edict that the first person who claimed to have brought peaches, but carried in yet more acorns or toads, would be hanged from the spire of the belfry.

The sabotier wanted to find out from his sons what this meant, but they were careful not to explain to him how their own discourtesy had caused the transformation of the peaches along the way.

The poor man could not get over their having lost such a good opportunity to marry a princess.

"I'd be glad to go, truly, if someone would send me there," said Little Peter. He seemed to be smarter than his brothers, but they were tall, with round, rosy cheeks, while he was skinny, weak, and pale. That was why he ws always called Cricket or Grasshopper.

"How likely is it that the Grasshopper will do better than his brothers?" the sabotier asked himself. "Besides, the princess would never want to marry such a cricket."

Even so, the reward was so tempting that after weighing it for a whole week, he decided to send Little Peter.

III

The boy, like his brothers, met the old granny at the Devil's Hole, and when she asked him what he was carrying in his basket, he answered politely: "Some peaches, dear woman, for the king's dessert."

"Oh well, my lad! I wish you may have the finest peaches ever seen."

"God grant it, Granny!"

And Little Peter continued on his way.

When he reached the door of the palace, the sentinel took pity on him and wanted to stop him from running to his doom, but he insisted so hard that in the end he was allowed in.

He left his sabots behind the door and went bravely into the dining room. As soon as he opened his basket —

"Godverdom! What beautiful peaches!" said the king, his eyes shining like stars.

And, in fact, the peaches were superb, white and rose colored, covered with a sweet down, and almost as big as the silver balls that we use for tennis games in our country.

The monarch, with his little gold knife, began to peel one, and licked his lips. The peach-flesh smelled so sweet to him, that he gobbled the peaches down then and there. Only he realized, as he ate the last quarter of the last peach, that he had forgotten to offer any to the queen and the princess.

When his napkin was full of the kernels, he noticed Little Peter standing there. He eyed him from head to foot and said, with a frown, "What are you doing there, manikin?"

"I'm waiting, Sire," said the Grasshopper.

"What for?"

"For the reward your Majesty promised."

"Ah!—What's your name?"

"Little Peter."

"What kind of work do you do?"

"I make sabots, Sire."

"But I don't want to be a sabotier's wife!" said the princess.

"Oh!—but I'll change what I do, my lady, if you don't like my job."

"You'll learn how to be a king?" asked the monarch.

"Yes, Sire, if your Majesty will be so good as to teach me."

"Ah, well, my lad!—you're going to start your apprenticeship this instant!"

The King of the Low Countries' nose was more refined than his conscience was. When you've eaten the tidbit, as the saying goes, you're not hungry for it anymore, and that's why he was looking for a decent excuse to break his promise.

He whispered to a servant, who went out and came back with a case holding twelve little white rabbits.

"Listen, manikin," said the king to the Grasshopper, "kings are just like shepherds. But men, you know, are harder to herd than sheep. You see these twelve little rabbits. Go take them to feed in the woods. If, at the end of three full days, you can bring the whole troop back to us, it'll show that you have a gift for the job of being a king, and that someday you'll be able to wield our scepter as a shepherd does his crook."

A general burst of laughter followed this elegant speech. Little Peter could see that the monarch was making fun of him, but having no one to defend him, he said boldly, "I'll try," and, making his bow to the king, he started for the woods, followed by a servant carrying the rabbits.

IV

When they got to the Devil's Hole, the servant opened the basket, and the rabbits bounded out of it and went zooming off in all directions.

"Goodbye, all thirteen of you," the servant said mockingly to the herd-boy, who didn't seem to hear him.

Little Peter didn't think it would be much fun to go running after his flock. Meditatively, he watched them flee, and, when the last one had disappeared, he slowly started back toward Boschfort.

He thought to himself that the princess was very pretty and that it would have been pleasant to succeed in herding the rabbits, if only to get even with them for laughing at him, and pay back the king in his own coin. He hadn't taken twenty steps when the old granny was there in front him, all of a sudden.

"Well, then, my little lad," she said, "did you get a good tip for service?"

"Not very good, Granny. The king had hardly finished eating my peaches when he sent me out to herd—rabbits!"

"So you didn't try to do that?"

"I did, too."

"Well, then?"

"Well, then! The moment I let them out in the woods, they made tracks."

"You'll have to call them back."

"But how?"

"With this." And she handed him a little silver whistle.

Soon the twelve rabbits came running back, in leaps and bounds, fast as their paws would go. He tried the experiment over again, two or three times, and every time it worked just as he wished.

Peter, enchanted, left his flock to browse on the thyme—both garden-thyme and wild—and he went to a nearby inn, the Black Sheep, to drink a pint and smoke a pipe.

That evening, who looked a fool?—the king did, when he saw Little Peter coming back, pushing twelve rabbits ahead of him, and whistling loud.

"Is the clown a sorcerer?" the monarch asked his courtiers. "Even so, you know, it's just not possible for a manikin like that to wed the heiress presumptive to the throne of the Low Countries."

"If your Majesty will allow me," suggested the lord of Nivelle, "I'll make sure that tomorrow the manikin won't come back with the whole herd."

"Yes, do, my friend," said the sovereign, "and if you succeed, I'll give you my daughter, even though you're by no means a king's son, you know, and it seems to me you're too fat to make her happy."

The lord of Nivelle was, indeed, as fat as a barrel, but even so all he needed was a chance like that for him to dare to try laying claim to the princess's hand.

The next day, he went to the woods with his dog, and started looking for Little Peter.

V

The Grasshopper, to pass the time, had cut a branch of elder wood and was busy making it into a blow-gun, or rather, as we say around here, an arbute, when he saw the fat lord coming toward him. Quickly, he blew on his whistle and summoned the flock.

"Sic 'em, Miraud, sic 'em!" cried the lord to his dog.

Miraud was a famous greyhound. His master was counting on him to frighten the rabbits so much that they would run away to the very devils. But what a strange thing! They stood with their feet planted waiting for the dog, and far from running after the game, Miraud kept close to the lord's heels, with his tail and his ears hanging down.

Seeing that his trick had failed, the lord followed the example of hunters when they're coming back with nothing in the game-bag. He went over to the Grasshopper.

"Herder," he said, snorting like an ox, "You have plenty of nice rabbits. Do you want to sell me one?"

"My rabbits can't be sold or given away," said the Grasshopper. "They can only be won."

"Oh!—and how can I win one?"

"Let me borrow your face so I can practice aiming at a target."

"I don't understand."

"It's simple enough. I'll aim at your full moon of a face, and your big nose will serve for the little black bull's-eye, or maybe a red one."

"What! you dwarf, how dare you—"

"There it is, my lord. That's my plan."

"Oh, come on, no more joking! How much do you want for your rabbit—a thousand silver pieces?"

Peter, without replying, proceeded to load his blow-gun with little balls rolled out of poplar bark.

"Ten thousand?"

He shrugged his shoulders.

"Twenty thousand?"

He shot a pellet at Miraud's nose.

The lord realized he wasn't going to get him to change his mind. He told himself that a moment of shame is soon over, and, anyway, if you're unlucky enough to look like a jug big enough to hold several swallows, you can't pay too much for the pleasure of marrying a princess as beautiful as the day.

"So, then, are you going to give me one of your rabbits?"

"Yes, my lord, as soon as I manage to hit the mark."

The lord of Nivelle looked all around and didn't see anyone coming. "All right," he said, "but hurry it up."

He wiped his forehead and took his stand at the desired distance.

While the rabbits browsed on the grass, running about, and playing hide-and-go-seek, Peter gravely amused himself with shooting a hail of little pellets at the fine round face of the fat lord. They bounced off his skin like balls on a net.

Minaud watched the scene from a distance, sitting philosophically on his rear.

The Grasshopper, mischievously, aimed now at the right eye, now at the left, now at the mouth. He never landed one on the nose.

"You hit it!" cried the lord of Nivelle.

"No, my lord."

"You did, too."

"I won't play anymore if you're going to cheat, and you a child of God!"

After a quarter of an hour, Peter was starting to run out of ammunition, and he landed one on the little target, and gave one of the rabbits to the lord, who left without staying around to ask for any more.

He hadn't even gotten out of the range of a cross-bow when he heard a whistle sound, Poof! The rabbit leaped to the ground.

"Hey, Minaud, come here!" cried the lord of Nivelle to his dog, who had set off without waiting for him.

But instead of obeying, Minaud ran as fast as his legs would carry him. That's the origin of the common proverb:

"That's the dog of John of Nivelle.

He runs away as soon as you call."

The lord returned to the palace with his little dishonor, and he didn't breathe a word about being shot at as a target.

Nevertheless, it was in memory of this great deed that the people of Nivelle later erected an iron statue on the tomb of Saint Gertrude, and to this day you can see the hours sounded on it by a mallet striking it.

VI

"If I could be allowed to go," the princess suggested timidly, "it seems to me I wouldn't come back empty-handed."

"Go, my daughter," said the monarch. "Save the honor of the crown, and prove to the world that you were not born to be a sabotier's wife, godverdom!"

A few hours later. Little Peter saw a fresh young milkmaid coming toward him. She had on sabots, a red skirt, a black shirt, and a white pinafore. On her head she was carrying a jug, or, rather, a yellow copper can that shone like gold in the sun.

"Here's something new," he thought.

And he whistled to his rabbits.

The princess went by him, calling out in a clear, slow voice, "Don't you need any milk?"

"Hey! pretty milkmaid, can you sell me a sou's worth?" said Little Peter. The game appealed to him, and he couldn't see any reason not to play along.

"I'd be glad to, gentle herdsman."

The false milkmaid poured some milk into the can's lid and handed it to the Grasshopper.

"Oh, what nice white rabbits!" she said, pretending to be surprised. "Give me one, please."

"The rabbits in my pack can't be sold or given away," said the Grasshopper. "They can only be won."

"And how can I win one?"

"By kissing the herdsman."

The princess, shocked at such boldness, almost gave herself away, but then she considered that as the little sabotier thought he was dealing with someone in his own class, his claim wasn't at all offensive. Flirting with a peasant-girl wouldn't have any consequences, so after all if ever a kiss was innocent, this one would be, and it would only be given to get rid of the poor herder.

She turned red, but she put her cheek out to be kissed and held out her apron, then sped away as swift as an arrow, carrying her jug and her rabbit.

She had not gone a hundred paces when, poof! the rabbit had jumped out of the apron. The princess caught it in its flight, but it scratched her so hard that she had to let it go.

An hour later, the Grasshopper had his troop all together again.

"For a hunt you need old dogs," said the king. "Tomorrow's the last day. I will go myself, and we'll just see if I come back empty-handed."

VII

The next day, Little Peter saw an abbot riding on a mule on the road between the trees. The presence of the holy man, just a few steps from the Cambre Abbey, seemed natural enough to him. Even so, he stayed on his guard and called his rabbits.

When the abbot was near, the Grasshopper took off his cap and crossed himself devoutly. The good father gave him his blessing. Little

Peter noticed that he had his cowl pulled down low, as if to protect him from the sun.

"What are you doing there, my little lad?" asked the abbot, who seemed to be speaking in a disguised voice, in the same way that his face was hidden.

"As you can see for yourself, my father, I'm watching over my flock."

"Ah! You're a shepherd."

"Yes, a shepherd—like your Reverence, or like the king, our master, or like our Holy Father the Pope, except that my sheep are rabbits."

"Cute little rabbits, too, godver—Would you sell me one?"

"Now I know you, even in that fine disguise," said Little Peter to himself. Then he said aloud, "My lord Abbot, my rabbits can't be sold or given away. They can only be won."

"And how can I win one?"

"As in Heaven, my lord Abbot, by humility. If you were to ask a favor of our Holy Father the Pope, what would you do?"

"I'd throw myself at his feet."

"And then?"

"Then I would kiss his slipper devoutly."

"Well, my lad! Here's ours—kiss it."

And he impudently stick his wooden shoe in front of the monarch.

"Godverdom!" cried the king.

But then he stopped short. Like the lord of Nivelle, he offered him gold, and begged and entreated him, and conjured him in the name of all the saints in Paradise. Little Peter wouldn't even listen.

So the king had to dismount, kneel, and kiss the wooden shoe of the mischievous manikin. After the humiliating ceremony, he climbed back on the mule, carrying a rabbit in the pocket of his cassock.

He had hardly gone the length of his crook, when, poof! the rabbit jumped out of his pocket. The king jumped off his mule to run after the rabbit, but he fell so heavily that he landed flat in the very middle of a large puddle of cow-dung, and he got back to the palace in a state that was completely unmajestic, godverdom!

VIII

Little Peter gathered up his rabbits for the last time.

He came with his flock to the room where the king was holding council, seated on his throne.

"Sire—" said the Grasshopper.

But he was suddenly interrupted by a great noise. The door flew open, and the princess burst into the hall, crying: "My ring! Someone's stolen my ring!"

"Shut up," said the king. "Don't deafen us!" Then, catching the ball on the bounce, he swung around toward Little Peter. As he no longer wanted him at all for his son-in-law, he said: "You've done very well, my lad, coming to the end of the first test, but the job of being a king is not simply one of guarding the king's subjects. He must also, you know, maintain law and order throughout the realm. Let's see if you're able to do that. Someone has stolen my daughter's ring. I will give you three days to bring me the thief."

"What does your ring look like?" asked the Grasshopper.

"It's gold, with a diamond as big as a pea," said the princess, looking at him in a way that was no longer so disdainful.

"The hunt's on, Manikin," added the monarch, rubbing his hands together. "And to make sure that the prey is within your reach, I'll order that you be given a room in the palace and served as well as I am myself. No one's going to say that I don't do things properly."

The Grasshopper was led at once to a nice apartment and given his supper. He wasn't served quite as well as the sovereign would be, as there was only a single servant standing behind him to wait on him. But the supper was exquisite, such as I'm willing to bet you've never had in your life, even on the feast-day of our patron saint.

Little Peter, who was a man of taste, licked his fingers, and thought to himself that the job of being king was a pleasant one. If he had a supper like this every evening, it would not be long before he had fine balouffes—I mean, fine full cheeks, like his brothers.

The next day, he went out for a walk, at the break of day, toward the Devil's Hole, but he did not find the old granny.

"Bah!" he said to himself, "I'll do just as well by myself, maybe. You have to go looking for something to find it."

At noon, he returned to the palace, as hungry as a hunter, dreaming about the supper he'd had the evening before. Like a true Flamand, he figured that even if he didn't get a chance to marry the princess, he would at least have had the pleasure of three excellent dinners. The dinner was, as it should be, even better than the supper.

When Little Peter had swallowed the last mouthful, he wiped his mouth with his napkin and said loudly, "That was really number one!"

At those words, the servant attending him jerked back.

He was the rascal who had stolen the ring, working together with one of his friends.

The next day, the Grasshopper went for a walk by the palace, looking at everybody's faces, but without finding the thief. He wasn't discouraged, though, but went to the dinner table when noon sounded, and did full honors to the dinner. When he had finished he clicked his tongue and said, "That's number two!"

The servant, who was none other than the second rascal, turned pale and dropped a pile of napkins.

"Suppose I go pay a visit to my rabbits," thought the Grasshopper. "They might give me some ideas—godverdom!, as our sovereign would say."

He lit his pipe, and went down to the barn-yard.

IX

While Little Peter was petting his rabbits, the two thieves were talking together, for they were very worried about the way things were going.

Since it looked as if the jig was up, wouldn't it be better to confess instead of waiting to be forced to spill it? On the other hand, were they that sure that the manikin was some kind of sorcerer?

To find out, they thought up a test that they thought would prove it. It was to stuff the ring in a little pellet of bread and then take a fine tom-turkey, strutting around among the ducks and chickens and hen-turnkeys like a new assistant leader in a Corpus Christi Day parade, and make him swallow it. "If he looks as if he's going to look there," they said, "he must really be a sorcerer, because there couldn't be a better hiding place."

Leaving his flock, Little Peter noticed the big tom-turkey. He'd never seen anything like it.

"Hey! Master Baptiste!" he cried, "What a fine fowl you are! I ought to have you in for dinner tomorrow—what do you say?"

"Gobble! gobble! gobble!" said Master Baptiste, innocently.

"All right with you? Well, then! I'll go and ask them to wring your neck today."

The thieves, interpreting the Grasshopper's words to fit their own theory, no longer doubted that he was a sorcerer.

They fell at his feet and, quivering in every limb, said, "We can see that you know it all, Mynheer Manikin, but—for the love of God!—don't destroy us."

Peter jumped like a real grasshopper. "What do you think I know?" he asked.

"Oh, good grief!—you know that we made Master Baptiste there swallow the princess's ring."

This unexpected revelation stunned Little Peter, but he instantly recovered his presence of mind.

"Oh! you rascals!" he said, with a severe, majestic air, "you thought you could fool me! You should have known that you couldn't hide anything from someone like me. But I'm a merciful prince, and since you've confessed it all, I mean to pardon you. But as for you there!—you're going to go and be hanged!" He picked up the turkey and ran to the king. "Sire," he said, "here's the thief."

"Who? Master Baptiste there?"

"The very one."

"Oh, nonsense! I've always heard people say that magpies steal— But I would never have believed that turkeys—But, after all, when you're at court—"

"At court you have to be ready to be in court, and you can see, Sire, that Master Baptiste and I are the proof."

Poor Baptiste was executed on the spot, and without a trial. And they found the ring in his crop.

All the same, he was entirely innocent, and his example proves again that we shouldn't condemn people on circumstantial evidence.

"The scoundrel!" cried the king. "We'll eat him for dinner. You're invited, Manikin, and this time we'll have a serious conversation."

X

The dinner was splendid, a veritable engagement-dinner. The king had invited all the lords and all the ladies of the court. They drank a pot and a half of local beer and twenty-seven casks of beer from Brussels. The turkey, stuffed full of chestnuts, was exquisite, they declared, and Little Peter greeted everyone cordially.

The princess's greeting to Little Peter was welcoming, and the monarch, for his part, smiled on him now.

"Decidedly, this funny fellow must be a sorcerer," he said. "And if he is, and if he doesn't insist on the sabot-trade, I'll give him my daughter! It'll be the first time we've had a sorcerer on the throne. As for the rest, that remains to be seen."

He whispered something to his squire, who left.

For dessert, two covered trays were brought in. On one was the princess's ring, which Little Peter presented to her, kneeling before her. They were about to uncover the other one, when the king cried: "Stop!"

Then he turned to the Grasshopper. "If you're a sorcerer, guess what's in that one."

"This time, I've had it," thought Little Peter, and he stared at the tray with a pitying look, and said, "Poor Grasshopper, I see you're in a fix."

"You rogue of a manikin!—you're right!" cried the monarch, and gave him a tap on the shoulder that could have felled an ox.

The tray was uncovered, and to Little Peter's astonishment, there really was a cricket—or, if you prefer, a grasshopper—sitting there.

XI

"Oh, well! since you're a sorcerer," cried the monarch, who was tipsy with wonder—also the Brussels beer, "give me some magic into the bargain. Fill up three bags for me full of tricks."

"Listen to that! He's starting to annoy me, this monarch. I'm going to make him shut his beak," said Little Peter to himself. His confidence was growing with his success so far.

"Three bags full of tricks—I agree!" he cried. "I can cover the cost. Bring three bags, as big as you have."

When the bags were brought, he said: "First bag! Once upon a time there was a little sabot-maker who was keeping watch over some rabbits. A fat lord came puffing up to him and asked him for one. The shepherd gave him one, but only on condition that the lord let him borrow his fine red nose and turn it white, shooting at it. The nobleman agreed, and—" As he spoke, the Grasshopper seized his blow-gun, and poof!—he hit the mark.

"Bravo!" cried all the courtiers. "Into the sack, Lord Nivelle, into the bag!"

The poor man climbed into the bag, raging.

The Grasshopper went on, "Second bag! After the fat lord, there came a cute little milkmaid.

"'How much are your rabbits, dear little shepherd?'

"'One kiss, pretty milkmaid.'

"The pretty milkmaid leaned forward, offering her cheek, and—"

"What! How dare you!" cried the king. "That's not true!"

"Yes, it is, Papa," said the princess, turning red.

"Into the bag! Into the bag!" cried all the court excitedly, and the princess curled herself up in it with the best grace in the world.

"Third and last sack!" said the Grasshopper. "The pretty milkmaid was followed by a venerable abbot.

"'Manikin, what do I need to get one of your rabbits?"

"'You have to kiss—'"

"Hush! You can have her," cried the king, shutting the manikin's mouth.

The Grasshopper invited his father and brothers to the wedding. To make sure that they'd look their best, he was careful to have them put some hay in their sabots, as the saying is, which means—have some money with them.

The wedding was magnificent. For dessert the monarch ate a whole quertinée—or, if you prefer, a whole basketful—of peaches, and died of indigestion.

The little shepherd at once changed his shepherd's crook for the scepter of the deceased king. Even though he'd had barely a week of apprenticeship, he ruled with rare wisdom, all the same.

People gave the credit for it to his cleverness with the marvelous whistle, but I think myself that his secret consisted quite simply—as it had in the wood of Boschfort—in smoking his pipe calmly, and in letting his rabbits—his subjects, I mean—amuse themselves as they chose.

And that is why the Belgians, in gratitude, erected, right on the corner of Oak Street—where he had stopped for a moment coming out from the celebration of his wedding, which he dedicated to Saint Nicholas—a little bronze statue, which people baptized with the name of the *Manikin-pis*.

Being practical people, who know how to unite the useful and the pleasant, they turned it into a sort of public fountain, and after his death, they made it pour a jet of water into the fountain, because when he was alive he poured out prosperity throughout the land.

The Manikin-pis is the oldest and finest citizen of the good old city of Brussels—though not the most decent.

Every year, during the kermis-fair, they dress him up from head to foot, like a Swiss Guard in front of the cathedral, in a little cocked hat, a little embroidered tunic, little trousers, and a little sword. They don't spare any expense, you understand, because it's because of the Manikin-pis that Belgium is the finest country in the world, godverdom!

The Guerliche's Nutmeg-Balls

In olden times, in the village of Erchin, on the Douai side, there was a little scamp who was called the Guerliche, after the little fish, because instead of going to school, he used to spend the whole blessed day in merrily depopulating the pools and fishponds of the neighborhood. Carp, pike, tench, burbot, perch, to him they were all fair game, right down to the little guerliches and loaches, which among us are good for nothing except to show when they put their heads up that it's raining. He was as naughty as he was skillful and agile, and he slid like a fish between the hands of the village constable, and so he had a double right to his name of the Guerliche.

He was the only annoyance that fretted Sans-Souci, the mayor of Erchin, a rosy, fat farm-owner who was wise enough to leave each person to act in his own way and the world to turn on its string as God wills. Not a day went by without someone coming to bother this good fellow, even when he was in the middle of a game of cards, to complain about the pranks of this little good-for-nothing. One fine evening, he swore by the heavens above that he would stuff him in jail at the very next escapade.

The day after next, at the time when everyone was out working in the fields, the mayor was smoking his pipe in the doorway, sitting on his caquetoire, or, if you prefer, his gossip-bench.

He was half asleep, when a little noise made him open his eyes. What did he see? The bold thief, sitting on a wall as if on horseback, was impudently catching his ducks with a rod-and-reel, out of the pool in the farmyard.

"You just wait a second, my boy, until I can get up!" cried the mayor. But the Guerliche did not wait, and, preferring sun to shadow, decided it would be prudent to get out of town and not come back to Erchin.

II

A long time later, on a Monday during the feast-day of their patron saint, the mynheers of Erchin, their heads a little heavy from drinking too much the night before, were silently smoking their pipes at the Good Convent, when—guess what!—a tall, funny-looking fellow stopped in front of the inn. He was dressed in a velvet jacket embroidered with spangles, like the kind of clown people call Soupy John.

He begged the landlady to lend him a table, and put a tablecloth on it. Then he took out of his bag a black wand, some trick glasses for conjuring, and some nutmeg-balls of the right size to make disappear. Then he sounded his trumpet and addressed himself to the honorable audience in these terms:

"Gentlemen and ladies, you see before you the incomparable Brambinella, conjuror in chief to His Highness the great sultan, also to the caliph of Bagdad, the shah of Persia, His Majesty the King of the Low Countries, and other crowned heads. The illustrious conjuror is going to have the honor of doing his work before your eyes, and, if you are pleased and satisfied, the spectacle will cost you no more than a little spare change."

The incomparable Brambinella then performed different tricks with the glasses, to the great astonishment of the Erchin villagers, who were primitive sorts, and just barely civilized. Besides the nutmeg-ball tricks, he juggled gold coins, rings, watches, even the canary of Marie-Joseph, the landlady of the Good Convent. The canary turned up in Mayor Sans-Souci's hat.

"You're clever with your hands, my boy," said the mayor, with a wink of his eye. "But I have a notion that you were even cleverer when you were making people's ducks disappear with your hook."

So you recognized me, Mayor?" said the Guerliche—for that's who the conjuror was.

"Good Lord, yes!"

"And you still have those ducks weighing on your heart?"

"Yes. The only way you can make me put up with that prank is to show us the finest trick in your bag."

"The one I reserve for all the crowned heads? I agree, good master. What would you like to be startled with? Animals or people? Speak, and I'm ready to serve."

"Oh, well! Here's Tony Balou, our shepherd, who's going to take his sheep to graze in the thicket by the Chapel. Do you think you can make something of his disappear?"

"His whole flock, if you wish."

"All of them?"

"All of them."

"I'll bet a hundred florins you can't do it."

"I can match that."

"You've got that much, do you?"

"Yes—in your money-bag. Send for a pitcher of beer. I'll bring you back your sheep in less than an hour."

The Guerliche took a back road and got to the little wood ahead of the shepherd. The thicket formed a sort of triangle surrounded by stretches of grass, stones, or waste ground.

When Tony Balou neared the trees, suddenly he saw the body of a man lying on the branches of an oak.

"Jesus! Myn God!—a hanged man," he said. He crossed himself devoutly and drove his flock away without daring to look back.

Two hundred paces farther along the way the line of the trees made a turning. Another hanged man was there.

"Another one!" said Tony Balou, and felt cold sweat running down his back. Two hundred paces more took him to another turning and another hanged man. Tony Balou couldn't take any more. Wild terror seized him, and he fled like a thief, scattering behind him his cloak, crook, bread-bag, and hat, so he could run the faster.

The three hanged men were really only one man, one in good health, the Guerliche, who promptly gathered up hat, bread-bag, crook, and cloak, put them on, rounded up the sheep, and returned to the village, shouting "Hurrah! Hurrah!" at the top of his voice.

III

"You won that one," said the mayor. "It's true that Tony Balou is as stupid as a goose, as timid as the moon, and it's certainly not his doing if shepherds generally pass for sorcerers. I'm going to give you some other tricks to try."

The mayor, along with Greenwood, a butcher from Douai, was busy taking the innards out of a duckling. Greenwood had come to the village expressly to buy a sheep from the mayor. Greenwood was lame and as bad-tempered as a hunchback might be. Having agreed on their bargain, the mayor took the Guerliche aside and said, "Here's a rabbit who won't let you skin him as easily as that clumsy ox Tony Balou did."

"And how much—?"

"A hundred florins that you can't make off with his sheep."

"Agreed!" said the Guerliche, and he set to work on it on the spot.

He had in his case a fine pair of new shoes. He tossed one in the sunken road that went to Douai, which was the way the butcher would have to go, and the other a little farther along, at the place where the road made a turn.

"Look at that!" said Greenwood, when he saw the first one, "a good shoe, and brand-new. It's too bad the owner forgot to lose the other one with it." And he passed it by. Less than three shots of a cross-bow further on, he found the other one.

"These two are a pair," he thought. "My word! I'm not going to have it said that I found some new shoes and left them for a wolf to gnaw!"

He tied his sheep to the stump of a birch-tree and retraced his steps. The Guerliche, who had been on the watch, untied the sheep and took a short cut to bring it back to the mayor.

Three hours later, Greenwood showed up, looking sheepish, with two pairs of shoes, but no sheep. He told the mayor about his misadventures, and the mayor, pretending to sympathize, let him choose another sheep from the flock, just like the first one, at half-price.

"Half-price—that's too good a bargain," said the Guerliche, and set off again.

Crossing through the Douai wood, near the place called the Round Hole, Greenwood suddenly heard a voice in the thicket crying, "Baa! Baa!"

"Hey! That's my rascally sheep," he said to himself. "How'd it manage to get here?"

The butcher was no fool, and, besides, the cat that's been scalded is afraid of even cold water. He didn't want to let go of his sheep, but the bleating seemed to be getting farther off, and the cursed beast was pulling back on the rope and wouldn't go in among the trees. Tired of the battle, Greenwood tied it, like the other, to a tree. He plunged into the wood and followed the bleating. The noise led him so far astray that when he got back to where he'd started from, there wasn't anything there.

The sheep had gone to rejoin its brother in the mayor's pen, and Greenwood was more than a little surprised to see them both there. He took hold of them, but no one could persuade him that he wasn't fighting against the Evil One himself.

"You're too valuable for me to let you leave here," said the mayor to the Guerliche. "Do you know how to read and write?"

"Reading, writing, and arithmetic—I'm as learned as a whole synagogue. There's nothing as broadening as travel."

"Very good! Settle down at Erchin. You'll govern the community in my name. Tall William, my registrar, is getting into his dotage. He's not good for anything anymore except sitting in the Old Folks home. I'll give you his job."

"Thanks to my time with the wand, I know something about conjuring tricks," said the Guerliche. "But a place at Erchin won't bring in much. I'd like to add to it a job as a grain-seller. Lend me a few thousand ecus to build a mill, and I'll accept. I'm getting tired of running around the countryside, and, besides, I have an idea I'd like to take a wife."

"It's a bargain," said the mayor.

The Guerliche had a mill built in the Erchin hills, near the path to Roucourt, close to the mayor's farm. And that's how the conjuror became the town registrar and a miller—I won't say a thief. I have to do him the justice to say that he no longer stole things, at least, not any more than his colleagues, and he contented himself with taking a double fee for every sack he ground, in accord with the usual custom.

Well, now, it happened one day that the King of the Low Countries came to Douai to see the procession that honors Gayant. Taking a walk the next day in the wolves' sunlight—that's to say, in the light of the moon—he noticed the mill and the farm, which were among the finest in all the Flemish territory.

"Whose mill is that?" he said.

"That's the Guerliche's mill, sire."

"And the farm?"

"That belongs to Mayor Sans-Souci."

"Sans-Souci—Without-a-Care! There's a citizen who's happier than his monarch. Hold on a minute! I'm going to give him something to worry about, my boy. Send out an announcement for me to tell him that I'm going to be here for a week, waiting for him to tell me three things: first, what does the Moon weigh, second, how much am I worth, and third, what am I thinking? If he comes and gives the wrong answer, too bad for him—he'll be hanged."

The King of the Low Countries sometimes had singular ideas, but the job of being a king isn't as easy as being a mayor, and some whims have to be allowed to the unlucky ones who are sentenced to the task.

When the mayor came to drink his pint at the Good Convent, he had a sad face, like a rainy day, and his mind was so preoccupied that he lost one after another five hands of the Marriage card-game.

"Here you are looking very pensive," said the Guerliche—his master had not seen him enter. "What's the problem running through your head?"

"The problem, my boy, is that I can't sleep at night, and in a week I'm going to be hanged. It's inescapable."

"Hanged! My God! But why?"

And the fat mayor told the Guerliche what the king was demanding of him.

"The Devil you say!" said the Guerliche, and tapped him on the belly. "So it's a question of saving you from the gallows. I've already conjured lots of tricks, but I've never run across a nutmeg-ball of that caliber. But it's all the same. Let me go there in your place. They don't know what you look like. And we'll just see what comes of it. Leave it to me! The noose that could be your necktie hasn't been twined yet."

On the day named, the Guerliche presented himself at the palace. The king was in a really good humor, having had a good dinner. He was sitting on his throne, digesting his food, and smoking his pipe, with all his courtiers around him. He gave the order for the mayor to be brought in.

"So you're the one they call Mayor Sans-Souci," said the king.

"I hardly deserve the name, Sire."

"Oho!—Cheery fellow, aren't you! Did you take the trouble to find out how much the Moon weighs?"

"Of course, Sire."

"And how much does it weigh?"

"One pound."

"One pound!" said the monarch, and frowned, thinking that the mayor was making fun of him. The courtiers' faces all grew dark.

"I can prove it. A quart is a fourth, and a quarter is a fourth, and a fourth equals a fourth. A pound has four, and the Moon has four, and it adds up to the same," said the Guerliche.

"That's true," said the king, smiling, and all the faces around him grew bright, too. "And were you bothered enough to find out how I'm worth, to the exact amount?"

"The exact amount—Twenty-nine deniers."

"Very funny," said the king. He took his pipe out of his mouth, and all the courtiers started whispering to each other.

"But it's true! Consider, Sire, that our Lord Jesus Christ was sold for thirty."

"Ah! Very good!" said the monarch. He blew out a big puff of smoke, and the echo ran round the courtiers:

"Very good! Very good! Very good!"

"Silence!" said the king, "And now let's see about the third question. Can you tell me what I'm thinking?"

"Oh, good heavens, yes, Sire! Your Majesty thinks that I'm Mayor Sans-Souci, and I'm only his servant."

"And I name you my prime minister!" cried the monarch, rising from his throne, "I don't know where I'd find anyone sharper."

But the Guerliche humbly begged His Majesty to excuse him, contenting himself with the rank of being the King of the Low Countries' Miller. That was the grandest proof of his wit that he gave during his life—as grand as the one he gave after his death.

IV

When the Guerliche was almost ready to take the final plunge, he told himself, "Having taken a wife has its consequences. It's given me a purgatory on earth, and therefore I have every chance of going to paradise. But a trickster doesn't get there directly, and neither does a miller. I'm much afraid that I'll be forced to win my place by a final conjuring trick. Let me see! The prize is worth some pains."

And he let his head sink down into the pillow.

It was then Saint Sylvester's day, the evening of New Year's day, and they were making waffles in all the Erchin homes. At the end of less than a quarter of an hour, the Guerliche said, "Wife, why aren't you making waffles? It's the custom."

"Waffles! Jesus and Mary! You can barely swallow the saliva in your mouth."

"That doesn't matter. If I can't get them down, you can stuff them in my coffin."

The miller's wife obeyed. In the time it takes to say the prayers for the dying, she kneaded together some flour, butter, and brown sugar, and put the waffle iron on the fire.

The Guerliche sighed his last breath just when the last waffle was being flipped over. Ten minutes later, when he'd been put into the earth, he arrived at the gate of paradise, with his little packet under his arm.

"Knock! Knock!"

"Who's there?"

"The miller Guerliche."

The noise of shoes shuffling over the floor could be heard, and the wicket was opened.

"On your way, my boy—there's no place here for thieves."

"A thief! How about you, dear sir, did you yourself always behave well all the time? Isn't it true—with all due respect—that you denied God three times?"

Saint Peter couldn't come up with an answer and went to make his report to God the Father. "At the gate," he said, "we've got a thief of a miller who wants to come in, in spite of everything, and he's insulting everyone."

"You go, my honest Saint Paul," said the good Lord, "and see what you think."

Saint Paul went.

"Knock! Knock!"

"Who's there?"

"It's me, the miller Guerliche."

"You've got the wrong door, child of God. We don't take thieves in."

"Bah! Bah! If I stole sometimes, I never persecuted anyone, or killed poor people, and it wasn't me who held the cloaks for the people who were stoning good Saint Stephen, if you know what I mean, Mister Saint Paul."

Saint Paul went on back, crestfallen. "I've never seen the like. He talks your ear off!" he said.

"We must have someone who can speak up for himself," said God the Father. "Have someone run and get Saint Augustine, our most famous preacher."

"Knock! Knock!"

"Who's there?"

"The miller Guerliche."

"Alas, my dear brother, you can't come in here! I'll give you three reasons which shall be the subject of this oration. The first is that Jesus Christ said: 'Blessed are the poor in spirit. The kingdom of heaven is theirs. Now, you don't seem to me to be sufficiently provided with that humility, that simplicity—"

"You've never seen anyone so simple, dear sir, as it seems to me."

"The second is that you never led a life free of sin all your days—"

"Oh, come on, now, cut it short, my boy. You didn't have all that clear a conscience when you got here, and if Saint Monica, your venerable mother, hadn't turned on the waterworks of her eyes so often, perhaps indeed—"

But Saint Augustine had stopped listening and was already far away.

"What's to be done?" said the good God. "Unless we send him the Holy Innocents, I really don't see—"

And they sent the Holy Innocents.

"Knock! Knock!"

"Who's there?"

"The miller Guerliche."

"No entry! No entry!"

"Oh, you're here, are you, my little dears. You're just the ones I came to see. Don't people reproach me for having cheated some of the wheat out of my customers by my tricks? What I did was simply to bring you a packet of my nice sugared waffles. Open up right now, and hold out your hands, my children."

The Holy Innocents opened the gate and poured out in a crowd, their hands stretching out toward the Guerliche, who went on in, freely distributing waffles right and left.

Someone ran to tell the news to God the Father.

"Have someone call out the constables!" he cried.

But it was in vain that they looked all through paradise. They couldn't find a single constable.

V

And that is how, after giving everyone a share, the incomparable Guerliche entered roundabout into paradise. But you'd do well not to follow his path, because there's no horse so good that it never stumbles, and, after all, to get up there, the shortest road is the straight line.

Death's Godson (II)

In olden times, it happened one day that Death was feeling bored. It wasn't that the old reaper had nothing to do—it was just that he had taken a dislike to the work.

Even so, it was a regal task, and he must have enjoyed being able to make shepherds and potentates equal with one sweep of his scythe. But people are so made that no one is content with his job.

"Always destroying," the poor fellow said to himself. "In all the six thousand years gone by since the world became the world, always mowing down heads—what an existence! Oh! how happy I'd be if I could rest for a while! God the Father rested on the seventh day, after creating Man.

"Creating!—what a divine word! Even the least of creative craftsmen can have a son who takes after him. I alone am condemned never to live again in my children. In return for my six thousand years of service, God the Father, dear God, you ought to give a son to your servant!"

"I never correct my word," replied God the Father. "You were put into the world to destroy, not to create. All that I can do for you is to grant you the favor of becoming the godfather to a child whose father you will meet tomorrow, on the way home from your day's work.

The next day, Death ran into John-Phillip, the big farmer of Chêne-Raoult, whose wife had just given birth to their thirteenth son.

John-Phillip, wanting a just man to be his son's godfather, chose the universal reaper, and Death gave to his godson the name of Macaber, which in Arabic means "graveyard."

Each evening, on the way home after the day's work, Death paid a visit to his godson. He bounced him on his knees, covered him with kisses, and brought him sugar cookies and little windmills that he would buy on the way through Condé.

Soon the boy was sent to school, and Death paid his tuition. The child showed extraordinary intelligence. By the time he was eighteen, he had passed his courses in the humanities with brilliant success. It was time to think about finding him a profession.

"Be a physician," Death said to him, "and you will become rich and famous—because that's a profession that depends on me. Life is a lamp with only so much oil—it can't be refilled. So you can't heal someone whose lamp is about to go out, but I'm going to show you a way to predict at first sight whether your patients are to recover or die. That will be worth a lot to you.

"When you see me standing at the head of the sick person's bed—and I shall be visible to you alone—you can swear to it that the patient is as good as dead. If, on the contrary, you see me at the foot of the bed, you can say boldly that he'll pull through.

"As for medicines, just prescribe whatever the usual remedies are, and you can laugh at them all, as your colleagues in the profession do."

II

Macaber followed his godfather's advice. Soon he became the most famous physician in all of Flanders, and became a serious rival to Our Lady of Mercy, who helps the sick.

Well, it happened that the daughter of the King of the Low Countries fell ill. All the physicians in the kingdom were summoned. They agreed in saying that the young princess had gone into a decline and was dying of it; but none of them could offer any remedy for it.

The King sent for Death's godson and promised him a barrelful of gold if he succeeded in working so difficult a cure.

Macaber bent down to observe the patient's face. In spite of her pallor, the sleeping Princess was marvelously beautiful, and so at once he fell madly in love with her.

Raising his head, he saw Death standing by the head of the bed.

At the sight, the doctor turned pale; but he recovered himself in a moment, and asked to be left alone with the Princess.

"Save her, I beg you, Godfather," said Macaber.

"You know very well that's impossible."

"I love her madly."

"What do you want me to do about it?"

"People are right when they say Death has no pity!" cried Macaber; "but I know how to deprive him of his prey!"

He went to the door and said to the King, "I know only one way to heal your daughter; it's to make a definite change in the way her bed is oriented. Order your servants to put the head of the bed where the foot is, and the foot at the head."

Although it seemed an odd remedy, the King whistled on his silver whistle, and at once four servants appeared. They hurried to carry out his orders.

"When Death finds himself at the foot of the bed," thought the doctor, rubbing his hands together, "the Princess will escape him, and my godfather will lose her."

But, alas!—no matter how quick the servants were, Godfather Death was faster, and the Princess died while they were turning the bed around.

All the physicians agreed in saying that it was the ill-timed movement that had killed the patient, by sending a flow of too much blood to the heart.

The King fell into a violent rage. He ordered his servants to seize the ignorant doctor and throw him into the sea.

The order was carried out immediately; but, as Macaber's lamp was still full of oil, he was buffeted about by the waves for three days and three nights, and then came to land on an unknown shore.

Macaber cursed his fate. In losing the Princess, and his love, he had lost everything. Life became intolerable to him. He couldn't even find the energy to stand up, and just lay on the sand in the sunlight, waiting for Death.

Death appeared. "What are doing there, my son?" he asked.

"Waiting for you, Godfather."

"To do what?"

"To take me to the Princess."

"But your hour hasn't come."

"I know how to hurry it up."

"How? You could see that the ocean didn't want anything to do with you."

"I know a more voracious monster."

"Who is that?"

"Starvation! A man is always free to keep his lamp from getting fed!"

The old reaper trembled. He adored his godson and could not accept the idea of losing him so soon.

He scolded, he begged, he wept, he pleaded: his godson was unshakeable.

"Unhappy child," he said at last, "look, let's talk this over. What do you want of me?"

Macaber made no reply.

"Do you want gold? Do you want a bushel of diamonds?"

"Could you bring my Princess back to life?"

"You know very well that it's not my job to resuscitate people."

"Then—"

"Besides, her nose was too short. Would you like ten princesses, all lovelier than that one?"

Macaber shrugged. "It's easy to see that you've never been in love," he said.

Death would have torn his hair out, if his skull hadn't been as bald and shining as glass.

In his wrath, he struck a great blow with his scythe against an enormous rock, muttering, "Accursed scythe!" The rock split in two from top to bottom, then collapsed into dust.

Macaber suddenly stood up. "I agree to live," he said, "on one condition: you must entrust to me the instrument that robbed me of my love."

"My scythe?—but God the Father would never allow—"

"In that case, let me die in peace." And he lay down again, without another word.

"God the Father," cried Death in despair, "isn't this child asking for the impossible?"

"Let him have what he asks," said God the Father.

God the Father was tired of hearing men complain incessantly about Death. He wanted to condescend, once and for all, to put the great scythe into the hands of a mortal.

"Oh, very well!—take it," said Death to Macaber, "but swear to me that you won't use it on yourself.

Macaber swore, took the scythe, and went away.

III

Death's godson was by nature good and sympathetic, and sorrow had not embittered him. He had demanded the great scythe only in order to do good to others like himself.

"I will reap," he said, "those who want to die, or those whose life will be a burden to others. I will be good to humanity—that will help me to forget my sorrow."

He soon ran across a poor old man, sitting on the edge of a ditch, paralyzed in every limb, and gnawed by vermin.

"O Death! when will you deliver me?" cried the vagabond.

"At once!" replied Macaber, and with one stroke of the scythe he delivered him.

But the soul was no sooner separated from the body than it muttered, "What rotten luck!—maybe my body could have been cured, and who knows but we might have got rich!"

"Let that teach me a lesson," the reaper said to himself. "I have been sufficiently educated on people who complain about life and how disgusted they are with it."

And he continued on his way.

As he passed through a village, he noticed, on the threshold of a little hut, a peasant woman holding in her arms a child so weak and puny and ugly that he could hardly bear to look at it.

Its legs were hardly bigger than its arms, and its arms were hardly bigger than its fingers. It couldn't stand up, and its breathing sounded like a series of groans.

"Poor little withered heron," the mother was saying, "what will become of you, when I am no more? Ah!—the good Lord would do well to call you back to him!"

The reaper reached out, and believed that this time he was acting wisely in delivering mother and child with a single stroke. But when the mother saw her son was dead, her grief was all the more lively.

The unhappy woman went mad, for she had loved this child ten times more than she would have loved another. She loved him for all the trouble he cost her, and all the more because he was weaker and uglier!

IV

Macaber reflected. "I'm going the wrong way," he said to himself. "The best way to make mortals happy is not to deliver them from life, but to rid them of the worst."

To make sure he was not mistaken, he went back to Flanders, where he had known people for a long time.

In those days there was a burgomaster in Maubeuge who had a bad reputation, well known for ten leagues around. This burgomaster did nothing but evil with his powers, to the point where there was a common saying among the people: "God keep us from war, plague, the pains of death, and the burgomaster of Maubeuge!"

So Death's godson resolved to begin his course of executions with this man, and he cut him down in full flower, as you'd root out a poisonous weed. Macaber thought to himself that this stroke of the scythe would be hailed with the blessings of all the town.

His surprise was great when he saw running to attend the funeral of the departed the crowd of those who had loathed him until then; his surprise grew even greater, when he heard magnificent speeches pronounced over the tomb, in which all his most odious vices were transformed into striking virtues.

This last experiment left him discouraged. He decided to go back to his godfather and give him back his scythe, since he could not manage to put it to good use.

Meanwhile, the rumor had spread far and wide that Macaber, of Chêne-Raoult, had at his disposal a supernatural power by which he could purge the world of the wicked.

Now, the town of Condé was at this time the prey of a hypocritical judge who, under the mask of religious devotion, falsely weighed the justice he handed out. He feared that Macaber might punish him, and he started dreaming of ways to forestall the avenging scythe. He had him arrested and indicted in his tribunal.

The reaper could have closed the proceedings with a single blow, but he wanted to see just how far the wickedness would go of the people for whom he had sought nothing but happiness.

The great scythe was seized and became Exhibit A in the proceedings of his trial. In less than an hour, the benefactor of humanity was accused of witchcraft, judged, and condemned to be burned alive.

On the day of execution, the town-square in Condé was flooded with a crowd of decent folk who were overjoyed at getting to come and see such a fine punishment.

Death's godson was barefoot, wearing only a shift, with a rope around his neck, while the bell rang out loudly.

He was greeted with an immense din of curses, and climbed onto the platform with the stake, which was as tall as the bell-tower.

The executioners lit the fire and threw the great scythe on it, so that it would undergo the same fate as its master. The fire burned for three days and three nights.

On the morning of the fourth day, while the ashes were still smoking, a man could be seen standing there, holding a scythe in his hand. It was Death's godson! At this sight, the townsfolk fled in terror.

Macaber considered that, if it was true that no one is a prophet in his own country, still, they had done him quite an honor in taking him for a witch, and he did not want to go taking vengeance on his fellow countrymen.

Only, he commanded that the lying judge be seized, and, to punish him for having maintained the balance of the scales of Justice so badly, he made them forge a scale twenty feel tall. He suspended it from the beak of the cock that perches on top of the bell-tower.

In one of the scale's basins he set the judge, and his enemies in the other. The first basin was at once raised as high as the balance beam, from the weight of the second, and Macaber condemned the abominable magistrate, who had been muttering his prayers so hard it was funny, to pray all night and all day until the two basins hung at the same level.

The people make sure that the balance is always at the top of the bell-tower, and the peasant-women of Fresne, Old Condé, Macou, and Thinvincelles, as they go to the market, stare wide-eyed at it, but in vain, for the judge's basin never budges.

Every hundred years, the basin gets one line lower, so they say, and it's still only halfway down.

V

"Decidedly!" thought Macaber, "I'm not going to meddle anymore trying to make people happy. It's a fool's game, and I've found out by experience myself that every good deed deserves its punishment. All the same, I want to make use of my scythe to win happiness for myself. Let's have honors and power for me! The King of the Low Countries behaved very badly toward us, so let's begin by dethroning him, and put ourself in his place. Being on the throne has got to be more comfortable than being in the middle of the Condé town-square."

So he left, and his fame preceded him. The King of the Low Countries fled at his approach, and Macaber found all the palace-doors wide open. He ascended the throne, put the crown on his head, and was proclaimed king by all the people of the Low Countries.

He promptly notified all the sovereigns of the world of his accession to the throne, addressing them as his dear cousins. But the sovereigns had no intention of admitting into their ranks a vagabond who had been burned as a witch in the Condé town-square.

They had of course heard tell of Macaber's power, but they didn't believe a word of it, and they sent all his ambassadors back again, loaded with scorn. Macaber declared war on them.

The general at the head of his army came to offer him his services. But he told him, "I've no need of you," and, indeed, left all alone, except for his scythe.

All the kings of the world gathered their troops together in an immense plain, and waited, firmly fixed, for the King of the Low Countries and his army. The sun had never risen on such an assembly of warriors.

Every sort of warrior was there, from those who march without any armor to those who won't go unless they're in a shell of iron; from those who fight on foot to those who fight on horseback or mounted on elephants; from those who shoot arrows or hurl javelins to those who fire bullets and bombs.

When the kings saw Macaber arrive alone, with his scythe, they burst out laughing and sent a message to him to ask if he took them for a field of barley.

"He laughs best who laughs last," said Death's godson. "You can give the signal to begin the dance."

His enemies at once shot off a hail of darts, arrows, balls, bullets, bombs, shells, and other projectiles. But he pressed forward without suffering any more than a shepherd would feel leading his flock through the rain. You might even say he was amusing himself, batting the balls back with his hand.

Then he took off his coat, rolled up his sleeves, and, like a reaper going into a meadow, penetrated their ranks and set about reaping with his great scythe, swinging it back and forth, slowly and steadily.

He cut off a thousand heads at each stroke, and, after an hour of this exercise, he was no more tired than if he'd only been cutting grass.

His enemies turned to flee, but as they kept getting in each other's way, and Macaber, with his scythe, overtook even the fastest horses, he left them with no recourse except to throw themselves at his feet and ask for mercy.

The conqueror pardoned them, on condition that the conquered kings would pay homage to him. He was named emperor of the universe there on the battlefield and became, by this single victory, more powerful than Alexander, Caesar, and Napoleon ever were.

On the summit of the highest mountain in the world, he had an immense palace built, glittering with gold and diamonds, and shut himself up there in his glory.

The conquered kings begged him on their knees for the honor of serving him, and His Majesty Macaber the First was adored as a god by all the peoples of the world.

He spent each day on a massive gold throne, which certainly must have been an agreeable way to spend each day. He wore an enormous gold crown, three cubits round, studded with emeralds and carbuncles. He held a scepter in one hand and the orb imperial in the other.

Behind him stood his guards, arranged according to height, from the smallest dwarf, about as big as the Pissing Mannikin, to the giant ten feet high. He never went out except in a palanquin carried by kings and preceded by a hundred drums.

The fields, the coasts, the forests, the lakes, and the seas of the whole world were called on to provision his table, and when he dined he always had delightful music playing.

His Majesty ate tarts and drank beer from Louvain at every meal.

Like King Solomon, Macaber had a thousand wives, of rare beauty; and, as he could have had them put to death with a wave of his hand, he was able to govern them with less pain than we go through trying to govern just one.

Sometimes, for diversion, he would beat them, and—it was astonishing and almost unbelievable!—none of them deceived him.

Everyone trembled before him. Yet he had only smiling faces under his eyes, and, no matter what evil deeds he did, he heard nothing but a concert of praises.

VI

If ever a man tasted happiness, that man really ought to have been Macaber. Alas!—no, Macaber was not happy at all. He had all he could want—all but one thing, a common thing, such as the least of men could have. Even the animals could. There was no one who loved him, no one he loved. That was enough to poison all his pleasure.

He saw the smiles on the lips of all around him, and he sensed the hatred deep in their hearts. He had no friends—only servants.

Out of fear, the whole world groveled at his feet, and this universal base cowardice raised his scorn and caused his despair.

He would have given the command of the universe to have one of his flatterers dare just once to tell him the truth to his face.

It was a frightful torture for a man who had been led by love to this extremity of wanting to be adored like a god!

At last, one night, when he was weary of all the false faces, all the lies, all the groveling, and all the hatred, Macaber took off his imperial robe, put the clothes of a peasant back on, and left his palace by a secret door, without telling anyone.

He fled like a criminal, for fear of being recognized and thrust back onto his throne.

He didn't stop walking until he got to the threshold of the hut where Death was sitting at rest, his arms folded.

"Oh! Godfather," said Macaber, "here!—take your scythe back and leave me to live like the least of mortals. I'll be happier then."

"Be it so," Death answered; and he took up his assigned task on the spot.

Macaber no longer even wanted to practice the profession of medicine, which reminded him too much of his former power. He set about gardening to see if he could produce something, at last, after having destroyed so much!

He settled down in the little town of Chêne Raoult, married an honest peasant-woman, and had ten children.

Death's godson lived for more than two hundred years. It was the most remarkable case of longevity that had been seen since the days of the patriarchs.

In his old age, sometimes he would tell his marvelous history to the grandchildren of his great-grandchildren, who would laugh quietly, thinking to themselves deep down that the good old man was wandering in his wits—for people then were already like people nowadays, laughing at everything, and believing nothing.

Martin and Martine

In olden times, in the country of the Moors, not far from here, there was a little prince who was marvelously handsome. He was so handsome that after his birth people were predicting that if ever the king, his father, came to see him, he would lose his eyesight.

The monarch, who wanted to keep his eyes, had his son brought up in the back of an old castle in a deserted spot. But when the child was hardly ten years old, bored with his solitude, he eluded the vigilance of his guardians and escaped.

He was taken in by one of those wanderers who go around with a jackass to the four corners of the world, crying, "White sand for sale!" or "We trade cherries for scrap-iron!"

This wanderer was particularly devoted to Saint Martin. He gave the little prince the name of this patron saint of honest drinkers and took him everywhere with him. They traveled for several years in this way, and then the wanderer was seized with a longing to return to the land of good beer and big pint-pots.

This was not the concern of young Martin, The boy found our sky too grey, our people too ruddy, or I might say rosy, and it annoyed him to see them sneer at his dark face.

His adoptive father, besides, was going more often than he had in the past into chapels dedicated to his patron saint, and, when he had re- cited more than enough of the prayers there—or, in other words, when he had drunk too many pints, in too many taverns, he would sometimes start landing strokes with a birch-rod on the shoulders of the poor little prince. So it happened one fine day, around twilight, that Martin deserted him near Cambrai and fled into the forest of Proville.

He kept walking until after dark, until, worn out with fatigue and dying of hunger, he spotted a lonely house. He beat on the door, and a girl came to open it.

"Would you be so kind," he said politely "as to let me stay here overnight? I'm ready to drop with hunger and weariness."

"What's your name?" the girl asked gently.

"Martin, at your service."

"What a coincidence! As for me, my name is Martine."

"Really! My pretty Martine, surely you won't let a poor wanderer be left to pass the night among the wolves, who are out in what they call the day."

"You're wrong. I'm not pretty," said Martine, "but I have a good heart, and I'll prove it to you. Unfortunately, my father is an ogre, and he'll be back any minute."

The boy took a step back. Martine added briskly, "Bah! Come on in. My mother is charitable, and we'll find a way to manage to hide you somehow."

Martin was so ravenous that he judged that hs most pressing need was to get something to satisfy his hunger, even if it meant running the risk of being something to satisfy his host's hunger later on. He entered boldly.

II

Martine's mother welcomed him gladly, gave him some supper, and made him tell them how he came to be there. He had hardly finished telling his story when they heard someone knocking violently at the door. It was the ogre, coming home. At once, his wife opened up the clock-case, and Martin curled up inside.

The ogre sat down at the table and ate half a veal, which he washed down with three big pitchers of dark beer. When he got to the dessert, he flared his nostrils—to the right, to the left—and then turned to the clock and said, "Look! The works have stopped."

"Don't worry about it, Father," cried Martine. "I can wind it up in an instant."

But the ogre was a methodical man. He got up and went to open the case. "Oh!" he said, "what a fine black man. That's why I was smelling fresh meat!

Martine flung her arms around his neck.

"Dear, good father, spare him, I beg you. He's so nice!"

"He'd be better still, with plum sauce!" said the ogre.

He seized a big knife and began sharpening it.

"That's just like you," his wife said then. "Our daughter is old enough to be getting married, and because of your depraved appetite, no one will want her except Big William. Now a king's son falls to us out of heaven who could become our son-in-law. But you've nothing better to do with yourself than to put him on the spit. Such a bad father!"

The ogre was, at bottom, not a bad man, and he felt this reproach. Besides, the prospect of having a prince for a son-in-law pleased him a lot.

"Oh! He's a king's son," he said. "Well, well, if he'll promise to marry Martine, I agree to let him escape me, even though he seems to have been cooked brown already."

Martin had no wish to get married. He looked at Martine. The girl was not at all pretty, but her face showed so much kindness that she won your heart anyway.

The boy decided that it would be less disagreeable to make the girl happy, rather than her father. "I'll marry her," he said, and Martine's face shone.

The young prince had pleased her from the first moment, and she loathed Big William—an old bachelor who wanted her for her dowry.

But the ogre was conceited through and through. He thought the prince's answer was cold, and it had taken him too long to give it,

"It's not enough to just say 'I'll marry her'," he said. "We have to find out if you're worthy of a father-in-law like me. What can you do?"

Martin was very embarrassed. He didn't know how to do anything. In that respect, the wanderer had truly given him the upbringing of a prince. He resolved to try audacity, and answered bravely, "Give me any command, and I'll carry it out."

"Oh, well! Tomorrow, at day-break, we'll go into the forest, and you will cut down a hundred measures of wood. Until then, go to bed, boy, sleep well, and don't have any bad dreams."

III

I don't know what dreams Martin had, but Martine tossed and turned twenty times in her bed, without getting the Sand-Grandmother to come with her sand and close her eyes for her.

"The poor boy will never succeed in such a task," she said. "If only my godfather were here. He would help us out of this trouble."

Her godfather was Cambrinus, the Duke of Brabant, the Count of Flanders, and the founder of the city of Cambrai.

During the period when Cambrinus brought the brown liquor to the world, the ogre, who was a hard drinker, was the first to recognize and proclaim the excellence of the wine that's made of barley. The result was that Cambrinus made an alliance with him, in spite of his bad reputation. He was even willing to be godfather to the ogre's daughter, and to choose as his counterpart the Fairy of the Hop-poles.

As she did not have her godfather to hand, Martine tried invoking her godmother. "Dear Godmother," she said, "come to our aid and save my husband-to-be, I conjure you!"

The fairy appeared, crowned with the leaves and flowers of the hop-plant. "Are you sure he really loves you, my poor child?"

"Save him, Godmother. I will love him so much that he'll have to love me back."

"Be it so. Here is my wand. It will carry out all your wishes on the spot. But be careful not to lose it, and especially not to let anyone else take it."

Martine thanked her godmother warmly and went to bed feeling reassured. When she woke, she went to tell her mother all about it.

IV

The next day, the ogre led Martin to a dense thicket, a hundred paces from the house. Handing him an ax, he said, "Get to work, my lad. I'm giving you three hours to get this clear."

And he left, smiling in his beard.

He lit his pipe, went down into the cellar, heaved a barrel of beer onto his shoulder, brought it to the dining room, took a pint-pot out of the sideboard, then went up to his cupola to see how poor Martin was getting on.

Martin did not even try to strike the first ax-blow. He was thinking about running away when Martine came to join him, gliding from tree to tree.

"Stand in back of me," she said, "and hide me so my father can't see me."

And, with that, she touched the trees with her wand, and the elms, the hornbeams, the aspens, the plane trees, the bushy beeches, the ashes with their long, thin branches, the pale poplars, the silver birches, the century-old oaks, the chestnuts, the maples, the wild cherries, the cornel-berries, fell with a frightful din.

The birds flew away in flocks, calling out in terror, and, in a panic, the roe deer, the fallow deer, the red deer, the foxes, the wolves, and the boars fled, too.

From the height of his cupola, the ogre contemplated this immense tree-felling. He opened his eyes as big as chariot wheels and could not believe what he saw. His surprise was so great that he forgot to drink his beer, and let his pipe go out.

But he had too much vanity to show his astonishment, and, when the little fellow came back with his ax, he said to him mockingly, "You're not bad at putting the squirrels to flight, but you've give me only a quarter of the day. Now you need to dig out a fishpond for me in the spot you cleared out just now. Here's a spade—let's see if you can wield that as well as you did the ax." Then he added, to his daughter, "As for you, Miss, you're going to come with me and sing your prettiest songs to keep me awake while this fine rabbit digs his burrow."

He thought he had spotted a white dress during the great massacre of the trees, and he was a little suspicious of his daughter.

V

Martin returned to the clearing and, counting on Martine, he began to dig, as if it were no more than digging a hole to plant an ash-tree.

At first, Martine sang her gayest songs: then little by little her tempo slowed, so much that at last the ogre let his pipe fall to the ground, his head drooped on his shoulder, and he fell into a deep slumber.

The little fairy came running then, light as a sparrow. With a few taps of the wand, she cleared the ground, dug out the soil, made springs of water shoot out, and filled the basin with a fine sheet of water, which shone like an immense steel plate in the sunshine. The ogre, when he woke up, was dazzled by it.

He came down grumbling. No one could have been more mortified. Noon had just rung, so he found the household at the table. He complained that the soup was too cold, the roast burnt, the beer running low, and kept on hunting for any pretext to get into a quarrel with poor Martin.

At last, he had an idea. "What fish did you put in the fishpond?" he asked.

Fish! Martin, who was not a fisher, had completely forgotten to mention this point to Martine, He didn't know how to reply.

"Aha! My fine fellow," said the ogre, enchanted to have caught him out. "You were supposed to make a fishpond, and you've forgotten to stock it! You're a real ne'er-do-well, you are!"

"He can go fix it," said Martine.

"Bring my coffee and my bottle of brandy to the cupola! We'll go and watch that."

And the ogre went on up, rubbing his hands gleefully. His daughter followed him, but this time she hardly had to begin a single song. Her father always dropped off to sleep after dinner. Soon he was snoring.

In two jumps, Martine was with Martin. Unfortunately, they needed more time to stock the fishpond. You can understand how it wouldn't be so easy, even with a fairy's wand, to create live fish as it was to cut down trees or dig out the soil. For a long time she kept tapping the water, but without hatching out so much as a catfish.

Finally, at the end of an hour, golden carp, perch with purple fins, greedy pike, eels coiled in green rings, gudgeons, minnows, loaches, and guerliches began to sport in the water. Martin forgot everything in watching them, and Martine in watching Martin, when all at once —

"Oh! I've got you now, you hussy!" cried a terrible voice. It was the ogre who had crept up on them, silent as a wolf. He grabbed hold of each by an ear and led them back to the house.

"Give me my knife," he told his wife, "and I'll soon have this young tom turkey cut up for cooking."

His wife saw that it would be useless to fight him directly.

"You'd do better to wait until tomorrow," she said. "It's the Sunday of the festival of the town's patron saint, and we've invited a couple of your friends to dinner. It's not every day you sink your teeth into a prince."

"True! That would really be what you'd call a kingly dish."

And he locked him in his larder. I mean, he shut Martin in a room at the top of the house.

VI

That evening, after supper, Martine, as usual, stayed behind to cover the fire. She took her spinning wheel, put it in front of the ash-pan, then touched it with her wand and said, "Wheel, wheel, my pretty wheel, when they call for me, don't forget to answer for me."

Then she put her distaff on the first step of the staircase, went up to her room, put the spindle on her bed, and gave them the same order. By then, she was at the young prince's room. She touched the door with her wand, and the door opened at once.

"I've come to rescue you," she told Martin, "but we have to escape together. Without me you don't know how to get past my father."

A little after the curfew-time, the ogre woke up, and, wanting to be sure his daughter was in her bed, he called, "Martine! Martine!"

"Here I am, Father," said the spinning-wheel. "I'm covering the fire, and then I'll go to bed."

An hour later, he woke up again, and cried, "Martine! Martine!"

"Here I am, Father," said the distaff. "I'm just going upstairs."

An hour after that, he woke again and called again, "Martine! Martine!"

"I'm in bed, I'm going to sleep, good night!" said the spindle.

"All's well," said the ogre to himself. "No need to try to sleep with one ear pricked." And soon his snores were rumbling away like an organ.

Who wound up looking sheepish? It was that child-eating ogre, when he woke the next morning and saw that his daughter had taken a powder with that little bit of a prince he'd intended for his dinner table. Quickly, he commanded his wife to bring him his seven-league boots, and set off in pursuit of the fugitives.

They were a good ways off, but the seven-league boots took the ogre so fast that, even with the time it took him to figure out which way they'd gone, he soon caught up with them.

Martine saw him coming when he was still some ways off, at a turning in the road, and with a tap of her wand she changed Martin into a chapel. She transformed herself into the likeness of one of those little girls who, for the festivals when all the bells are rung, erect little altars on the street-corners and run after people, carrying a collection-plate in their hands, and shout, "For the Holy Virgin's altar! For the Holy Virgin's altar!"

"You haven't seen a boy and girl pass by, have you, child?" said the ogre.

"For the Holy Virgin's altar! For the Holy Virgin's altar!"

"I asked you if you'd seen a boy and girl go by."

"For the Holy Virgin's altar! For the Holy Virgin's altar!"

"Oh, devil take it, I've nothing to give you," grumbled the ogre impatiently.

He continued on his way, beat the bushes all around in vain and finished by going back home. His wife, who was expecting him to come back empty-handed, was not annoyed at getting the chance to tease him a bit.

"Didn't you find them?" she asked.

"I certainly thought I saw them, but they vanished at a turn in the road, and all I found was a chapel and a little girl asking for alms."

"Stupid as an ox, Husband! By Heaven, that chapel was the little prince, and the little girl was your daughter."

"I'll go back there!" cried the ogre, "and if I catch them, I swear to God I'll fricassee the one and marry the other to Big William. And that won't be the least punishment the two of them will get!"

He set out again, and didn't find the chapel. But farther along he found a magnificent rose-tree with a beautiful white rose. He knelt down to pick it and carry it back home, when it occurred to him that the flower would have enough time to droop and fade, and he would do better to pick it on the way back.

He traveled for a long time, but it was a long time without finding the fugitives. At last, tired out with so much running, he retraced his steps, forgetting about the rose. He didn't remember it until he was telling his better half about his search.

"Oh, that's rich!" she said, snorting with laughter. "What! Didn't you see that the rosebush was Martin, and the rose was Martine!"

"I'll catch them," said the ogre, "if I have to tear up all the rose-trees for a hundred leagues around!"

VII

He set out a third time through the countryside and uprooted all the rose-trees along the way, but the fugitives had already returned to their own shapes. They gained a lot of ground, but their persecutor caught up to them at the edge of a great lake. Martine only had time to change Martin into a boat and herself into a boat-woman.

"Have you seen a swarthy young man and a girl dressed in white come this way?" asked the ogre.

"Yes, indeed," said the boat-woman. "They followed the shore for a while, then went off through the willow grove." And pushing back with her oar, she got out into the open water.

The ogre followed the way she had pointed out to him, but found no one. Evening fell, and he felt all worn out.

He returned home, going through Cambrai, and stopped at the Great Saint Hubert inn to drink a pint and play a hand of cards with his pal Cambrinus.

Being a father doesn't stop you—a father is still an ordinary man, and a man who knows what he's about doesn't go to bed without emptying a few bottles. The ogre drank forty, as his custom was.

While he drank, he told the story of his misadventure to his old friend, who did his best to console him.

"Don't get yourself in a temper," he told the ogre. "My goddaughter will lead her little prince by the nose through here one day or another."

"You think so?"

"Lord, yes! Anyway, it's your own fault! Why do you have the bad habit of eating poor kids? If it weren't for that sad defect, I would have made you a suggestion long since."

"What?"

"Well, look here, my boy. My fine town of Cambrai is prospering nicely, and could get along without my help. I've given the people of Cambrai both beer and bells. They lack nothing to be happy, and that is why I've been feeling that I'd like to retire to Fresnes, my native town, and plant cabbages. To do that, I'd need to have a good man here who could replace me as the burgomaster."

The ogre had always dreamed of honors. He saw at once where his old friend was going, and his vanity was so tickled that he forgot about the fugitives completely.

"Did you consider asking me?" he said.

"Yes, but Devil take it!—there's your passion for young flesh. People would hardly dare to get married, and that would be bad for the population."

"Oh, that's not a problem, my lad. If I have to, I'll promise to respect the little brats."

"Word of honor?"

"Spit my tongue out if I don't!" cried the ogre, pinching his chin. Around here, that is the most solemn oath.

"Oh, well! Let's drink on it," said Cambrinus. "Come have supper with me next Monday. I'll invite all the best people and install you at the end of the meal—between the pears and the cheese."

VIII

It didn't take the ogre long to become an excellent burgomaster. His method was quite simple. It was like the fat mayor of Erchin's, and consisted of leaving each person to live as he chose and the world to spin on its axis, as God wills.

In addition, he chose Big William for his assistant, who had formerly been Martine's suitor and was the fat mayor's ex-registrar. He was an old hand who understood how things are done and how to keep the routine going, steady as a blind nag turning the wheel at a brewery.

There was only one problem that plagued Monsieur the Burgomaster. Swollen with Cambrinus's dark beer, the mynheers of Cambrai could not get themselves going at closing time. It was like a barge that's run up on the bank—at night it needed nothing less than jacks and winches to get these live barrels of beer moving.

It was no use to warn them that curfew had rung, and it was time to cover the fire. The mynheers, plunged in sweet drowsiness, would just look at you, waggling their sleepy heads and turning a deaf ear.

"They don't hear any better than so many dead men," said Vasse, the town constable.

"I'll make such a noise round them that they'd hear it even if they were at the very bottom of their beer," cried the ogre, and, pleased with his joke, he ordered a magnificent clock from the best clockmaker in Cambrai and had it put under an enormous belljar under the dome of the town hall.

The clock marked the hour as exactly as a Fresnian's growling stomach. All they had to do was to choose someone to ring the bell. Unfortunately, the job seemed so monotonous that no one wanted to take it on, no matter how well it paid.

Perhaps the mynheers of Cambrai had some hidden reason for this universal repugnance.

It was in vain that his honor the burgomaster and his registrar searched for a way out of the difficulty. To think it over at leisure, the ogre took his duck-gun and sat down behind a blind in the lights—what we call the marshes—of Palluel.

IX

Hidden by an immense cask surrounded with reeds, he had been there three hours, but his game-bag was as empty as his head, when he spotted on the horizon a black dot that grew larger, little by little, and became, to his astonished eyes, a swan with such a great wingspan that he had never seen its like.

With his head hidden under his barrel, he waited for the prey, then suddenly threw off the mask and took aim.

"Don't shoot! Don't shoot!" cried the bird.

The ogre, utterly astonished, let his weapon fall. He had indeed heard that swans sing when they are about to die, but no one, so far as he knew, had ever heard one talk.

He recognized at last, sitting on the swan's back—guess who!—his daughter. Martine's white gown had blended in with the swan's white wings, and that's why the ogre hadn't at first seen who was there.

Not knowing what changes had been going on during her absence, Martine had chosen this method of transportation to take refuge at Cambrai with her godfather Cambrinus.

"Come down from there, or I'll break one of your steed's wings," cried the hunter.

The swan came to rest a few steps away.

"Where have you been, my girl?" the ogre went on, severely. "Is this the conduct of a well-brought-up girl, to go travelling around through the air on a swan's back?"

The traveler, at these words, looked down and made no reply.

"And your prince, what've you done with him? I told you he'd leave you in the lurch!"

"No, he's right here, Father," cried Martine, pointing to the bird. "That's Martin,"

"Oh! That's Martin! Well, now, I may have sworn not to eat any more children, but I didn't make any promises about swans!"

He seized his duck-gun. That would have been the end of the poor boy, if Martine, faster than lightning, hadn't turned him back to his original form.

Her father, furious, tore the wand from her hands. It promptly disappeared, and Martine, disconsolate, remembered her godmother's warning. The poor girl now had no way to protect the one she loved. The ogre ordered them to walk ahead of him, and he returned to Cambrai in a very bad humor.

X

He was especially vexed because he didn't know what to do. A sensible father wouldn't have hesitated a minute—he would have had the guilty pair married off at once. But the ogre was not the sort of man to pardon the trick his daughter had played on him.

In the town square, they ran into Big William, who was standing around, idly watching the crows, trying to come up with an idea. With his eyes turning to the clock, he seemed, as usual, to be trying to find mid-day at two o'clock.

Big William was so called because he had big feet, big hands, a big mouth, a big nose, and big ears. In short, he was big all over, except in brain and heart.

The ogre explained the situation to him in a few words. The old bachelor thought he saw in it a roundabout way to marry Martine himself. He scratched his knee—I mean to say, his head—and, for the first time in his life, managed to come up with an idea.

"What you need," he said, "is a bell-ringer. And look!—here's one all ready for it!"

"Of course! I'll station him up high. That'll teach him to run away." And the ogre at once gave the order for Martin to be set up next to the bell. Alas! Poor Martine! What had become of her wand!

The ogre had the prince chained to one of the columns, a heavy mallet in his hand, and the order given to him to ring the bell exactly on the hour, on pain of being left to die of hunger.

Big William told an ex-prison-guard who was a friend of his, named Riboulet, that he would be responsible for throwing the prince's food to him and above all to keep watch over him day and night to keep him from going to sleep.

"As for that pretty child," he said in the ogre's ear, "if she's a problem for you, I know a good fellow who would be happy to take charge of all that."

The registrar winked one eye, and the burgomaster understood who the good fellow was that he was talking about, and he felt humiliated to the very depths of his soul.

He closed Martine behind triple bolts, and pleased, overall, with his day's work, he went to drink a pint at the *Great Saint Hubert*. Martin rang the curfew at ten o'clock precisely, and, although it was by moonlight, his cheeks turned a purple as magnificent as if he'd been sunburnt.

The next day, the ogre woke late and went to visit his prisoner. He found the cage open and the bird flown. He asked his wife what had become of his daughter.

"Did you tell me to watch her?" she said, with a shrug of her shoulders.

He wondered if the mother and the daughter were in a plot against him together, but he didn't like quarrels in the house, so he didn't breathe a word, and went away to let his anger die down.

As he crossed the square, he noticed a crowd of people, noses pointing up in the air and eyes fixed on the clock. He lifted up his nose like the rest, and what did he see?—there was Martine next to Martin.

He was shaken with a terrible fit of rage. If he'd had his duck-gun, no doubt he'd have aimed right at his daughter as he would at a teal. When he could command himself enough to speak, he cried: "Since that's where the hussy wants to be, she can just stay there!"

And without waiting to hear a word, he gave orders for her to be chained up on the other side of the bell.

XI

Martin and Martine spent a year in this way, exposed to all the harm severe weather can do. Under the fires of the sun, the girl's face eventually became almost as dark as her companion's. People noticed, as a marvelous thing, that the more her complexion bronzed, the more fine and regular her features seemed to be. Her soul rose up, as it were, came into flower at the surface, and her whole figure bloomed. The gentle majesty of self-sacrifice gleamed about her head like a halo.

The poor girl suffered much less from her hard punishment than Martin did. Separated from him by the enormous bell, she could not see him or even speak to him. Every time the unfortunate pair tried to exchange a word, Riboulet's gallows-face popped up.

Martine's devotion had profoundly touched the young prince, and now he loved her as much as she loved him. Perhaps their eternal separation played a part in it.

The mynheers of Cambrai contemplated the two victims while smoking their pipes, and, although they were getting heavy with drinking beer, they felt moved by pity and could not keep from sorrowing over them. Sometimes they even tried begging for forgiveness for the guilty pair, but the burgomaster invariably replied with these words, which the registrar had put into his mouth: "My daughter is free. As soon as she agrees to come home to her father, I'll hack off her chairs on the spot!"

Soon they got so used to the spectacle that they stopped noticing it, and the most obvious result of Big William's jealousy was that at ten o'clock precisely all the inns emptied out, as if by enchantment, when curfew sounded.

Martine's mother was the only one who could not bear the torture of her daughter. Even an ogre as completely an ogre as her husband would have ended by yielding to her tears, except for the detestable influence that Big William had over him. But the day of reckoning came, and Big William could no longer get away with it.

Cambrinus felt a whim, one fine day, to pay a visit to his good city of Cambrai. Passing the square, he heard the bell ring, and raised his head. He was much astonished to see his god-daughter beside it.

"What are you doing there?" he asked.

"Alas! Godfather, you see before your eyes two of the unhappiest creatures!"

And the poor girl burst into tears.

Their savage guardian soon appeared, but a glance from Cambrinus forced him to take cover, and the whole story came out. Cambrinus understood all the torments of love, having felt them himself, and he went at once to find his friend.

"Are you out of your mind," he asked him, "to make such a spectacle of your daughter? Since these children love each other honestly, why haven't you married them off, instead of leaving them to die over a slow fire?"

The ogre tried to argue back with a thousand reasons, each more absurd than the other. The King of Beer refuted them victoriously.

"You're going to upset all our customs," the burgomaster said in conclusion. "They ring the bell so well! It's only since they've been up there that I can have peace and have everyone know for sure when it's ten o'clock."

"So that's where the saddle pinches," said Cambrinus. "But remember that the King of Beer was also the inventor of the carillon. I'll undertake to make two mechanical bell-ringers who look as much like those poor martyrs as one drop of ink looks like another. What does it matter to you whether the curfew is struck by a Jack or a Martin, as long as you have a jackanapes to hit the bell at the right time?"

"But what will Big William say?"

"Who? Your dumb-bell of a registrar? He's already said only too much, and, anyhow, it was all twaddle. The Mayor of Erchin made a good decision letting him go. Decidedly, the best thing is to send Big William away!"

"Of course! The youngsters have been roasting over a slow fire for long enough!" cried the Burgomaster, converted by this argument.

And he sent Big William and his friend Riboulet away, to stay away forever.

XII

Cambrinus made two mechanical bronze bell-ringers, and they can be seen to this day striking the hour under the dome of the town-hall of Cambrai. They took the name, as they had taken the places and the forms, of Martin and Martine.

On the same day that the mechanical figures were installed, their predecessors were married in great splendor, and they proved, in spite of the vanity and jealousy of fools, that spirit and constancy are sometimes rewarded here on earth.

They held a superb feast, presided over by the King of Beer, and the Fairy of the Hops. In memory of his old trade, Martin invited the peddlers of Quevaucams, Grandglise, Strambruges, and other places. They all rode in on their jackasses, superbly dressed in bottle-green velvet pants.

Cambrai was a country full of donkeys, but even in Cambrai they'd never seen such a fine reunion of jackasses. I went to it, like the rest of the people, but I wasn't one of the wedding guests, so I came home again, my belly empty, trailing after my dog's tail.

The people of Cambrai tell the story of Martin and Martine in another way. The reason for that is that they're out of their heads altogether, and they've lost their memory of the past. That's why it's a common proverb: "Everyone in Cambrai is marred by Martin's hammer."

The Candle of the Kings

I

In olden times, near Douai, by the village of Lécluse, on the top of the hill where the enormous block of sandstone can be seen that the people roundabout call the *Devil's Stone*, there lived a fat farmer named Antoine Wilbaux, who, according to the census, held half the properties in the neighborhood.

One year when the harvest had been magnificent, it happened that, on the night before the day when they should have been bringing the crops in, a fire took hold in the farmer's barn, the finest barn there was for seven leagues around. It was entirely burnt up, along with the hay and rye stored inside.

Antoine's farm stood alone—he could not resort to the barns of any neighbors. So he had to leave his harvest lying spread out on the fields, for, in those days, they had not yet invented the technique of bundling the wheat in shocks.

Old Matthew Lænsberg's reliable almanac had predicted for that date a whole week of rain.

In this distress, Wilbaux had the idea of going that same evening to consult his friar, who lived at Hendecourt, about two leagues off.

When he got to the place where the path crosses the great road to Arras, suddenly he saw before him a man dressed in a brown cloak, with a sword at his side, and a red feather in his hat.

"Where are you off to?" said the stranger.

"What's it to you, sir?" said the farmer, who was in no mood for a chat.

"No, the question is what's in it for you, and what I know, for I alone can save you from ruin."

Wilbaux at this time was a long way behind in the rent, and the fire would be, in fact, total ruin for him. He noticed tha the stranger had no whites to his eyes.

His two orbs were so completely black that they seemed to have been carved from a lump of coal. And by this feature, he saw that it was Beelzebub.

"And how are you going to save me?" he asked.

"I'll rebuild your barn."

"With all its contents?"

"With all its contents."

"But when?"

"This very night."

Antoine hesitated a few seconds, then, choosing which side he was on, he said, "I accept."

"In that case, my friend, sign this."

And Beelzebub handed the farmer a quill pen and a scrap of old parchment, marked with cabalistic signs.

"What do those words mean?" asked Wilbaux.

"They mean that you will belong to me, body and soul, in fifty years' time, if by cock-crow I've rebuilt your barn as good as new."

Antoine pricked his finger and signed with a drop of his own blood. The Evil Spirit disappeared.

Reaching home, the farmer wanted neither supper nor sleep. He said not a word to his wife, and did nothing but go out, come back in, and out again, all night long.

Worried by this behavior, his wife in the end followed after her husband, and, from the threshold, she saw a strange sight.

A crowd of little creatures with faces the color of flame, and crooked nails on feet of mud, were silently at work rebuilding the barn.

"What's all that! Lord Jesus!" said the farmwife, trembling.

"That, my poor Françoise," said Antoine, "is our salvation in this world, and my eternal damnation in the other."

And he admitted it all to her.

Françoise was a sensible, God-fearing woman. She went right back to her room, fell to her knees, and fervently asked Heaven for a way to save her husband.

When she stood up, her face was bright. She seized the box of kindling, struck a light, and set on fire the old kindling, which was half burnt up.

Then she took one of those long matches of hemp coated with sulfur, which we call buhottes, and then the big candle of multi-colored wax that the candle-maker had given them on the day of Epiphany.

Armed with these objects, she crossed the courtyard and came to the hen-house.

The barn was almost rebuilt. The roofers had come up as high as the ridge of the roof.

Suddenly a bright light flooded the henhouse, and Chantecleer the rooster, thinking day had come, crowed loudly, "Cock-a-doodle-doo!"

At once the devils took off, tumbling head over heels, like a flock of little birds surprised by the reaper. It was in vain that Beelzebub, who had been setting the last tiles on the roof, tried to hold his troop there. In a rage, he flung away the cutting knife and fled, shouting out blasphemies.

The next day, what a strange thing! Where the simple sandstone boulder had been, they found in the next field an enormous stone, about thirty feet long, six feet high, and two feet thick. It had sunk into the ground to a depth of almost ten feet.

Wilbaux's farm is no longer standing nowadays, but the devil's stone remains in the same place, and, on the side facing Hamel, you can see three little furrows. These, people say, are the marks left by Beelzebub's claws.

Antoine returned to the harvesting and tried to finish rebuilding his barn, but in vain.

Meanwhile, the days of rain that had been predicted by the almanac had arrived on the day predicted. The rain that fell from the sky kept coming into the barn, like a donkey turning a mill round and round. The grain rotted in all that water, and the farmer found himself even closer to an end—and I mean a bad end—than before.

II

One night, when the rain was still coming down in torrents, Wilbaux, without telling his wife anything about it, went back to the place where he'd met Beelzebub. But even though he waited long enough to satisfy all the devils, our one particular devil didn't come walking by.

Antoine resolved then to force him to appear, and to do that, he had recourse to the all-powerful cabalistic ingredient, the Black Glaine, as taught in the *Veritable Red Dragon, or, the Art of Commanding the Celestial, Terrestrial, and Infernal Spirits.*

About eleven o'clock that evening, he went to find a young glaine— that means, a black pullet-hen that hasn't started laying eggs yet. He was careful to grab it by the neck, so that it couldn't cry out. Then he went back to the place where the roads crossed.

There, when midnight sounded, he traced a circle with a wand of cypress-wood, stepped inside it, and tore the pullet in two, while he repeated three times: "*Eloïm! Essaïm!*"

A flame rose up out of the earth, and Beelzebub appeared.

"What do you want of me?" he said.

"I want to make a pact with you."

"Oho! my fine fellow, did you think the devil was the sort of man to let himself be played for a fool by some oaf of a peasant?"

"But it wasn't me, it was my wife—"

"Enough. What do you want?"

"That you'll allow me to finish your work."

"I agree to that on one condition, that you hand over to me the child your wife is going to give you."

"No—not the soul of my child—my own child!"

"Yes, your own child. I don't mean to take much trouble to get it. But I need your daughter. Anyhow, she won't be the loser by it. I'm going to make a princess of her."

Wilbaux resisted for a long time, but he was terrified by the idea of seeing himself, and his wife, too, reduced to begging their bread, and in the end he agreed.

"Go complete your barn," said Beelzebub then, "and in three months look to keep your promise."

III

Three months later, on an evening in November, Antoine was smoking his pipe by the light of the fire. The potatoes were sizzling in the pan, and Françoise was humming a lullaby, "*Do do, Ninette*," to a ravishing little girl with an angelic smile, lying in her crib.

Outside, the snow was swirling, and the wind was howling. Suddenly a plaintive voice was heard outside the door.

"Good people, let a poor pilgrim in!"

"Don't open it!" cried Antoine, trembling at the sound of that voice.

"Oh? Why? The weather is frightful out there."

And Françoise lit the candle, which they had left on the mantelpiece, from the last Epiphany, the feast-day of the Three Kings. She carried it as she went to open the door, saying, "Come in, child of God."

143

On the threshold was a man wearing a woolen robe, with cockle-shells sewn on it. He had a broad-brimmed hat on his head, a purse hanging on his belt, a begging-bag at his back, a drinking-gourd on his shoulder, and a staff in his hand.

The stranger was wearing the pious costume of a pilgrim, but far from looking humble and contrite, he eyed the room with a hard and insolent expression. His eyes, like two balls of jet, flamed.

"Back, Satan!" cried Wilbaux, leaping forward to meet him.

"Oh! what a worthy man!" laughed Beelzebub—for that's who it was. "Is this how you keep your promise?"

"What do you want?" asked Françoise, beginning to tremble.

"I want my child. She's mine."

"My daughter—?"

And the mother flung herself over the cradle.

"Farmer," said Beelzebub, "Tell your wife to keep quiet, or else—"

Antoine was silent, and Françoise, her eyes gleaming, drew herself up in front of her daughter, like a lioness protecting her cub.

"Is it true," said the Accursed One, "that you promised to give me your daughter if I let you finish re-building your barn?"

"It is true," said Wilbaux, almost choking on the words.

"But I didn't promise you anything—not me" said Françoise, "and the child belongs to the mother as much as the father."

"The man is the master," said Beelzebub. "Hurry it up—I need to be going."

And he took a step forward.

Françoise saw that all resistance was useless. "Oh! have pity!" she cried, her hands clasped together. "Leave me my child."

"No."

"Only till tomorrow."

"No."

"Dear Lord, help me!" the poor mother whispered. Then, noticing the Candle of the Kings, she was struck by a sudden idea, and said, "At least, give me a moment to kiss her one last time—only for as long as it takes this candle to burn down all the way!"

"Agreed!" said Beelzebub. Not feeling sure of his place, he thought it prudent to compromise.

He took a chair, seated himself by the fire, and proceeded to fill his pipe.

Suddenly Françoise blew out the candle, shut it in the sideboard, and pulled the keys out of the lock.

In a rage, Beelzebub snapped his pipe and rose up, saying: "Woman, I'll teach you to try tricks on the devil! Your daughter herself, in spite of you, will be the one to finish burning that candle."

"I'll find a way to destroy it before anyone can light it," said Françoise boldly.

"Don't you dare," said Beelzebub. "Your daughter will die the same hour!"

And he disappeared, never doubting that, having seduced Eve, he would easily get the better of one of Eve's great-great-granddaughters.

IV

The next day, they had the child baptized and gave her the name of Jillette. Jillette grew up, and for several years they had no news of Beelzebub.

She was very pretty, but from the very start she was as capricious as a kid, and as scatter-brained as a minx—fit to out-do the devil, as the folk of Lécluse put it.

When she was about seven years old, an extraordinary adventure happened to her. She was a child who was always running and jumping and rummaging around, and one day she noticed a sort of oblong box hidden at the bottom of the sideboard, under a pile of napkins.

Jillette was not slow to ask what was in it; each time, she was told that it wasn't for children. That only made her more curious.

One day, when she had been left alone in the house, she found a little key. She ran at once to the sideboard, opened the box, found in it a maplewood case, and in the case a big Epiphany candle.

The candle must have been there for a long time, because the wax had yellowed. Jillette lit it. Suddenly, someone appeared in the room. He wore a scarlet mantle, with a flame-colored feather in his hat.

"Mama!" cried the frightened child.

"Don't be afraid. I'm your friend," said the stranger, gentling his voice. "What would you like your good friend to give you? Would you like some toys?"

"Yes, some toys," said Jillette, somewhat reassured.

At once the stranger drew from under his cloak some dolls from Nuremberg, miniature Swiss chalets, balloons, and hoops, so many that they filled the room.

"Oh! What pretty toys!" cried Jillette, clapping her hands.

"When you want more," said the man in the red cloak, "all you have to do is light that candle." And he disappeared.

Jillette started to play with her dolls, with the candle still alight and burning.

Just then her mother came in. She gave a cry, ran to the light, and put it out.

"Wretched child! Who told you to light that candle?"

"I don't know." And Jillette told the whole story to her mother.

"The one you are calling your good friend," said Françoise, "is the one who wants the greatest evil for you. He wants to lead you to hell, so that you shall burn there eternally with him."

She took the toys and threw them into the fire, in spite of Jillette's tears. Then she hid the candle so well that it was in vain for the child to look for it—she could never discover it.

Ten years later, Wilbaux died, and the following year his wife went to join him in the cemetery.

When Françoise felt that her last hour was near, she begged to be left alone with Jillette, and, in a grave and solemn voice, she revealed the fatal secret to her.

"Nevertheless, my poor child," she added, "you are the sole mistress of your destiny. No matter how much desire for it should seize you, swear to me that you will never light that accursed candle."

Jillette wept and swore to obey. Her mother turned the little key over to her, and died.

Her uncle d'Hendecourt came to live with her and run the farm.

When her sorrow had eased a little, she began to think about the Candle of the Kings. Soon, the memory obsessed her. It wasn't that she wanted to light it—she was just curious to see it again.

She remembered, in every detail, the scene which had taken place ten years earlier: the apparition of the man with the flame-colored feather and the room full of toys.

One evening, trembling like a leaf, she took the box, drew out the case, opened it, and immediately closed it again. She believed she had seen the devil in person.

The next day, she began again, and grew bolder: she dared to look steadily at the old yellow wax. It still looked quite long to her. Only a third had been consumed.

From that moment on, every time that she was alone, she took the candle out of its case.

At last, unable to resist, she lit it.

Beelzebub appeared.

"What do you want, my pretty child?" he said.

"Nothing. Go away!"

She blew out the candle, and the devil disappeared.

The poor mother wept, up in heaven.

The festival of Lécluse's patron saint arrived, and Jillette, having finished her chores, went to the ball. She was, undeniably, the prettiest of all the dancers; but the mayor's daughter had richer clothes, and through all the village the people talked of nothing but the beautiful robe of the mayor's young lady. Jillette felt jealous.

The following Sunday found her up before daybreak. She had not closed an eye all night. Her resolution was taken. She lit the Candle of the Kings.

"What is your wish, dear young lady?" said Beelzebub, showing himself at once.

"A robe finer than—"

"I understand. Here it is."

"Good. Go away."

She put out the light, and the Evil One obeyed.

The wax had hardly burned for a second, and Jillette calculated that it could last a long time yet.

Her dress was magnificent, and she looked ravishing in it. She was the wonder of the ball, and she who wore it was perfectly happy; only, when she was getting undressed afterward, she felt a drop of water fall on her hand. It was her mother's tear.

V

One day, when Jillette was playing shuttlecock in front of the farm gate, the son of the King of the Low Countries happened to pass by with his retinue.

She thought him so dashing and handsome that she was seized with a sudden irresistible desire to have him for her husband. She ran to the candle and lit it.

Beelzebub appeared.

"I want the Prince of the Low Countries for my husband," said Jillette.

"You shall have him, my beautiful princess," said Beelzebub, rubbing his hands together. "Sit down at your spinning wheel: blackbirds are lured with piping, and husbands with spinning."

Jillette put out the light and sat down at her spinning-wheel. As she spun, she sang:

"Run, little spindle, bring him back!
Find the Prince of the Low Countries!"

What a marvel! The spindle suddenly jumped out of the spinner's hands and flung itself out-of-doors. Astonished, Jillette watched it go. It went capering over the fields and left behind it a long thread of gold.

When it was out of sight, the girl took her loom and shuttle and began to weave, singing,

"Shuttle, follow the spindle's track!
Wave your bright weaving upon the breeze!"

At once the shuttle jumped away in its turn and wove, before crossing the threshold, a beautiful, richly-colored cloth.

Jillette took her needle then, and sang:

"Stitch, little needle—find the knack!
To hang my walls with tapestries!"

The needle escaped in its turn and ran through the room, draping the chairs in dark, garnet-colored velvet, the table in bright red, and the walls in tapestries of damask.

The last stich had just been sewn, when Jillette saw through the window the white plumes of the prince's hat. He entered the room, passed through the tapestries, right to Jillette, and said: "Would you like to be my wife?"

"Gladly," said Jillette, lowering her eyes.

She made a packet of the best of her old clothes, and hid in it the Candle of the Kings, said goodbye to her uncle, climbed onto the prince's horse, and settled herself behind him. He brought her to his palace.

The king welcomed her as his daughter-in-law, and the marriage was celebrated with splendor a few days later.

When Jillette's mother saw from on high that her daughter had become a princess, a deep sadness fell over her. Here's why:

On the day she died, as she arrived in Heaven, Françoise had met the Queen of the Low Countries at the gate into Paradise. Like Françoise, the Queen was a woman after God's heart.

Saint Peter came out with his keys, and, after peering through the wicket, he opened the door, let the Queen in, and told the farmer's wife to wait a few moments.

Soon she heard a great noise of bells, then the sound of harps, and the songs of the seraphim. She looked through the wicket, still half open, and saw a superb procession coming to the Queen.

When that ceremony was over, Saint Peter opened the gate wide for Françoise. She imagined that the music would begin again, but there wasn't any.

Only two angels came forward and welcomed her cordially, without singing. Françoise was so astonished that, in spite of her modesty, she couldn't keep from saying to Saint Peter, "Saint Peter, why isn't there music for me was well as for the Queen? I'd always been told that in Paradise everyone is equal,"

"So they are," said Saint Peter, "and you'll be treated no less well than the Queen. But consider, my child, we get people like you here every day, while the great ones of the earth hardly come here once in a hundred years."

Here's why the poor mother was so sad. In her desolation she went to find God the Father, and she said to him, "God the Father, when my daughter was only a simple peasant, the unfortunate child gave way— alas!—only too easily to the temptations of the Evil One. He said one day she would be a princess—there was no way she could win the struggle. By the seven sorrows of the Virgin, the mother of your son, help me, God the Father, to go to her rescue!"

"Go, poor mother, protect your child," said God the Father. "But to keep the angel of darkness from complaining that's not fair, you will appear among the mortals in another form. Your daughter won't recognize you, and no matter what happens, you must not reveal to her that you are her mother."

Françoise, then, found herself all at once on earth, on the edge of a clear fountain, in a wild, uninhabited place. She saw herself in the water of the fountain, and didn't recognize herself.

She was admirably beautiful and seemed to have grown fifteen years younger; but this metamorphosis didn't matter to her at all. She was thinking of nothing but her daughter.

She wanted to set out right away on the road to rejoin her; unfortunately, she didn't know which way to go.

Night fell. A shining face appeared in the sky and looked at her with big, curious eyes. Françoise remembered the old song which, when she was little, she used to sing to the moon at night: Fair one, fair one, where are you going?"

And she said: "O Moon, you see everything, fields and forests, mountain-tops and valley-bottoms. Fair One, show me the road to the Low Countries."

"Gladly," said the Fair One, "but you must sing me the lullabies you sang over your daughter's cradle when she was little."

"I'll sing anything you like but don't delay me, I beg you."

"Sing!" said the Moon.

And the poor mother began to sing. After three songs, she asked: "Is that enough?"

"More," said the Moon.

And the unfortunate mother, weeping, began to sing again.

When she had sung three more songs, she asked again: "Is that enough?"

"More," said the Moon.

And the unfortunate mother, weeping, began to sing again.

When she had sun three more songs, she asked again: "Is that enough?"

"No," said the unrelenting Moon.

And the unfortunate mother began to sing again, sobbing, and wringing her hands.

Finally the Moon took pity on her and said: "Follow me; and when you can no longer see me, keep going straight ahead."

And Françoise walked night and day.

Soon she came to a harsh and dreary country where it was always winter. She crossed a gloomy forest of pines and came to a crossroads. The poor woman did not know which road to take.

"Oh! who will show me the road to the Low Countries?" she said aloud, in anguish.

"Warm me up next to your heart, and I'll show it to you," said a thorn-bush, its branches all covered with a coat of icy snow.

And the mother pressed the bush to her heart to warm it up. The thorns pierced her flesh, and her blood ran out in big drops.

Then, what a wonder! The bush grew green again, and pretty white flowers bloomed among the leaves. Such is the strength of the warmth of a mother's heart.

And for her pain, the bush showed her the road to the Low Countries.

She came to the seashore; seeing neither ships nor boats there, such as she would need to rejoin her child, she lay down on the shore, so that she might drink the sea dry.

"You'll never get to the end of that," said the Ocean; "but I adore pearls, and I don't know any more precious than a mother's tears. If you want to give me all the tears from your eyes, I'll carry you to the kingdom of the Low Countries."

The unhappy woman had only too much reason to cry, fearing that she would never get there in time.

She sat on the shore, and her tears ran silently down into the waves, where they were changed into pearls of great price.

She cried so much that her eyes dimmed, and she became blind. Then the Ocean lifted her up like a boat and carried her to the opposite shore, in the kingdom of the Low Countries.

The poor blind woman stepped forward, feeling her way, across the countryside—sad, but not despairing.

"Where are you going, alone and unable to see?" asked an old woman.

"I'm going to the home of the Princess of the Low Countries," said Françoise.

"Which princess?"

"The Princess Jillette."

"You mean the Queen. The old king died three days ago, and his son succeeded him on the throne."

"Lord! Lord! let me get there soon," murmured Françoise, "for her danger increases every hour." Then, addressing the old woman, she said: "Lead me to the Queen, I beg you."

"What will you give me for my trouble?"

"Alas! I have nothing left to give; but, if you wish, I will go on a pilgrimage on your behalf, barefoot, to Our Lady of Charity."

"No. Give me instead your long black hair. I'll give you my white hair in exchange."

"Is that all? Take it, take it!" said the mother.

She changed her beautiful hair for the old woman's, and the old woman led her to the palace door.

The two women had hardly arrived, when they heard a carriage rolling up.

"There's the Queen!" Françoise said to her companion.

"How do you know that—you can't see!"

"I feel it here," said Françoise, putting her hand to her heart. Then she murmured, "Holy Virgin, Mother of God, make me able to see her!"

And her prayer was so fervent that the light that had gone out of her eyes suddenly shone there again, with extraordinary brilliance.

She had recovered her sight.

She came close to flinging herself at the Queen and crying: "My daughter!" But she restrained herself.

Meanwhile, Jillette stepped out of the carriage, with the King. She was so much changed that her mother, seeing her so thin and pale, could not keep from weeping.

The Queen, seeing these two women, the one so old with her head crowned with magnificent black hair, and the other young and beautiful, with her hair all white, asked what they wanted.

The old woman told her how they came to be there.

As the story was told, big tears fell from Françoise's eyes.

"Since you wanted to see me so much, would you like to enter into my service, my good woman?" said Jillette.

"Oh! yes, my lady," said Françoise.

"Good! Come back tomorrow, and we'll find a position for you to take."

Françoise came back the next day; and, as her clothes were worn with travel and hardly more than rags, she was hired simply as a dishwasher.

VII

Jillette was Queen, and yet she was not at all happy. Her husband had at first showed all the signs of being very much in love, but he had married her under the influence of a spell, and through Beelzebub's influence, the spell lost some of its power every day.

And the candle was growing shorter, little by little.

Each time the Queen was in too much pain from her husband's coldness, she would call Beelzebub to her aid. He was careful now to make her wait, so that the wax would burn away the more quickly.

One day, when the candle had been burning in vain for more than a minute, the King walked in suddenly.

Jillette blew it out, but her husband, who suspected there was some mystery involved, pressed her with so many questions, that she let the fatal secret escape her.

He naturally wanted to turn it to his own profit. Ambition flamed in his heart, and he wanted to be the most powerful monarch in the universe.

He waged wars against his neighbors, and forced his wife to ask Beelzebub to give him the victory.

The accursed candle was three-fourths gone when Jillette, worn down with anxiety, fell gravely ill.

Working in the palace kitchens, Françoise knew all that was happening. The unfortunate mother was wild with grief. "Oh! if only they would let me take care of the Queen," she kept saying, over and over, "I swear I could save her!"

Meanwhile, the sick Queen came to a crisis so violent that they thought she would never recover. Everyone wept, for the Queen was much loved, and within an hour, the palace was in the greatest disorder.

Françoise took advantage of the confusion to steal into Jillette's room. She leaned over and whispered in her ear: "Oh! come back, come back, poor child!"

At these words, Jillette revived. Her cheeks grew a little less pale; she opened her eyes, and smiled at the young woman with the white hair, whose voice reminded her of her mother's.

Jillette was saved. From that time on, Françoise never left the Queen, who soon loved her so much that she got to the point of revealing to her the terrible secret of the King's candle.

"Trust it to me," she told her. "I promise you that, while I live, no one shall light it."

But the King had locked it away. However, he no longer talked about using it, and that's why Jillette was clearly getting better.

VIII

Unluckily, it happened that all the sovereigns of Europe had leagued together against him, conquered his troops in the course of several battles, and advanced by forced marches to lay siege to the kingdom's capital city,

In a peril so pressing, the King shut himself up with his wife, and, in spite of all her pleas, forced her to light the accursed candle.

Françoise was on the watch. She looked for a way to get into the room. She got an idea: she set the curtains on fire in the next room, and ran out crying, "Fire! Fire!"

The King came running. Françoise raced into their room, seized the candle, put it out and fled from the palace into the forest.

Her trick was soon detected, and the King, in a rage, sent his men at arms to scour the woods and hunt the fugitive down like a deer.

She let herself be taken without trying to fight; but, when they asked her what she had done with the Kings' candle, she refused to answer. They searched for it without success, and it was in vain that they went through the whole forest.

She was put on trial, and condemned as a sorceress to be burnt alive. Jillette tried to beg mercy for her friend. Far from heeding her prayers, her husband wanted her to attend the execution herself.

Meanwhile, the word spread that they were going to burn a sorceress. Crowds of people came flocking from the town to the place where the stake would be set up, and the unfortunate woman climbed onto it, followed by cries of rage, and curses.

The fire was lit.

Some people were sure that they saw a white figure escape from the stake and rise into the air, scattering flowers on the executioners, but the truth is that the sky, where the sun had been shining without a cloud, began to pour, as if weeping for the innocent victim.

The water put out the fire, and it was impossible to relight it.

"Stone her!" cried the people.

"Do it!" said the King. And he himself flung the first stone,

He demanded that the Queen follow his example. Jillette refused. The King, beside himself with rage, grabbed her wrist and, with an iron grip, shook her fiercely.

The presence of her daughter strengthened Françoise's soul. Standing erect at the stake, her face shining, she watched her with a tenderness too deep for words.

Suddenly she saw that someone had put a stone in the Queen's hand. The poor mother felt her heart breaking.

"Oh, no! Not that! Dear Lord!" she cried, with a gesture of supreme grief.

Jillette saw the gesture, and, even though the King gripped her hand in his gauntlet, she let the stone fall.

An hour later, Françoise's body had disappeared under an enormous heap of stones, and the crowd melted away in silence.

Back in the palace, the King called for the peasant's clothes Jillette had worn when she came to the court, and said to her: "Put on your clothes and go back to your village. I repudiate you."

Jillette left the same evening. She had suffered so much on the throne that left it with no regrets.

Before setting out on the road to Lécluse, she wanted to make a pious visit to the heap of stones. When she got there, she wanted to see her friend, and she lifted the stones off, one by one.

When the poor murdered corpse appeared, she fell on it, weeping, took it in her arms, and covered t with kisses.

Suddenly, oh joy! The body seemed to waken. The mother came back to life under the caresses of her child.

Françoise opened her eyes. She found herself healed as if by enchantment.

"Let's get out of here!" said Jillette.

"Follow me, first," said Françoise.

And she led her into the forest. She dug at the foot of a tree and unearthed the Kings' candle.

"Now that you are no longer Queen, will you keep it intact?" said Françoise.

"Yes! Yes! I swear it!"

Françoise then pressed her daughter to her heart for the last time—and disappeared.

IX

Jillette returned to the village of Lécluse. It was in vain that Beelze-bub tried again to tempt her; she was insensible to all his lures, and never again lit the Kings' candle.

She lived in this way for ten years, after which God called her to him, and she was struck down by a singular malady. She went out slow-ly, like a lamp burning down.

Her uncle called in the best physicians in the country. They were unable to understand her illness.

Meanwhile, they heard that a strange doctor had come to Lille, who could work miracles. Jillette's uncle ran to find him and brought him back the same evening.

The doctor, like his colleagues, wore a long robe and a vast periwig, but they noticed that under his gold-rimmed glasses his eyes were as black as a crow's black feathers. He drew near the sick woman. "She is very ill!" he said. "I won't know how to cure her unless I'm left alone with her."

They hurried to obey him.

He took a little key that hung around Jillette's neck, opened a cup-board, found a casket inside, drew out a box, and in the box found the stub of a candle, the Kings' candle.

Then he lit a match and put it in the sick woman's hand and ordered her to light the candle. Jillette, her eyes closed, obeyed him, without knowing what she was doing.

One final thought was wavering in her head like a feeble light: the desire to live.

By the power of the candle, this wish was fulfilled.

She opened her eyes, saw at the head of the bed the hateful figure of Beelzebub, and closed her eyes again at once. But then she opened them again and stared with terror at Beelzebub, holding the candle.

Beelzebub cackled, and the candle burnt on.

Jillette wanted to speak, but her tongue was frozen; and yet she felt her strength coming back to her. At last, a cry burst from the pit of her stomach: "Mother!"

"Be quiet, you miserable fool!" shouted the Evil Spirit.

"Help me, Mother!" cried Jillette, and this time so loud that every-one came running.

The candle, almost burnt down, threw out bright beams of light.

Suddenly three heavy blows were heard, struck on the front door below.

"Don't open it!" said the physician.

But the door swung open.

Someone came swiftly up the stairs, and then three more blows fell, on the room-door.

"On pain of death, don't open it!" cried the doctor again.

But the door swung open.

A young woman came in, pale and robed in white. She was marvelously beautiful, with silver hair.

She went straight to Jillette's bed and said, "Do you want to come to Heaven and be with your mother?"

"Oh! yes!" said Jillette.

And she died.

As the candle was still burning, and Jillette was in a state of grace, the dead woman's final vow was completed.

The pale woman leaned over her, took her in her arms, and opened the window. Beelzebub could not even try to stop her.

"Oh! that woman!" he said, wringing his hands, "that accursed woman—she's beaten me again."

Françoise replied: "No, not the woman," she said, "the mother!"

The Kings' candle went out, completely burnt up, and the mother and the daughter rose up, radiant, toward the stars.

Misery's Pear Tree

I

In olden times, in the village of Vicq, on the banks of the Escaut, there was a good woman called Misery who went begging from door to door, and who looked as old as Original Sin.

In those days, the village of Vicq was hardly more than a hamlet: it stagnated on the edge of a swamp, and there was nothing to be seen there but some barren fields covered with reeds.

Misery lived off to the side in a poor shack made of clay, where she had no one at all for company except a dog called Faro. Her only goods were a staff and a begging bag, which all too often was three-fourths empty when she brought it home.

To tell the truth, though, she still owned a little enclosure back of her hut, where she had one single tree. It was a pear tree so fine that its like had never been seen since the famous apple tree in the Earthly Paradise.

The only pleasure that Misery got to taste in this world was eating the fruits of her garden, that's to say, of her pear tree; unfortunately, the naughty boys in the village would come to raid her enclosure.

On all the days in God's calendar, Misery would go out begging with Faro; but in the fall, Faro stayed at home to guard the pears, and that was heart-breaking for both of them, because the poor woman and the dog loved each other dearly.

II

Once, there was a winter when for two months the weather was cold enough to crack a stone. Then so much snow fell that the wolves came out of the woods and tried to break into the houses. There was terrible hunger in the countryside, and Misery and Faro suffered more than the rest.

One night the snow fell and the wind howled. And this unhappy couple were huddled together, trying to keep each other warm, by the unlit hearth, when someone knocked at the door.

Whenever someone came near the hut, Faro would bark angrily, thinking it those little boys come on a raid. But this night, on the contrary, he started yapping gently and wagged his tail joyfully.

"For the love of God!" said a plaintive voice, "open your door to a poor man dying of cold and hunger.

"Lift the latch!" cried Misery. "I won't have it said that in weather like this, I would leave one of God's creatures outside."

The stranger came in: he looked even older and more miserable than Misery was. All he had to cover himself was a ragged blue smock.

"Sit down, my fine fellow," said Misery. "You're in a sad state, but I still have something to warm you."

She put the last log on the fire and gave the old man three bits of bread and one pear that she still had. Soon the fire flamed up, and the old man ate hungrily; while he was eating, Faro licked his feet.

When her guest was done, Misery wrapped him up in her old cotton blanket and made him lie down on her pallet, while she herself sat down to go to sleep with her head pillowed against a wooden stool.

In the morning, Misery was the first to wake: "I don't have anything more to give my guest," she said, "and he'll need some breakfast. Let's see if I can find a way to go begging in the village."

She stuck her nose out the door; the snow had stopped falling, and a bright spring-like sun was shining. She went back in to take her staff and found the stranger risen and ready to leave.

"What! are you leaving already?" she said.

"My mission is complete," said the stranger, "and I have to go report on it to my master. I am not what I seem to be: I am Saint Wanon, the patron saint of the parish of Condé, and I have been sent by God the Father to see how my faithful practice charity, which is the first of the Christian virtues, I knocked at the doors of the burgomaster and the Condé townsfolk. I knocked at the doors of the noble lord and the farmers of Vicq; the burgomaster and the townsfolk of Condé, and the noble lord and the farmers of Vicq left me shivering at their gates. Only you had pity on my need, and you were as needy as I was. God will repay you: make a wish, and it will be fulfilled."

Misery crossed herself and fell to her knees: "Great Saint Wanon," she said, "now I'm not surprised that Faro licked your feet, but I wasn't being charitable to get a reward. Anyway, I don't need anything."

"How can you not have anything to wish for," said Saint Wanon, "when you have so little as it is. Come, tell me, what would you like?"

159

Misery was silent.

"Would you like a nice farm with a granary full of wheat, a wood-shed full of logs, a bread-bin full of bread? Do you want treasure, do you want honors? Do you want to be a duchess, do you want to be the Queen of France?"

Misery shook her head.

"A saint who has any self-respect shouldn't have to be in debt to a beggar-woman," said Saint Wanon, sounding annoyed. "Speak, or I'll think you're turning me down out of pride."

"Since you insist, great Saint Wanon," said Misery, "I will obey. I have a pear tree in my garden that gives me the most beautiful pears; un-fortunately, the naughty boys in the school come to rob me, and I have to leave poor Faro outside the house to stand guard. Make it so that anyone who climbs up my pear tree won't be able to come down again without my permission."

"Amen!" said Saint Wanon, smiling at her naivety, and after he had given her his blessing, he went on his way.

III

Saint Wanon's blessing brought happiness to Misery, and from that time on she never came back to her house with her bag empty. Spring followed winter, summer followed spring, and autumn followed summer. The little boys, seeing Misery go out with Faro beside her, climbed up the pear tree and filled their pockets; but when they tried to go down, they were trapped.

Misery, on her return, found them perched in the tree, left them there a long time, and let Faro chase hot on their heels once she was ready to free them. They didn't dare come back, the town's-people avoided going near the enchanted tree, and Misery and Faro lived happy as could be in this world.

Towards the end of the autumn, Misery was warming herself one day in the sun, out in her garden, when she heard a voice that cried: "Misery! Misery! Misery!" The voice was so sad that the good woman started to tremble in every limb, and Faro howled as if there was a tres-passer in the house.

She turned around and saw a tall, thin, old man with parchment-yellow skin, as old as one of the Patriarchs. This man carried a scythe as long as a hop-pole. Misery knew him for Death.

"What do you want, man of God?" she said, in a changed voice, "and what have you come to do here with that scythe?"

"I've come to do my job. Let's go, my good Misery, Your hour has sounded, and you must follow me."

"Already!"

"Already? But you ought to thank me, as poor as you are, and old and decrepit."

"Not so poor and old as you think, Master. I've got bread in the bread-bin and logs in the woodshed; I'll only be ninety-five years old come Candlemass; and as for being decrepit, I'm as firm on my legs as you are, no insult intended."

"Oh, go on! You'll be better off in Paradise."

"We know what we'll lose, and we don't know what we'd gain in the move," said Misery philosophically. "Anyhow, it would be too hard on Faro,"

"Faro will follow you. Come on, now, make up your mind to it."

Misery sighed.

"Give me at least a few minutes to put on something a little nicer. I wouldn't want to feel ashamed in front of the folks over there."

Death gave his consent.

Misery put on her pretty flower-print calico gown that she'd had for more than thirty years, her white bonnet, and her old cloak, of sturdy Silesian cotton, much worn, but spotless and untorn, the one she used to wear to the festivals when the carillons were rung.

When she had put these on she cast a last glance around her cottage, and noticed the pear tree. A singular idea came into her head, and she couldn't keep from smiling.

"While I'm getting ready, would you do me a favor, man of God?" she said to Death. "Would you climb my pear tree and gather the three pears for me that are still there?"

"Very well," said Death, and he climbed into the pear tree.

He gathered the three pears and wanted to come down, but, to his great surprise, he couldn't get to the bottom.

"Hey! Misery!" he cried, "help me get down. I think this damned pear tree has a spell on it."

Misery came out on the doorstep. Death made superhuman efforts with his long arms and long legs to free himself from the tree, but no matter how he tried, the tree, as if it was a living person, held him tight and wrapped its branches around him. It was so funny to see that Misery burst out laughing.

"My faith!" she said, "I'm not in all that much of a hurry to go to Paradise. You're fine where you are, my good man. Stay there. Humankind will owe it to me to light a nice candle in my honor."

And Misery closed her door, leaving Death up the pear tree.

IV

At the end of a month, with Death no longer providing his services, everyone was astonished to see that no one had died in Vicq, Fresnes, or Condé. The astonishment was doubly great at the end of the following month, especially when they learned that it was the same at Valenciennes, Douai, Lille, and all of Flanders.

They'd never heard of such a thing, and, when the new year came, they learned from the almanacs that it was the same everywhere—as much in France, Belgium, and Holland, as among the Austrians, the Swedes, and the Russians.

The year went by, and it was established that during the past fifteen months there hadn't been a single death anywhere in the world. All the sick people got well, and the physicians didn't know how or why: not that that stopped them from giving themselves the credit for all of the cures.

That year went by like the one before it, with no one dying. When Saint Sylvester's Day came round, from one end of the earth to the other, people were hugging each other and congratulating themselves because they'd become immortal. They held public rejoicings, and in Flanders they held a festival such as had never been seen since the world began.

The good Flemish, no longer afraid of dying of indigestion, or gout, or apoplexy, ate and drank their fill. It was calculated that in those days each man had eaten a bushel of grain, not counting the beans and the meat, and each one had drunk a vat of beer, not counting the gin and brandywine.

I would add for my part that I can scarcely believe it, but in every land people had never been so happy, and no one suspected that Misery was the cause of this universal happiness. Misery didn't boast about it, being a modest woman.

All went well for ten, twenty, thirty years; but at the end of thirty years, it was not unusual to see old folks of 110 or 120 years, which is usually the age of the worst feebleness. These old folks, overwhelmed by infirmities, memory fading, blind and deaf, their senses of taste, touch, and smell gone, began to find that immortality was not such a great blessing as they'd thought at first,

People saw them dragging themselves along in the sunshine, bent over their staffs, hair all white, heads nodding with palsy, eyes dimmed, coughing, spitting, flesh withered, shrunken, shriveled, looking like enormous slugs. The women were even more horrible than the men.

The old folks who were the weakest stayed in their beds, and there was hardly a house where you couldn't find five or six beds filled with grandparents, whimpering, to the great pain of their great grandchildren and their great-great-grandchildren.

People even had to gather them together in immense hospices, where each new generation no longer took care of anything except taking care of the preceding generations, whose lives were never going to get any better.

In addition, since people had stopped making wills, there were no more inheritances, and the new generations had nothing of their own: everything belonged by right to their great-grandparents—or great-great-grandparents—who could no longer enjoy it.

Under the rule of invalid kings, governments grew weak, laws were not enforced; and soon the immortals, sure that they weren't going to hell, gave themselves up to every sort of crime: they pillaged, robbed, raped, started fires, but, alas!—they couldn't assassinate anyone.

In every realm the cry of "Long live the king!" became a treasonous cry, and it was forbidden, under pain of all the most severe punishments—all, that is, except pain of death.

And that wasn't all: as the animals weren't dying any more than the people were, soon the earth was so full to bursting with life that there wasn't enough food to feed them all; a horrible famine started, and people were left running half-naked about the countryside, without a roof to shelter their heads, and suffering cruelly from hunger, without being able to die.

If Misery had known this frightful disaster, she wouldn't have wanted to prolong it, even if ending it would be at the cost of her own life; but she had been so used to having so little over so many years, and so much sickness, that she and Faro suffered less than the others did. Then they became deaf and blind, and Misery no longer knew much about what was going on around her.

Then people feverishly started trying to find ways to die that in the old days they would have tried to avoid, instead. Some tried poisons or murderous snares; but the snares and the poisons only hurt them, without killing them.

People declared great wars. Out of a common agreement to do each other the service of mutual annihilation, nations fell upon each other; but they did each other frightful harm without killing a single person.

They held a Death Congress: physicians came from the five parts of the world; some were white, some yellow, some black, some copper-colored, and they all searched together for a remedy against life, but they couldn't find one.

A reward of ten million francs was offered to anyone who discovered it: all the doctors wrote brochures about life as they had about cholera, but they couldn't cure the one malady any more than the other.

This calamity was even more frightful than the Flood, because the epidemic raged so much longer, and no one could tell when it would come to an end.

V

Now, at that time, there was a very learned physician in Condé, who almost always spoke in Latin, and who was called the Doctor De Profundis. He was a very honest gentleman who had helped many people in the good old days, and felt desolate at not being able to help anybody anymore.

One evening he came after dinner to visit the Mayor of Vicq, but as he had drunk one cup too many, he got lost in the marsh. Chance brought him to Misery's garden, and there he heard a plaintive voice that said, "Oh! Who will free me and free the world from immortality, which is a hundred times worse than the Plague!"

The learned Doctor looked up, and his joy was equaled only by his surprise—for he recognized Death.

"Ha! Is it you, my old friend?" he said. "*Quid agis in hac piro perch?*"

"I'm not doing anything here, Doctor De Profundis, and that's what grieves me," said Death. "Give me a hand to help me down."

The good Doctor stretched out his hand, and Death tried so hard to pull loose from the tree that he lifted the Doctor off the ground. The pear

164

tree seized the newcomer and wrapped its branches around him. De Profundis could debate it all he liked, but he had to keep Death company.

People were astonished when they didn't see the Doctor on the next day or the day after. As he gave no signs of life, they put up posters and listed it in the gazette, but to no avail.

De Profundis was the first man who had disappeared from Condé in many a long year. Had he then found the secret of dying, and had he, always so generous in the old days, kept the secret for himself alone?

All the townspeople poured out of Condé in search of him; they ransacked the countryside so thoroughly in every direction that they arrived at Misery's garden. At their approach, the Doctor waved his handkerchief as a distress signal.

"Over here!" he cried, "over here, my friends—here he is, here's Death! As I put it so well in my brochure, he would be found in the Vicq marsh, the true birthplace of the cholera. I still hold that, but *non possumus descendere* from this accursed pear tree."

"Long live Death!" cried the townsfolk in chorus, and they gathered around without hesitating.

The first to get there stretched out their hands to Death and the Doctor, but, like the Doctor, they were pulled off the ground and tangled in the branches of the tree.

Soon the pear tree was covered with people. What an extraordinary thing! The more people it seized, the bigger it grew. The people who came next took hold of the first-comers' feet, and ones who followed were suspended from the rest, and together they all formed links in long chains of people, extending as far as the cross-roads. But it was in vain for the last ones, whose feet were still on the ground, to try with all their might—they couldn't pull their friends off the accursed tree.

Someone had the idea of knocking the pear tree down—they went to find axes and started chopping at it all together; but, alas! there was not even a sign of the blows to be seen.

They looked at each other very sheepishly, and they didn't know what saint to call on, when Misery heard the hubbub and came to ask what it was about. They explained to her what had been going on so long, and she understood the harm she had done without meaning to.

"I alone can free Death," she said, "and I agree to do it, but on one condition, that Death won't come looking for us, Faro and me, until after I've called for him three times."

"Agreed," said Death. "I'll ask Saint Wanon to arrange it with the good Lord."

"Come down—I give you permission!" cried Misery; and Death, the Doctor, and all the rest fell down from the pear tree like over-ripe pears.

Death set about his work without a pause, and hurried off the most urgent cases; but each one wanted to be the first to go. The good fellow saw it was too much for him to handle. So he raised an army of physicians to help him, and named Doctor De Profundis the commander-in-chief.

A few days were enough for Death and the Doctor to rid the earth of the excess of living beings, and put everything in order. All the people over a hundred years old had the right to die, and they did die, with the exception of Misery, who stayed very quiet, and has not, in the days since then, ever called on Death three times.

And that, so they say, is why Misery is always to be be found in this world.

Walnut John's Thirty-Five Encounters

I

In olden times, there was a little cow-herder in the village of Saint-Saulve, near Valenciennes. He was called Walnut John, because no one knew who his parents were, neither his father nor his mother, and he had been found, one fine morning, under a gogué, which in our parts is the same thing as a walnut tree. He was also called the Ninoche, the Simpleton, because he was as simple and innocent of spirit as a suckling calf.

Walnut John had never in his life stuffed his belly except with potatoes, and he had only one wish in the world: to eat some roast goose.

Now, four leagues from there, on the way to Condé, there was a village where they had such magnificent flocks of geese that in all the country no one made a fuss about any goslings except the goslings of Hergnies.

"When I get big," said the Ninoche, "I'll go to Hergnies and have some gosling to eat."

In fact, one evening in autumn, he left his cows behind and took off unheralded, without either a tambourine or a trumpet to announce him.

Whether he came back as he had left, and just how far a love of poultry could take a dimwit ninoche, is something we'll find out in due course.

He walked a little way, at random, asking for directions. At nightfall, he reached Escaupont, and came to Vivier's farm, which, as everyone knows, is next to the wood of Raismes.

"Could you show me the road to Hergnies?" he asked the farmwife, who was sitting down to supper.

"Of course, my lad; but you're out very late. Is your business that urgent?"

"Oh! I think so, ma'am! I've been longing to eat some roast goose for more than ten years, and so you can understand—"

The farmwife, astonished, looked him over from head to foot. "What are you called?"

"The Ninoche."

"So I can understand! Oh! yes, I understand!" she said, and burst out laughing. "Listen, child of God, you're tall and strong, and you seem to me like someone with an honest heart. Jack, our servant, has just left us to take service with the King. Would you like to take his place?"

"Can you give me some goose to eat?"

"No later than Sunday. What I need is exactly someone to go to Hergnies, to my cousin Berlutiau. You can leave tomorrow at daybreak, and you can bring me back a fat goose. We'll have a feast on your return to honor Saint Calisstus' day, when the Grise will take us to see the parade to celebrate him. Is that all right with you?"

"Yes, ma'am."

"In that case, pull up a chair to the table."

And John, who had a good appetite after his walk, hardly gave himself time to say grace before starting in at once on his duties.

II

The next day. Which was Saturday, the farmwife went to wake up the Ninoche, asleep in the stable.

"Hey! come on, now, up with you!" she said, shaking him. "Don't you hear Chantecleer cock-a-doodling? That's a sign that it'll be good weather to hang out the infant Jesus's diapers to dry, which the Holy Virgin washed last night."

She warmed his heart with a cup of chicory, and cut off an enormous piece of bread he could eat on the way, for breakfast, and then said to him: "Look, there's your road. It'll take you straight to Odomez; from there you'll go to Our-Lady-of-the-Wood, then to Bruille, where you can take the ferry across the Escaut. When you get to Hergnies, ask for Berlutiau's mill, and from there you bring me back, along with the fat goose, seven vassiaux and a pint of wheat-seed."

A vassiau around here means about twenty-five liters.

Master Chantecleer finished sounding reveille on the thatch of the roof, and Beauty—it's the Moon that I mean—was watching over him with her pale yellow eye when John left the farm.

Although he was thinking all the time about the pleasure he would have eating some roast goose, he kept in mind what the farmwife had told him. In fact, to make sure he didn't forget, he was repeating at the top of his voice: "Seven vassiaux and a pint! Seven vassiaux and a pint!"

"Seven vassiaux!" someone cried, who had been calculating in his head just how much his field ought to yield. "Seven vassiaux! Well, thank you very much! But I wish you'd say, child of God, that I ought to get a hundred!"

These words rolled around in the Ninoche's brain, and, as he had never in his life been able to keep track of more than one idea at a time, instead of saying "Seven vassiaux and a pint!" he continued on his way, repeating: "I ought to get a hundred! I ought to get a hundred!"

In crossing Our Lady's wood, he passed by Fat Thomas, the shepherd at Fresnes. Fat Thomas was even more crimson in the face than usual, and he seemed to be as proud as a cock that's been treading a hen, or, rather, a pullet. A wolf had come prowling around his flock, and his dog had throttled it.

"I ought to get a hundred! I ought to get a hundred!" said Walnut John.

"What! You fool! Are there a hundred coming!" cried Thomas, thinking he was talking about wolves. "You should say: I'll trap the next one!"

"Trap the next one! Trap the next one!" said the Ninoche, like an echo, in his confusion. All the while talking in this way, he noticed a bell-tower that he thought was the one at Bruille.

III

He heard from a distance the notes of joyous music, and he turned toward it. Soon he saw a crowd of people gathered.

It was a wedding party, in front of an inn behind a green hedge. The fiddlers were playng "Mathurin's Ronde," and everyone was dancing.

Walnut John passed through the dancers, still repeating "Trap the next one! Trap the next one!"

"Who's trapped?—me?" cried the young husband, and he started to throw himself at Ninoche. He was rolling up his sleeves to give him a black eye, when the maid of honor, who approved of marriage, stopped him and pushed the intruder away, hissing at him:

"You imbecile! What you ought to say is—everyone should go out and do the same."

"Everyone should go out and do the same! Everyone should go out and do the same!" Walnut John repeated, getting more and more confused.

He left the village, and came to a haystack that was on fire.

The fire brigade was working valiantly as directed by their captain, who had run out of water. He had collared a poor devil who was accused of having started the fire.

"Everyone should go out and do the same! Everyone should go out and do the same!" said the Ninoche, still thinking about his goose.

"What are you saying? Are you trying to get more people starting fires! I ought to arrest you, you scoundrel!" exclaimed the captain, who did not approve of barefoot beggars, and knew how to talk sense to them.

John trembled like an aspen leaf.

"You should say instead: May the good Lord put it out," the corporal whispered to him.

"May the good Lord put it out! May the good Lord put it out!" the Ninoche repeated, and ran off as if his pants were on fire. He didn't so much as breathe again until he got to a village that he thought was Hergnies.

He passed in front of the marissau's forge, or, if you prefer, the blacksmith's forge. The marissau was in a terrible temper. He had been blowing on the embers for three hours without getting the fire to start!

Just when he had managed to get a little blue flame going, as thin as a cat's tongue, he heard these words just outside his door: "May the good Lord put it out! May the good Lord put it out!"

Furious, he grabbed his hammer, flung it at the mocker he thought was making fun of him, and stretched him full length on the pavement.

IV

John was not dead. The good Lord had other plans for him. The marissau's neighbor, who was threshing in his barn, came running with his servants to the rescue. They carried John into the farmhouse, where he soon recovered his senses.

Such a hammer-blow could have split open a head ten times as thick as John's. But the Ninoche only had a lump on his forehead, and it was this very lump that later on made people think there was genius in him.

The farmer asked where he'd come from and where he was going.

"I've come to Hergnies to get some goose to eat."

"You think you're at Hergnies! No, I'm sorry to say, you're more than three leagues off!" cried the farmer, who knew the countryside, having more than once served Saint Calistus by taking part in the Procession of the Rejoicers.

To console him, he made him a present of some wheat-grain. Then he set him off on the right road, but it didn't take John long to get himself lost again.

On the stroke of noon, he stopped alongside an enclosure. He sat down on the ground, his back against the hedgerow, set his packet of seed at his feet, pulled out his piece of bread, and cut off a hunk.

After he had eaten it, as he was all tired out, he fell asleep. A cock happened to come by who, for his part, dined, along with his hens, on the grains of wheat.

The Ninoche, when he woke up, found that he had nothing but the straw left, and started to cry. The owner of the field was a good-hearted fellow, and, taking pity on him, gave him the cock to make up for his loss.

It was only half-grown, but when you get a gift-horse, you're not supposed to look in its mouth.

"Thanks very much," said John. He took the cock, tied its feet together, and carried it off.

At four o'clock, his stomach advised him that it was teatime, and he ought to have a bite to eat. He set his cock on the ground inside the fence around a pasture, and set himself down on the fence, one leg on this side and one on the other. Alas!—while he was having his snack, an unwelcome cow wandered by that stepped on the cock and crushed it.

John began complaining bitterly. "I always have to have bad luck!" he sighed. "If I'm given some grain, a cock eats it. If I'm given the cock, here comes a cow to trample it!"

"Bah! Don't cry over it. I'll give you the cow," said the lord of the village, who was going by, his rifle under one arm and his gamebag on his back.

"Thank you, my lord," said the Ninoche joyously, and he walked on with his cow until it was getting dark.

He asked at a farm if they could put him up overnight, and they sent both him and the cow to sleep in the stable.

The farmer had a méquenne, that's to say, a servant-girl, a tall, handsome girl, as strong as the ropes on a mill.

"A cow that's been walking all day," he said, "must have a full udder." And he ordered the méquenne to go milk Walnut John's cow.

The cow's udder was so full that she was in pain. She lashed her tail against the méquenne's face so hard that she saw stars.

She was a girl with a quick temper, and, in a fit of rage, she seized a pitchfork and slashed open the cow's belly, and the cow fell dead.

And with that, John started unreeling his pitiful litany again: "I always have to have bad luck!" he repeated, sobbing. "If I'm given some grain, a cock eats it. If I'm given the cock, here comes a cow to trample it. If I'm given the cow, here comes a méquenne to rip open her belly."

"Oh, well! Take the méquenne, and stop squawling," said the farmer, who'd had enough of a servant-girl like that.

Walnut John didn't need to be told twice. With the farmer's help, he grabbed the méquenne, who didn't dare to kick up too much of a fuss, for fear that she'd be beaten. John tied her arms and legs, put her in a sack, and carried her off on his back.

"When I get to Hergnies," he thought, "I'll marry the méquenne, and we'll have goose to eat."

The result of getting lost was that he finished now by getting on the right road, and he followed it to the Bruille road. The méquenne was heavier than the Moon, which weighs only a pound, if we can believe the incomparable Guerliche. So, when he got to the village, the sack seemed to him, speaking with all due respect, like a load of dust and ashes in his belly.

He went into the *Esclipette* inn to lay the dust with a pint of new beer, and he left his sack beside the door.

V

As it happened, there were four Condéens from Capelette Square, a neighborhood known to have the biggest practical jokers in the country, gathered together inside, sitting around a table: Tuné, Nanasse, Polydore, and his dog Rombault.

Polydore, a tailor by trade, had come to Bruille to deliver a jacket to one of his customers. Nanasse and Tuné, who had just finished a week's work, had come with him, along with Rombault.

It was a matter of needing to stop and relax a bit, play a game of cards at the *Esclipette*, and drink some of Our Lady's beer, as the little birds in Valenciennes would say.

Tuné left the inn—I don't know just why. He noticed the sack, and, seeing that something was moving about inside it, he felt curious enough to open it. He was more surprised than a bell-maker at finding a pretty girl inside, tied up like a sausage.

He freed the méquenne, and she explained to him in a few words how it had happened. Then, having no wish to marry the Ninoche, she headed right back to her own village.

"Now, what shall I put in her place!" Tuné said. "By God!—I'll stuff our friend Rombault into it. He'll be trapped for sure!"

Rombault was a handsome yellow mastiff, very gentle and intelligent. He'd been given his name by the Capelette Square jokers to annoy the Rombault Square folks.

Tuné called him over, then popped him in the sack.

The Ninoche, having finished his drink, picked up the sack again, not suspecting anything, and set out on his way. Tuné walked with him for some distance. That made Rombault stay quiet, feeling that he had a friend there protecting him.

Walnut John came at last to Hergnies, by way of the plain that's called the Priest's Marsh, which is not to be confused with the Germans' Marsh.

John's idea was to go straight to the parish priest, but it occurred to him that he'd forgotten to ask for the girl's consent. He put down the sack, and just as he opened it up a whistle blew, echoing loudly.

"Well, now, Méquenne," said the Ninoche, "Would you like to have the two of us get married?"

A heavy growl was the answer. Frightened, John dropped the cord, and the sack fell all the way open. Rombault jumped out, fuming with rage, and looked as if he was going to go for John's throat.

The Ninoche had just time to climb into a willow, which happened to be there, luckily enough. But the willow was hollow and rotting away inside, and it cracked under his weight and broke in two with a frightful crash!

The tree and the man fell on top of the dog, who was waiting for John, and they were almost scrambled together. That was enough for Mynheer Rombault, who saw how things were going, and ran off.

Was he obeying that blast of the whistle, or was it that, having been trained in Condé, he remembered that the town gates would be closed at ten o'clock, and if he was late, he might have to spend the night with the beautiful stars?

VI

With Rombault gone, John got himself untangled from his tree. He checked on his limbs and was relieved to see that they were all there.

All at once, he spotted something in the hollow center of the tree that gleamed in the starlight like a lumerote, that's to say, a will o' the wisp. He reached his hand in and drew out a goose with feathers of pure gold.

He had lost a woman and found a goose. I know some ill-wishing people who would say that he hadn't lost anything by the exchange.

John wasn't that cynical, but all the same, he was delighted by what he'd found.

"Here's the goose I wanted!" he cried. "The good Lord has sent it to me! I'll have it cooked right away." He meant to have it done at the Paradise tavern, the best in the village.

He had completely forgotten the farmwife at Vivier, who, late as it was, was still waiting for her seven vassaux and a pint of wheat-grain.

The Paradise was full of pilgrims who were there to take part in the procession of the Rejoicers on the following day.

The innkeeper hardly knew which way to turn first, and, when the Ninoche showed him the goose, he hardly paid attention. He sent him away, saying that, since it was made of gold, they couldn't put it on the spit.

"Since they can't help me out here," said Walnut John, "I'll present it to Saint Callistus. The devil's in it if he won't give me one in return that can be put on the spit!"

And, after having some supper, he took his goose and went to sleep in the stable.

VII

The Paradise innkeeper had three daughters who were as curious as Eve, their grandmother. All night long they tossed and turned in their bed, thinking about the golden goose and tormented with the desire to examine it to their satisfaction.

At the first cockcrow, the oldest girl got up and said: "It's very hot. I can't sleep," and she went down to the stable, stealthy as a wolf, so as not to wake the Ninoche.

In the light of the beautiful Moon, the marvelous bird shone like a star. When she had looked her fill, the girl wanted to pull out one of its feathers.

She reached out a hand to touch it, but to her great surprise, she couldn't let go of it again.

At the second cockcrow, the younger girl got up and said, "There's a flea biting me. I can't sleep anymore." And she ran to join her sister, but as soon as she touched her, she found it impossible to budge from the spot.

At the third cockcrow, the innkeeper's youngest girl said, "There's Chantecleer wishing Good day to Saint Callistus—it's time to get up." And, like her sisters, she went to the stable.

"Look out! look out!" her sisters cried, but she didn't understand why, and thought, "Nonsense! If they're there, I can be there, too!"

She had barely touched her sisters when she found that she had joined the goose's train of followers.

A quarter of an hour later, the Ninoche woke up, rubbed his eyes, stretched, shook the straw out of his hair, and, taking his goose under one arm, he set out, without taking any notice of the three girls who were pulled along behind him.

They tried to stop, but John thought they were trying to take his goose away from him, and began to run. So the girls ran, too, forced to follow as fast as their legs could go.

When they had left the village, as they were out of breath, they begged him to slow down, which he said he'd gladly do, on condition that they showed him which way to go.

The sun was well up when the company came to the hamlet of Queue-de-l'Agache.

VIII

Just then the Condé priest came by with his two curates, his choristers, his jackass—oops! I meant to say his sacristan, Bourla. And there was old grandfather Jacob, the bell-ringer; Vilain, their fatso of an organist; Trogniez, who played the serpent-trumpet, or cornet-horn; and the children who sang in the choir, too, in their red surplices.

These fine folks were on their way to sing the High Mass for Saint Callistus.

In those days, the Condé priest was as round as a barrel, and he stuttered almost as badly as our friend Jocko, the Devil's bailiff, the one Cambrinus, the King of Beer, played such a good trick on.

But that didn't make him any the less a holy man, and very strict in matters of morality.

At sight of the three girls marching at the Ninoche's heels, he cried: "Aren't you ashamed, you g-girls with no sh-shame, to run like that over the f-fields with a b-boy?"

He grabbed the youngest by the skirt, to get her away from there; but he had hardly touched the skirt when he was stuck there, and had to join in the goose parade.

"Reverend father! reverend father! Where are you going like that!" cried Bourla the sacristan, who was as tall and skinny as a heron. He ran to catch hold of him by the cassock, and found himself attached to it.

The priest ordered the others to come and free them. The next moment, the curates, the choristers, the bell-ringer, the organist, the cornettist, and the little red-surplices, all hand in hand, were being dragged by John, who kept going on his way, and they found themselves, willy-nilly, following after the goose.

IX

Saint Callistus was at the time as greatly venerated in the Flemish country as Our Lady of Mercy is nowadays. His chapel had been raised near Bernissart, on the spot where a farm of the same name can still be found today.

The pilgrims would go there in crowds from Lille, Douai, Valenciennes, Cambrai, Mons, and Tournai. And, as Saint Callistus was famous for healing the sick, they would form the oddest procession that ever was.

All you'd see there were hunchbacks, one-eyed people, cross-eyed or squinting people, the blind, the one-armed, the lame, the halt, the limping, the bent, the knock-kneed, and the legless, and the spectacle was so funny that, inside the chapel, they had to arrange the saints who kept the blessed Saint Callistus company so they were back to back. If they'd been left face to face, and seeing such a collection of bizarre and misshapen creatures, it would have been impossible for them to look each other in the face without laughing.

What made the whole thing so very amusing was that none these good people were cripples at all. Quite the contrary, they were former sufferers who had been miraculously healed by the saint, and who in gratitude came to serve him this way every year. They delighted in imitating their former ills, to recall the image of what they had been to all the on-lookers there, the better to rejoice in their present good health.

When the Mass was done, they took off their bandages and wrappings, cast away their canes and crutches, and went off on a binge, even if the Devil should rise up in arms against it. And that's why the pilgrimage of Saint Callistus was always called the Procession of Rejoicing.

X

As you know, at this time the King of the Low Countries had a daughter who was as beautiful as the day, but who had never laughed once in her life. She was as sad as the bell that's rung for the dead, the mourning bell, as we call it, and that's why people called her the Fair Mourner.

As she was the King's only daughter, she had been stuffed with sweets, and toys, and all sorts of ornaments, even when she was still in her cradle. It's no doubt because she was cloyed with all that while she was so young that the poor thing was so sad that nothing could cheer her anymore.

It was in vain that they sent to the four corners of the earth for the most famous acrobats, tumblers, clowns, punsters, jokers, grimacers, grotesques, and comedians.

No one could put a smile on the pale lips of the Fair Mourner—not Punch, not Pierrot, not Harlequin, not Scaramouche, not Bobeche, not Guignol. Not the Soupy John clown, not even the scamp who was called the Guerliche, the incomparable Guerliche himself, no act whatever, no matter how amusing it might be.

The courtiers' funniest displays had no effect. The Fair Mourner had watched them throw their long arms around each other, gnaw themselves with their white teeth, bow right down to the ground, jump high up, walk on all fours, crawl along flat on their bellies, in short, cut all the most astonishing capers, the most extraordinary pirouettes, and turn all the most surprising somersaults, but even the most marvelous buffooneries could not so much as lighten her lovely features.

She would not laugh for an empire, and even if someone put his head on the executioner's block, that wouldn't have raised any more of a laugh from her.

The King, in despair over her incurable sadness, sent out an edict to declare that anyone who succeeded in making his daughter laugh, would make her his wife.

As the funniest fellows in the world had passed in front of her, and she had watched them with indifference, no one now came forward to try. So her father, with no idea which saint he should make an offering to, thought of taking her to Saint Callistus.

XI

All the court, since early morning, had been watching the Rejoicers march past—the lame stragglers, hobbling along, the hunchbacks, the one-eyed people, the squinters, the blind, the one-armed, the lame, the halt, the limping, the bent, the knock-kneed, the legless. There were some twisted into the shape of an X or a Y or a Z, with still others like S's, or even K's. The whole alphabet was passing by there—all but the letter I. The funniest were the ones marked by nature as B's.

The courtiers laughed fit to split their sides, and the King even louder than the rest. The Princess gaped like a nice little carp caught in the sunlight.

Perhaps it was just as well that at that moment she had better things to do. The poor little thing, after all, was risking nothing less than having to marry a former hunchback or an ex-legless man, and you have to admit that it was no time for laughing.

The court was getting ready to go home, and the King, judging it was enough of a test, had already given the signal to leave, when all at once Walnut John, who had been urged to hurry it up, appeared with his goose and his following.

When the Princess saw the Ninoche, the three girls, the fat priest, the sacristan as skinny as a heron, the two curates, the choristers, the bell-ringer, the organist, the cornettist, and the little red surplices all attached one to another, running close on one another's heels, she was seized with such a wild fit of laughter that she collapsed in the arms of the Queen.

The King, enchanted, threw his arms around the Ninoche's neck and cried: "You shall marry her! You shall marry her!" And all the courtiers threw themselves into each other's arms, crying, "Noel! Noel! He'll marry her!"

John went with his following, which included the monarch now, to put his goose at the feet of Saint Callistus. At once, the King, the three girls, the priest, and his acolytes were able to unhook themselves. The spell was broken.

The marriage was held a week later, at the castle of Bernissart. The guests were served a whole troop of geese from Hergnies, they drank two vats of beer from Fresnes, and they laughed fit to split their sides.

During the dessert, the Condé priest started stammering out a long discourse that almost put everyone there to sleep; in his turn, the Bernissart priest, who was a witty fellow, woke them up by singing "The Holes in the Trousers," the best song ever made in the Low Countries.

XII

After the death of the King, Ninoche succeeded him, and he really didn't govern any worse than his predecessors.

The people of Valencienne often recalled that he had been found under a walnut tree, and laid claim to the honor of giving him birth.

In all ages, the people of Valenciennes have had a weakness for putting great men on their bell-towers. They had statues carved, in walnut wood, of Master Walnut John, and put them on a tower where they rang the hours on the most magnificent clock you've ever seen.

In those days, the Valenciennois were not rich in illustrious men. Since then, they've had plenty of them, and they've demolished Master Walnut John's tower and put his statue in storage—a mistake, in my opinion.

The Ninoche was a great man like other great men. I've known more than one in the world who during his lifetime didn't know how to do anything more than repeat other people's ideas, and, like him, owed his good fortune to lucky encounters, and, also like him, reached the pinnacle—without doing it on purpose.

Notes

"Cambrinus, King of Beer" provides an origin for Cambrinus (or Gambrinus), a figure well known in pictures over northern Europe and elsewhere, but not otherwise provided with a story.

"Death's Partner" follows the first half of the Grimms' "Godfather Death," but the godson's dramatic and rebellious death is assigned instead to his father, leaving to the godson, in the sequel, "Death's Godson," a quieter, more ironic fate. The insistence on finding a just person for the godfather and the brief appearance of the Wandering Jew are Deulin's additions.

"The Inn of the Seven Deadly Sins" seems to be original with Deulin. The Seven Deadly Sins belong rather to literature than to folklore, whether presented literally, as abstract ideas, such as Dante used to organize the geography of Hell in *The Inferno*, or allegorically personified as individuals, as in Marlowe's *Doctor Faustus*. There are no examples of folktales about the Seven Deadly Sins listed in the *The Types of the Folktale* (enlarged and translated by Stith Thompson from Antti Aarne's *Verzeichnis der Märchentypen*). Along with "Misery's Pear Tree," this story was singled out for praise by critic Augustin Sainte-Beuve, and his letter, the publishers said, was what made them decide to bring out a second collection of Deulin's fairy tales.

"Green-Jeans, The Conqueror of the Lumçon" follows the plot, very loosely, of the Grimms' "The Story of the Youth who went forth to learn what Fear Was," adding to his exploits with the castle ghosts the encounter with the Lumçon, which is presented as the origin of the Belgian festival of that name, in which the parade spirals in (like a limçon, a snail-shell) on the monster.

"The Little Soldier" appeared, somewhat abridged, in Andrew Lang's *The Green Fairy Book*. Its opening resembles the Grimms' story of "The Raven," although the Grimms' princess under a spell has the shape of a raven, not a snake, and it is the hero's failure to obey directions, not her treachery, that makes him sleep through her three drive-bys. (The Grimms' story of "The King of the Golden Mountain" has a princess transformed into a snake, but is not otherwise like "The Little Soldier.")

A collection of Belgian folktales from a couple of decades later, *Contes Populaires du Pays Wallon* (1891), by Auguste Gittée and Jules Lemoine, has a story, "L'Arbre à Cornes ou le Cuisinier sans pareil" ("The Horn-Tree, or the peerless Chef"), which is clearly related to the second half of Deulin's story, but it is not so clear what the relationship is. The later published account might have been based on an earlier oral version known also to Deulin, or the later version might have been based on Deulin. The title seems to suggest that Deulin's story was the original, because there is no horn-tree in "The Horn-Tree." Instead of making horns grow on the forehead, the tree's magic plums cause the victim's nose to grow long.

"The White Sparrow" closely follows the Grimms' story "The Dog and the Sparrow," but with many added details.

The first half of "Manekin-Pis" follows roughly the first half of the Grimms' "The Griffin," omitting the visit to the Griffin that makes up the second half, and adding the thief-catching incident, modeled on the Grimms' story of "Doctor Knowall," instead. The story is set up to "explain" the origin of the famous fountain-and-statue. The saying "put some hay in their sabots" is an idiom meaning to "have money with them."

"The Guerliche's Nutmeg-Ball" is a tale of a trickster whose tricks end by getting him into Heaven. Examples (although not otherwise close to the Guerliche's story) in the Grimms' stories include "The Tailor in Heaven," "Brother Lustig," and "Gambling Hansel." There are many analogues to the Guerliche's answers to the king's riddles (Thompson and Aarne's *The Types of the Folktale*, under the heading of #922, "The Shepherd Substituting for the Priest Answers the King's Questions" lists many of them; Paul Delarue and Marie-Louise Tenèze, in *Le Conte Populaire Français*, comment that versions where one of the riddes is "How much does the moon weigh" are late, first becoming known around 1850.)

"Death's Godson" follows the second half of the Grimms' "Godfather Death." The Godson's attempt to deceive Death and save the princess is successful in the Grimms' story, although the Godson himself meets with a dramatic death, as punishment (assigned instead to his father, in Deulin's Part I). In Deulin's ironic interpretation, Death is not so easily fooled, and Macaber meets with an unromantic, quieter fate. Deulin's assertion that Macaber's macabre name comes from the Arabic word for graveyard is an accurate etymology, but dictionaries nowadays mostly prefer to explain the origin of "macabre" as a distortion of "Maccabees," growing out of the descriptions in Second Maccabees of the tortures inflicted on Eleazar and the Seven Brothers.

"Martin and Martine" is set up to "explain" the origin of the Cambrai bell-ringing figures. The theme of the flight of the young lovers, and the girl's use of magic, leaving enchanted objects to answer for her, and transforming herself and her sweetheart into unrecognizable shapes, is found in the Grimms' "Sweetheart Roland" (among many others). Deulin added from his own mythology the figures of the benevolent Cambrinus (in "Cambrinus, King of Beer") and the Hop Fairy. Ogres, with their latinate name, do not show up among the Grimms' stories (in "Sweetheart Roland" the adversary is a witch; giants generally fill the role of cannibalistic adversary). Ogres were popular among French fairy tales, as in Charles Perrault's "Puss in Boots" and "Hop o' My Thumb," or Mme. d'Aulnoye's "The Orange Tree and the Bee." Hop o' My Thumb's ogre, like Deulin's, owns seven-league boots (the witch in "Sweetheart Roland" has "many-league boots" instead). Deulin's ogre, with his mixture of fearsomeness and sociability, is a more complex character than the traditional French ogres. The Grimms' stories also omit the fairies (another word derived from Latin) so popular among the French fairy tales.

"The Candle of the Kings"—stories of deals with the devil were common in folklore (Deulin had already presented a more comic one in "Cambrinus, King of Beer.") The incident of Jillette's using her spindle, shuttle, and needle magically to bring the Prince to woo her follows the plot of the Grimms' "The Spindle, the Shuttle, and the Needle," and the incident of the difference between the receptions in Heaven of Jillette's mother and of the Queen follows the plot of the Grimms' "The Peasant in Heaven."

"Misery's Pear Tree" has passed into folklore, having been recorded as an oral folktale by twentieth-century collectors, in Greece and Puerto Rico, but it seems to be largely original with Deulin. (If it had existed as a folktale earlier, it would probably have been reported by some of the many nineteenth-century folktale-collectors). It is significantly different from such folktales as the Grimms' "Gambling Hans," in which the gambler Hans gets Death up an enchanted tree for only a short time, or "The Master Smith," from *Norwegian Folk Tales*, by Peter Christen Asbjørnsen and Jørgen Moe, in which it is not Death, but the Devil who is trapped in the enchanted tree. As Hans' Death is trapped only briefly, and the Devil is after the Smith only, their entrapment has none of the wider consequences and the Gulliver's-Travels-like horrors, of long-term deathlessness. Another version, "Le Bonhomme Misère et son Poirier," recorded in an undated pamphlet (published sometime late in the nineteenth century) may be later than Deulin and influenced by him. Like "Gambling Hans," it has a male protagonist and a Death who is trapped in the tree for only a short time, but the Goodman's feminine noun of a name, "Misère," sounds like Deulin.

"Walnut John's Thirty-Five Encounters," starts out with a simpleton on a journey of stepwise mishaps, like the one in the Grimms' "Going a Traveling," but instead of stopping with the simpleton's discouragement, he is sent dauntlessly on to his encounter with the practical jokers in the tavern, which leads him in turn into the same events as in the Dummling's journey in the Grimms' "The Golden Goose" and to a happy ending.

TALES OF KING CAMBRINUS

Preface

In olden days, in Condé-sur-l'Escaut, in the moonlight, these stories were told on street-corners and down in the cellars.

They were told by old women, or, rather, by story-tellers from the Marquette Estate, the home of Alexander Favier's grandmother.

This gentle friend refreshed my memory, one night in September, when we emptied a jug of dark beer, in his garden, among the ruins of the old Gayant castle.

And that's why these *Tales of King Cambrinus*, given that name because they were born under the inspiration of that heady monarch, are dedicated to Alexander Favier by his countryman and friend,

C. D.
Paris, 15 May 1873

The following letter, addressed to the author of the *Contes d'un Buveur de Bière*, made the publisher decide to publish this second series of Tales.

31 March 1868

I ought to have thanked you earlier, dear sir, for the interesting volume of Flemish Stories—interesting in fact for the material and the phrasing, and the lively good sense and drama of everyday life at play on every page. You have perfectly made these legends and popular tales your own: people might not expect to gather pure learning or the history of a culture from these simple roots, but it is the right way to go about it, through these stories which have gone from hand to hand to be written down and read at last. These primitive sketches can only gain from getting a skillful finishing polish done by a friend and by a region.

"The Hotel of the Seven Deadly Sins" is excellent. "Misery's Pear Tree" is admirable. I wonder if there has ever been in the field of the popular tale a sentence so lovely and yet simple: "Each new generation no longer took care of anything except taking care of the preceding generations, whose lives were never going to get any better." That's one example of what I call the finishing touches of the artist who know his craft and makes it look easy.

Please accept, dear sir, the assurance of my devoted sentiments,

Sainte-Beuve[1]

---

[1] Charles-Augustin Sainte-Beuve was a French literary critic and writer born in Boulogne-sur-Mer on December 23, 1804, and died in Paris on October 13, 1869. A representative of Romanticism, he is renowned for his literary criticism and the method of writing he employed.

Gayant the Bold

I

In olden days, it happened that a woodcutter from Cantin, near Douai, going to the woods to cut green branches, found in the forest five bearcubs rolling around in the mouth of a cavern.

At sight of him, the animals fled, except for one, who came up to him making little whining noises that resembled human cries.

Although the little creature walked on all fours and certainly looked like a bear, the woodcutter recognized with surprise that it was not a bearcub, but a human, like you and me.

He picked him up, and, afraid he might run into the mother bear, he hurried to get back to the village. He went right to the Mayor's house, where the neighbors came running, too, drawn by so odd a sight.

They had never heard tell of a child being brought up by a she-bear. Anyway, they baptized the little boy, dressed him from head to foot, and put him in the care of the woodcutter, who sent him off to school.

II

He was a little too big to be made to take the cross in God's name, and in fact his beard was beginning to grow out. Because of that the students made fun of him as if he were a big horsey.

He'd been named John Gelon, which was his foster-father's name. But even though they soon got him out of the habit of walking on all fours, his little friends thought he was so ugly that they always called him John Bearcub.

He was a calm boy, reflective, not saying much, and so gentle that he wouldn't hurt a fly. The naughty scamps put his good will to rough tests.

"Dance, John Bearcub," they'd say, "dance!" And they'd hit him with sticks pretending they were playing on flutes or tambourines.

John let them do what they liked. But he was as strong as a grown man, and they noticed that even though he didn't get any better looking, at least it was plain to see he was growing.

The little boys got to such a point of naughtiness that one day, while they were playing cafoums—that's to say, blind man's buff—they blindfolded his eyes and then threw stones at him, until his face was all bruised.

John Gelon finally lost patience. He tore off the blindfold, seized a stone as big as hazel-nut, and threw it so hard at the wildest of the group that the stone streaked through his head like a bolt of lightning.

The rascals screamed, and their fathers and mothers came running. They took hold of the murderer and tied him up to lead him to prison, He shook himself hard and broke the ropes. Someone ran to fetch some chains, and they handcuffed him, but—Crack! He broke that, too.

III

The villagers were talking it over, unable to decide what to do, when a herald, all dressed in velvet and riding a horse richly decked out, came galloping at triple speed into the village square. He sounded his trumpet three times, then made this announcement to them:

"Good people: His Majesty the King of the Low Countries makes it known that his two daughters, the Princesses Golden-Ball and Silver-Ball, have been stolen away by an infamous kidnapper, and he will give one of them in marriage to anyone who can rescue them—the victor can take his choice."

When he heard these words, John Gelon had an idea. "Go make me a good iron staff," he said to those who were keeping a close watch on him, "a staff as big as my arm. I'll try to rescue the princesses, and if I succeed, I'm inviting you all to the wedding."

The people of Condé could see that this was a way to get out of the fix they were in, and they approved of his speech, the longest that John Bearcub had ever spoken. They gathered together all the iron they could find in the village, and carried it to the marshal.

Once the staff was forged, John Gelon threw it into the air and caught it as skillfully as a drum-major. The mayor was so impressed that he cried out in a fit of enthusiasm: "You can't be called John Gelon anymore, my lad—you must be called Gayant. And I even believe that you're going to atone for your crime by marrying a princess and bringing honor to your village!"

"I'll try to, with the help of God and Mary Saguenon," the future hero said modestly.

I must tell you that around here "gayant" means "giant," but no one knows just why the boy gave his staff the name of Mary Saguenon.

Without losing so much as a minute, he took his bag, fastened his spats, lit his pipe—he smoked like a grown man already—and, with his staff in his hand, he set off into the forest.

IV

He had not walked for more than a quarter of an hour when he saw coming towards him a she-bear followed by four cubs. He recognized his foster-mother and threw himself into her paws' embrace.

The bear drew herself upright the better to welcome him. He hugged each of his foster brothers. Then the bear said to him, in her own language, "Where are you going with that staff?"

"To rescue the Princesses Golden-Ball and Silver-Ball."

"Do you know where they are, my dear?"

"Not so far."

"Well, follow me. I'll take you there."

And they started walking, putting one foot before the other, like weasels in the snow. The bear went first, with her four cubs, and Gayant followed, with his good staff.

After they'd gone a hundred paces, they heard a horrible crunching sound, and they saw in a clearing a big, cheerful youth, who was amusing himself by wringing an oak tree, like a washerwoman wringing out the linen after she's rinsed it in the stream.

"Good-day to all of you!" cried the wringer. "Would you like to give me a hand?"

"We're in too much of a hurry, my lad."

"Where are going?"

"To rescue the Princesses Golden-Ball and Silver-Ball."

"I'll come with you. My arm will rescue the princesses, and I'll marry Silver-Ball, or I'm not called Oak-Wringer!" And with that, the wringer was one of their company. Although there was a wide enough field for both of them to go harvesting, Gayant thought Oak-Wringer was taking his welcome too much for granted. Nevertheless, he accepted this new companion, without calling attention to his sin of pride.

Soon the forest became too thick for the travelers to go any farther. The trees were brushing against each other like ears of wheat.

"We're getting close," said Gayant's foster-mother.

With the help of Oak-Wringer and his staff Mary Saguenon, Gayant cleared a trail, and at last they came to a splendid castle.

"That's where the princesses are," sad the bear to the adventurer, and, after wishing him "Good luck!" she kissed him and left at a gentle trot, with her four cubs.

V

The two companions rang the doorbell, ting-a-ling, ting-a-ling, but no one came to answer, so they decided to force it open and search the castle from top to bottom. But they didn't find a living soul.

In the kitchen they saw a magnificent cauderlat—that's to say, a handsome row of cauldrons and saucepans—gleaming all along the wall like so many full moons. There was also an enormous spit, but unfortunately they didn't find anything to put on it.

Looking about for food, they found a box of salt and a butter-dish with some butter in the pantry, and a batch of loaves of dark bread in the kneading-trough. Gayant went down into the cellar and brought up a pitcher of old beer.

"Let's drink a cup, he said. "That will clear our heads. Now here's what I propose. As there isn't anything else in the pantry, one of us is going to have go out hunting, while the other stays indoors to get some soup started."

"That's me—I'll stay here!" cried Oak-Wringer. "And if the thief dares to show so much as the end of his nose, I won't need either a staff or a club—I'll just hit him with my fist and knock him out!"

"All right," said Gayant. He had often heard tell that the worst wheel of a carriage is the one that squeaks the loudest. "Just be careful to ring the bell when the cuckoo says it's noon."

Left alone, Oak-Wringer lit the fire, went to gather some herbs to put in the soup, and set the soup on to cook, after which he put some tobacco in his pipe. The pot began to bubble, when all at once the cook heard a sound in the chimney—tick! tick! tick!

Then he saw a little old grandfather come down past the hook. He was dressed all in yellow, wore a little three-cornered hat, a little robe cut in the French style, a little pair of knee-breeches, and little shoes. This little old grandfather was carrying a little bowl in one hand, and, in the other, in spite of the fact that it was still broad day, he held a little lamp that was lit up. There was nothing big about him, except his nose and his chin, which were so long that they met at the tips, like a nutcracker.

"Who are you, fellow, and what do you want?" cried Oak-Wringer.

"I'm Little Father Bidoux, my dear sir, and I've come to ask you to give me a little soup, for the love of God!"

"You earthworm—scram!"

Oak-Wringer had not even finished these words when Little Father Bidoux set down his bowl and his lamp and jumped forward, like a rubber-band being stretched, caught him around the knees with an irresistible force, bashed his head against the wall, and dragged him out of the kitchen over to an enormous heap of firewood and pulled it down on top of him. Then he picked up his bowl and lamp and ran away, shouting, "The little gentleman still lives!"

It was in vain that the hunter pricked up his ears around noon—the bell didn't ring. Tired of waiting, he returned to the castle. He found the stew-pan upside-down on the ground and the fire almost out, but nothing else.

He ran from room to room, calling, "Hey, Oak-Wringer, hey!"

Oak-Wringer didn't appear. His companion decided to go and get dinner by himself.

He went to look for a log to get the fire going again. As he drew near the log-pile, he heard Oak-Wringer's voice, crying: "Help me, my friend!"

Seeing his friend lying under the pile of logs, he set to work right away to free him.

When that was done, seeing that no one was asking him for an explanation, Oak-Wringer said, sounding a little confused: "I was tugging at the wood when the whole heap collapsed on me."

Gayant did not reply. They passed up the soup, and ate the two hares and the pheasant that the hunter had brought back. They stood guard all that night, turn by turn, but they didn't see so much as a cat.

VI

The next day Gayant stayed in the kitchen. He leaned his staff against the corner of the chimney and took care of the housework.

Toward noon, when the soup was ready, he got up to go ring the bell. Suddenly he heard a noise—tick! tick! tick! He turned around and saw Little Father Bidoux, with his little lamp and his little bow.

"Give me a little soup, for the love of God!" the little man said sweetly.

The cook took his Mary Saguenon in one hand, and with the other he took the lid off the pot, keeping, as the saying goes, one eye on the stove and one on the cat.

Suddenly this little-bit-of-a-man leaped at him to grab him around the knees, but one blow of Gayant's good staff stopped him cold. Gayant thought he'd crushed his head and was astonished to find that he'd only broken an arm off.

Taking advantage of his surprise, the little man quickly gathered up his arm, which he tucked under his other arm, grabbed his lamp, which hadn't gone out, and fled into the forest, shouting, "The little gentleman still lives!"

Gayant pursued him, and he was about to catch up with him, when he saw him disappear down a fussiau's hole—or you might say—a polecat's hole. He shoved his staff into it with such force that he almost lost his hold on it when it met only empty space inside.

Oak-Wringer returned to his side just then. With his help, Gayant pulled up the covering of weeds that had hid the opening to a vast, deep well.

"If we had a rope," he said, "we could go and see what's going on down there."

"Let's begin by eating the soup, and then we can get our flutes tuned up. Get something in your pants before you dance!" said Oak-Wringer, who didn't seem to be in a hurry to catch Little Father Bidoux.

VII

While his companion was eating, Gayant searched all through the castle, without finding even a bit of string. He thought about peeling the bark off the big linden-trees that grew along the entryway and trying to twist that into a rope.

When Oak-Wringer was full, he rejoined Gayant and set about with unbelievable strength and speed wringing the bark that Gayant had pulled off the great linden-tress, to twist it into a rope.

They worked for three days and three nights without stopping until they had a cable a thousand feet long.

"Who should go down first?" asked Oak-Wringer, uneasily.

Gayant was silent out of modesty. Seeing that, he companion suggested, "Let's draw straws."

"All right."

And chance, which would not choose otherwise, selected Oak-Wringer to try the adventure first.

Oak-Wringer set out with reasonably good grace. He tied the rope to his belt, hooked the dinner bell on, and carried a piece of rock to use to sound the depth of the well. When they'd unrolled six hundred feet of rope, the bell rang, and Gayant pulled his companion back up to the light.

"I dropped the stone," he said, "and I'm sure we'd need another five hundred feet."

"If we needed a thousand, I'd go, just the same," cried Gayant.

He left the bell, took his staff in one hand, and with the other grabbed hold of the rope, which took him down, down, down, until it had unrolled entirely.

At that point, our hero let go of the rope and let himself fall into the void, under God's protection. He reached the bottom broken, black and blue, and beaten up. The fall had been about fifty feet.

VIII

He stood up and dragged himself along, hobbling toward a light that was shining at the end of a long gallery. Soon he could see that it was a lamp, and two human forms were crouched next to it. He crept forward and recognized one as Little Father Bidoux.

An old, white-haired woman, who looked more than a hundred years old, was putting a bandage on his arm. She rubbed it with some ointment she was taking from a little sandstone pot. This task so absorbed the man and the woman that they didn't hear anything.

Gayant noticed how careful the little grandfather was to keep his lamp lit. Realizing that his power was in that, he put it out quickly, gathered all his strength for a supreme effort, and this time flattened Little Father Bidoux's head with a blow of his staff.

The old woman let out an exclamation that sounded more like a cry of joy than a cry of terror.

The conqueror relit the lamp. "What's in that pot?" he said.

"It's an ointment, good master, to heal wounds."

Gayant rubbed some of it all over his hurts. At once, as if none of his limbs had failed him, he felt hale and hearty. Having used up half the ointment, he shut the rest in his sack.

"Now, then! you wife of the devil!" he said, "you're going to tell me where the Princesses Golden-Ball and Silver-Ball are."

"Yes, right away. Look around you."

The adventurer looked and saw a vast system of cellar-rooms

"In these cellars," said the good woman, "are the princesses you seek. Open the first one on the right. There you will find the Princess Golden-Ball—but be sure to be on your guard!"

He pushed at the bronze door, which opened at his touch.

At once, from the back of the cave there came a frightful hissing, and a serpent longer and thicker than a poplar tree slid toward him, with gaping maw. Gayant plunged his staff all the way into the snake. Holding the creature, which was squirming horribly, out to the old woman, he said, "Now you could roast it. It's on the spit."

Putting his foot on the dying monster's head, he pulled out his Mary Saguenon. Then he went deeper into the cellar. He kissed the Princess Golden-Ball politely and offered her his hand to help her up to leave with him.

IX

The Princess Golden-Ball was as lovely as the sun, and it was only with difficulty that he could gaze steadily at her bright face. She held out her fingertips to her rescuer by way of a handshake and said haughtily, "This is all very well, young man. You're awfully ugly, but no matter. Here's my ball, Guard it as something precious, and when we're on the surface, bring me to my father the King. He'll reward this service."

"I won't fail you, fair lady."

"But how are you going to get me out of here?"

"Be patient! There's time for everything. The most urgent matter is to rescue my lady your sister."

"Do it!" said Golden-Ball.

And she sat down on a stool and straightened the folds of her dress.

X

Silver-Ball's cellar-room didn't have a door, but it was closed by an immense spider-web made of threads as solid as their master.

In a corner, behind the web, Gayant saw a frightening sentinel, a spider as big as a calf. The monster looked at him with its eight eyes, gleaming in the shadows, as bright as will o' the wisps. It rose up silently on its fore-feet, ready to leap at the reckless man who would touch its threads.

Gayant went boldly forward and broke the spider-web with his staff. The spider jumped out through the opening. Gayant wasn't afraid, but finding himself faced with eight long legs about to twine around him, he stood still for a moment, dazed.

The poor boy would have been lost, if Mary Saguenon had not come crashing down all by itself, like a thunderbolt. Four legs fell at the first blow, and the second crushed the foul creature's head.

Silver-Ball gleamed like the morning star, modest and simple. She flung her arms around her rescuer's neck, saying, "I beg you, save my sister, too."

"That's already done!" said the conqueror.

And he went with the Princesses to shout to his companion to let down the rope. Gayant, seeing that the rope was too short, stood lost in thought.

XI

"What!" said Golden-Ball, "Don't you have a ladder? Do you really expect me to go up on a wretched rope that's—"

"Alas! Yes, Princess, unless you would prefer to stay here."

While speaking, he brought out his knife, skinned the snake as he would an eel, cut the skin into strips, and fastened them together, end to end. He picked up from the ground the fragment of rock that Oak-Wringer had dropped, tied it to the end of this new kind of cord, and shouted to his companion, "Hey, up there! We're going to bring the Princesses up. Here's an extension for the rope,"

And he threw the enormous stone on up.

With this extra length, the rope reached all the way to the bottom. Gayant fastened it to Princess Golden-Ball's belt and called to his companion to pull her up. The precious burden was raised up without any mishap. The rope came down again and went back up, carrying Princess Silver-Ball, who had likewise given her ball to her rescuer.

XII

When he saw that Silver-Ball had reached the hands of his companion, Gayant called. "Now it's my turn. Hey, up there! Let down the rope!"

The rope descended.

An idea suddenly occurred to him, and instead of tying the rope to himself, our hero tied Mary Saguenon to it. The rope started up again.

It hadn't even reached the halfway point, when it fell back down, landing right on Gayant, who was nearly squashed.

The situation was disturbing. Gayant was looking sadly at the two balls, when the old woman said to him, waggling her head, "Will you promise to follow all the directions I give you, to the letter? I will show you a way to get back up above,"

"I promise," said the adventurer.

She called, "Come here, Hummingbird!"

And he saw a giant bird appear, three times bigger than an eagle—but it was nothing more than a crow.

The bird opened its enormous beak, and let out a formidable Caw!

"Wait a minute! my gentle Hummingbird," said the old woman. "You're going to have a beakful." She took the lid off a salting tub. Inside it was some beef.

"Take this into your care," she said, "and climb on Hummingbird's back, and each time he cries Caw, be sure you stuff a bit of the meat into his beak. That's the only way he'll be able to fly to the top without weakening. When you get there, send him back again."

XIII

The adventurer thanked the good woman warmly, then led the crow to the well and climbed on his back, taking the salting tub, too, and not forgetting Mary Saguenon. The crow spread out his enormous wings and said, "Caw!"

Gayant closed his beak with a hunk of meat.

"Caw!"

A second beakful.

"If I'd thought you were such a chatterbox," thought the rider, "I'd have brought along a whole barrel-full."

The bird was not yet halfway up, and the pieces were getting visibly fewer.

Gayant took out his knife and cut the morsels in two, but the Caws only became more insistent.

He was almost at the opening at the top, when he gave the bird the last beakful.

"Caw!" went the crow.

"It's no good yelling, my lad. I don't have any more."

"Caw!"

And the bird's flight grew slower.

"Caw! Caw!"

"Just a little more courage, my gentle Hummingbird!"

The bird made a desperate effort. He was just about to reach the very top, when he hit his wing, and could go no higher. To keep him from sinking down, the adventurer put his good staff across the width of the well.

In this extremity, Gayant remembered the story of the princess who, crossing the Red Sea on a griffin, let a gold beechnut fall into the waves, and at once an immense beech-tree sprang up out of the sea, and the tired bird-beast rested there. If only he had such a marvelous beechnut!

The rider did not know what saint to pray to. Suddenly an idea came to him, Without hesitating, he cut off a piece of his thigh. He crammed the slice into the crow's beak, and the bird started going up again.

"Caw!"

Gayant, in spite of his pain, cut off a steak from his other leg, and the bird reached the edge of the well at last.

"I look a sight, don't I!" he said to himself. "No matter! You go back to your mistress my good Hummingbird."

And the crow spiraled back down the well, turning in circles like a vulture descending on a ring-dove.

Our hero unfastened his sack to look for something to bandage his injuries. There he found the old woman's pot, which he had forgotten.

He made such good use of it that he could feel his flesh growing back together. Deciding to carry out the adventure to its end, he set out at once on the road to the capital of the Low Countries.

A pleasant reflection encouraged him—not the thought of Princess Golden-Ball, but the image of the lovable Princss Silver-Ball. He couldn't help but think that Little Father Bidoux had given a proof of his good taste in putting her under the guard of the spider, the more horrible of the two monsters.

One fine morning he reached the capital city.

As he was strolling along the streets, trying to find a way to get in to see the King, he saw a lord come out of a goldsmith's shop.

He recognized him at once as Oak-Wringer, in spite of the magnificent clothes the rascal had on

When Oak-Wringer had gone around the corner, Gayant went up to the goldsmith, who was leaning against his door.

"Isn't that the young lord," he said, "who rescued the King's daughters?"

"Yes, in fact, it is," said the goldsmith, "and he's just been to order some work from me that won't be easy at all."

"What's that, if it please you?" said Gayant.

"What's that to you?"

"Perhaps I'd be happy to help you."

"You're a goldsmith?" asked the other, smiling. "You don't have the air of a goldsmith."

"It isn't the air that makes the song," said Gayant.

"Oh, well! The Princesses had two balls, one of gold and one of silver. They lost them on the way here, and I've just been ordered to make duplicates for them. The King doesn't want his daughters to get married without them."

"Why is that hard for you to do?"

"What makes it hard, my boy, is that I've never seen the wretched things. All I know is that one is engraved—"

"With the figure of the sun, and the morning-star on the other."

"Who told you that?"

"These jewels came from the workshop of the great Saint Eligius, your patron. It was Saint Eligius, when he came to preach in this country, who made a present of them to the father of the present King. They had been made by his son Oculi, my master, and the holy goldsmith's best workman,"

Gayant had rarely made so long a speech, and, for the first time in his life, he was telling a lie, so great was his desire to see Silver-Ball again.

"And you know how to make jewelry such as that?" said the goldsmith.

"Give me the gold and silver needed, and a workroom where I can be alone."

"What salary do you want?"

"Not much. Just give me a sack of walnuts, in advance."

XV

The goldsmith accepted, laughing at the bizarre bargain, and installed Gayant in a room. Once he was alone, our hero set to work cracking the nuts—he had inherited from his foster-mother a great liking for them.

The goldsmith's wife, who was as curious as Eve, went several times to listen at the door of the workroom, but all she heard was the sound of Gayant cracking the nuts.

"I don't know if your new workman is getting through much of the work," she told her husband. "When you go by the door, all you hear is crick-crack, crick-crack."

Around eleven o'clock, the goldsmith went to see how the work was getting along. Going into the room, he was met by the eternal crick-crack, and he surprised our hero sitting at a table in front of a good heap of shells.

"Well, my friend!" he said, "how do you like my walnuts?"

"They're excellent, Master, and here are your balls."

"Finished already?"

"Do you see anything left to do on them?"

"On the contrary—they're superb."

"In that case, I'm going to take them to the palace right away."

XVI

Gayant presented himself as the representative of the crown goldsmith, and the sentinel let him in. Just inside the entryway he encountered the whole Court, coming in from their promenade.

Oak-Wringer had Golden-Ball on his arm, and the King had Silver-Ball, and the courtiers were following them, two by two.

Without saying a word, our hero started juggling the balls: they glittered in the sunlight so brightly that the people thought they were seeing a couple of noonday stars.

"My ball! my ball!" cried Golden-Ball and Silver-Ball, and they dropped the arms of their escorts in a rush.

"I'd be glad to give them to you, my ladies," he said, "when you've told my lord your father why you confided them to me,"

"He's lying!" said Oak-Wringer. "I don't know this fellow with a face like a bear!"

"But how does it happen?" said the King, "that he has the balls?"

"He must have stolen them!"

Our hero was going to throw them at the impostor's head. The monarch stopped him with a gesture.

"What do you have to say about it, my ladies?" he said, turning to the princesses.

The princesses were silent. Oak-Wringer had made them swear on their hope of eternal salvation never to reveal the truth.

XVII

At that moment, a frightful Caw! rang in the air. They saw a crow bigger than an ostrich appear, with a little old woman riding on its back and stuffing bits of meat into its beak.

"It's the good Maglore!" said the monarch, with surprise, and he hurried to open the window to let in these new arrivals.

"Yes, sire, the fairy Maglore, whom this young hero saved, along with your daughters, from the clutches of Little Father Bidoux."

"Come to my arms—my son-in-law!" cried the King, "and, as you can't marry both girls at once, choose one."

"I choose the lovable Silver-Ball," said Gayant, "if she's even willing to take a lumbering bear like me."

Silver-Ball blushed right up to the whites of her eyes—which is the best way to answer in such a case. Her rescuer seemed to her so good and so brave that, far from thinking him ugly as a bear, she thought him handsome as a lion.

"As for this fine lord," added the monarch, "instead of giving him the hand of our daughter, we will give him the arm of the gallows."

"No, Sire, he helped me with this, and, besides, he has touched the heart of your young lady."

"You think so?"

"See for yourself."

Gold-Ball in fact was edging near to Oak-Wringer, who had turned as pale as someone escaped from the grave.

"Unless I'm much mistaken," thought Gayant, "the poor devil is going to be properly punished by being married to my haughty sister-in-law."

XVIII

The double wedding took place a week later. Gayant invited all the people of Cantin, who got themselves there in carts, in char-a-bancs, in wagons, in dogcarts, and in barous—that's to say, in garbage-trucks.

When they were all ready to set off, up came the bear and her four cubs, who put themselves at the head of the parade.

Then came the fairy Maglore, looking so much younger she seemed perhaps only sixty years old, dressed in magnificent clothes, and riding on the crow, who, for the occasion, was transformed into a hummingbird—an actual hummingbird—a gigantic hummingbird. Gayant, always a modest fellow, came at the end of the parade, with Silver-Ball and Mary Saguenon.

It was a splendid feast. They had gingersnaps and the kind of gingerbread nuts we call pimperboles, and apple turnovers to eat, and they drank beer from Louvain. The King opened the ball with Gayant's foster-mother, and that amused everyone mightily.

They were so glad and joyous that, when it came time to go to bed, in passing the match to light the candles, they invented that pleasant game that's called, after the boast of the naughty little grandfather, "The little gentleman still lives."

And, in recognition of these memorable events, in that place, every year, during the festival of Douai's patron saint, they hold a Parade for Gayant. Our hero comes promenading triumphantly through the streets, with his wife and children, followed by a band playing.

He has become as handsome a hero as he was ugly in his lifetime. They present him in a figure twenty feet tall, and Madam Gayant—who, by a bizarre confusion, they call Mary Saguenon—is almost as tall as her husband.

John Gelon, called Gayant, is as much celebrated in Flanders as Green Jeans, called the Knight of Saint George, and the saint's feast in Douai is just as gay as the one in Mons. Gayant's Parade is just as famous as Green Jeans' Combat of the Lumçon. Whenever you find someone from Douai or Mons, all you have to do is hum the tra-la-la of the celebrated parade, or the toot-toot of the illustrious tourney, and you will see these good people weep for joy at the memory of their ancestral grandfathers Gayant and Green Jeans.

The Tailors' Flag

I

In olden days, there was in Solesmes a little tailor named Warlemaque, who was as curious as a woman. Sitting cross-legged by his window, tugging his needle in and out, he kept his eyes and ears open.

Moreover, his ten fingers were very nimble. He was perhaps even more of a thief than he was a tailor.

Rarely did Warlemaque cut out a dress or a pair of pants without dropping in the kind of chest that's called the hollow-of-the-wave, or else the hell-hole, a good piece of cloth to make himself a waistcoat.

In this way, he had assembled the finest collection of waistcoats ever seen. He had white ones, black, blue, green, and many-colored, and others brightly flowered, such as the people of Vendegies and Bermerain like to wear for the feasts of their patron saints.

II

Warlemaque went on committing his robberies shamelessly for a long time, but then one night he had a singular dream. He dreamt he was standing before God's court. God was surrounded by an imposing retinue of angels and archangels.

Suddenly, Warlemaque heard himself called. Trembling, he came forward.

One angel detached himself from the group, took several steps into the middle of the space in front of them, and, without saying a word, spread out a great flag of a thousand colors.

Warlemaque recognized all those pieces of cloth he had stolen, and was seized with such fear that he gave a start, waking himself up.

The next day, he told his dream to his two apprentices, and said to them, "You have to be really mad as can be to damn yourself for a few miserable pieces of cloth! Each time you see me throw some cloth that I've cut off into the hollow-of-the-wave, make sure to shout at me, without fail: 'Master, remember the flag!'"

"We won't fail you," said the apprentices.

III

From that day on, Warlemaque corrected one of his faults: he was still the most curious tailor in Solesmes, but he became a scrupulously honest tailor—and that annoyed his colleagues enormously.

His customers were astonished that he could outfit them using so little fabric.

"How can you do that?" his neighbor, old mother Perpetua, asked him.

"Oh," said Warlemaque, "it's because people have grown so thin. It's strange how thin everyone in Solesmes has grown of late! It's all the fault of those rogues the brewers who brew such bad beer!"

A good three months passed, and the little tailor had not thrown anything down the hell-hole. Then one morning the lord of Solesmes sent for him and turned over to him a length of magnificent cloth-of-gold to make into a ceremonial robe.

Never had Warlemaque seen anything so beautiful.

He carried the cloth home and spread it out on his workbench. The more he handled it, the more he felt the itch to give himself a piece of it.

At last he looked around out of the corner of one eye to make sure his apprentices weren't watching him, and crack!—he let a half an ell fall into the hollow-of-the-wave.

"Master, remember the flag!" cried the apprentices, who'd been looking at him sidelong.

"Yes, the flag, I know perfectly well," said Warlemaque. "But it occurs to me that what it was lacking was eactly a piece of cloth-of-gold."

IV

After that, the little tailor went back to his favorite vice, and, as usually happens in such a case, he stole ten times as much as before. He stole so much that one night he saw again the flag of a thousand colors.

This second dream kept him honest for several days, but soon he started feeding the hell-hole again, while waiting for the time when he would go down there himself.

A third dream had even less effect. The next day, while folding a piece of fabric, Warlemaque had the nerve to say: "Good!—another piece for the flag!"

His bad reputation was thus so well re-established, that, in no time at all, people wouldn't trust him with enough to stitch a pair of gaiters. Every customer wanted to keep his eyes on him while he cut out enough to make a pair of pants.

Old Mother Perpetua insisted on it, too, one day when she came to bring him a length of olive-green cloth to make a full suit for her husband.

"I'll have some of your cloth all the same," thought the sinful little tailor.

And he thought of a clever trick.

First, he cut off a large strip and threw it out the window, saying, "That isn't good for anything."

"What! Not good for anything! I know very well how to make something out of that!" cried old Mother Perpetua. And, while she ran into the street to pick up that piece of cloth, the tailor quickly hid away a half-ell of the rest.

Unfortunately, it happened at just that mment that someone broke a window-pane in the house across the street. It was the shoemaker, who was having an argument with his wife, and so put the cat, as the saying is, among the pigeons.

Warlemaque, feeling curious, looked up, but still went on cutting the cloth with his scissors.

He cut, alas! so clumsily that he cut open an artery, and died within the hour.

V

Although he certainly deserved to roast in hell, the little tailor nevertheless followed the road to Paradise.

When he got there, the weather was so fine that day that God the Father had gone for a walk in the gardens of heaven with the angels, the apostles, and the saints.

There was no one at home but Saint Peter, and the Lord had ordered him not to receive a living soul.

Warlemaque knocked softly.

"Who's there?" said Saint Peter, opening the wicket.

"Little Warlemaque, a poor and honest tailor."

"Honest! honest!" muttered Saint Peter. "It's got crooked hands, your honesty! With the cloth you've stolen, I could—God pardon me!—make a carpet long enough to go from here to hell."

"Oh, really, Saint Peter!—for some wretched pieces of cloth that fell off the workbench, that even the rag-sellers wouldn't have bothered to pick up in the street!"

"A fine story! Be off with you—your place is not in here. Besides, God the Father forbade me to let anyone in while he wasn't here."

"I beg you, dear milord Saint Peter, don't force me to go back down that road. Tailors are so bad at long walks that my feet are all blistered. Open the door—I'll sweep the floors, I'll amuse the children, and, into the bargain, I'll mend your old clothes."

VI

The doorkeeper's heart was touched. He opened the door halfway—just enough for Warlemaque to step into Paradise.

"Now you go sit there," he said, "in that corner, behind the entryway, and stay there, and don't whistle, so that when God the Father returns he won't see you."

The tailor obeyed and made himself so small that you couldn't have found him in a box of mice.

At the end of an hour, Saint Peter needed to leave for a moment. Warlemaque, whose feet felt itchy, stood up from his hiding-place, opened a door, tried peeping in, then took a few steps inside, then grew bold, and so at last went bravely from room to room to visit Paradise.

He put off trying to find out if there was something there from his dream, and if the flag of a thousand colors really existed.

He didn't see the accusing flag anywhere, but he came to a round hall, magnificently decorated, with a great number of seats, each with a footstool in front of it.

In the middle of the room there shone a marvelous gold throne, studded with precious stones, where God the Father would sit with his feet on a gold footstool, to see what was happening on the earth.

VII

Astonished, the tailor stared with all his might for a long time at the throne. In the end, he could not resist his longing to sit on it. From there he saw at a glance what people were doing all over the world, and you could say that never had someone so full of curiosity enjoyed such a spectacle as that.

When the little tailor was tired of examining the whole world, he said to himself, "Let's try looking a little at what the people are doing in Solesmes." He turned his gaze in that direction, and at once he saw shirts hung out to bleach in the curoir, or if you prefer, in the village-green.

Old Mother Perpetua was there, busy gathering up her linen. Lo and behold, all of a sudden our tailor noticed that the old woman was taking two of the handsomest shirts, shirts that were Warlemaque's, and she was carrying them off with her own things.

"Stop thief!" cried the tailor, but as the old woman didn't turn back, he grabbed the footstool, and he threw it down out of the sky right at her head.

With the footstool gone, Warlemaque felt that he'd done something very stupid. As he could not go to look for it, he jumped as fast as he could to the base of the throne and went back to curl up in his place behind the door.

VIII

He was just in time, because a moment later the door swung open, and God the Father came back in, with the angels, the apostles, and the saints. The little tailor was so well hidden that no one noticed him.

Unfortunately, God the Father went right to his throne to sit down. He didn't find the stool in front of it for him to put his feet on, and he called Saint Peter.

"Where has my footstool gone?" he asked.

"I don't have any idea, Lord God," Saint Peter replied.

"You didn't let anyone in, did you?"

"No one at all, except a little tailor, who's over there behind the door."

"Let him come forth!" said God the Father.

IX

Little Warlemaque came forward, trembling like a leaf.

"Haven't you seen my footstool?" the Lord asked him.

"Yes, indeed, Lord God," said the tailor.

"And what have you done with it?"

"Oh! Lord God, such a disgrace!—I was looking at the earth, and what did I see but old Mother Perpetua stealing my shirts! I was so disgusted that I threw your footstool at her head."

"What, you scoundrel, you threw my footstool out! Instead of sending you warnings that didn't do any good, if I had been as quick to punish as you, all in good time I would have no footstool, no tongs, no poker, no shovel for the fireplace! Just try to save yourself, you wretched boy!"

Little Warlemaque took to his heels and ran right to Purgatory; and, since then, tailors have become so honest that the good Lord has left their flag to be eaten by worms, and this song has been written about them:

Hallelujah for the tailors!
The shoemakers are the thieves now.
The day will fall
We'll have them all.
Hallelujah!

The Devil's Stewpot

I

In olden days, on the road from Valenciennes to Condé, there was only one single village, or, rather, a hamlet, the hamlet of Escaupont. All the rest of the country was covered by the immense Charbonnière Forest, which belonged to the nobles. Even when there was plenty of deadwood about, the poor folk had to blow on their fingers when the north wind howled.

In those days, a marissiau, or farrier, lived at Escaupont. He was named John Hullos, but was generally called the Cacheux—which, according to some, meant the Hunter, because he liked to go poaching, but others said it meant the Searcher, because he always looked as if he was searching for something.

II

One winter's evening, when the Cacheux was wandering in the forest over Mount Anzin, he spotted a reddish light shining through the trees.

John headed in that direction, for it was very cold that night, and his teeth were chattering like a stork's beak.

Soon he came to a hut, peeped in the door, and saw a great fire burning on the hearth.

You'd have thought there were ten lamps lit up, the fire was so bright and clear, and yet it didn't seem to be built of wood, or peat, or straw, or dry leaves, but rather big black stones, which burned like stalks of colza.

Three men—three dwarfs—all of them black from top to toe, were sitting around the fire.

Someone else, in John's place, would have run away in a hurry, but the marrisiau had a fist like a vise and feared neither wind nor storm. But he was quite astonished, and started thinking that those stones really ought to go to him, to *him*, because he had so much trouble so often getting the heavy iron red-hot.

He drew out his pipe, and, as he came in the door, he said, as the custom was, "Is it all right to smoke, my boys?"

One of the three dwarfs beckoned him to come in, and, while he was stuffing his Borinage pipe, John took a look at his hosts.

They were completely naked, and furry as bears. "What's that you're burning there, my masters, if I'm not too curious?" John Hullos asked.

The three dwarfs looked at one another, grinning and making faces, after which the first said to the two others, pointing downwards, "If someone only knew what was down there, at the very bottom of the pit, treasure more precious than gold and diamonds!" Then he added, "When the cat's away, the mice will play." He made a face, and snickered.

"If someone only knew," said the second, "that someday the innards of the earth will burn in the sunlight, and carriages will go without horses, and boats will go without sails, and lamps will burn without oil!" Then he added, "When the sun's down, all animals are in the shade!" And, like his neighbor, he finished up by making a face, and snickering.

"If someone only knew," said the third, crooking his fingers to make horns, "that little by little his reign over the world will come to an end, and one day maybe his stewpot will be overturned!"

"Who? Who're you talking about?" cried John.

But suddenly a whistle blew, seeming to come from below. The three dwarfs jumped up as quick as squirrels and disappeared down a big hole the Cacheux hadn't noticed.

"By my pipe! I'm going to get to the bottom of this!" said he, and he flung himself after them into a bottomless shaft.

III

John Hullos found a steep ladder inside to climb down, and at the end of an hour, he came to a sort of round cave, with long, low passages going out of it, like the spokes of a wheel from the hub.

Countless lights were coming and going in the passages. The Cacheux realized that there were as many dwarfs as lights, and each one had his forehead lit with tongues of fire, and each one was busy with a strange task.

Some, squatting or lying on their sides, were breaking off immense slabs of black rock with blows from their pickaxes; others were loading them onto little carts, while others still drew them away through the passages.

They carried out their tasks with incomparable skill and dexterity, laughing, crying, gesturing, and jumping about like a troop of monkeys.

"What are you doing there, my boys?" John Hullos asked them.

"Oh, if someone only knew," said one of them, "just what it is he gets to cook with!"

"Who?—so who is it?" cried the Cacheux.

"Oh, if someone only knew! if someone only knew!" chorused his companions.

"By my pipe! someone will find out!" he said. And he made his way through one of the passages, following some of the carts.

The passage ended in a vast, open space, where enormous heaps of black rocks stood.

Near there ran a stream with yellow and green waves, and big barges, all loaded with these stones, going by.

John scrambled up one of the heaps to see further, and, on the other side of the stream, in a heavy cloud of smoke, he spotted an immense cauldron, where it seemed to him—a terrifying sight!—men like himself were being put in to boil.

"He's going to get himself burnt up! He's going to get himself burnt up!" cried the dwarfs, and they forced him down.

IV

Then the whistle blew again, and echoed from one passage to the next. All the workmen threw down their tools, sat down in a circle, and filled their pipes. John realized that it was a rest period, and started to smoke with them.

Big foaming pitchers of beer were brought to them. The black workers offered some to their guest. A true Flamand would never refuse a glass of beer, even if the devil in person offered it: Hullos took it without haggling.

"To your good health, my masters!" he said, and emptied his glass.

Nothing worried him, except the possibility that the beer might have a burnt taste. On the contrary, it was fresh and strong, as good as the beer of Escaupont.

The result was that John emptied his glass so many times that he drank one draught too many and fell asleep.

Whether it was the effect of the hops—or some other cause?—the Cacheux had a dream, and it was an extraordinary dream.

A great stewpot was bubbling away in front of him, and perched on top of it was a horned giant with the muzzle of a billy-goat, the eyes of a polecat, and the wings of an immense bat.

Armed with a long spoon, the winged giant was stirring the stewpot, when John Hullos, himself, drew boldly near, and, with the bucket from his forge, moistened the black stones burning underneath.

They smoked and went out, but the giant seized an enormous bellows and in a rage blew up the fire again.

Next, the infernal cook and his stewpot faded away, little by little, and all John could see was two eyes shining in the darkness, like a glassmaker's furnace.

Then he heard a voice which said: "Not yet! not yet! Don't touch the stewpot yet!"

And it seemed to him that he was shut into a coffin of lead, and he slept like lead for all eternity.

V

When the Cacheux woke up, he found himself in the forest.

The moon was fading, and day was starting to break, but no birds were singing, because it was winter. He looked all around, rubbed his eyes, and tried to get his thoughts in order.

"What a funny dream!" he said, stretching. "I thought I was done for. But what an idea to sleep in the sun like a woodcock when it's cold enough to freeze a blood-pudding on the grille! Brrr!—my Johnnie must be worried!"

He got up to go home. How strange!—he didn't recognize where he was, not at all: where it had been thick with underbrush the night before, now he saw open clearings, and the whole forest seemed to him much thinner.

Not understanding these changes at all, he looked around to get his bearings, as he would have done in a strange country, and went down the mountain with a feeble and faltering step.

At the end of a half-hour he came to a village. That surprised him even more, for Escaupont, as everyone knew, was an hour away from Mount Anzin.

He saw a shepherd and his sheep coming from the distance.

The Cacheux knew all the shepherds around there. He didn't recognize this fellow at all.

"What do you call this place?" he asked him.

"Here? Why, old man, it's Bruai," said the shepherd, in an accent that didn't sound at all like the native one.

John also couldn't figure out why he was calling him "old man," when he wasn't even thirty years old. "Well," he said, "I felt sure it wasn't Escaupont."

"Escaupont is where you can see that bell-tower, down that way, another half a league."

The Cacheux set off and came to Escaupont.

He didn't recognize a single one of the buildings in the village, except for the church, which was cracking all over and going to ruin. Another, bigger one was going up beside it.

"Is my dream already coming true?" he wondered. But the carriages he saw going by were drawn by horses, and he didn't see anywhere the black stones he'd seen flaming under the earth.

He reached his hut, or, rather, the spot where it had been: in its place was a pretty little cottage in the shade of an oak.

He remembered that, six months earlier, at the birth of his daughter, he'd planted an acorn in his yard. By some incomprehensible means, in six months the acorn had become an enormous oak.

VI

John Hullos didn't know if he was dreaming, or if he'd been dreaming—if he was still dreaming at the bottom of the earth, or if, in reality, he'd been dealing with Satan in person.

He went into the cottage and saw a woman holding a child in her arms. But it wasn't his wife, or his daughter, either.

"What do you want, goodman? We don't have anything to give," said the young woman.

"I don't money, I want Johnnie."

"Johnnie who?"

"The Cacheux's Johnnie, John Hullos's Johnnie."

"I've never heard those names in my life."

"But this is Escaupont—isn't it?"

"Of course."

John dropped down on a chair and broke out laughing. "Oh, I must be mad—it's obvious!"

The woman was frightened by his outcry. "Look, you just go away," she said. "You don't look like a nice person, not a bit, with a beard an ell long: you look like the Wandering Jew."

John put his hand to his chin and realized that he did in fact have a long white beard. There was a miroulet, a little mirror, hanging by the chimney; he looked into it and gave a cry of despair. He snatched up a calendar, glanced at it, and fell back on the chair, ready to faint.

The poor man had just realized that he'd aged a hundred years in one night.

The woman ran to tell her neighbors that the Wandering Jew was in her house. Everyone came running.

Meanwhile, the Cacheux came to himself again. He put his head in his hands and sat motionless, like a man who's been wiped out.

"Where do you come from?" asked the women.

"Escaupont."

"Was it a long time ago when you left?"

"One night, but the village and me—we've grown a hundred years older."

"What did you do in that one night?"

"I went to the bottom of the earth."

"To the bottom of the earth! What did you find there?"

"The devil's stewpot."

"He's a sorcerer!" a voice exclaimed.

At these words, the women scattered. Curiosity gave way to fear, and then to rage.

"A sorcerer! a sorcerer!"

The mayor showed up with the rest, and he just barely managed to drag the old man from the hands of the mob, who wanted to stone him. He brought him to Valenciennes himself, under the escort of the rural guard.

VII

They shut Hullos in the prison to be judged the next day; but, as it happened, the head provost died suddenly that day: the trial was put off for a week.

When the marissiau came before the tribunal, the poor old fellow was so bowed by age and suffering that he hadn't even the strength to raise his head.

"Is it true that you went to the bottom of the earth and saw the devil's stewpot?" asked the new judge.

"That's true," said the Cacheux.

"And what else did you see there?"

"Treasures more precious than gold and diamonds."

"What treasures?"

"Stones that burned—that'll make carriages go without horses, someday, and boats without sails, and lamps without oil."

"Only magic could do wonders like that. This man's a sorcerer!"

The judge spoke these words with so much hate that John raised his eyes.

The head provost looked just like the terrifying personage Hullos had seen under the earth, feature for feature, except for the tail; the only difference was that he'd hidden his horns under his hat, his bat-wings under his robe, his muzzle under a bushy beard, and his polecat eyes under his glasses.

The judge and the accused looked at each other. The eyes of the judge grew wide, as if it had been night-time. At the sight of those two flames, the Cacheux felt he was lost.

The provost then spoke a good deal. All that John got out his discourse was the end: "Let him be brought to punishment tomorrow!"

And John was led back to prison, followed by the curses of the crowd.

The next day they came to lead him to the gallows in the town square.

VIII

It was a Saturday, marketday, and there were a good many women from the countryside roundabouts selling butter and eggs or drinking light beer in the bars.

There was John, the rope around his neck, hardly able to drag himself along. No one there had ever seen a man so old going to pay the penalty, and the women couldn't help but feel sorry for him.

As for John himself, he was resigned. After all that he had suffered since the night when his fatal curiosity had led him to the bottom of the earth, he would just as soon die as live.

All the same, he felt more than a little bitter over his fate. He held in his hands a secret which could make the whole world happy, and he was carrying his secret to the grave!

All at once, among the crowd that lined the way, he saw a young country-woman nursing a child.

The unlucky man gave a cry: "Johnnie! Johnnie, my dear!"

And, before they could stop him, he ran to take her in his arms.

He covered the mother and child with kisses, and his tears ran down the length of his white beard. The mother and child looked so exactly like his wife and daughter that John forgot that both of them had been dead for years.

The young woman was seized with pity for the old man and while she let him hug her, she was weeping herself.

"So you remember John Hullos, John the Cacheux?" he asked her.

"John the Cacheux? I've often heard my grandmother speak of him, for he was her grandfather."

"But it's me—*I'm* John the Cacheux!"

IX

An old woman, more than 80 years old, drew near just then.

"If you are John Hullos, otherwise known as John the Cacheux, I am your grand-daughter, and this is your great-grand-daughter's daughter.

John pressed his grand-daughter to his heart.

"So you're the daughter of my poor Jeanette," he said, "and when I left her she was at her mother's breast. Alas! what's become of her, my pretty little girl?"

"She's been dead these twenty years. She lived to be eighty."

Everybody wept to hear these words.

"How come you don't live in Escaupont anymore?" John Hullos went on.

"My grandmother often told me how after my grandfather was gone, she left her village to go settle at Aulnoy, on the other side of Valenciennes."

"To the gallows!" cried a voice, the judge's voice.

216

But the women were on the condemned man's side now, and they all shouted at the same time: "He's not a sorcerer, not a bit! it's John the Cacheux, Jeannette's grandfather, and you'll have to have us all killed before you put him to death!"

And the men, for their part, were saying, "The old fellow knows a place where there's treasure buried."

And they delivered him from the hands of his guards.

"Listen to me, my brave friends," said John Hullos then, "and you won't have to perish with cold in the winters anymore. Under Mount Anzin lies an enormous heap of black stones that burn like colza stalks. The day will come when, thanks to these stones, carriages will go without horses, and boats without sails, and all people will live in joy and prosperity."

"And you wanted to deprive of us all these fine things, you cursed judge! To the gallows with the judge!—to the gallows with him, the scoundrel!"

And the crowd seized the head provost, throttled him, put him up on the gallows, and then into the fire —

—when lo and behold! all of a sudden, the day grew dark, and a heavy cloud descended on the flame, and they saw the judge transform himself into a gigantic bat, which took flight, soared for a while over the city, dropped down onto the belfry, gave three sinister cries, and headed straight for Mount Anzin.

X

The next day, twenty or so resolute men, guided by Hullos, met at Mount Anzin, with picks and shovels.

They found no hut, no hole, no ladder there; but they dug in the spot John pointed out, and discovered coal, which they named houille, pit-coal, after Hullos.

They dug a shaft and brought up to the sunlight the entrails of the globe.

The devil, to avenge himself, sometimes lights a fire in the pit-coal mines, which people call a firedamp explosion; but it doesn't help him, for the workers continue to ransack his stores boldly, and to bring up from there the world's joy and prosperity.

The Twelve Dancing Princesses

I

In olden days, in the hamlet of Montignies-sur-Roc, there was a little cowherd, with neither father nor mother. His name was Michael, but people called him Crowboy because when he was leading his cows through the waste country he would stop and gaze idly at the crows in the fields.

As he had fair skin, blue eyes, and curly blond hair, the village girls would shout at him, "Hey! Crowboy, what are you doing?"

"Nothing," Michael would say, and he went on his way without paying any attention to them.

The truth is that he thought they were ugly, with their sunburnt necks, their big red hands, their heavy wool skirts, and their wooden shoes.

Michael had heard stories about girls somewhere in the world who had fair necks, slender hands, and clothes of silk and lace, who were called princesses. When he sat with his friends around the fire, imagining shapes in the flames, as the logs burned, they only saw more big black cows in their herds, but he dreamed about what a joy it would be to marry a princess.

II

One time, around the middle of August, just at noon, when the sun was blazing hot, after he had eaten his hunk of dry bread, he fell asleep under an oak tree and dreamed that he saw before his eyes a beautiful lady in a robe of cloth-of-gold.

This lady said to him, "Go to Beloeil Castle, and you'll marry a princess."

That evening, the little cowherd told his dream to the other farmhands. He rather liked the idea of following the advice of the lady in the robe of cloth-of-gold. But the good folk there made fun of him, understandably.

The next day, at the same time, he fell asleep again under the same tree. The lady appeared and said to him for the second time, "Go to Beloeil Castle, and you'll marry a princess."

Michael again told his dream, but they laughed in his face even harder.

"I don't care!" he said. "If the lady appears to me a third time, I'm going to obey her."

The next day, people in Montignies-sur-Roc were a good deal surprised, when about two o'clock they heard someone shouting:

"Ho, there, ho!
See the cows and the calves go!"

It was the little cowherd leading his cows back to the stable.

The farmer, in a rage, went in after him, but Michael simply told him, "I'm leaving," made a bundle of his things, said goodbye to them all, and set out boldly.

There was an uproar in the village, and, from the hall, the townsfolk watched him go, laughing to split their sides, as the Crowboy marched bravely through the valley of the Honneau, his bundle tied to the end of a stick.

They had good cause to laugh.

III

It was, in fact, something well known for twenty leagues round that there really were twelve princesses in Beloeil Castle. They were marvelously beautiful, but they were equally proud, and, moreover, they were so delicate and so truly princesses, that if you had put a pea at the base of their beds they would have felt it right through the mattresses.

Besides that, people said they lived the lives of real princesses, sleeping late every morning, and not getting up until noon. They had twelve beds, all in one room, and—an astonishing thing!—even though they were shut in with triple locks, every morning their satin shoes were worn through.

When they were asked what they had been doing all night, they said that they'd been asleep. And, indeed, no one had heard any noise in their room, and no one could understand how their shoes were getting worn out all by themselves.

The Duke of Beloeil had sent out his trumpeters to announce that whosoever could discover how his daughters were wearing out their shoes could choose one of them to marry.

A crowd of princes had presented themselves to undertake the adventure—they had kept watch on the princesses from behind the door, kept ajar, but when morning came, the princes were no longer to be seen, and no one could say what had become of them.

IV

When he got to the castle, Michael went right to the gardener and offered him his services. The gardener had just sent his previous assistant away.

Although the Crowboy did not seem to him a sturdy lad, he hired him, thinking that his cute face and curly blond hair would please the princesses.

He warned him first of all that when it was time for the princesses to get up, he was to bring each of them a bouquet.

Michael figured that this was definitely not the most disagreeable task he'd ever had.

He stationed himself at the princesses' door with his dozen bouquets in a basket, and presented one to each of the sisters. They took them haughtily, without looking at the boy, but Lina, the youngest, fixed her large eyes, as soft as velvet, on him, and cried, "Oh!—what a darling he is, our new flower-boy!"

The others burst out laughing, and the oldest sister told her that a princess should never lower her eyes to take in a gardener's boy.

Michael was not unaware of what people said about the sisters. But even so, thanks to Princess Lina's lovely eyes, he felt a fierce desire to undertake the task.

Unfortunately, he did not dare to put himself forward, fearing that people would make fun of him, and might even, as penalty for his presumption, put him out the door.

V

Meantime, the Crowboy had a new dream. The lady in the robe of cloth-of-gold appeared to him, holding in her hand two young laurels—a cherry-laurel and a rose-laurel—and in the other hand a little golden pick-axe, a little golden pail, and a silken towel. She said to him, "Plant these two laurels in two big pots, dig them in with the axe, water them with the pail, and dry them with the towel. Then, when they have grown as tall as a fifteen-year-old girl, say to each of them, 'My beautiful laurel, with the golden axe I dug you in, with the golden pail I watered you, and with the silken towel I dried you.' Then ask of them what you wish, and the laurels will give it to you."

Michael thanked the lady in the robe of cloth-of-gold, and when he woke, he found the two laurels there, so he did exactly what she had told him.

The shrubs grew fast, and when they were as tall as a fifteen-year-old girl, he said to the cherry-laurel, "My beautiful laurel, with the golden axe I dug you in, with the golden pail I watered you, and with the silken towel I dried you. Give me a way to make myself invisible."

At once a pretty white blossom appeared on the laurel. Michael picked it, and put it in his button-hole.

VI

That evening, when the princesses went upstairs to go to bed, he followed after them, barefoot, so that his steps would not be heard, and hid himself under one of the twelve beds, leaving the floor clear.

The princesses at once set about opening their closets and storage boxes. They took out magnificent sets of jewelry, put them on in front of their mirrors, and turned around to admire the results from every angle.

In his hiding place, Michael couldn't see anything, but he could hear, and he heard the princesses laughing and jumping about with glee. Finally, the oldest princess aid, "Let's hurry, Princesses—our dancers are going to be getting impatient."

After a while, when the Crowboy didn't hear any more noise, he risked peeking out and saw the twelve sisters superbly robed, with their satin shoes on their feet, and the bouquets he had brought them in their hands.

"Are you ready?" asked the oldest princess.

"Yes," her eleven sisters replied in chorus, and they got into a line behind her.

The oldest princess clapped her hands together three times, and a trapdoor opened. All the princesses disappeared down a secret staircase, and Michael hurried to follow them.

As he was walking right at the heels of the Princess Lina, he accidentally stepped on the train of her dress.

"There's someone behind me!" cried the princess. "Someone's pulling back on my dress."

"Oh, you little fool!" said the oldest princess. "You're always worrying. It's just a nail you've snagged your dress on."

VII

They went down, down, and came at last to a corridor with a door at the end that was latched shut. The oldest princess opened it, and it led them into a beautiful little wood where the leaves were spangled with drops of silver that gleamed under a bright full moon.

They crossed into another grove, where the tree-leaves were dotted with gold, then a third, where the leaves glittered, covered with diamonds.

Finally Crowboy saw a big lake and, on the shore, twelve little boats with flags flying, holding twelve princes who, the oars in their hands, were awaiting the princesses.

Each princess got into one of the boats, and Michael slipped into the boat with the youngest one. The boat glided rapidly away, but Lina's boat, more heavily loaded than the others, lagged behind.

"We aren't going as fast as usual," she said. "What's the matter?"

"I don't know," said the prince. "I'm rowing with all my strength."

On the far side of the lake, the little gardener's boy saw a handsome castle, brilliantly lit up. The joyous noise of violins, kettle-drums, and trumpets poured out from the windows.

They hurried to the shore, and they leaped out of the boats. The princes moored the boats, then offered their arms to the princesses, and led them into the castle.

VIII

Michael followed and so made his way behind them into a ballroom. It was all bright with chandeliers, candelabras, mirrors, damask tapestries, and baskets of flowers. The Crowboy was dazzled.

He drew back into a corner, admiring the grace and beauty of the princesses. Some had brown hair, some yellow, some light chestnut and some dark, and some fair hair as bright as gold. Never on earth had anyone seen such a beautiful gathering of princesses; but the one who looked the sweetest and loveliest to the cow-herd was the little brown-haired princess with eyes as soft as velvet. How joyfully she danced! Leaning on her partner's shoulder, she let herself be swept away as if in a whirl-wind. Her cheeks flushed, her eyes sparkled, and it was not hard to see that the dance was for her.

The poor boy envied the luck of their handsome partners, with the youngest princess dancing so gracefully in their arms. He did not think to wonder if he had much reason to feel jealous.

These handsome partners, in fact, were some of the princes—more than fifty of them, now—who had undertaken to discover the princesses' secret. The princesses had made them drink a potion that froze the heart, leaving no love, except for dancing.

IX

They danced until the princesses' shoes were full of holes. When the cock crowed for the third time, the violins stopped, and servants brought out a delicious supper, with sugar-cakes, gingersnaps, waffles, round cookies, bar cookies from Lilles, and other delicacies which, as everyone knows, are the usual food of princesses.

After the supper, the dancers went down to the boats, and the Crow-boy climbed into the oldest princess's boat. Again they passed through the wood with leaves spangled with diamonds, the one with leaves dotted with gold, and the one where they glittered with droplets of silver.

As a proof of what he had seen, the boy broke off a twig from a tree in the last grove. Lina turned around at the noise when it snapped.

"What's that?" she said.

"It's nothing," said the oldest sister. "It's the screech-owl that nests in the castle towers."

X

When he had made the bouquets, Michael hid the twig with leaves dotted with silver in the bouquet he presented to the little princess.

Lina, finding the twig, was astonished. She said nothing to her sisters, but when she encountered the boy, as she was walking in the shade of the arbors, she stopped as if to talk to him, but then started abruptly on her way again.

That evening, the twelve sisters went to the ball again. The Crowboy followed them as before and crossed the lake in Lina's boat. It was the prince this time who complained that the boat seemed heavy.

"It's the heat," said the princess. "It seems hot to me, too."

During the whole ball, she kept looking around for the little gardener, but in vain.

In returning, Michael gathered a twig in the grove with leaves spangled with gold, and, this time, it was the oldest princess who heard the noise when it snapped.

"It's nothing," Lina told her. "It's the cry of the screech-owl that nests in the castle towers."

XI

When the princesses arose that day, Lina found the twig in her bouquet, and when her sisters went down, she lagged a little behind, and asked the little cow-herd, "Where did this twig come from?"

"Your highness knows very well," said Michael.

"So you followed us?"

"Yes, Princess."

"How did you do that? We never saw you."

"I was hidden," said the Crowboy simply.

The princess was silent for a moment, then all at once she said, "You know our secret. Keep the secret—here's money to pay you for your pains."

And she threw a purse full of gold at the boy.

"I don't sell my silence," said Michael, and he walked away without picking up the purse.

For three nights, Lina did not see or hear anything extraordinary. On the fourth night, she heard a noise in the wood with leaves spangled with diamonds. At noon, there was the twig in her bouquet.

She drew the Crowboy away from the others and said to him harshly, "Do you know the reward my father has promised to pay for our secret?"

"I know it, Princess," said Michael.

"Aren't you going to reveal it to him?"

"That's not my plan."

"Because you're afraid?"

"No, Princess."

"Then why are you keeping silent?"

Michael did not answer.

XII

Lina's sisters had seen her talking to the little gardener, and they made fun of their little sister.

"What's to stop you from marrying him?" said the oldest sister. "You'll be the garden-girl. It's a nice profession. You'll live in a hut at the end of the park, you'll help your husband by drawing water from the well, and when the rest of us rise, you'll be the one who'll bring us our bouquets."

Princess Lina was furious. When the Crowboy brought her bouquet to her, she received him in the most disdainful way.

Michael bowed to her respectfully. He never raised his eyes to look at her, but all that day she felt that he was at her side, although she could not see him.

In the afternoon she resolved to tell her oldest sister.

"What!" said the oldest princess, "that rascal knows our secret, and you've waited so long to warn me! I'm going to get rid of him for us."

"What will you do?"

"Oh, Lord, I'll have him sent to the tower and dropped into one of the secret dungeons."

In olden days, that was how pretty princesses got rid of people who were over-curious.

But what an astonishing thing!—the youngest sister did not care at all for this way of closing the mouth of the boy who, after all, hadn't told on them.

XIII

They decided to discuss the question with their other ten sisters. The others all had the same opinion as the oldest. Then the youngest sister declared that if anyone touched a hair of the little gardener's head, she would go to their father herself and reveal the secret of the worn-out shoes.

In the end, it was decided that they would invite Michael to try to test him—they would invite him to the ball and at the end of the supper they would pour out for him some of the potion to enchant him as it had the others.

They had the Crowboy called and asked him how he had managed to pierce the mystery, but he was silent.

Then the oldest of the sisters told him imperiously what they were ordering him to do. He answered simply, "I will obey."

He had been present invisibly at their meeting and had heard everything. He had decided to drink the potion and sacrifice himself to the happiness of the girl he loved.

He did not want to cut a poor figure at the ball next to the other dancers, so he went at once to the laurels and said, "My beautiful rose-laurel, with the golden axe I dug you in, with the little golden pail I watered you, and with the silken towel I dried you. Give me some clothes so I can dress like a prince."

A beautiful rose-red flower appeared. Michael picked it and found himself all at once dressed in velvet as black as the little princess's eyes, with a cap, and a feather in it pinned on with a diamond, and a rose-laurel flower in his buttonhole.

That evening, he presented himself to the Duke of Beloeil in his fine new clothes and got his permission to keep watch to discover his daughters' secret. He looked so fine that it was hard for anyone to recognize him.

XIV

The twelve princesses went upstairs to go to bed. Michael followed them and waited behind the half-open door until they gave the signal to leave.

He didn't put himself in Lina's boat. He gave an arm to the oldest sister, danced with each of them in turn and danced so gracefully that they were all delighted with him.

Then came the moment for him to dance with the little princess. With her, he danced the best of all, but he did not dare to speak a word to her.

While he was escorting her to her seat, she said to him, mockingly, "Now you've had all your wishes granted—you've been treated like a prince."

"Don't worry," said the Crowboy gently, "you will never be a gardener-boy's wife."

The little princess looked at him uncertainly, and he withdrew without waiting for an answer.

When the satin shoes were worn out, the violins stopped, and the servants set the table. Michael was placed at the right hand of the oldest sister, opposite the youngest.

They were served the finest foods, and strong wines were poured in their glasses. They showered him with flattering compliments to turn his head even more.

He didn't let himself be swept away by either the wine or the compliments.

XV

At last, the eldest sister gave the sign, and one of the pages brought in a big golden cup.

"The enchanted castle has no secets from you anymore," she told the Crowboy. "Let's drink to your triumph."

He cast a final look at the little princess and lifted the cup to his lips, not even turning pale.

"Don't drink!" cried the princess suddenly. "I'd rather be a gardener-boy's wife,"

And she burst into tears.

Michael spilled out the contents of the cup, leaped up from the table and over it in one bound, and fell at Lina's feet.

All of the princes likewise fell at the princesses' knees. Each princess chose one of them to marry, and gave him her hand to raise him. The spell was broken.

The twelve couples climbed back into the boats. It took several more voyages to bring back the other princes.

Together, they all went through the three groves, and when they had passed the subterranean gate, they heard a great noise, as if the enchanted castle had collapsed.

They went right to the room of the Duke of Beloeil, who had just then awakened. Michael was still holding in his hand the gold cup, and he revealed the secret of the worn-out shoes.

"Choose, then," said the Duke, "the one you would like."

"My choice is made," said the little gardener, and he offered his hand to the little princess, who blushed and lowered her eyes,

A week later, they were married, and each of the princesses married one of the princes now freed from their enchantment.

Princess Lina did not become a gardener's wife—it was the Crow-boy, on the contrary, who became a prince. But before the ceremony the bride demanded her husband-to-be tell her how he had managed to uncover the mystery.

He showed her the two laurels that had helped him. Being a prudent and sensible girl, she judged that they would give her husband too great an advantage over his wife. She had them cut off at the base and threw them in the fire.

And that is why the girls around here and elsewhere sing this song:

We'll go no more to the woods—
The laurels were cut down

when they dance in circles, in the summer, by the light of the moon.

The Lady of the Lights

I

In olden days, in Paluel, near Cambrai, there was a poor weaver, whose wife was soon going to give him a child. Then, one night, she dreamed that if she ate some of the herb speedwell, which we also call wild veronica, she would bring into the world a girl who would have the most marvelous hair ever seen. According to her dream, the veronica had to be gathered while midnight was sounding, from the garden of the Lady of the Lights. We call water-marshes lights. At that time, these lights extended from Paluel much farther than they do nowadays.

They were bordered on three sides by forest, and in the middle of the lake, on a little island, there grew an enchanted garden, so people said.

For fear of annoying the Lady of the Lights, no one would dare approach her domain. But the weaver's wife so tormented him that on a night as black as the heart of the chimney, he took a boat and rowed toward the island.

He landed there safely, crept as quietly as a wolf into the kitchen-garden, and by the light of a dark-lantern, he gathered some shoots of speedwell, the tenderest he could find.

He had just finished filling his basket, when suddenly the Lady of the Lights appeared.

"What are you doing there?" she said.

"Please forgive me, good madame," he said, "I'm gathering a little speedwell for my wife, who is dying of longing to eat some."

"I will forgive you on one condition—that you give me that which will be born tomorrow in your house, at the same hour as now."

The weaver was not expecting the baby so early, and he had a goat almost ready to give birth. He promised the lady what she demanded and carried away his salad of speedwell.

His wife ate it right away, and the next day, as midnight was sounding, she brought into the world a girl who had beautiful hair, as golden as wheat. The nanny-goat didn't give birth until an hour later.

The weaver and his wife were devastated, but what could they do? Anyhow, they both died in the plague the following year, and Veronica—for that was the name they had baptized the child with—was taken in by a charitable neighbor.

II

Veronica grew up without ever hearing about the Lady of the Lights, but one day when she was on her way to school, her little schoolbag on her arm, she encountered a pretty lady with green eyes, wearing a dress that was damp around the hem.

This lady took Veronica by the hand and led her to her own domain, where she shut her in a crystal tower that had neither door nor staircase. The only way in was through a single window, at the very top.

The tower was so transparent that, whether in sun or shade, it was like so much air, and from a distance, you could not even tell it was there.

III

The Lady of the Lights installed the little girl in the very top of the tower, in front of a table covered with pieces of gossamer cloth.

"You are going to earn your living," she said, "by cutting and sewing my shirts. I like them very fine, and I give them a lot of use. It's a skill I shall quickly teach you."

Indeed, Veronica soon became very good at it, and she spent several years in this way. During this time, her hair went on growing, thick and silky. By the time she was seventeen, her hair, as yellow as fine gold, fell to her heels, and, strange to say, it grew longer still when she wished.

The Lady often came to see her, and she would call from the foot of the tower, "Veronica, let down your hair so I can climb up!"

Veronica would unbind her long golden tresses, wind them around one of the window hooks, and let them fall down outside the tower. Her hair grew longer as it fell, until it reached the ground, and the Lady climbed up this new kind of ladder.

The prisoner's only amusement, when her day's work was finished, was to comb her hair and watch the teals and swans and mallards that swooped down on the tranquil mirror made by the lights.

The poor girl was terribly bored—she thought that she would never get married, and that she would live alone forever in her tower. It seemed to her that if she could get married as other women do, she would have a loving and faithful husband, and that she would make him happy.

Sometimes she sang to ease her boredom—she had a pure, silvery voice that could be heard far out in the forest, and people who were bold enough to venture out that way thought they were hearing the voice of an angel.

IV

One evening, coming home from the hunt, the young Count d'Oisy passed beside the lights. He heard Veronica's song, looked all around him, but could not tell where the enthralling voice came from.

The next day, he returned at the same time and heard the same voice. By nature he was never fearful, and he took a boat and rowed out toward the island of the Lady of the Lights.

When he got close enough, he saw above him, over the water, a girl of marvelous beauty, combing her long golden hair in the purple gleam of the setting sun.

He could not make out the form of the tower, because it was completely transparent, and the girl seemed to him to be suspended in mid-air.

For some minutes he was so astonished that he did not even move, but then he hurried to pull ashore on the island, realizing that the lovely girl with hair of gold was not really suspended over the earth and the water, but was shut in at the top of a crystal tower. He searched for the tower-door, and found there wasn't any.

Suddenly he heard the sound of footsteps and saw the Lady of the Lights, who was coming to visit Veronica. He hid behind a tree. The Lady called:

"Veronica, let down your hair so I can climb up!"

Veronica let down her hair and, to the great surprise of the young Count, it fell all the way to the bottom of the tower, and the Lady climbed up it.

He waited for some time, but seeing that the visitor wasn't ready to leave the girl, he returned to his castle, musing over this strange adventure.

V

The next day, he came again to hang around the shore, and when night was near, he called out, imitating the Lady's voice: "Veronica! Let down your hair so I can climb up!"

Veronica unrolled her sweet-scented hair, and the Count climbed up. At sight of him, the girl gave a cry of fright. Nevertheless, he jumped into the chamber, and, falling on his knees, he tried to reassure her—he succeeded without any trouble.

The evening before, Veronica had seen him, and he seemed to her handsome and elegant in form; and she said to herself, in her heart, that the woman he married would be very happy.

He proposed to free her and bring her to his castle, where they could get married. His words were so gentle and so tender that she was soon persuaded.

The prisoner agreed to have him return the next day with a rope-ladder. They tied it to the window-bar, and both got out that way. Then they got into his boat, and the Count started to row hard.

At the moment when they touched the ground, and found themselves outside the Lady's reach, they looked back and saw her standing on the surface of the water, a few steps behind them.

"Count d'Oisy," she said, "you've carried off my prisoner! Woe unto you, if I catch you again in my domain."

VI

When they reached the castle, the Count d'Oisy married Veronica, as he had promised. The pair loved each other ardently, and heaven blessed their union. Nine months later, the beautiful, golden-haired woman gave her husband twin sons, boys of a rare beauty.

The Countess loved nursing them and singing to them. She spent all her days playing with them, dressing them, and admiring them.

As soon as they could walk without leading strings, she kept watch over them all the day, like a hen with her chicks, keeping them where she could see them, and there was nothing so charming as seeing her walk in the park, followed by her two children, who held on to her by her long golden tresses.

This happiness lasted for five years, but at the end of that time one of the twins happened to die. There was great despair in the castle, and the Countess wept until she had no tears left.

She could not accept the idea that the little body was lying in the cold, damp earth, and so her grief was inconsolable.

VII

One night, the dead child appeared to her: he sat down in his usual place and began to play. He stayed there until morning, and all the night long the Countess wept and watched him.

Some days after, while she was still weeping, the child appeared again. He was wearing the little tunic they had dressed him in when they put him in his coffin, and his head was crowned with a wreath of white roses. He sat down at the foot of the bed.

"Mother," he said, "my little death-shirt is wet with your tears, and that keeps me from sleeping in my grave. Don't weep any more, Mother dear, but transfer all your love to my brother."

Veronica stopped weeping, but her other son fell ill, and slowly got worse. The mother's despair knew no limits. The dead child appeared to her again. This time he held in his hands three golden apples.

"Mother," he said, "here are three apples from the garden of Paradise: give them to my brother when his illness makes him suffer too much."

She took the apples, and when the child started crying, she gave him one. The child played with the apple, and when he was cheerful again he handed it back to his mother, who stored it away as a precious treasure.

VIII

To distract himself from his grief, the Count spent almost every day hunting. He started out at the hour when the cats start hunting and went deep into the woods.

The Countess had not forgotten the memory of the Lady of the Lights. Every morning she said, "Be especially careful, my husband, not to go hunting on the edge of the marshes, I beg you."

And the Count would answer, "Don't be afraid, my dearest, I'll never go there."

One day he startled a doe that was brilliantly white, who fled before him for four hours, always seeming almost ready to let him catch up to her. Carried away by his eagerness, he didn't notice that she was leading him little by little to the edge of the marshes.

Suddenly, through a gap in the bushes, the doe broke through to the lake and plunged panting into the water. The Count fired, wounding the animal, which sank, struggling, to the bottom.

Without stopping to think, he jumped into the water to seize his prize, but he was no sooner in than the lady with green eyes wound her damp arms around him. She drew him so swiftly to the bottom that the mirror of the water was hardly disturbed.

But Veronica started to worry when the Count did not return. Toward midnight, she had the servants take torches and search the forest. When day came, they went on searching, but it was in vain.

In the evening, the Countess thought that, in spite of his promise, the Count must have gone to the shore of the lights as he hunted. She went there, weeping and wringing her hands, and called her beloved by name, but no one answered. She went all the way around the lake and was not afraid to call out to the Lady herself, but there was no answer.

The mirror of the water was motionless, and the horns of the notched disc of the moon were reflected there without a ripple.

Deciding to face the worst, she climbed into a boat and had it rowed to the crystal tower—the tower was no longer there. She ordered the servants to search the whole lake, but she found no husband there, either living or dead.

IX

She went into mourning and wept for forty days and nights. She looked to her child's caresses for some consolation in her grief, but she always had before her eyes the image of her dearly-beloved husband. Every evening she would wander with her son along the lights, unable to get the thought out of her head that he was there, the one she had lost.

One evening when the full moon shone in the sky, the child began to weep and cry so hard that the Countess took out the gold apple to quiet him.

He played with the apple and made it roll along the edge of the water. Suddenly the water started bubbling, a wave rose up that ran in as far as the apple, and carried the apple away with it in receding.

The child ran to recapture his toy. Fearing that her son would be dragged off by the wave, the mother threw herself forward and quickly pulled him back.

The apple had hardly arrived at the bottom when the Count's head rose out of the water. He said nothing, but he stared at his wife with a long, sad look.

Another wave rolled in and covered the husband's head. Then it all disappeared. The lake became as calm as before, and the Countess could not see anything but the peaceful face of the full moon on the water.

Veronica was so moved that she felt ready to faint. She sat down on the dark earth and tried to recover herself. She knew that her dearly-beloved was still alive, and she gave thanks to Heaven.

Sadly, though, he was at the bottom of the lake, in the power of the Lady of the Lights, and it was in vain that the poor wife had the lake searched again.

X

If she threw another gold apple into the water, she had the faint hope of seeing him again, but then she would have only one left to bring joy and health to her little boy!

"Is it really enough," she asked herself, "for him to show his head above the level of the lake? If he can't come back to me, isn't it even crueler than if I didn't know where he is?"

And yet the unfortunate woman couldn't resist the longing to see her husband again. The child began to cry again, and she gave him the second apple.

He rolled it along the edge of the lake, as he had the first. The waters started bubbling, a wave rose up and ran in toward the shore, taking the apple with it when it receded. Almost as soon as the water opened, the Count rose to the surface as far as his belt and stretched out his arms to his wife.

Suddenly another wave roared in, covered him, and took him out of sight.

"Alas!" said the Countess, "Dearly beloved, what good does it do me to find you again and lose you again at once?"

Even so, she felt a longing even stronger to see him again. She had no doubt that this time he would completely appear.

But now one gold apple was all she had left, a single one, and if she sacrificed it, how would she be able to amuse and cure her little boy?

XI

The poor woman looked back and forth, from the lake to her son's pale face, not knowing what to decide.

All at once she lifted him in her arms and fled, crying: "No, no, I must not sacrifice my child's life for the joy of seeing my husband!"

The little boy began to whimper and cry so hard that you might have thought an invisible hand was whipping him until it drew blood. Veronica stopped, set her son on the ground, and, judging that he was far enough from the water to be out of danger, she gave him the last gold apple.

He no sooner had it in his hand, than he ran toward the lake and, before his mother could stop him, threw the apple into it, crying, "Father! Father!"

At once the Count appeared, completely out of the water. Swift as lightning, the Countess threw her long golden hair at him. The Count grabbed hold, slid over the water, and, with one bound, jumped ashore.

He folded his wife and child in his arms, and all three hurried back to the castle of Oisy. Appeased by the gift of the apples from Paradise, the Lady of the Lights let them alone after that.

They lived a long time in happiness, and people say that it's since then that, in memory of her work as a girl weaving in the tower over the lights, Veronica has become the patron of linen and silk workers. Since then, also, in memory of the Countess's great and constant love, veronica has been the flower of fidelity.

The Nettle-Spinner

I

In olden days, in Quesnoy, there was a nobleman named Burchard, but the people around there called him Burchard the Wolf. This nobleman was so hard and cruel that he harnessed the peasants to his plough, so they say, and made them till the earth in their bare feet, urged on by the whip.

His wife, quite the reverse, was good and kind to the unfortunate.

Each time that she got wind of one of her husband's misdeeds, she would go in secret to heal the evil. So all the people of the country blessed her, and as much as they hated the Count, they adored the Countess.

II

It happened one day, when he was hunting near Locquignol, in the forest of Mormal, that the nobleman noticed, in the doorway of an isolated cottage, a girl of rare beauty, spinning hemp.

"What's your name, girl?" he said.

"Renelda, my lord."

"Doesn't it get boring to live like this in a corner of the woods?"

"I'm used to it, my lord, and I'm never bored."

"All the same, come to the castle. I'll make you the Countess's chambermaid."

"I can't do that, good my lord. I have to take care of my grandmother, who is ill."

"Come to the castle, I tell you. I'll expect you this evening."

And the nobleman continued on his way.

Renelda realized that his intentions were bad, and it was not only to take care of her grandmother that she was reluctant to obey him. Besides, she was engaged to a young woodcutter who lived nearby, named Gilbert.

Three days later, the Count passed by the cottage.

"Why haven't you come to the castle?" he asked the pretty spinner.

"I told you, my lord, because I have to take care of my grandmoth-er."

"Come tomorrow. I'll make you the Countess's maid of honor."

And he went away.

This offer was just as ineffective. Renelda didn't go to the castle.

"If you're willing to come," said the Count, a few days later, "I'll divorce the Countess and marry you."

Two years earlier, Renelda's mother had died, after a long illness. The Countess had sent things to the cottage to help them out during all that time. Even if the Count had seriously wanted to marry her, Renelda would have refused him.

III

Burchard stayed away for some weeks without coming to the cot-tage again. Renelda had started to think she was free of him, when one day he came by the cottage-door, with his duck-gun under his arm and his game-bag on his shoulder. Renelda this time was busy spinning, not hemp, but flax.

"What are you spinning, girl?" he said gruffly.

"My wedding dress, my lord."

"So you're going to get married?"

"Yes, my lord, if you allow it."

In those days the peasants couldn't get married unless their lord gave his permission.

"I'll give permission on one condition. Do you see those big nettles over there, that grow on the tombs in the cemetery? Go pick them, and spin enough to make two fine robes. One will be your wedding dress, and the other my winding-sheet. You can get married the day I'm buried in the ground."

And the Count went away, with a laugh and a sneer.

Renelda trembled. No one in Locquignol had ever heard tell of spinning thread from nettles. Besides, the Count had an iron constitution and, glorying in his strength, he had often said that he expected to live to a hundred.

Gilbert came to visit every evening, after his day's work, to visit his bride-to-be. That evening he came to visit, as usual. Renelda told him what Burchard had said,

"Would you like me to ambush him," he said, "and split open his head with a blow of my axe?"

"No," said Renelda, "I don't want blood on my wedding bouquet. Besides, the Count is sacred to me—the Countess was so good to my mother!"

The old woman spoke up, the mother of Renelda's grandmother. She was more than ninety years old, and she would spend the whole day resting in her armchair, bobbing her head up and down without saying a word. "My children," she said, "as long as I've lived, I've never heard of a use for nettles, but if that's what God wants, people can do it. Renelda, why don't you try?"

II

Renelda tried, and, to her great surprise, the mildewed nettles, when peeled, produced a soft, light, sturdy thread. Soon Renelda had spun enough for the first robe, the marriage robe. She wove it and cut it out right away, hoping that the Count would not force her to start on the other one. She had just finished sewing it when Burchard the Wolf came by.

"Well," he said, "how are you doing with the robes?"

"Here is my marriage-robe, my lord," said Renelda, handing him the robe, which was one of the finest and loveliest.

The Count paled, His only reply was to say harshly, "Good. Start on the other."

The spinning-girl went to work on it at once. On his way back to the castle, the Count felt a shudder and felt, as we say around here, that death was standing just behind him. He wanted to eat supper, and couldn't. He went to bed, trembling with fever. He slept very badly, and in the morning he couldn't get up.

This sudden illness, that kept getting worse, disturbed him. No doubt Renelda's spinning-wheel came to his thoughts. Perhaps the body would be ready at the same time as the burial-robe?

Burchard at once sent an order to her to stop the spinning-wheel.

Renelda obeyed. That evening, Gilbert asked: "Has the Count consented to our marriage?"

"No," said Renelda.

"Go on with the work, dear heart. It's the only way we'll get his consent—he said so himself."

V

The next day, when she'd done the household chores, the spinning-girl sat down at the wheel again. Two hours later, some men-at-arms came and found her spinning. They seized her, tied her arms and legs, and carried her to the edge of the Rhonelle, which was swollen by the rains.

When they got there, they threw her in the river and watched her sink to the bottom. Then they went away, but Renelda floated up to the surface of the water, and, although she didn't know how to swim, she managed to get to the bank of the river.

She returned to the cottage and went back to work spinning the thread.

The men-at-arms seized her again, took her to the river, tied a stone around her neck, and flung her like a dog into the water.

When they left, the stone came loose, and Renelda again waded to shore, returned to the cottage, and set to work at her spinning-wheel again,

The Count resolved to go himself to Locquignol. As he was much weakened and could not walk, he had himself taken in a litter. Meanwhile, the spinning-girl was still spinning.

Seeing that, Burchard aimed a bullet at her, at point-blank range, as if at a wild beast. The bullet ricocheted and did no harm to the spinning-girl, who went on spinning.

Burchard rushed inside, in a fit of fury so strong he almost died of it. He broke the wheel in a thousand pieces, and fell fainting on the ground. They carried him back, unconscious, to the castle.

The next day, the wheel was fixed, and the spinning-girl was spinning again. The Count, feeling that his life was coming to an end, ordered his guards to go tie her hands and keep a watch on her.

The guards fell asleep, the ropes dropped off by themselves, and the spinning-girl went on spinning.

Burchard had all the nettles uprooted for three leagues around, but they had hardly been uprooted before they sprouted up again and grew tall so fast the eye could see it happening.

They sprouted up as far as the cleared ground around the cottage, and as they were picked as fast as they grew, the wheel's distaff was always fully loaded with dank nettles peeled and ready to spin.

Meanwhile, the Count grew worse and worse, and he could see his end was near.

VI

Moved with pity for her husband, the Countess finally learned the cause of his illness. She begged him to allow himself to be cured. The haughty lord refused even more sternly than before to give consent to Renelda's marriage.

The lady decided to go without telling him to beg the spinning-girl to help him. In the name of Renelda's dead mother, she begged her to stop the work. Renelda promised her she would, but that evening Gilbert, in his turn, came to visit her.

Seeing that the fabric wasn't any further along that evening, he asked why that was. Renelda admitted that the Countess had begged her to let her husband live.

"Has he agreed to our marriage?"

"No."

"In that case, let him die!"

"What will the Countess say?"

"The Countess will understand that it's not your fault, not at all—the Count himself is to blame for his death!"

"Let's wait. Maybe his heart will change."

They waited a month, two months, six months, a year. The spinning-girl stopped spinning, and the Count stopped persecuting her, but he still didn't agree to her marriage. Gilbert grew impatient.

The poor girl loved him with all her soul—she was even sadder than she'd been before, even though the Count was no longer having her tormented.

"Let's make an end of this," Gilbert would say.

"Let's wait a little more," said Renelda.

The young man was tired of it. He came more rarely to Locquignol, and soon he stopped coming at all. Renelda felt death in her soul, but she was steadfast.

One day, she happened to meet the Count. She clasped her hands together as if standing before the Holy Virgin and said, "My lord, please, please!"

Burchard looked away and passed her by.

She could have lowered his pride by going back to her spinning wheel, but she didn't.

Some time later, she learned that Gilbert had left the country. He did not come to bid her goodbye, but she knew the day and the hour when he left, and she hid herself along the road to see him one last time.

When she got home, she saw that her wheel was standing empty in the corner, and she wept for three days and three nights.

VII

Another year went by in the same way. One time, the Count fell ill. The Countess thought that Renelda, at the end of her strength, had gone back to spinning. She came to see her and found the wheel empty.

The Count's malady grew so much worse that his physicians said there was no hope. They rang the bells to call for his soul's pardon, and he awaited the hour to go to God. Yet he was not dying as quickly as they had expected.

His case seemed desperate, yet it went on and on without a change.

He could no longer live, but he could not die. He suffered horribly, and begged Death to come and take him.

In this extremity, he remembered that he had told the little spinning-girl long before: if Death was slow in coming for him, it would be because he was not ready to follow him—because his winding sheet was not finished.

He sent a servant to fetch Renelda to his bedside, and ordered her to go on spinning his robe.

She set to work, and the Count at the same moment felt his pains greatly eased.

Then he felt his heart soften. He regretted all the evil he had done out of pride, and asked Renelda to pardon him. Renelda pardoned him, and went on spinning, night and day.

With the nettles spun, she wove the cloth on her loom, then cut out the robe and started sewing it together.

The more she sewed, the more the Count felt his suffering—and his life—weakening. His last sigh came when the needle put in the last stitch.

VIII

At the same hour, Gilbert came back, and, as he had never stopped loving Renelda, they were married a week later.

He had lost two years of happiness, but he consoled himself by keeping in mind that he had married a clever spinning-girl and, something even rarer, a good and valiant woman.

La Ramée's Tale

I

In olden times, there was an old soldier named La Ramée, who had been freed from the service and was on his way home.

It has to be supposed that at that time the King was not rich, for all that brave La Ramée had been paid for his long service was a ration of bread and sixteen sous.

Having put the bread in his sack and the sous in his pouch, the veteran set out on the road to Boucaude, the village where he had been born. He had not covered more than half a league when he ran into a blind beggar who asked him for alms.

Being a good devil of a fellow, he shared his ration of bread and his sixteen sous with the beggar.

Half a league farther along, he saw another beggar. This one, like the first, was blind, and, what was more, he had only one hand.

La Ramée was moved with pity, and he gave the poor wretch half of the bread and four of the eight sous he still had left.

Traveling another half a league, he saw a third beggar on the road. This one was blind, one-handed, and lame, into the bargain. He shared with the poor fellow the rest of his bread and his coins.

"Now all I have left," he said, "is a hunk of bread and two sous to drink a pint. Well, let's hurry to a tavern, because otherwise if I meet another poor soul on the way, I'll be running a great risk of having nothing but memories to eat."

He went in, put his sack on the floor, and when he had eaten—not as well as a prince would have—he lit his pipe and started on his way again.

II

He had walked for hardly a quarter of an hour, when he saw coming toward him from the side an old soldier who seemed to have left the service. This soldier looked vaguely like the three beggars who—something La Ramée had not noticed before—also had a family resemblance.

"Comrade," said the old soldier, "I'm guessing your sack is as well filled as your belly—wouldn't you have the kindness to share a pint of beer with me, and a slice of bread to go with it? I'm dying of hunger and thirst!"

"It's too late to have supper, my boy," said La Ramée. "This morning I had sixteen sous and a ration of bread, but I shared them with three blind men I met along the way. Now my sack and my pouch are both empty, and—"

"—and like me you're trying to find a way to fill them?"

"Exactly."

"Suppose we go see if we can find some friends."

"I wouldn't say no, my boy. What's your name?"

"Peter. And you?"

"La Ramée. Well, then, it's a bargain. We'll go begging."

"No, let's not. It's a nasty profession—makes the farm dogs bark."

"Do you have another?"

"I know a little about medicine, and sometimes that brings in a little money. Come with me, and we'll share."

"Agreed!" said La Ramée, who was not in any hurry to get back to Boucade, and they set off on their way together, on foot, like the King's dogs.

III

When they got to the forest of Vicoigne, they came to a little house and heard cries and groans coming from inside.

They went in and saw a woman tearing her hair out beside the bed of her husband, who was sick and dying. Weeping, she told them that she'd been told that his belly had been gashed open by a wild boar.

"Is that all?" said Peter. "Don't cry, good woman—I'm going to save him."

He dug into his pouch and pulled out a little box of ointment. He rubbed some on the dying man, who, the next moment, jumped out of bed. He and his wife fell at the knees of their benefactor.

"How can we repay you?" they cried. "What can we give you?"

"Why, nothing," said Peter. "You don't have all that much for yourselves, good people."

La Ramée made a face at Peter's reply. He had a charitable nature, but when your stomach's hollow and your pockets empty, you really don't want to work for free.

"What kind of song are you singing?" he said, jogging his companion's elbow. "Always accept something, my boy—we aren't exactly rolling in gold ourselves."

But Peter wasn't listening to him, and the more the good couple urged him, the more he refused.

Finally, the peasant brought out a hare he'd killed the evening before and absolutely insisted that Peter take it.

"Take it, you imbecile," whispered La Ramée. "That'll do to fill our sack."

"I'm not stopping you from taking it," said Peter impatiently, "but I warn you, I won't be responsible for it."

"I'll be responsible for it, if you won't," said La Ramée. He stuffed the hare in his sack, and they left.

IV

On their way through the forest, they spotted in a clearing a fire of wood shavings, or rather, scraps of wood left by some sawyers.

"It's high time we had a bite," said La Ramée, "My stomach feels as if it's lined with cobwebs. Suppose we put the hare on a spit to roast?"

"Yes, let's," said Peter, "but I'm not one to meddle with cooking. You get the meal ready, and, as for me, I'm going to take a little nap over there, under that big beech-tree. Just be careful to keep the hare's heart for me—that much will be enough for me."

When his companion had left, La Ramée skinned the hare, cleaned it, lit the fire, and set about roasting the hare. While he was turning the spit, and turning it, he was wondering, "Why the devil did he tell me to keep the heart for him?"

When the hare was done, he took it off the fire and looked for the heart, and set it aside. He ate one thigh first, then the other, then the back. After that, he glanced at the heart out of the corner of his eye.

"It must be a nice morsel," he thought, "or maybe it's that my friend has no appetite. Or maybe—who knows?—there's some special power in a hare's heart."

He took a bit of it no bigger than the head of a pin, held it on his tongue, and found it tasted so good, he couldn't resist eating the rest. It made one mouthful.

Peter came back when La Ramée had just finished swallowing it.

"Good, isn't it!" he said, "but where's the heart?"

"The heart—oh, yes!—I looked for it, but you were making fun of me, my boy. You know very well that hares don't have hearts."

"What! Hares don't have hearts! But all animals have them—everyone knows that."

"Oh, nonsense! Don't people say that a coward has no more heart than a hare? So, as a child of God, surely you must see, hares just don't have hearts."

"Well, all right," said Peter.

La Ramée packed the rest of the meat into his sack, and they lit their pipes and set out again.

V

Right in the middle of the Arnonville marsh, La Ramée stopped with a cry of surprise. At the spot where a little stream normally ran, this time there was a great torrent foaming past that barred the way.

"After you, my boy," said Peter.

"Not me! After you," said La Ramée. And he thought to himself: "If there's no solid footing, I'll stay on this side."

Peter then waded into the torrent and crossed it.

Seeing that the water only came up to his knees, La Ramée stepped forward, but the water rose suddenly, and he was in up to his shoulders.

"Help!" said the poor man.

"Admit it," said Peter, "you ate the hare's heart."

La Ramée, ashamed of the lie, didn't want to agree to this. "I swear to you," he said, "I didn't eat it."

The water kept rising, and the unlucky man was in up to his chin.

"Admit that you ate it," Peter said again.

"No, I didn't eat it," said La Ramée.

But the last word went unheard, because he swallowed a big gulp of water, and it made him sneeze like a cat that's lapped up a bit of vinegar.

The water started going down then, and the stubborn old fellow got away unharmed, except for the fright he'd had.

VI

They went on walking. Three arrow-shots' length from Péruwelz, they heard that the only daughter of the burgomaster was sick and like to die. The burgomaster, people said, had so much money he measured it by the shovelful, and his daughter was as dear to him as his eyes.

"Look here," said La Ramée, "this is our lucky day. If we can cure the girl, it's sure and certain that her Papa will put enough in our sack for us to live on for a long time. Come on, a clever fellow like you! The bells are ringing for us—let's get a move on, so that we get there ahead of the Grim Reaper."

But his companion did not put one foot in front of the other any the faster. They had hardly got into town, when they heard the sick girl had just died.

"Now see what you've done—this is your fault," grumbled La Ramée. "You're like a conscript who's being forced to mount an attack."

"Bah! Trying to go too fast just makes it take longer," said Peter. "Don't get in a stew, my boy! Besides, I know something better than healing the sick—I have something in my pocket that can wake the dead."

"You can wake the dead! You old fox! That's not small beer. Are you a sorcerer, then?"

"Quite possibly."

"Oh!—but then our fortune is made!" cried La Ramée, dancing a little jig. "Mynheer Burgomaster is going to fill our sack with gold louis."

"Filling the sack is all you ever think about," said Peter. "Remember that there'd be more profit in thinking a little about eternal salvation."

"Fine! Eternal salvation!—we'll have plenty of time to think about that, my boy. But before we start worrying about dying well, we need to pay attention to living well. If the sack would fill itself all by itself, I wouldn't say no. But there's no need to be in a hurry to get to Paradise."

VII

They walked along, laying their plans, and at length arrived at the house of death, and asked to speak to the Burgomaster. Peter proposed to him to bring his daughter back to life. As he had nothing else to try, and nothing could make matters worse, the father agreed to let them try the experiment.

Peter made everyone go out of the room, except for La Ramée. When they were alone, he took a little vial out of his bag, and poured a few drops into the dead girl's mouth. Then he said three times: "In the name of the Father, and the Son, and the Holy Ghost, arise!"

On the third time, the dead girl rose up, shining with freshness and beauty. Her father was overjoyed.

"Name your own reward," he said to Peter, "anything you like—I'm ready to give it you, even if it's half my fortune."

"That would be too much, Mynheer," said Peter. "Twenty coppers is all it's worth."

"Twenty coppers for waking the dead! That's crazy!" cried La Ramée. "Take what's offered you, you triple idiot!"

The Burgomaster insisted on giving them more, but all Peter would accept was twenty coppers, neither more nor less.

Seeing that arguing was useless, he fell back on La Ramée, and filled his sack with florins.

VIII

Going on from there, they headed toward Brussels in Brabant. When they got into the forest of Baudour, Peter struck a light, lit his pipe, and said to his companion: "Now we're going to divide the florins between us."

"Oho!" said La Ramée. "So you've stopped spitting on money? Yes, my boy, let's divide them up."

Peter emptied the sack, counted the coins, and made three heaps.

"He's made three piles, but there are only two of us," thought La Ramée. "Who the devil does he want to give the third share to?"

"I've divided it up," said Peter. "Here's yours, here's mine, and here's the part for the one who ate the hare's heart."

"That's me!" cried La Ramée, and presto! he pocketed the coins.

"What, my boy!—so it was you? But you know very well that hares don't have hearts."

"Who sang you that song, my dear fellow? Yes, of course, hares have hearts. Don't we say of a coward: He has the heart of a hare? So you can see that hares do have hearts."

"That's great. Take the lot," said Peter. "I don't want any more of your company. You're too bad for me."

"If that's what you want, my boy—have a safe journey!" said the old soldier, and they went different ways. "I'm not sorry he's gone," thought La Ramée. "He's definitely an odd duck!"

IX

When he got to Brussels in Brabant, La Ramée had nothng more urgent to do than to make his coins skip. Like a true Flamand, he spent his days at the tavern, drinking pale ale from Louvain in the morning, plain local beer in the afternoon, and strong Belgian beer after supper. He started gambling to pass the time, and soon he had managed, as we say around here, to eat up the sack and all the contents.

Meanwhile, it happened that the son of the Duke of Brabant suddenly fell deathly ill. "Here's a good opening," La Ramée said to himself, "just in time for me to feather my nest again! I'll bring him back to life, and they'll give me a fine reward."

He had long since learned his paternoster prayers, and so he had easily memorized the words his companion had pronounced in healing the Burgomaster's daughter. Also, he found that he accidentally put the little vial in his sack.

So he went to see the Duke of Brabant and proposed to resuscitate the young prince. The Duke had heard tell about how a soldier who was out of the army was running around the country bringing life to the dead. He naturally thought that it was La Ramée and told him to go ahead.

Only, as he didn't want to be tricked, he warned him that if it didn't work, the doctor would be hanged from the highest belfry.

La Ramée, sure of himself, accepted this condition.

X

Left alone with the dead, the doctor opened his sack, drew out the vial, poured a few drops on the boy's mouth, then said three times, loudly, "In the name of the Father, and the Son, and the Holy Ghost, Amen."

The dead body didn't budge.

La Ramée, surprised, repeated the formula, but the dead body stayed still.

The doctor then remembered that the last word pronounced by his companion had not been Amen, but something else that began with A.

It was in vain that he tried the invocation several more times—the rascally word wouldn't come. Poor La Ramée tried "Ascend!—Appear!—Alive" He didn't think of trying "Above!"

Finally, in a rage, he exclaimed, "In the devil's name, stand up, or I'll brain you!"

But the dead boy was as unbudging as a brick.

XI

The unlucky doctor had the look of a dying hare, when all at once he saw his comrade Peter only two steps away.

"Would you believe," he told him, "that this pigheaded dead boy doesn't want to come to life? Yet I made him drink your elixir, and I spoke the words!"

"Fine words," said Peter, "calling him to come to life in the devil's name! I'm happy to get you out of this scrape, just this once, but I warn you, if you do it again, I won't get you out of it. Furthermore, I forbid you to take more than twenty coppers in payment."

Peter cried three times: "In the name of the Father and the Son and the Holy Ghost. Arise!"

The young prince stood up, and Peter disappeared.

The Duke was beside himself with joy. "What reward would you like?" he asked La Ramée.

"Twenty coppers," he said, with a sigh. But under his breath he said, "What an absurd animal that sorcerer is! What he gives you with one hand, he takes back with the other."

But the Duke laughed at him, and had an enormous purse full of gold louis brought. La Ramée's eyes shone like stars, but he kept his promise.

"Above all," he cried, "don't put that purse in my sack!"

So naturally the Duke's treasurer did just that.

He buckled the sack and fastened it by force on La Ramée's back as he left.

XII

The doctor had hardly passed the first turn in the road when he found himself face to face with his comrade.

"What a frightful old clutch-fist you are," Peter said. "I told you not to take more than twenty coppers, and here you are, carrying a bushel of gold."

"Is it my fault," said La Ramée, "if they put the gold in my sack by force?"

"Your sack! your sack! You never think of anything but that damned sack, and you don't worry about your salvation any more than if you were a horse or a dog! You were worth a hundred times more when you had only sixteen fine sous. Then you shared your money with the poor, but now you're going to spend it all on drink, and making a mess of everything, and leading a life that will lead you right to the great devils of hell."

"I tell you again, my boy, I don't think emptying my sack can do anything to prevent me from being saved—it's the need to fill it up again that might do that. How can you honestly expect a poor man to find the time to think about the other world, when he's always in danger of dying of hunger in this one? Ah! if all I had to do was say: 'I want that in my sack!' I'd give you my word that I'll go straight to Paradise, with my sack on my back."

"You're sure of that?"

"You're a sorcerer—you could put it to the test. You'll see that I'll be as prettily behaved as a nun who's just taken her vows."

"Very well," said Peter. "But I warn you—look out for stormy weather! Keep in mind that a sack bursts when it gets too full. Farewell—you will not see me again in this world."

"So be it," said La Ramée. And he muttered under his breath: "Go away, you old misery—go away, you preacher, and go hunt for iron to shoe the flies in the Baudour marshes. You won't find much!"

XIII

La Ramée planned to be economical in spending his money, but the local beer, the strong Belgian beer, and the pale ale from Louvain soon got the better of his good intentions. He began by throwing the whole house out the windows, then made every day a seven-chandelier festival, and ended by turning it all into so much dust.

Six months later, all he had left of his fortune was a few louis. He decided to set out for Boucaud and go into planting cabbages there.

On the way he stopped at all the taverns, regular as a brewer's horse. In this way he emptied many pint-pots and the rest of what he had in his sack, so completely that he had only sixteen sous when he got to Saint Ghislaine, in the Borinage.

He stopped at the inn called Great Saint Julian, after the patron saint of boatmen, and ordered a bottle of beer, two sous worth of bread, and six of ham.

It was precisely the day of the saint's festival, and every time that the door to the kitchen was opened, the scent of geese roasting on the spit filled the building.

When he'd finished his meal, La Ramée was still hungry. All the while he was lighting his pipe, he kept a watch on the kitchen out of the corner of his eye, and he saw four fat geese browning on the fire.

"Ah!" he sighed. "I'd be so happy to get a couple of those geese, if all I had to do was say: I want that in my sack."

XIV

He paid the tavern-keeper, picked up his sack, and left.

When he got outside, it seemed to him that his sack was a lot too heavy for an empty sack. It didn't help to shift it from one shoulder to the other—it still felt heavy.

"Let's take a little look," he said, "and see what's going on in there."

He opened it and was astonished to find two geese inside.

"Well, isn't that nice," he thought. "If all I have to do to get the sack full again is to make a wish, I must surely be on the road to Paradise, maybe even getting before that to the Earthly Paradise."

He walked about thirty paces along the Hayne, sat down on a bridge-piling, chose the fattest of the geese, and bit into it eagerly.

He had not been tearing into it for three minutes when two barge-men, or, rather, two downstream tow-men, happened to pass by. They didn't have a sou to spend to celebrate Saint Julian's day, so they had their fishing-poles out to catch enough to make a feast of sorts.

At sight of the old soldier, still gobbling his fine Saint-Martin's-goose, they stopped. "What a guinse!" one of them cried. That's what we say around here for "What good grub!"

"You'd like a taste, hey, my boy?" said La Ramée.

"We wouldn't say no, city-boy," said the other. He was a bold, sarcastic fellow. Seeing that La Ramée went on stuffing his belly without offering them any, he added, "By the way, my boy, do you know why geese, as long as they live, never stop cackling?"

"No, my boy. Why?"

"Well, my boy, it's because they asked the fox to hold off eating them until they finished praying. The fox agreed and gave them his word. So one of them started off: cackle, cackle, cackle, cackle; another took up the verse, cackle, cackle, cackle; a third and fourth followed, and so on forever, and that, my boy, is why geese are not as dumb as foxes, and boatmen are not as foxy as city-boys."

La Ramée seemed so pleased with this explanation that he gave the other goose to the tow-men and told them to go to the town and drink to his health.

Actually, he was annoyed at having a boatman make fun of him and treat him like a foolish city-boy, and that gave the rascal an idea.

XV

The tow-men had appetites that gaped as wide as a lawyer's purse. They hardly took the time to thank La Ramée, and hurried off with the goose to the tavern, where, to moisten each mouthful properly, they asked for a good bottle of wine.

The tavern-keeper served it to them, and they fell to on their goose as poverty does on the world. The tavern-keeper was astonished to see a couple of tow-men with such a feast and went into the kitchen to make sure his four geese were still on the spit.

Finding only two, he went over to the tow-men, still eating away, and said to them, with his fists on his hips, "That dinner didn't cost you much, hey?—that dinner you've got there!"

"Only the trouble of putting out a hand to take it, my boy."

"That's just what I thought. But you're going to pay me for it right now, or I'll beat you up."

"Pay for what?"

"My goose, by God!"

"This isn't your goose. An old soldier gave it to us."

"Nonsense! He left here empty-handed, that soldier—I saw him."

"Empty or full, it's all the same to us. We didn't take anything from you, and we won't pay for it."

"We'll see about that, you scamps!" The tavern-keeper grabbed a stick and started drubbing the tow-men.

Hidden behind a big tree, La Ramée watched the fight from a distance and burst out laughing.

But then he remembered that he had promised to be good, and he set off again to Boucade, planning to go straight there.

XVI

It was a long time since his household had fallen apart—that's to say, there was no longer anyone at home he knew, no father, no mother, no brother, no sister to welcome him back.

He set up house in a little deserted hut and thought about ways to get an honest living. It wasn't an easy matter.

When he found himself alone with a fine chicken or turkey, his mouth watered, and it was hard to keep from crying: "I want that in my sack."

He managed, however, and instead of cheating others, he contented himself with going fishing or hunting to fill his sack. All he had to do was say: "Fish swimming in the water, birds flying in the air, I want you in my sack," and pheasants and pike-fish would fall into the trap.

He soon put together enough coins to build a little house, and he would have lived there as cozy as a chicken in a pie-crust, if only the devil, who never sleeps, had not tempted him again.

XVII

One morning he had gone to Mortagne to sell a bunch of partridges, and at the market he ran into a pretty young butter-seller, as fresh as new cream. Her sweet face made him think it was time to take a wife.

He confided this thought to her, but she didn't think he was young enough. She laughed in his face and said he was too late.

When he found he couldn't persuade her to follow him to see the priest, La Ramée again forgot to care about his salvation. He glared at the butter-seller, and whispered, "I want you in my sack!"

With a crack! there she was, and the delighted veteran carried her off to Boucade.

Unluckily, he was dealing with a girl who was a handful. Furious at his clever trick, she resolved to be revenged.

When they got to the old soldier's house, she winked her eye at him and said, "The rats aren't going to eat your hat, my boy."

"Why is that, my girl?"

"Because you've got a tomcat under it."

"You think so?" said La Ramée.

"And what's more I really believe you're going to make your wife happy. But how did you manage to stuff me in your sack?"

As she spoke, she gazed at him, looking so sweet and coaxing that the old soldier let himself be persuaded without fighting it, and he told her what the sack's power was.

The artful butter-seller seized the sack then, and, fixing a malicious look in her turn on her kidnapper, she said, "I want La Ramée in the sack!"

And there he was in the sack.

Without losing a moment, the naughty girl went and threw the sack down a well.

And ever since then, when a man who's too old for it takes up with a young wife and dies during the honeymoon, it's a common saying, that "he fell down the well."

XVIII

Once he was dead, in order to get to either Hell or Paradise, La Ramée first had to get out of the sack. Then he put it, dripping wet, on his back, and went bravely off to ring the bell at the gate of Paradise.

Who was surprised?—our friend La Ramée, when the gate-keeper turned out to be his old traveling companion Peter.

"Well, well!—So it's you!" he said. "You've got a famous position here, my boy. And there I was, taking you for a sorcerer! What luck! I hope, son of God, that you're not going to leave an old friend at the door?"

"I really have to, son of God," Saint Peter said, holding the door barely half open. "Why did you only think about filling your sack, instead of your salvation?"

"But I did think about it—about my salvation! I just didn't think about it all the time."

"Nicely put! And look at what you got by that game—you didn't even managed to get here with a full sack!"

256

"You just wait, you old loudmouth, I'm going to fill my sack up," La Ramée said under his breath, and then added, aloud, "Once, twice— aren't you going to open the gate for me?"

"No, my boy, no."

"In that case—I want you in my sack!"

And there was Saint Peter in the sack!

"Now, see here, you rascal," cried Saint Peter, "is that how you abuse—"

But La Ramée had stopped listening. Sack on his back, he marched boldly into Paradise.

Finding the door open, at once all the sinners who'd been wandering, like souls in torment, along the walls, came slipping in behind him.

At the sight of these not-so-very-Catholic people streaming in: "Who are all those Christians there?" cried God the Father. "Why isn't Saint Peter at his post? Someone go find him!"

But it was in vain that they rooted through every nook and corner. No one could find the doorkeeper-saint anywhere.

XIX

God the Father was starting to feel worried, when La Ramée came bravely forward.

"Lord God," he said, "I know where Saint Peter is. Promise me that you'll keep me here in your Paradise, and I'll tell you."

"Tell me this instant," said God the Father.

"Oh, well!—it's a question of what's in my sack," said La Ramée, unbuckling it.

"Scram, you scoundrel!" cried Saint Peter, jumping out of the sack.

"No," said God the Father, "let him stay! I gave him my word."

"What! Lord, are you going to pardon that rogue?"

"I pardoned the Wandering Jew, when he gave his five sous to a poor man! If La Ramée has sinned, he has also practiced charity, which is the first of all the virtues."

XX

And that is how, as it's been told, that that devil of a La Ramée entered, with his sack on his back, into Paradise.

257

The Wolf-Oak

I

In olden days, at the foot of Mount Péruwelz, on the side facing Belgium, in a hollow, there was a big oak covered with ivy that people called the Wolf-Oak. This oak rose opposite the steep slope, and its height matched the hill so exactly that from the top you could step directly into the branches.

One morning, an extraordinary—in fact, unbelievable—thing happened. A wolf that was chasing a hare jumped out too far from the hill and landed in the tree, caught its hind foot in the tangles or twists of the ivy vines, and, in spite of all its efforts, could not get loose.

In those days, people weren't going on pilgrimages to Our Lady of Bon-Secours, Mount Péruwelz was deserted, and there wasn't a living soul to be seen there. The wolf had to hang there through two full rounds of the clock, and his guts were growling in his belly like a load of pebbles in a wheelbarrow, when he thought he heard a noise some ways off.

He put up his two forepaws in front of his muzzle, summoned up all his strength, and cried, "Help!"

II

The man—for it was a man—ran forward, hearing that cry, and seeing the poor animal in such a pitiful state he burst out laughing. "What could anyone say you're doing there, my boy," he asked, "and since when do wolves go climbing trees and perching in the branches?"

"I didn't do it on purpose, good master," said the wolf. "I was chasing that skunk of a bandit who's been ravaging all the countryside. I fell into the tree, and my paw got caught in one of these damned vines."

"You've got to admit you make a fine starling, my boy."

"I can't dispute that, good master, but get me out of here right away, I beg you—if you don't, I'm a dead wolf."

"Who's to say that once I get you unhooked you won't feel like eating me up?"

"Oh! what do you take me for? Anyhow, I only eat harmful ani-mals—weasels, skunks, martens, ferrets. Far from eating people, on the contrary, I'm very useful to them"

"What good does that do me? I don't have a hen-house or a sheep-fold—I'm nothing but a poor basket-maker."

"A basket-maker! Oh!—now I recognize you! You live at Cigogne, just across from fat Medard, the shepherd. Get me out of here, good mas-ter, and I promise you I'll never touch any of honest Medard's sheep."

"It's all the same to me. Fat Medard's sheep get into the wheat."

"Oh! they get into the wheat! How well things turn out! If I should go right to the side of his sheepfold, you just see what will happen!"

"Do you swear you won't eat me?"

"I'll spit on it to seal the deal."

And with his free paw the wolf touched his muzzle, as the custom is around here.

The good basket-maker got him loose. Once he was on the ground, the animal yawned, stretched, licked one paw, tried taking a few steps and at last felt able to hobble away, hop and step.

The two friends set off toward the town of Cigogne, without a backward look.

III

After only a quarter of an hour, feeling his paw was now getting better, the wolf began glancing at his savior with a hungry look. "Do you know, my boy, that you're a fine-looking man," he said, "and they must eat well in Cigogne, if I can judge by your belly."

"Er—um—" said the man.

"Really a superb man—plump as a monk in Crespin's abbey!—and I'm so hungry!"

"Oh, come on, now! Let's not have any of your jokes, my friend." You know what you swore to me."

"I know, I know—but my guts aren't happy at all. They're ringing so loud that I can't hear the voice of my conscience. I really think I'm going to break my promise."

"Don't do that, my boy. What about gratitude? Remember, in all honesty, that wouldn't be fair. I don't think there's a wolf in the world who would be so ill-advised as to have an idea like that."

"That's what you think?"

"I could swear to it. Look, if you like, there's a good dog who's limping along towards us, who could be the judge. She's an old dog, so she must be a dog of experience."

"All right! Consult her, but hurry up."

And they stopped the dog.

"Madame Dog," said the basket-maker, "here's a wolf who had a paw caught in the oak by Mount Péruwelz. He would certainly have had to give up the ghost if I hadn't freed him. And now, for my pains, he wants to eat me. Is that fair?

"You're making a bad choice, Mynheer," said the dog. "I'm in no condition to judge. I served my master well and faithfully until today, and now, look!—in my old age he's thrown me out the door so he doesn't have to feed me anymore! Go find someone else to judge you."

And the dog, with a bow, took her leave.

"Good heavens!" said the basket-maker, "I know her. That's Fat Medard's dog. But where would you find anyone as miserly as Medard? Since she recuses herself, would you like us to submit the case to that honest mare browsing the grass over there in the pasture?"

"All right! But let's be quick about it," said the wolf, sharpening his teeth.

IV

They called the mare over, and the man explained the matter to her.

"You couldn't make a worse choice, child of God," said the mare. "I've spent my life plowing the earth for my master, and now that I'm not good for work anymore, he's talking about having me slaughtered. I would be a very bad judge of your dispute."

"Well, well! What do you say to that, child of God?" said the wolf.

"Servants are rascals—they're never content," said the basket-maker. "Look! There's a fox peeking out of his den. Let's call him—he's a free animal, and he'll judge between us with a free heart."

"I'd gladly consult with him, but I warn you that I have six long ells of empty guts inside me, and my teeth are getting larger and larger!—If my friend the fox condemns you, I promise you that you'll be in for it!

They cried to the fox to come over, and the man put the case to him.

V

Friend Fox thought for a moment. At last he said, "I understand the wolf's appetite, for it has to be admitted, my good man, that you make a fine morsel."

"Yes, doesn't he!" said the wolf, charmed by the beginning.

"But—I confess it to my shame—I don't understand equally well how you managed to get your paw caught in the branches. I don't think I can judge you without having seen with my own eyes how it happened. Take me to Mount Péruwelz."

"I'd be glad to," said the wolf.

When they got to Mount Péruwelz, in reach of the oak, the fox considered the tree for a long time. "Honestly," he said, scratching his ear, "I still don't understand how the wolf got hung up there."

"But it's very simple," said the wolf, without suspicion, "it was like this."

He jumped into the tree.

"And then?" said the fox.

"And then like this," said the wolf, and he let himself fall forward, head down.

"So that's how you were hanging?"

"Yes, my boy."

"Oh, well! Then you can stay there, my boy," said the fox.

"What superb judgment!—admirable judgment!" cried the basket-maker, enchanted. "This business is your doing, good master, and no one could be more sensible."

"Oh!" said the fox modestly, "it's not all that difficult. The wolf was an imbecile to try to compete outside his own territory. I had warned him before that one day or another he'd run into bad luck."

"That makes no difference. Just the same, I owe you more than I can repay, and I mean to prove to you how grateful I am."

"It was nothing, child of God."

"Yes, yes, it was, my boy. Meet me here tomorrow morning. I'll bring you two pullets."

"Fat ones?" said the fox, licking his chops.

"Fat and greasy," said the man.

"That sounds good, my boy. I'll be there."

VI

The next day, as the birds were leaving their perches, the basket-maker came back with a big sack. Master Fox was waiting under the oak where the wolf had come to the end of his life.

"Open the sack," said the man, "and you'll find something unexpected."

The fox opened it, and out came a big dog that killed Master Fox.

That is how this oak got its name the Wolf-Oak, and that's why it's been a common proverb among us ever since:

Do a donkey a favor, and I suppose
He will kick you in the nose.

Caillou qui Biques!

I

In olden times, when the charcoal-trade still covered much of Flanders, the village of Autreppe was already there, and it was, as it still is, blue all over.

As everyone knows, Autreppe has a great quarry of blue stones, and that is why not only the roofs and staircases of the houses, but the houses themselves, the pavement, and even the very dust are all blue.

In those days, there was a magnificent castle in the village, blue like the others, and the lord of the castle was always called the King of the Blue Country.

This king was a rough man. He had no greater pleasure than hunting, and he spent whole days in the part of the forest that belonged to his domain.

One day, one of his guards went into the forest, and when evening came he had not returned. When he didn't come back the next day or the day after, the king sent two more guards to look for him. An astonishing result!—they didn't come back, either.

The monarch called together all the hunters in the country and ordered them to search all through the forest. He sent them, but they didn't come back. Not even a single hound of the pack they'd brought with them came back.

Seeing this, the king forbade anyone to set foot in the dangerous forest. From that moment on, it was left silent, and its solitude was not troubled by anything except an eagle or a vulture that might soar now and then over the tranquil leaves.

II

The king no longer went hunting in that direction. But one day someone gave him a gift, an enchanted bullet, and when he went out tracking a wild boar, the boar led him into the forest. Soon he came to a deep pool, where the beast plunged in.

His dog was in front of him, and hardly had it touched the water, when an arm rose up from the pool, seized the dog, and jerked it down to the bottom.

It happened so fast that the hunter didn't have time to aim his gun. He fired blind. Suddenly, at the contact with the enchanted bullet, the water began boiling and transformed into an opaque vapor that went up, and up, and went to increase the cloud-cover. And the pool was dry.

There in the mud the monarch saw a wild man whose body looked like a reddish-grey stone. This man had long black hair that covered his face and fell to his knees.

Just then, the king's huntsmen caught up with him. All together, they seized hold of the stone man, tied him up with ropes, and took him to the castle.

The monarch had him put in a big iron cage and set in the middle of the courtyard. Under pain of death, he forbade anyone to open the door.

"Give me the key, said the queen. "I'll put it under my pillow."

They gave her the key, and after that people could go into the forest in complete safety.

III

The King of the Blue Country had a son who was as handsome as a rosebush in flower. One day, when the young prince was amusing himself with archery practice, his arrow fell into the stone man's cage. It was a superb arrow. Its tip, or, rather, the arrowhead was made of silver, and at the foot it had feathers of many colors.

"Give me back my arrow," said the prince to the stone man.

"Open the door for me," said the stone man, "and I'll give it to you."

"I can't," said the boy. "The king has forbidden it under pain of death."

And he went away, leaving his arrow there.

The next day he came back to ask for it.

"Open the door for me," said the man.

And the little boy again refused. He could have asked his father to make him give the arrow back, but he was afraid he would be spanked for having shot at the stone man.

IV

The next day, as the king was out hunting, his son went to the cage and said to the man, "Even if I wanted to, it'd be impossible for me to open the cage for you. I don't have the key."

"The key," said the man, "is under your mother's pillow. There's nothing to stop you from going and taking it."

The child resisted for an hour more his longing to get his arrow back, and then he carried off the key and opened the cage-door.

The wild man came out, handed the child's arrow back to him, and fled. It was only then that the little prince understood how bad he'd been. He cried, "Hey! Wild man, don't go!—if you run away the king will have me killed!"

The stone man turned back. "It is much better," he said, "when a bird is in the woods than when it's in a cage. Come with me—that's the only way you might have to escape death. Anyway, your father's son won't lose anything by it."

The boy made no resistance, being so much afraid of his father, and the man put him on his shoulder and plunged into the forest.

When the king returned from the hunt, he saw the empty cage and asked the queen what had happened. She didn't know. She ran to her room and found the key was no longer there. Then they realized that their child had disappeared. They called him, they searched the house, they scoured the forest, but it was all useless. The king and the queen then realized what had happened, and there was great mourning in the royal castle.

V

The stone man carried the young prince into the very depths of the forest, to the place where to this day the Angre woods are green, and where the Caillou qui Biques—that's to say, the stone that stands out, raises its human-like head more than seventy feet high in the clearing.

The child noticed that the crest of the rock indeed looked like a human face, and that the face vaguely resembled the stone man's face.

The stone man caused him to fall asleep and plunged with him into the nearby Honneau Abyss, which people call the Devil's Hole. He opened the subterranean door—its hinges can be seen when the water is clear—and went farther down, coming at last to an immense gallery, where he set the little boy down.

He left him there asleep while he searched out what he wanted, and then woke him. He showed him his diamonds, rubies, sapphires, topazes, emeralds, chrysolites, and then told him, "These treasures are for you, if you know how to earn them. You will be richer than all the kings of the earth."

"What must I do?" asked the child, dazzled by the sight.

"You're going to learn."

The wild man brought him back up on top of the ground and led him twenty paces away from the abyss, to a fountain, with the water rolling out of it in spangles of gold.

"You will sit here and rest by the Fountain of Gold all day long, and you will take care that nothing falls on it to tarnish the mirror of its surface. Each evening I will come and make sure that you have carried out your instructions well."

And he plunged back into the Devil's Hole.

VI

The young prince sat down on the edge of the Fountain of Gold, and he took care that nothing fell on it. He stayed there for six full hours without budging, which was hard work for a child as lively and quick as a bunch of mice.

Meanwhile, the time went on, and he was getting as bored as a swallow in a cage. For something to amuse himself, he admired his image, which smiled at him in the stream.

He leaned over it, farther and farther, to see his eyes, and his long hair, which waved about his shoulders, and at last fell into the water.

He lifted his head out of the water quickly, but already his hair was gilded and shone brilliantly. No need for me to tell you how miserable the child was! He took his handkerchief and knotted it about his head so that the stone man would not notice what had happened.

The stone man came back before evening, and he already knew all about it. He said to the little boy, "Untie your handkerchief."

The gold hair streamed down over his shoulders, and it was in vain for the boy to try to excuse himself—the stone man pronounced his punishment just the same:

"Since you didn't know how to win a fortune, you are going to wander through the world to learn what poverty is. However, I don't want to abandon you entirely. When you have need of me, come here and say three times: "Caillou qui Biques! Caillou qui Biques! Caillou qui Biques!" And here's something you must be careful to remember: when you are going to be married, make sure that you are loved for yourself. That will bring you happiness, which is worth more than riches."

VII

Then the boy was left to wander through the depths of the forest. His soul was resolute, so he did not torment himself over his fate any more than the birds in the field would do, who have the Good Lord for their landlord. Soon he reached a pretty village, full of fountains that leaped and bounded surrounded by perpetual greenery.

Everything there seemed to be of a fresh young green, and even the houses had roofs green with moss, and the walls, from top to bottom, were crowned with climbing vines growing green. The castle was adorned with an immense green spread of ivy. It was reflected in a beautiful lake framed by the forest, and that was why people called it the Castle of Sebourg, which, in the language of those bygone days, meant the Castle of the Lake.

The little adventurer looked up and saw at the window a young princess, marvelously beautiful. "Couldn't she be the one," he thought, "who will love me for myself!"

He went into the castle and asked who its lord was. They told him it was the King of the Green Country. He asked if the King could give him any work.

The castle servants did not know if there was any work for him. But they told him to wait, because his fresh, rosy face pleased them.

Finally, the cook took him on as a servant, and the Prince of the Blue Country was set to hauling water, chopping wood for the fires, and cleaning out the ashes in the home of the King of the Green Country.

He always kept a cap on, pulled down over his ears, and when they asked him why he always covered up his hair so carefully, he said that he didn't have any hair, because it had fallen out when he was ill. So instead of calling him Clicquet, which was his given name, the castle servants called him Little Curly.

This name stuck with him, and whenever they saw him, no matter how far away, the servants, as a joke, would imitate the cry of the tomtit, which, as everyone knows, always says: "Li'l Curly! Li'l Curly!"

VIII

Now, it happened one day that the servants had taken a day off to go to the Sebourg fair, and the young prince stayed by himself with the cook at the castle and was told to carry the platters to the king's table.

When the king saw that he kept his cap on his head, he said, "When you serve at table, you have to take off your cap."

"I realize that, Sire," said Clicquet, "and if I'm keeping my cap on, it's because of the respect I owe you. I had an illness that made my hair fall out, and I wouldn't dare to come before you with my head all bare."

The king scolded the cook for having taken into service a boy with no hair. He ordered him to send him away, but the Cook took pity on the youngster and gave him to the baker, who hid him in the bake-house. The young prince helped out there for some time, out of the king's sight.

One morning in July, when he was tugging a load of water from the well, it was so hot that he took off his cap. His gold hair spread out on his shoulders, and the sunbeams fell on it and were reflected onto the window-panes of the room where the King's daughter, the beautiful Lauriane, slept.

The princess was awakened by this bright light. She got up, hurried to get dressed, and ran to the window to see what it was. She saw the young baker's boy, with his gold hair, and she was dazzled. She watched him until he put his cap back on, and then, although she was very proud and never talked with the servants, she called to him. "Hey, boy! are you going to be baking today?"

"Yes, my lady," said Little Curly.

"In that case, bring me a riboche."

That's what we call an apple covered with dough and baked in the oven.

IX

Little Curly went into the bakery and made a riboche.

"Who's the riboche for?" said the baker.

"For the princess—she asked me to get her one."

268

"Do you have to bring her a plain old riboche hardly worth a sou? Make her a gilded one, or a pie, or an apple-tart."

"No," said Clicquet, "If she asked me for a riboche, she must have wanted a riboche, not a gohière."

When the riboche was done, he brought it, with his heart beating fast, to the beautiful Lauriane, who said to him sharply: "Take off your cap. You're not supposed to keep it on in my presence."

"I can't, Princess," said Clicquet, "because I don't have any hair."

But she grabbed the cap by its tassel and pulled it off, and the gold curls rolled down on his shoulders. The young prince started to run away, but the princess caught hold of the sleeve of his jacket, and said, "Who are you? Why did you lie to me, and how does it happen that you have gold hair?"

To all these questions, Little Curly could only reply with silence. He did not want to confess his secret, and, besides, he felt unable to answer, because of the princess's great beauty. Seeing that she couldn't get anything out of him, Lauriane sent him away, but put into his hand a fistful of florins.

Clicquet returned to his work, and, running into the baker's children, he gave them the florins for them to play quoits with.

An hour later the princess noticed them playing with the florins. She asked them who'd given them to them.

"Little Curly," they said.

And the princess was much surprised.

X

Some time after that, the Lord of Sebourg got into a quarrel with the powerful lord of the Flamengrie, and war was declared.

The enemy came out in full force, and the King of the Green Country could not count on winning.

The young prince thought, "Now that I've grown tall, I ought to go to the war. That's the way to win the princess's heart."

He went to the men-at-arms and said, bold as a tomtit, "Give me a horse, and I'll come with you."

They burst out laughing, and told him, "We'll leave one for you in the stable. You can go take it after we're gone."

When they had set out, Little Curly went to the stable and led the horse out. It was broken-winded and limped so heavily that it seemed as if it had only three legs. He mounted it anyway and rode into the depths of the shadowy forest, until he reached the great crag with the human face. When he got there, he cried out three times: "Caillou qui biques! Caillou qui biques! Caillou qui biques!"

At once, the stone man came out of the Devil's Hole and said, "What do you want?"

"I want," said Clicquet, "a battle-horse that doesn't stumble, because I'm going to the war."

"Turn around and take a look," said the man, and he plunged back into the abyss.

Little Curly turned around and saw coming up the drive—I mean, the path through the trees—a stable-boy leading a fire-breathing stallion by its bridle. A squire was walking beside the horse and carrying the pieces of a full set of armor—helmet, breast-plate, arm- and thigh-guards, and a sword and shield.

Some twenty paces behind came a troop of men-at-arms with faces of stone, like the wild man's face. Their long-swords glittered in the sunlight, but they had no helmets, breastplates, or shields. They were naked down to the waist, and their breasts, like their faces, were of stone.

They marched one after the other in profound silence, and the earth shook under their tread. They looked like a troop of statues on the march.

XI

Little Curly put on the armor, gave the stable-boy his three-legged horse, mounted the stallion, and put himself at the head of the company.

He got to the field of battle at moon-rise.

A great many of the men of the Count of Sebourg had already bit the dust, and the rest were starting to give way.

Little Curly lowered the visor of his helmet and thrust himself forward with his troop, who looked like a living wall.

The bullets bounced off their breasts, and the broadswords could not cut into them.

The stone men, always in silence, penetrated into the enemy ranks, cutting and thrusting and trampling underfoot those who fell.

The others tried to flee, but the young captain pursued them, and woe to those who came in reach of his sword!

270

Instead of returning to the king, he turned onto a path that took a different way, led his companions into the forest, and cried three times, "Caillou qui biques! Caillou qui biques! Callou qui biques!"

"What do you want?" said the wild man.

"Take back your battle-horse and your troop of stone men, and give me my three-legged horse again."

The thing was done as Little Curly wished, and he returned to the castle on his three-legged horse.

In the meantime, the Princess Lauriane had run to her father to congratulate him on his victory.

"I didn't win the victory," said the king. "It was a knight who came to my rescue with his troop."

"Who was the knight?" asked Lauriane.

"I don't know. He galloped off in pursuit of our enemies, and no one has seen him since."

These words piqued the princess's curiosity. The next day, out walking by the bakehouse, she met the baker. I don't know just what news about the baker's boy she asked of him.

But the baker said, "He came back on his three-legged horse, and everyone started laughing. They were all whistling like a flock of tomtits 'Li'l Curly! Li'l Curly!' and they asked him, 'What hedge did you go hide behind to guard the moon from the wolves?' But he replied, 'I'm the one who won the battle!' And they laughed even harder."

Lauriane went away, deep in thought.

XII

The princess was very anxious to find out who the mysterious knight was. The king, who adored her, said:

"Winter is coming, shaking his cloak of snow, and already last night a skin of ice tightened the surface of the lake. As soon as it has frozen to the bottom, I'll give a skating party there. You will toss out a gold apple, and perhaps the unknown knight will come to try to win it."

Winter came, and they made great preparations for the party. The evening when it was going to take place, Little Curly, who was an excellent skater, went into the depths of the forest and called three times, "Caillou qui biques! Caillou qui biques! Callou qui biques!"

"What do you want?" said the stone man.

"I want to win the gold apple of the Princess of the Green Country."

"So you love the Princess Lauriane?"

"Passionately!"

"Does she return your love?"

"Not yet, but I'm working to make her love me."

"That's good. Turn around and take a look."

Clicquet again saw the stable-boy coming along the path through the trees and leading his stallion with fiery nostrils. But instead of armor the squire brought him an elegant suit of black velvet, with a cape and a veil of close-woven mesh to hide his gold hair.

XIII

Little Curly mounted his horse, and, with the squire following him, rode to the castle. A glance showed a scene like something out of fairy-land, Thousands of little lamps gleamed in the branches of the trees and framed the lake with fire. On the lake, some poles, set out at intervals, supported garlands of lights of a thousand colors. Some servants were walking over the lake, carrying torches that shone with a red light reflected in the ice.

In the middle were the skaters, richly dressed, making graceful turns, going back and forth, balancing, swaying, and criss-crossing like dancers. The windows of the castle were all lit up, and the king, his wife, and the ladies of the court were standing there, muffled in warm furs.

When he came to the shore of the lake, Clicquet left his horse in the squire's care, put on his skates, and with a bound launched himself onto the ice.

The skaters turned around to see the newcomer. He skated with grace and agility. Soon all eyes were fixed on him, and even the other competitors stopped short to watch him more easily. In the semi-circle that they formed, he set about tracing as he skated over the ice a handsome laurel, the emblem of Princess Lauriane, who was giving the party.

Lauriane guessed at once that the clever and gallant skater was the unknown knight.

She stepped forward and threw the gold apple. Everyone rushed for it, but Clicquet caught it in flight. Instead of going to greet the king and the court, he sped away like an arrow, gained the shore, mounted his horse, and plunged into the forest.

The following night, he came dressed all in blue. The skaters made a circle around him. This time it was Lauriane's name, garlanded with laurel branches, that he traced on the ice.

He seized the gold apple again and fled. But the king was much annoyed at this sort of behavior.

"This," he said, "is not the way a proper knight should act. If he comes again, and if he takes the apple and flees to safety like a thief, you must pursue him, and bring him to us, either willingly or by force, even if you have to injure him."

The third night, it was in vain that they awaited the stranger—he didn't appear. The princess was desolate. She waited until the last possible moment to throw the apple, but in the end she had to make up her mind to do it.

As her hand flung it, a terrible cry was suddenly heard on the shore of the lake. The skaters turned around and saw a great white phantom coming toward them. Struck with astonishment, they pulled apart to let him pass. He gathered up the apple and headed toward the forest, as quick as a boquet—that's to say, a squirrel.

The knights guessed that this was the mysterious skater. They hurried after him, and one of them followed so closely that the point of his sword scratched his armor.

The next day the king's daughter again asked the baker if he had any news of his assistant.

"The boy," he said, "is in his room. He went to the party last night, and he showed my children three gold apples that he won there."

The princess could no longer contain herself. Putting aside all pride, she went to his room, without pretending otherwise, where she peeped through the keyhole and saw Little Curly bandaging his arm. His long gold hair fell on his shoulders, and on the chimney gleamed the three gold apples.

No more doubts! Little Curly was the mysterious knight. But did he love the princess, and how did it happen that he had disguised himself as a baker's boy?

"I will find out," said Lauriane.

XV

Meanwhile, spring was coming, and the King of the Green Country said to his daughter, "It's time for you to be getting married—I'll leave the choice of a husband up to you."

"I will take," she said, "one who loves me with true love."

"How will you know him?" asked the monarch.

"I have a way," said the princess.

She had a path of gold constructed in the castle's main hall, and then she said to the doorkeeper, "The one who can urge his horse right down the middle of this road will be the husband I'm waiting for. You must let him enter—but don't open the door to the ones who follow along the side."

And the king sent out his trumpeters to announce that he had decided to get his daughter married, and suitors should come and present themselves.

They came in a crowd from all four points of the compass. At sight of the handsome gold pathway, each of them said to himself, "It would be a real pity to go riding on that. My horse's shoes might damage it."

So all the knights went along the sides off the path. But when they got to the door, the doorkeeper cried to each one: "Go your ways, Mynheer—the princess doesn't want anything to do with you."

XVI

When Little Curly heard the proclamation, his heart beat fast. He went into the deep forest and called three times: "Caillou qui biques! Caillou qui biques! Callou qui biques!"

"What do you want?" said the stone man.

"I want," said Little Curly, "the most spirited horse, and the richest suit of banqueting clothes."

"What for?"

"To ask for the hand of the Princess of the Green Country."

"Are you sure that she loves you for yourself?"

"I've done all I can to make sure."

"That's not an answer. As for the rest, we shall see. Turn around and look."

And Clicquet saw coming up the path through the trees a horse even finer than the others, and a squire who was carrying a splendid outfit of green velvet.

The young prince put it on, mounted the horse, and this time he did not leave the squire in the forest. The closer he got to the castle, the harder his heart was beating. He was afraid he might not meet with approval, and the thought so absorbed him that he rode right down the middle of the gold road, and came to the door before he realized it.

The door opened before him, and soon the ornamental plants beyond it quivered as he passed—then the flowers along the stairs bloomed, and rare birds filled all the rooms with joyous music.

In the great hall, all the court had gathered. This time Little Curly doffed his cap at the sight of the king. His long gold hair streamed down on his shoulders, and the sight was so dazzling that the sun itself was jealous.

"But aren't you our old kitchen boy," said the monarch, "the one they call Little Curly?"

"Yes, sire," said Clicquet, "and I am also the knight who won the three gold apples—" He took them out and showed them—"and the one who helped you in battle."

And while he was speaking, a sound of heavy footsteps could be heard, like statues on the march—it was the prince's escort, sent by the stone man to do him honor.

"So who are you?" asked the sovereign.

"I am the son of the King of the Blue Country," said Clicquet.

"In that case, there is no reason you should not marry my daughter, if she agrees."

"It is a long time now," said the princess, lowering her eyes, "since I realized he was a king's son."

"All we need now," said the monarch, "is the consent of our good cousin, the King of the Blue Country. Dine this night with us, and tomorrow you shall go to seek him."

The young couple had supper sitting next to one another. They ate hardly anything, even though it was the finest meal they'd ever had in their lives.

XVII

The next day, as soon as the squirrels were up and about looking for food, the prince left to cross the forest to seek his father's consent.

The King and Queen of the Blue Country were delighted to see their son again. They had thought he was dead, and, full of wonder, they set out on the road, with all the courtiers, to go to the wedding.

Clicquet, although a prince, was mindful of the gratitude he owed the stone man, and he made them pass by the Devil's Hole. When he got to the clearing, he stopped, and cried three times: "Caillou qui biques! Caillou qui biques! Callou qui biques!"

"What do you want?" said the stone man, suddenly appearing.

"To thank you, and to invite you to my marriage with the Princess of the Green Country."

"Are you sure she loves you for yourself?" the wild man asked again.

"She's glad to marry me!"

"That's not an answer. She is glad to marry the Prince of the Blue Country, but did she love Little Curly enough to want to make him her husband?"

Taken aback, the prince made no reply, and the stone man added, "We're going to find out."

He bent over the Fountain of Gold, took a little of the water in the hollow of his hand, and sprinkled the king, the queen, and all the lords and ladies of the court. All at once, they were changed into trees with gold flowers, growing in a dense thicket around the clearing.

XVIII

One day, two days rolled by, and in the Green Country they were astonished that they did not see the young prince return. The king secretly sent an envoy to the castle of the Blue Country to find out what had happened. His messenger found only the servants there. The king, the queen, and the young prince had left three days ago, and in the three days since they had had no news of them.

The monarch had the whole forest searched, but it was in vain. They could find no trace of the rulers of the Blue Country.

Princss Lauriane was in despair. One morning, unable to bear her grief and anxiety any longer, she slipped out by herself from the castle and plunged into the wood. When she got to the standing stone, she stopped, instinctively, and as if held there by a force greater than her own.

All was calm and silent, as if she were in a church. No wind rattled the leaves, no stream murmured, no ray of sunlight pierced through the dense foliage.

The princess leaned against an ebony tree with long gold clusters and walked around it sorrowfully. Her heart swelled. She heaved a sigh, and, thinking that her betrothed was lost to her forever, she let fall these words: "Shall I never see you again, my poor Little Curly? Alas! I would have been only too happy to marry you, even if you had stayed a simple baker's boy!"

Suddenly she thought she felt the tree moving. The bark became as soft as flesh. The little branches bent down toward her. The big branches turned into arms and embraced her. Lauriane raised her head, and, in place of the tree, she saw the handsome prince with gold hair, and she hugged him with a full heart.

Soon the neighboring trees changed into gleaming knights and lovely ladies, and, all together, they set out on the road to the Green Country.

The wedding was celebrated the next day. The stone man attended, dressed in magnificent clothes that gleamed with gems. He gave a part of his treasure to the young prince, but the most precious gift was the heart of the Princess of the Green Country, which, thanks to the stone man, Little Curly was now sure he had.

The Viol d'Amore

I

In olden days, there was a young countess named Cecile, who lived in a castle at Antoing, near Tournai. She loved music more than anything.

At that time, the organist at the Tournai cathedral was a young man named Roland, who was the son of a violin-maker, and who had showed such a genius for music that by the time he was fifteen years old, he could play every instrument known.

The Duke of Antoing often ordered him to come to the castle to play sonatas with his daughter, who was a very good harpist.

In those days, musical instruments were very imperfect, and although Cecile took great pleasure in hearing them, none of them—not the theorbo, the mandolin, the guitar, the harp, or the organ—went to her heart so keenly as to bring tears to her beautiful eyes.

"Oh!" she would often say, "if a musician could be found who would bring tears to my eyes, I would give him the loveliest rose in my bouquet, the finest ruby in my necklace, the loveliest pearl in my tiara!"

Cecile was a marvel of grace, and, in spite of the proverb, "Every sheep knows its like," Roland had not been able to resist her overpowering charm.

One day, when she came to repeat her favorite songs, Roland had disappeared.

II

Cecile missed the young musician, but she had plenty of other reasons for sorrow. For over a hundred years, the people of Antoing had been at odds with the people of Bitremont, their powerful neighbors.

The Count of Bitremont had noticed Cecile at a tournament. He was struck by her beauty, and asked her father for her.

The count was known to be jealous and hot-tempered. He had olive skin, hair as black as a crow's wing, and gloomy eyes under heavy brows.

Cecile was afraid of him, but her father greatly wanted this marriage, as it must bring peace between their two houses. The poor child gave way and was not slow to regret it.

Her husband soon displayed frightening jealousy. He would have liked to have his wife love nothing but him in the whole world, but he did nothing to win her heart.

Everything annoyed him, even Cecile's love of music. He suffered through it impatiently when she played the harp, and one day, in a fit of rage, he went so far as to break the instrument into a thousand pieces.

Poor Cecile often thought of the blessed time when she could play sonatas with Roland, in complete freedom.

III

One evening, when the Countess of Bitremont had come with her husband to the manor of Antoing, a servant announced that a minstrel was asking to play his instrument before the guests in the castle.

The Count of Bitremont waved his hand impatiently, but the Duke took no notice, and gave the order to have the stranger admitted—it was Roland.

At sight of him, the young wife's eyes sparkled. "What!—is it you?" she said, with a sweet smile. "Why, where have you been, you fine fugitive?"

"Lady of Beauty," said Roland, "you have often said that if a musician could be found who would bring tears to your eyes, you would give him the loveliest rose in your bouquet, the loveliest ruby in your necklace, the loveliest pearl in your tiara. I have had the good fortune to invent an instrument which, perhaps, will accomplish this wonder. Here it is."

And he held up the new instrument. Cecile considered it attentively, and then she said, "What do you call this marvelous instrument?"

"The viol d'amore!"

These words roused the Count's wrath.

"Why should we let beggars in?" he muttered, "—viol-players and rabble hoping for gold florins?"

"I'm not a beggar," said the violist, "and all I ask is the honor of amusing Madame the Countess."

Entirely absorbed by her own feelings, Cecile did not notice her husband's increasing rage. At a sign from her, Roland tuned his viol and began.

IV

The instrument, in fact, produced tones sweeter and tenderer than all those the Countess had ever heard before. The inventor played with a strange charm. At first astonished, then moved, the countess fell into a profound reverie.

Soon her heart was beating fast, the expression on her face showed a sorrowful delight, and when the artist fell silent, she gazed at him with moist eyes.

Then, forgetting everything, she stood up, took off the rose that decorated her corsage, and offered it to the young minstrel, saying, "Never, my dear friend, have I ever heard anything so touching! Play again, I beg you, for I want to carry out all my promise."

"You're not going to carry anything out, you traitor!" cried the Count. Overcome with rage, he drew his dagger and plunged it into his wife's heart, and she fell dead.

Roland cried out, leaped at the dagger, drew it out of her breast, thrust it into the Count of Bitremont's breast, and fled.

V

He stayed away twenty years without returning. People thought he was dead, and when he came back, no one recognized him. His back was bent, his eyes haggard, his hair and beard grey, his cheeks lined—how much he had changed!

Seeing Cecile murdered had driven him mad. He believed the young woman was still alive, but lost to him, and he searched for her everywhere.

From being a great artist he had become a poor fiddler. He went about playing the viol in taverns and inns, living on public charity, and warming himself at God's fireplace.

It was chance that brought him back to the place of his birth. Night had closed in when he found himself at the castle of Antoing. He looked at it, and suddenly he felt his mind clearing—by the white moonlight, he had recognized the old manor.

He went inside the walls of the park, and, a few steps farther, he saw a chapel, its door open. He went in.

In the middle of the chapel a tomb of marble had been raised, and standing on it was a figure of a young woman, marvelously beautiful. She was draped in a great ceremonial cloak, her forehead was circled by a countess's crown, her neck was ornamented with a ruby necklace, her arms were crossed, her eyes looked up to heaven, and she seemed to be hearing the concerts of the angels.

It was a statue of Cecile, and the artist had made it so like, that Roland gave a cry, and believed he was looking at Cecile herself, flesh and blood.

"I've looked for you for twenty years, and I've found you at last, Lady of Beauty!" he cried. "Oh! I still hope to touch your heart and win tears from your beautiful eyes!"

VI

He tuned his viol and drew himself up. He began with a song that was weird and sublime—a heart-rending wail sadder than any that ever poured from a desolate soul.

All at once—wonder of wonders!—the statue's stone face grew dim with profound sorrow. Her eyes filled with tears and looked at the musician with inexpressible tenderness.

When he had finished, the lady unfolded her marble arms, put a hand to her necklace, pulled off its most beautiful ruby, and gave it to Roland.

Trembling, the minstrel took the precious stone. Then the statue folded her arms again and was again motionless.

Overcome by love, Roland fell to his knees and cried: "Thank you! Lady of Beauty you've kept your promise, but is it only the artist who's had the happiness of pleasing you? Oh! I beg of you, speak one word to me—make some gesture that proves that the man touched your heart, too!"

But the statue remained mute and motionless, and Roland, in desperation, went away.

He wandered all the night and the following day through the countryside. That evening, overcome with weariness, he asked for lodging at a farm. They took pity on him, and put him in the hayloft.

In the morning, some men-at-arms came and searched him, and found the precious stone; they brought him before a judge.

When the magistrate questioned him, he said that the ruby had been given to him by the Countess. The judge thought that he was pretending to be mad, considered him capable of the crime of sacrilege, and sentenced him to be hanged, as an example, within the hour, in front of the chapel where he had committed his crime.

Followed by a great crowd of people, Roland went out between the guards. He did not understand where they were taking him, nor what they wanted with him,

When he got to the place where he was to be punished, he saw the statue of Cecile. A gleam of reason woke in his soul. He raised his head.

"It's the custom," he said, "for the last wish of a man condemned to death to be granted. Have someone bring me my viol, for I want to play again, one last time!

VII

His instrument was brought to him. He took his place in front of the statue and began to sing his death-song.

"It is for you, my lady, that I die," said the funereal lament. "I have no regret at losing my life, since you never loved me. But the memory people have of me will be weighed down with a crime of which, as you know, I am innocent. Will you allow that?"

And while the viol was lamenting in this way, he fixed his eyes ardently on the statue's mute face.

The more he played, the more his reason returned to him. Soon he realized that it was not really Cecile there before him, but her image, a cold statue of marble.

And the fiddler saw that she was not wearing either her ruby necklace or her pearl tiara. They had been removed out of prudence, so as not to tempt thieves.

"Oh! it's the end," said the viol, "and you won't be able to keep your promise in full. Now nothing can save me. Farewell, then, you whom I loved so much!"

At that moment, a voice cried, "Behold!" and a long shiver ran through the crowd.

The statue's face was dimmed with grief, and her look grew tender. Soon two tears appeared and fell slowly down her marble cheeks.

The statue unfolded her arms, held out her open hands, and caught the two tears. They turned into great pearls, which she presented to the poor string player.

VIII

The people cried, "A miracle!" and freed Roland.

Thenceforward his reason was completely returned, and he became a great artist.

The chapel soon became a place of pilgrimage, and musicians took Cecile as their patron saint, the tender daughter of the Duke of Antoing, who loved the viol d'amore so much that when she heard it, her eyes of marble wept tears of pearl.

Love's Desire

I

In olden days, in the time of King Cambrinus, there lived at Avesnes a nobleman who was the finest man among his friends, by which I mean that he was the fattest in all the Flemish country. He ate his four meals a day, slept his twelve hours, and touched no weapons except his bow—and the only use he made of that was to aim at little birds on the feast-day of the town's patron saint.

He was a bad shot, for his belly kept getting in the way. By then it had grown so round that he had to have a wheelbarrow along to carry it. And that's why the wags in the neighborhood called him Lord Barrow-Belly.

Lord Barrow-Belly had but one anxiety. That was over his adored son, who looked nothing like him, being thin as a cuckoo. What worried him was that the young prince, in the judgment of the young ladies in that land, had one very great defect: no matter how much he was offered, and no matter what tender looks their eyes could give him, he had no wish to get married.

Instead of chatting with any of them at twilight, he liked to plunge into the woods to talk to the moon. The young ladies considered that fantastic and chimerical. It did not make him seem any the less lovable—quite the contrary!—and, as he had been given the name of Désiré, they all called him Love's Desire.

"What ails you?" his father often asked him. "Here you have everything that brings happiness: a good bed, good food, and kegs full of beer. There's nothing lacking for you to become fat and jolly, except a woman who's lovely in your eyes. So get married, and then you'll be perfectly happy."

"I wouldn't ask anything better, Father," said Désiré, "but I've never found a woman who pleased me. All the girls around here are white and pink, and nothing bores me as much as their eternally rosy cheeks."

"By my belly! Do you want to marry an African girl and bring me a pack of grandchildren as dark as night?"

"No, Father, but there must be some women somewhere in the world who aren't like all these vermillion girls, and, let me tell you, I'm not going to get married until the day I find someone to my liking."

II

Some time later, it happened that the prior of the Abbey of Saint Amand sent the lord of Avesnes a basket of oranges, with a nice letter explaining that these gold fruits, then unknown to the Flemish people, came directly from the land of the sun.

That evening, at supper, Lord Barrow-Belly and his son tasted these golden fruits, and found them deliciously refreshing.

The next morning, at the break of day, Love's Desire went down to the stable and saddled his pretty white horse. Then he went with his boots on to the bedside of Lord Barrow-Belly, who was smoking his first pipe of the day.

"Father," he said gravely, "I have come to take leave of you. This past night I dreamed that I was walking in a grove where golden fruits were ripening. I picked one, and, when I opened it, I saw a princess with gold cheeks come out of it, who was marvelously beautiful. She is the bride I long for, and I'm going to seek her."

The lord of Avesnes was so flabbergasted that he dropped his pipe. Then, at the idea that his son wanted to marry a yellow woman—a woman shut up in an orange!—he burst out laughing.

Love's Desire waited, to finish saying goodbye, until the fit of mirth was over. But Barrow-Belly was not done laughing. The wine-skin that served him for a belly rose and fell, going up and down like a barrel tossed on the waves, and the poor boy stood there sheepishly, not able to get a word in.

Seeing that, he threw himself on his father's hand, kissed it tenderly, opened the door, and, in a blink of the eye, was at the bottom of the stairs. He mounted his pony nimbly, and he was already a quarter of a league away while Barrow-Belly was still laughing.

"A gold wife! He's crazy!—so crazy he should be tied up!" cried the good man, when he could speak at last. "Hey!—hurry!—run!— someone go and bring him back to me!"

His servants went running at his cries and jumped on horseback. As they did not know which way the lord's son had gone, they spread out on all the roads, except the right one, and, instead of the fugitive, all they brought home when the evening was growing dark was their horses, dead tired and hardly able to stand.

III

When Love's Desire thought he had gotten out of reach, like a man who has unwound a nice ribbon from his queue, he slowed his pony to a walk. He traveled easily in this way, by easy stages, through cities, towns, villages, up hills and down dale and across plains, and always heading in the direction where the sun looked brightest and hottest.

The sun at last became so burning hot that one day, as it touched the horizon, Love's Desire thought he must really have come to the right place. He was then in a corner of a wood, in front of a hut, where his tired horse had wandered of his own will. There was an old man with a white beard sitting out front to enjoy the cool breeze. The prince dismounted and asked for hospitality.

"Come in, my young friend," said the old man. "My house is not large, but it's big enough to let a traveler inside, and not leave him sitting in front of the door."

The traveler entered, and his host served him a simple meal. When the prince had satisfied his hunger, the old man said, "If I'm not mistaken, you come from far away—might I know where you are going?"

"I'll tell you," said Désiré, "although it's a safe bet that you'll make fun of me, as my father did. I dreamed of a land of the sun, where there was a grove of orange trees, and where I found inside an orange a marvelously beautiful princess, whom I must marry—I'm going in search of her."

"Why would I make fun of that?" said the old man. "To be crazy when you're twenty years old—that's being wise, yes? Go on, young man, follow your dream, and if you don't find the happiness you seek, you will at least have the happiness of having looked for it!"

IV

The next day, the prince got up early in the morning, and took leave of his host.

"The grove that you dreamed of is not far from here," said the old man. "It is hidden in the depths of the forest, and this road will take you there. You will find yourself in front of an immense park surrounded by very high, strong walls. In this park there is a castle, and a horrible sorceress lives there, who does not allow anyone to break into it. Behind the castle grows the marvelous grove. Go along the wall until you come to a heavy iron gate. Don't try banging against it, but grease the hinges with this." And the old man gave Barrow-Belly's son a little phial full of oil. "The gate will open for you by itself," he went on, "and an enormous dog that guards the castle will come running, with gaping maw. Throw him a little fine wheat bread. Next you will see on your right a woman baking over a hot oven—give her this broom. Lastly, you will see a well on your left—be sure you pull up its rope and stretch it out in the sunlight. When you've done that, don't go into the castle, but turn and go right to the grove of orange trees. Gather three oranges and take the road back to the gate as quick as you can. When you reach it, leave the forest, heading in the opposite direction.

"Now—pay close attention!—no matter what happens, do not open your oranges until you come to a river-bank or a spring. You will find inside the oranges three princesses, and you will choose your wife from among them. When you have made your choice, be careful not to leave your fiancée for a single moment, and keep in mind that the danger most to be feared is not the one that's known to be one to fear."

V

Love's Desire thanked his host warmly, and took the road he'd pointed out. In less than an hour he reached the foot of a prodigiously high wall. He jumped down, tied his horse to a tree, and soon discovered the gate of iron. Then he took out the phial and greased the gate-hinges. The gate swung open, and he saw an old castle and went boldly into the courtyard.

At once a ferocious barking resounded, and a dog as large as a donkey, with eyes as big as hockey-pucks ran straight at him, showing fangs like the teeth of a pitchfork. Désiré threw him some bread. The watchdog snatched it, and gulped it down—and let the young prince pass.

About twenty steps farther on, he found an immense oven with an opening full of flame, like the mouth of hell. A baker-woman, immensely tall, was leaning over the oven. Désiré went up to her and handed her the broom, and she took it without a word.

Lastly, he came to the well, drew up the rope, half rotting away, and stretched it out in the sunlight. With that done, he turned from the castle and entered the grove of orange trees. There he gathered the three most beautiful oranges and hurried to get back to the gate.

At that moment, a cloud came over the sun, the earth shook, and Love's Desire heard a voice that cried, "Baker, baker, take him by the feet and throw him in the oven."

"No," said the baker-woman. "For a long time now, I've had to clean this oven bare-handed. You cruel woman, you never gave me a broom! But he did. He can leave in peace!"

"Rope, rope!" cried the voice, "coil around his neck and strangle him!"

"No," said the rope. "For too many years you've left me to rot in the dampness! He spread me out in the sun. He can leave in peace!"

"Iron gate, iron gate," cried the voice, growling like thunder, "close on him and crush him!"

"No," said the gate. "For a hundred years you've left me rusting away, and he greased me. He can leave in peace!"

VI

Once he got outside, the young adventurer put the oranges in the sack hanging on his saddle-bow, mounted the horse, and sped out of the forest.

As he found he was longing to see the princesses, it seemed to take a long time to find a spring or a river, and it was in vain for him to push on ahead, for he still did not discover a spring or a river. Even so, his heart beat with joy, thinking that he had come through the hardest part already, and the rest would follow of itself.

Toward noon he came upon a dry plain, burning under the fiery sun. He felt ready to die of thirst, so he took out his drinking-gourd and raised it to his lips.

Alas! the gourd was empty. He had been so absorbed by his joy that he had forgotten to fill it. He went on riding, fighting against the tormenting thirst, but at last he could no longer get the better of it.

He let himself slip to the ground, and lay down next to his horse, his throat dry, his chest heaving, and his head ringing. Already he felt the approach of death, when his eyes fell on the sack bulging with oranges.

Poor Love's Dream, who had faced so many perils to win the lady of his dream, would at that moment have given all the princesses of the world, either red or gold, in exchange for a drop of water.

"Oh!" he said, "if only these oranges were real oranges, fruits as refreshing as those I ate while I was still in Flanders! And who knows?—maybe, after all—"

This idea roused him. He had enough strength to pull himself up and put his hand in the sack. He drew out an orange and opened it with his knife.

Suddenly, out sprang a canary, the loveliest ever seen.

"Give me something to drink! I'm dying of thirst!" said the golden bird.

"Wait," said Désiré, so much surprised that he forgot his own suffering. To find something for the bird to drink, he took a second orange and opened it without stopping to consider. Another canary hopped out, and she, too cried:

"I'm dying of thirst! Give me something to drink!"

Barrow-Belly's son now realized how foolish he had been, and while the two canaries took wing and flew away, he fell to the ground and, worn out by this last effort, he fainted away.

VII

He came to himself with a pleasant feeling of coolness. It was night, with great stars coming out in the sky overhead, while the ground beneath him was covered with dew.

The traveler, refreshed, mounted his horse, and soon, with the first white glimmers of the dawn, he saw from far off the light rippling on a stream, where at last he could quench his thirst.

He felt he no longer had the courage to open the one orange he had left. He considered, however, that he had failed to obey the old man's directions the night before. Who knew if that irresistible thirst might have been a trap set by the crafty sorceress, and if the third orange, opened beside the stream, might hold the princess he sought?

He took his knife and opened it. Alas! as with the first two, a pretty little canary hopped out of it, and said to him, "Give me something to drink! I'm so thirsty!"

Poor Love's Desire felt mortified. But he did not want to let the bird fly away as the others had, so he quickly dipped up some water in the hollow of his hand and poured it into her beak.

The canary had hardly finished drinking when she changed into a gorgeous young woman, with an agile figure, fine features, big dark eyes, and golden skin. Désiré had never seen anyone so lovely, and he stood silent before her, in ecstasy.

She herself seemed dazzled at first. She took a few steps in every direction, with delighted looks, and when she stopped in front of her liberator, her gaze held no sign of fear.

He asked her what her name was, and she told him she was Princess Zizi. She seemed to be about sixteen years old, and the wicked sorceress had been holding her, in the shape of a canary, shut inside the orange, for a good ten years.

"Well, then, my charming Zizi," said the young prince, in a fever to marry her, "let's hurry and get on my horse and escape the wicked sorceress."

Zizi wanted to know where he was taking her.

"To my father's castle," he said.

He mounted his pony, took Zizi up in front of him, and holding her carefully in his arms, he set out.

VIII

Everything the princess saw was new to her, and as they crossed mountains, valleys, towns, and villages, she asked him a thousand questions, revealing an innocent, naïve soul. Love's Desire felt an infinite charm in answering her. It is so sweet to teach someone you love!

As it was a long way, she leaned lightly back against him in order to rest, and his heart beat fast with delight.

Once she asked him what the girls were like in his country.

"They are white and rose-red," he said, "and their eyes are blue."

"Do you love that color?" said the princess.

Love's Desire thought this was a good occasion to find out what Zizi felt in her heart. He didn't answer.

"No doubt," said the princess, "one of them is waiting there to marry you?"

He kept silent. Zizi sat up straight.

"No," he said at last. "None of the girls in my own country please me, and that's why I came to the country of the sun to look for one who did. Was I wrong, my charming Zizi?"

Now it was Zizi's turn to be silent, but then the horse stumbled on a stone, and she let herself fall gently back against Love's Desire, leaning against him as before.

IX

Chatting together in this way, at length they drew near the castle of Avesnes. When they were four slingshots' length away, they thought they would stop to rest in the forest, at the edge of a clear fountain.

"My dear Zizi," said Barrow-Belly's son, "we can't show ourselves in my father's castle as if we were just coming in from going for a walk. We should make an entrance that's worthy of us. Wait for me here, and in less than an hour I'll bring back an escort befitting your rank."

"Don't be long," said Zizi, and it was with tears in her eyes that she saw him leave.

Left alone, the poor girl felt afraid. For the first time in her life she found herself left alone outdoors in a great forest.

All at once, she heard a noise of footsteps coming through the trees. Fearing that it might be a wolf, she hid herself in the midst of a thicket, in the branches of an old cropped willow that hung over the fountain. She climbed all the way in, leaving only her charming head still visible, reflected in the mirror of the water.

It was not a wolf that appeared then, but something just as ugly and ill-willed. And here's what it was.

X

Near there, in the town of Roquette, there lived a family of brickmakers. Fifteen years earlier, the head of the family had found in the wood a little girl who'd been left behind by nomads. He carried her to his wife, who took pity on her and raised her with her own children.

The little nomad girl relied on strength and trickery much more than on wisdom and grace. She had a narrow forehead, a flat nose, a wide mouth, thick lips, untidy hair, and skin not gold like Zizi's, but a muddy yellow.

Because people made fun of her color so often, she had become as naughty and shrill as a bluetit. Because of that, and no doubt also because of her muddy features, they called her Masinque, which is our word for the bluetit.

The brickmaker often asked her to go get water from the fountain, and the chore made her feel humiliated.

This was the one who, coming there with the pitcher on her shoulder, had frightened Zizi. The moment she leaned over the water, she saw reflected there the gorgeous image of the princess.

"What a pretty face!" she cried. "But, by heaven!—it's mine! So why do they all say I'm ugly? Oh, I'm definitely too beautiful to fetch water for them."

And with that, she broke her pitcher and went home.

"Where's your pitcher?" said the brickmaker.

"Oh! what can you expect? If you keep taking the pitcher to the well—"

"—eventually it gets broken. Well, well!—here's a pail. That won't break."

Masinque went back to the fountain, and, seeing Zizi's face again, she said, "No, I'm not going to put up with this job of hauling around a bucket."

And she threw the pail over her shoulder, so hard and so high that it landed in the branches of an oak.

Seeing her come back a second time empty-handed, the brickmaker asked her what she had done with the pail.

"I met a wolf," she said, "and I smashed it over his muzzle."

The brickmaker did not ask any more questions, but called for a broom, and administered to her some blows to humble her pride.

Then he took an old milking-can made of copper and gave it to her, saying, "Bring that back full, or look out for your bones—because I'll break some in the end if you don't!"

XI

Masinque left, rubbing her bruises.

This time, she did not dare disobey, and she bent unwillingly over the fountain.

It was not easy to get water into the milking-can. Her round belly got in the way when she tried to plunge it in, and Masinque had to try several times.

Her arms got so tired that when the canister was almost full of water, she didn't have the strength to pull it out, and she let it fall to the bottom.

Seeing the canister disappear, she made such a funny face in her sorrow that Zizi, who'd been watching her struggles, burst out laughing.

Masinque looked up and realized the mistake that had fooled her. She was so angry that she wanted vengeance right away.

"What are you doing up there, lovely lady?" she said to Zizi.

"I'm waiting for my betrothed," said Zizi, and, with a naivety pardonable in a girl who until then had been only a charming little canary, she told Masinque her history.

Masinque had often seen the young prince pass that way before, when he'd gone out with his rifle strapped to his shoulder to gawk at the crows. She'd been too insignificant and ragged for him to notice her, but, for her part, she thought him a fine figure, if perhaps a little on the skinny side.

"Now, look here!" she said to herself, "if he likes yellow girls—Well, I'm yellow, too, and if I could just find a way—!"

It didn't take her long to think of a way.

"Hey!" said the crafty Masinque, "if people are going to be coming here in state to fetch you, aren't you afraid to show yourself, with your hair all in a snarl, in front of so many handsome lords and lovely ladies? Come down quick, my poor child, and I'll do your hair."

And the innocent Zizi came down next to Masinque. Masinque began to comb her long dark hair, then all of a sudden she took a pin from her dress, and, in the same way that a bluetit stabs its beak into a linnet or a hedge-sparrow, Masinque stabbed the pin into Zizi's head.

Zizi hardly had time to feel the sting before she changed back into the form of a golden bird, and took flight.

"That's a good job!" said Masinque. "The prince would have to be really clever to find his pretty girl again!"

And, straightening her dress, she sat down calmly on the grass to wait for Love's Desire.

XII

Meanwhile, the prince hurried back at full speed on his little white horse. In his impatience, he was fifty paces ahead of the ladies and lords Lord Barrow-Belly had sent to meet Zizi.

At the sight of the ugly Masinque, he stopped, mute with surprise and horror.

"Ah!" said Masinque, "don't you recognize your poor Zizi? The wicked sorceress came here during your absence, and look how she's

293

transformed me! I can only get my beauty back if you have the courage to marry me just the same."

And she started weeping hot tears. Désiré was as good and trusting as he was adventurous.

"Poor girl," he said. "If she has become so ugly, it's not her fault—it's mine. Why did I leave her alone? Why didn't I follow the old man's advice? Anyhow, it depends on me for her enchantment to be broken, and I love her too much to let her go on suffering in this condition."

And he presented Masinque to the nobles attending him, and told them of the terrible misfortune that had happened to his beautiful betrothed.

They acted as if they believed him, and the ladies set about the task of dressing the false princess in the rich robes they had brought for Zizi. Then they perched her on a superb palfrey, and the procession started on the road to the castle.

Alas! these ornaments only heightened Masinque's ugliness, and it was with a grieving soul and a blushing face that Love's Desire made his triumphal entry with her into the fair city of Avesnes.

The bells in the clock-tower rang a full peal, the carillon played all its tunes, the townsfolk crowded onto their doorsteps, and they stared at the singular bride, unable to believe their eyes.

To do them honor, Lord Barrow-Belly had come to the foot of the grand marble staircase to meet them. At the sight of the horrible creature, he thought he might fall over backwards.

"What! Is that your marvelous bride-to-be!" he cried.

"Yes, Father, she is," said Désiré sheepishly, "but a wicked sorceress has transformed her, and she will regain her beauty only when she becomes my wife."

"Is that what she told you? Well, well! if you believe that and drink plenty of plain water, you'll get good and fat," said Barrow-Belly, joking and sorrowful.

But he adored his son, so all the same he gave his hand to Masinque to lead her into the dining hall, where the betrothal feast was ready to serve.

XIII

The feast was exquisite, but Love's Desire hardly touched his food. The other guests ate so heartily they had to undo some buttons to make it at least look like a happy occasion. Barrow-Belly, who never lost his appetite over anything, stood out over all the others, wielding his fork magnificently.

When it came time to serve the goose, or, rather, the roast gander, there was a pause. As a friend of Cambrinus, Barrow-Belly knew how to make use of the delay to catch his breath, but soon, as the roast still hadn't made its appearance, he sent his carving-squire to see what was going on in the kitchen.

Now, this was what was going on.

While the gander was turning on the spit, a darling little canary was pushing in at the edge of the open window.

"Good-day, dear cook," she said in a high, flute-like voice, to the head-cook, who was watching over the roast.

"Good-day, lovely golden bird," said the head of the kitchen staff, a man who'd been well brought up.

"I pray to heaven to make you sleep," said the golden bird, "so that the gander will burn, and there won't be anything for Masinque to sink her beak into."

And sure enough, the head-cook fell asleep, and the gander burnt black as coal.

When he woke up, seeing what had happened, he ordered another gander to be plucked and stuffed with chestnuts and put on the spit.

While it was browning on the fire, Barrow-Belly asked again where the roast was. The head-cook went up to the dining hall himself to make his excuses and ask his lord to have patience, but Barrow-Belly's patience didn't stop him from scolding his son.

"It isn't enough," he said, gritting his teeth, "that this fine fellow has to go and lose his head over a hag without a cent—but then the gander has to get burnt! That isn't a woman you've brought here—she's Famine in person!"

XIV

Now, in the absence of head-cook, the golden bird came back and perched on the window-ledge, and said in its high little voice to the kitchen-boy who was watching the roast, "Good-day, good kitchen-boy."

"Good day, lovely golden bird," said the kitchen-boy, for in his dismay, the head-cook had forgotten to warn him.

"I pray to heaven to make you sleep," said the canary, "so that the gander will burn, and there won't be anything for Masinque to sink her beak into."

And the kitchen-boy fell asleep, and at his return the head-cook found the gander as black as the heart of the chimney.

Furious, he woke the kitchen-boy, who told him what had happened, to excuse himself.

"Accursed bird!" said the head-cook, "it's going to get me fired. Come on, the rest of you, go hide yourselves. If it comes back, trap it for me and wring its neck."

He put the third gander on the spit, lit a fire as hot as hell, and stationed himself next to it.

The bird re-appeared and said to him, "Good-day, good cook."

"Good-day, lovely golden bird," said the cook, as if nothing was the matter. And, at the moment when the canary started to say, "I pray to heaven to makie you sleep," a kitchen-boy, who had hidden himself just outside, slammed the shutters. The bird took flight through the kitchen.

At once, all the cooks, kitchen-boys, and sauce-mixers went chasing after it, trying to hit it with their aprons. One of them trapped it just at the moment when Barrow-Belly, followed by all the court, came into the kitchen, brandishing his scepter. He had come to see for himself why the gander wasn't ready.

The kitchen-boy, who was just going to wring the canary's neck, stopped short.

XV

"Will someone tell me what this means?" cried the lord of Avesnes.

"My lord, it's this bird!" said the kitchen-boy. And he handed it to him.

"What the plague!—what a pretty bird!" said Barrow-Belly, and he stroked it gently—and felt the pin that was stuck between its feathers. He drew it out, and—snap!—the canary changed into a pretty girl, with gold skin, who dropped lightly down.

"Plague and pest!—what a pretty girl!" cried Barrow-Belly.

"But that's her, Father! That's Zizi!" said Love's Desire, who had come in at that moment.

And he took her in his arms, saying, "My dearest Zizi, how glad I am to find you again!"

"What's that? Then who's the other?" asked the lord.

Masinque tried to make for the door.

"Stop her!" cried Barrow-Belly. "We'll sit in judgment on her here and now."

He sat himself gravely down on the stove, and, from the height of this throne, he condemned Masinque to be burnt alive. After he had made this judgment, all the nobles and the kitchen-boys lined up around them, and Barrow-Belly put Zizi's hand in Désiré's.

XVI

The marriage was celebrated a few days later. All the boys of Avesnes were there, armed with wooden swords and decorated with gold-paper epaulettes, like Saint Gregory, and they sang in the streets:

No one's ever seen
  Saint Gregory of old,
  No one's ever seen
  Saint Gregory so bold!

Zizi begged for mercy for Masinque, who was sent back to the brickmaker's, chased by them all. So it's not because, as people commonly say, that the bluetits betrayed God, but because of Masinque that the neighborhood boys even today hunt bluetits and throw stones at them.

The evening of the marriage, all the cupboards, all the kneading-troughs, the wine-cellars, store-rooms, and tables of the townsfolk, rich or poor, were magically stocked with bread, wine, beer, cakes, pies, and even roasted geese, ortolans, and larks. This was done so that Barrow-Belly could not possibly complain that his son was marrying Famine.

From that day on, abundance never ceased to reign in that land, and that is also why, since then, in Flanders, a country known for rosy-cheeked women, there are some lovely girls with gold skin, dark hair, and dark eyes.

The people of Avesnes have lost the memory of these events, but it is not very long since the pot-bellied people of Valenciennes would mark the close of the Carnival season by lighting fireworks off the Bridge of Great God that lit up in the shape of Barrow-Belly's paunch, the friend of King Cambrinus, and the patron of hearty eaters.

The Champion Crosse-Player

I

In olden times, in the village of Coq, near Condé-sur-l'Escaut, there lived a carlier—that is, a wheelwright—named Roger. He was a good friend, as reliable in pleasure as he was in pain, and as skilled at getting control of a crosse-ball with a stroke of his stick as he was in putting together a cart-wheel.

As everyone knows, the game of crosse-ball is rather like field hockey. You try to get a cholette—a ball made of dogwood—into the goal, by hitting it with a stick that has a crosspiece at the end, shaped like a crozier, a sort of little iron shoe without a heel.

For my part, I don't know any game that's more fun. Besides, when the field has been somewhat cleared of snags, all the people—men, women, and children—go out, striking at the ball with their staves—or their crosse-sticks, if you will. And nothing is so cheery as seeing them on a Sunday, speeding out like starlings in flight, across the turnip-fields, over the ploughed furrows.

II

Well, it happened one Tuesday—it was Fat Tuesday, the Mardigras—the Coq Carlier put down his chisel and put on the smock he wore to go drink a mug of beer in Condé, when two strangers came into his place, crosse-sticks in hand.

"Would you put the shoe-piece back on my crosse-stick, good sir?" said one of them.

"How can you ask that, my friends, on a day like today! I wouldn't undertake a snip of the scissors for a bar of gold. Anyhow, who plays crosse-ball on the Mardigras? You'd do better to go see the shows being performed in the main square in Condé."

"We don't feel like going to see the shows," said the stranger. "We were challenged to a game, and we want to finish the match. Won't you come along and help us?—they say you're one of the best players around here."

"Oh, if it's a question of taking a side in a match, that's different," said Roger.

He rolled up his sleeves, fastened his apron, and with a flick of the wrist, he adjusted the cross-piece.

"How much do I owe you?" asked the stranger, taking out his purse.

"Nothing at all, my boy—it was no trouble."

The stranger insisted, but in vain.

III

"You're being altogether too honest, my good fellow," he said to the wheelwright, "leaving people in your debt like that! So I'll grant you three wishes."

"Don't forget to wish for something good," added his companion.

At these words, the carlier smiled, incredulously. "Do you belong to the Capelette Birdies?"

The Birdies of the Capelette town-square were considered the biggest jokers in Condé.

"What do you take us for?" said the stranger, severely, and with his crosse-stick he touched an iron axle-tree, which changed on the spot to an axle-tree of pure silver.

"Who are you?" cried Roger, "—if you can turn iron into silver like that!"

"I am Saint Peter, and my companion is Saint Anthony, the patron of crosse-players."

"If you would be so kind as to come in, gentlemen," said the Carlier of Coq quickly; and he made the two saints go into the inner room. He offered them chairs and went to pull a pot of beer from the cellar. They had a drink, and then they lit their pipes.

"Since you are so good, gentlemen and saints," said Roger, "to let me have three wishes, for a long time, you know, I've wanted three things. First, I would like to have it so that anyone who sits down on the stump of the elm tree beside my door would have to stay there until I say they can go. I love company, and I get terribly bored when I'm alone."

Saint Peter shook his head, and Saint Anthony gave him a nudge.

IV

"When I go out to play cards, on Sunday evenings, at the Bold Rooster inn," the Carlier went on, "it's hardly struck nine o'clock when the village cop comes in and tells the drinkers that it's time to clear off. I wish that whoever has his feet set on my leather apron can't be chased away from the place where I had it spread out."

Saint Peter shook his head again, and Saint Anthony said solemnly, "Don't forget to ask for something better for you."

"Better still," said the Carlier of Coq, "I'd like to be the best crosse-player in the world. Each time that I meet my match, I feel as if my blood is running black as soot, like the heart of a chimney. So I'd like to have a crosse-stick that will hit the ball as high as the Condé bell-tower and win me the game, without fail."

"So shall it be!" said Saint Peter.

"You would do better," said Saint Anthony, "to ask for eternal salvation."

"Bah!" said Roger, "there's plenty of time for me to worry about that—I'm not ready yet to shine my boots for the great journey."

The two saints left, and Roger followed them, curious to get to see so unusual a game. But all at once, near the chapel of Saint Anthony, they disappeared before his eyes. The Carlier then went to see the shows being put on in the main square of Condé.

When he got back, around midnight, he found in the corner of his doorway the crosse-stick he had asked for. To his surprise, it was nothing but a miserable little iron stick fitted with a misshapen old cross-piece. However, he picked up the gift from Saint Peter and held it carefully.

V

The next day the Condé folk spread out in a crowd over the countryside to play crosse, eat smoked fish, and drink beer, to clear the clouds out of their heads and recover from the fatigues of the carnival.

The Carlier of Coq also came with his sad-looking stick and hit five blows so sharply that all the players left their own games to watch him. The following Sunday, he was even more skillful. Little by little, the word spread through the country. The players came running from ten leagues around to play against him, and it was then that people started calling him the Champion Crosse-Player.

Every Sunday, he spent the whole day playing crosse, and in the evening he would relax by playing a game of Marriage-cards at the Bold Rooster. He spread out his apron under the players' feet, and the Devil himself couldn't get them to leave.

On Monday mornings, he would stop the pilgrims who were going to serve Our Lady of Bon-Secours and persuade them to rest on his gossip-seat. And he wouldn't let them go until they'd made full confession of their stories.

In short, he was leading the pleasantest life a good Flamand could imagine, and the only thing he regretted was that he hadn't been able to wish that it would go on forever.

VI

Well, it happened one morning that Paternoster, the strongest crosse-player from Mons, was found dead at the side of a ditch. His head had been cracked open, and his crosse-stick was beside him, red with blood. No one knew how he had come by that gash, and, as Paternoster had often said that in a game of crosse he feared neither God nor Devil, they supposed that with these words he had offended Mynheer van Beelzebub, and that that was who had bashed his brains in, to punish him.

Mynheer van Beelzebub is, as everyone knows, the best player there ever was, on or under the earth, but he's especially fond of the game of crosse. When he made rounds in Flanders, he was almost always to be found with his crosse-stick in hand, like a true Flamand.

The Carlier of Coq had been good friends with Paternoster, who, after him, had been the best crosse-player in the country. He went to attend his funeral with some other crosse-players from the villages of Coq, Cigogne, and the Queue of Agache.

Coming back from the cemetery, they went into a tavern to drink, as we say around here, to the dead man's brains, and they forgot their sorrow in chatting about the noble game of crosse. When the evening grew dark and they started to go their separate ways, the Belgian crosse-players said to each other, "Safe journey!—and may Saint Anthony, the patron saint of crosse-players, keep you from meeting the Devil on your way!"

"I laugh at the Devil!" said Roger. "If he attacks me, I'd soon knock him off the field!"

The companions stopped in at tavern after tavern, without running into any bad luck, and it was not until long after the Condé belfry had sounded the hour of the wolves and time to be getting home, that each of them got back to his own place.

VII

As he was putting the key in the lock, the Carlier of Coq thought he heard a burst of mocking laughter behind him.

He turned around and saw in the shadows a man six feet tall who again burst out laughing.

"What are you laughing at?" Roger asked him, annoyed.

"What am I laughing at? Why, at your confidence in boasting just now that you'd dare to go up against the Devil."

"And why not, if he attacked me?"

"Oh, well, then, get your crosse-stick out. I am attacking you!" said Mynheer van Beelzebub, for that's who it was. Roger recognized him by a certain smell of sulfur that this lord always carries around with him.

"What's the wager?" he said boldly.

"Your soul?"

"Against what?"

"Whatever will please you."

The Carlier considered. "What have you got in your sack there?"

"The week's loot."

"Is Paternoster's soul in there?"

"Oh, heavens, yes!—and five other crosse-players like him who died without having made their last confessions."

"I'll play for my soul against Paternoster."

"It's a deal!"

VIII

The two opponents went into the nearby field, and chose as the goal the door of the Condé cemetery.

Beelzebub put his ball on a waroque—that's to say, a frozen clod of earth—and then said the customary words: "To get there, there from here, how many times three strokes will you need to get it there?"

"Two times," said the Champion Crosse-Player.

"Very good!" said Beelzebub.

302

He touched the ball with his stick, and it shone brightly all of a sudden, in the shadows, like an enormous glow-worm.

"Heads up!" cried Roger.

He touched the ball with the end of his crosse-stick, and it flew up into the sky like a star going to rejoin its sisters. In three strokes, it had covered three-fourths of the distance.

"Very good!" said Beelzebub, twice as astonished as before. "Now it's my turn!"

With a stroke of the flat of the crosspiece, he launched the ball over the roofs of Coq, close to the White House, a half-league away.

The stroke was so violent that the iron struck sparks out of a stone.

"Good Saint Anthony!—I'm lost, unless you come to my aid," murmured the Carlier of Coq.

Trembling, he hit the ball. And even though his arms seemed uncertain, the crosse-stick seemed to have acquired new strength. At the second stroke, the ball flew, as if by itself, and knocked against the gate of the cemetery.

"By my grandfather's horns!" cried Beelzebub, "I'm not going to have people saying that a son of that simpleton Adam beat me. Give me a return match."

"What shall we play for?"

"Your soul and Paternoster's against two crosse-players' souls."

IX

The Devil defended himself passionately. His crosse-stick at each stroke set off a shower of sparks. The ball flew from Condé to Bon-Secours, to Peruwelz, to Leuze. One time there was a trail as far as Tournai, six leagues away.

It left behind a luminous track, like a comet, and the two crosse-players followed, so to speak, along the trail it blazed. Roger never knew how he could run—or, rather, fly—so fast, never getting tired.

In short, he did not lose a single set, and he won the souls of the six deceased crosse-players. Beelzebub's eyes glowed like an angry tomcat's.

"Shall we keep going?" said the Carlier of Coq.

"No," said Beelzebub, "they're expecting me at the witches' sabbat, on top of Mount Copiémont. "That crook there," he thought to himself, "could empty out my whole game-bag."

And he disappeared.

When the Champion Crosse-Player got back home, he shut the souls he'd won in a sack and went to bed, enchanted at having defeated Mynheer van Beelzebub.

X

Two years later, the Carlier of Coq had a visit that he hadn't been expecting. An old man, tall, thin, and yellow, came into his work-room, carrying a scythe on his shoulder.

"I see you're bringing me your scythe to have a new handle put on, sir."

"No, my boy, my scythe never needs a new handle."

"Then what can I do for you?"

"You must follow me: your hour has come."

"The Devil!" said the Champion Crosse-Player. "Can't you just wait a bit while I finish up this wheel?"

"All right. I've had a lot of work to get through today, and I think I deserve a moment to sit down and smoke a pipe."

"In that case, sir, sit down there, on the gossip-seat. I can offer you some of our famous Belgian tobacco—seven pence a pound."

"That sounds good, my boy—but hurry it up."

And Death lit his pipe and sat down by the door on the elm-tree stump.

Laughing in his beard, the Carlier of Coq went back to work. At the end of a quarter of an hour, Death shouted, "Hey, my boy! aren't you done yet?"

The Carlier turned a deaf ear and went on planing the wood, while he sang:

> *"Wait for me on the elm-tree stump.*
> *You'll wait and wait and never jump!"*

"I don't think he heard me," thought Death. "Hey, my friend, are you ready?"

> *"See if the guests are coming, dear,*
> *Go and see if the guests are here,"*

replied the singer.

"Is that lout making fun of me?" said Death.

And he tried to stand up.

304

To his great astonishment, he couldn't free himself from the gossip-seat. He realized then that he was the pawn of a higher power.

"Now, look," he said to Roger, "What do you want in return for freeing me? Would you like me to give you ten more years of life?"

"I've good tobacco in my pouch,"
sang the Champion Crosse-Player.

"How about twenty years?"

"It's raining, shepherd, raining hard.
Get your white sheep in the yard."

"Lucifer take you, Carlier—how about fifty years more?"

The Carlier of Coq sang out at the top of his lungs:

"Sail away safe, dear Dumello
Land yourself safe, at Saint-Malo."

Meanwhile, the clock in Condé had just sounded four o'clock, and the boys got out of school. The sight of this big, skinny heron of a fellow struggling on the Carlier's gossip-seat, like a devil caught in a basin of holy water, surprised and then delighted them. They suspected that although he was sitting at the old man's gate, Death was lying in wait for the young, so it amused them to stick out their tongues at him and repeat in chorus:

"Sail away safe, dear Dumello
Land yourself safe, at Saint-Malo."

"How about a hundred years?" shouted Death.

"Hmmm—a hundred years more of life, you say? I accept gladly, sir, but let's be clear: I'm not so stupid as to ask that you just lengthen my old age."

"What do you want, then?"

"What I want from age is the experience that it gives, little by little. 'If youth knew—if age could!' says the proverb. During that hundred years, I want to keep the strength of a young man as well as acquiring the knowledge of an old man."

"All right!" said Death. "I'll be back in a century—to the day."

"If you'll just take the trouble to stand up, dear sir," said Roger, with a sarcastic smile.

Friend Death didn't need to be told twice. He rose up, as obedient as a blind man's guide-dog, and withdrew, his scythe on his shoulder, while the naughty little boys escorted him away, singing at ear-splitting volume:

"Sail away safe, dear Dumello

Land yourself safe, at Saint-Malo."

XI

The Champion Crosse-Player took up his new life. He played then with perfect happiness, made even greater by knowing that it would be a century before it came to an end. Thanks to his experience, he was so good at running his affairs that he was able to put down his hammer and leave his shop-door closed.

However, he found there was one annoyance that he hadn't foreseen. His prodigious skill at crosse ended by frightening off the other players. At first, even that delighted him, but later it meant that no one would play against him.

He left the canton and began wandering through French-speaking Flanders, through Belgium, and all the countries where the noble game of crosse is held in honor.

At the end of twenty years he returned to Coq to win the admiration of a new generation of crosse-players, and then set out again, returning another twenty years later.

Alas! in spite of its obvious charms, this life soon became hard to bear. It was boring to win all the time, and besides that, it was wearisome to keep passing, like the Wandering Jew, across the generations, and to see the sons, the grandsons, and the great-grandsons of his friends dying, each in their turn.

He had to keep making new friends, and then lose them to age and death, like everyone else. Everything kept changing around him—he was the only one who didn't change.

He grew impatient with his perpetual youth, which condemned him to keep tasting the same pleasures, and sometimes he wished he could know the calmer enjoyments of old age.

One day he was surprised to find himself standing in front of his mirror, trying to see if his hair might be turning white. Nothing seemed as handsome to him now as the snowy locks of old men.

XII

And besides that, experience had soon made him wise—so wise that nothing at all amused him anymore. If, sometimes, in a tavern, he got a notion into his head about using his apron to spend the night playing cards, his long experience would whisper to him, "What good is too much! Making the days go by faster isn't enough—what's needed is a way to keep from getting sick of it."

It got to the point where he refused the pleasure of drinking his pint and smoking his pipe. After all, why plunge into pleasures that weaken the body and weigh down the spirit?

The unhappy man went even further, and gave up playing crosse. Experience had convinced him that the game of crosse is dangerous. The players get over-heated—just the thing to lead to a runny nose, a sore throat, rheumatism, and pneumonia.

Anyhow, what good is it—even if there's no glory so fine as being known as the finest crosse-player in the world?

What good is glory—isn't it just smoke, as pointless as the smoke from a pipe?

When experience in this way had taken all his illusions from him, the unlucky crosse-player felt bored to death. He realized that he'd been mistaken, that illusion is worth something, and that the greatest charm to being young might be its inexperience.

And so he came to the date set by the contract, and, as he had not found Paradise below, on the earth, he examined the wisdom he'd acquired through so much pain to see if there was some clever way he could win it up above.

XIII

Death found him at Coq, at work in his shop. Experience had at least taught him that work, after all, is the pleasure that lasts longest.

"Are you ready?" said Death.

"I am."

He took his crosse-stick, put twenty crosse-balls in his pockets, threw his sack over his shoulder, and buckled his over-shoes, without taking off his apron.

"What do you need your crosse-stick for?"

"Oh!—why, to play crosse in Paradise with Saint Anthony, my patron-saint."

"Do you think I'm going to lead you to Paradise?"

"You'll have to, because I'm carrying half a dozen souls in my sack that I saved long ago from the claws of Beelzebub."

"You'd do better to try to save your own. Let's be off—'dear Dumello'!"

The Champion Crosse-Player understood that the old Reaper was still angry at him, and that he was going to lead him straight to the Paradise of black chickens.

Sure enough, a quarter of an hour later, the two travelers were rapping at the gate of Hell.

Knock-knock.

"Who's that?"

"The Carlier of Coq," said the Champion Crosse-Player.

"Don't open it!" cried Beelzebub. "That rascal wins every stroke—he could depopulate my whole empire."

Roger smiled in his beard.

"Oh, don't think you're saved," said Death. "I'm going to take you where you won't be feeling cold ever again."

In less time than it takes a poor man to empty out the alms-box, they were at Purgatory.

Knock-knock.

"Who's that?"

"The Carlier of Coq," said the Champion Crosse-Player.

"But he's in a state of mortal sin," cried the angel standing guard. "Take that parishioner away from here."

"I can hardly leave him hanging about between Heaven and Earth," said Death. "I'll take him back to Coq."

"—where they'll take me for a spook, thank you very much! Don't we still have Paradise left to try?"

XIV

They were there in less than an hour.

Knock-knock.

"Who's that?"

"The Carlier of Coq," said the Champion Crosse-Player.

"Ah, my boy," said Saint Peter, opening the gate a crack, "I'm really terribly sorry. Saint Anthony warned you, you'd have done better to ask for your soul's salvation."

"That's true, my lord Saint Peter," said Roger sheepishly. "And how is he, that joyous Saint Anthony? Couldn't I come in, just for a little minute, to repay the visit he paid me long ago, with you?"

"There he is just coming now," said Saint Peter, and he swung the gate wide open.

In a blink of an eye, the sly crosse-player flung himself into Paradise, unfastened his apron, let it fall to the ground, and sat down on it.

"Good-day, my lord Saint Anthony," he said politely, bending low. "As you can see, I found the time to think about Paradise—because here we are, all of us!"

"What! You and who else?" cried Saint Peter.

"Yes, me and my company," said Roger, opening his sack and shaking the souls of the six crosse-players out on the ground.

"Be so kind as to clear out, all of you!"

"Impossible!" said the Champion Crosse-Player, pointing out his apron.

"This joker's making fun of us," said Saint Anthony. "Come on, Saint Peter, in memory of our game of crosse, let him come in with his souls. He really did his time in Purgatory while he was still on Earth."

"It's not setting much of a good example," muttered Saint Peter.

"Bah!" said Roger, "when you're getting such a fine crosse-player in Paradise, where's the harm?"

XV

And that is how, after having lived a long time, played a lot of crosse, and emptied lots of mugs of beer, the Carlier of Coq, called the Champion Crosse-Player, was admitted to Paradise. But I wouldn't advise anyone to copy him, because that's not at all the way to go, and Saint Peter could hardly be in such a good mood all the time.

Caracol Bistécol

In olden times, in the days when the Belgian lion wandered through the forests of Flanders, in company with bears and panthers, there was a little hunchback who lived in the village of Waudrez, near Binche. He was a broomier by trade—I mean, he made brooms and besoms for chimney sweeping, and he earned enough to live in poverty with his old mother.

People called him the Caracol, which is the name around here for the colimaçon snail, and no doubt they bestowed that name on him so that his name would match his figure.

Hunchbacked and lame, he looked so funny when he was out walking with his cane that people could not help laughing when they saw him.

Since childhood, his figure had been a subject of perpetual mockery. He was hardly six years old when a witch predicted to his mother that he would marry a princess, when his hump grew on the front, under his nose. Later still, whenever he went to Binche, he couldn't go by the Hurtebise Inn without having that jokester of an innkeeper sing the well-known song of *"Caracol, Bistécol"* after him:

> *Caracol,*
> *Wry-neck,*
> *Show us your horns,*
> *Your horns.*
> *I'll tell you when you'll get an orgy:*
> *At Mons, or at Tournai,*
> *At Lille, or at Douai,*
> *In the street of Georgie-Porgie.*

Caracol never tried to answer the jeers that fell like hail on his hump all the livelong day. Often people could hear him whistling the tune of *"The Song of the Caracol"* himself. And that was why people felt that his soul was fairer than his figure.

They couldn't say as much for the other hunchback, who was like Caracol for ugliness, and who was the seneschal of the Baron of Binche. His title was Lord of Malicorne. To make fun of him, though, jokers around there always called him Bistécol—Wry-neck. As he held the rank of a swordsman, Bistécol did not bear their raillery with patience. He realized that he owed his nickname to his resemblance to Caracol, and so he hated him with all his heart.

His hatred grew to such a point that one day he resolved to arrange to have the poor devil disappear. Under the pretext that the forest was haunted by wild animals, he ordered a set of big, deep ditches to be dug, with vertical sides, and covered over with leaves, so that the animals would fall into the trap.

They were dug in secret, at night, in the place where Caracol always went early in the morning to look for birch-twigs. The seneschal hoped that the broom-maker, walking in the shadows before sunrise, would fall in and break his back.

He even wanted to see with his own eyes that his orders were being faithfully carried out. So he went to the chosen place well before day-break.

He was so caught up in dreaming about how happy he'd be to be rid of this nightmare that he was going along without watching where he was going, when suddenly—crash!—he fell in the trap. He hadn't ex-pected any ill fortune, but now he shouted in vain, for no one came run-ning to help him.

After a few moments, he heard a noise overhead, and a hare fell in next to him. Soon after, he heard another noise, and a bear, and then a lion, came to keep him company.

Well, you can imagine how much at his ease Bistécol felt in that so-ciety. He thought he would die of fear, when he heard someone whistling the tune of the "Caracol."

He realized it was the broom-maker, whistling his favorite song, and although he felt humiliated at having to owe his life to the one whose death he'd tried to engineer, he started calling for help again.

"Who's there?" asked Caracol, coming near.

"It's me, the chief seneschal!" said Bistécol. "Throw me a rope so I can get out of this damned hole."

"I don't have one here long enough," said Caracol, "but have pa-tience, my lord, and I'll go back to the village and find one."

"Hurry it up—the ditch is full of wild beasts, and it's a miracle that I'm still alive."

311

The broom-maker ran as fast as he could to his house, which was on the edge of the village, right next to the forest. He took the rope out of his well, tied a slip-knot in it, and returned lickety-split to throw it in the hole. Pulling it back out again, he sensed that there was something enormously heavy on the other end.

"You're pretty heavy, my lord!" said Caracol.

"That's not me going up," said Bistécol. "It's a lion."

"A lion! Good God!" said Caracol.

And he let the rope fall back.

"What are you doing?" cried Bistécol.

"I'm not supposed to be pulling up a lion," said Caracol. "It's supposed to be you. So grab hold of the rope—"

"I can't. The lion won't let me take his place. Pull him up—I can come next."

"Suppose he eats me?—I'm the sole support of my old mother."

"Get me out of here, and I swear to you that you and your mother will never again be in need of anything."

And, as Caracol seemed to be still hesitating, Bistécol added, "Hurry it up, or you'll make the lion lose patience."

Caracol reflected that he would have a chance of escaping the lion's teeth, but it would certainly gobble up Lord Malicorne. He tied his rope around an old hollow oak and pulled up the lion, winding the rope around the tree trunk.

When he saw the lion had reached the top, he hid himself behind the tree and hurried to climb on up, but the King of the Animals said to him, "Many thanks!—you will soon have proof that you haven't helped an ungrateful animal."

And with a bound he plunged away through the forest.

"Your turn now, my lord!" cried Caracol to the seneschal.

He sent the rope down, but it was the bear that it brought up. Like the lion, the bear said, before going on his way, "Thank you—you haven't helped an ungrateful animal."

"Finally, it's my turn!" cried Bistécol, but just when the broom-maker was throwing the rope down, he noticed a fly caught in a spider web, in the hollow of the oak, buzzing in distress. Already the spider had come out of its lair when Caracol swept the web aside with his hand and freed the fly.

"Hurry up!" cried the seneschal.

The broom-maker let down the rope, and the seneschal climbed up.

"You kept me waiting too long!" he said, in a surly tone.

"Pardon me, my lord. I was saving someone whose plight was more urgent than yours."

"Who?"

"A fly struggling in a spider web."

"You call that a good excuse?" said the seneschal. And he left without thanking his deliverer.

Thinking he had emptied the ditch, Caracol was setting about his work, when he heard a thin little voice that cried:

"Hey there! What about me? Aren't you going to have the courtesy to pull me out, too?"

"Is there someone still there?" asked the hunchback, leaning over the hole.

"Yes," said the voice, "someone who begs you for help in the name of all the saints in Paradise."

Caracol paid out the rope, and brought out the hare. After thanking him, as the other beasts had done, the hare raced away.

"That's almost half the day gone by!" he said. He tried to go faster to make up for lost time, for he didn't want hs mother to suffer because of other people's clumsiness.

Unfortunately, in his haste he gashed his thumb with his billhook, and had to go back home to bandage it.

He wasn't able to work the rest of that day, and as the household was so poor that they could only live day to day, the next day they had no food.

III

Caracol felt miserable.

"Why don't you go see the seneschal?" said his mother.

"That's right," the hunchback thought, "he promised me a fine reward."

He went to the castle and knocked timidly at the gate.

"What do you want?" asked the gatekeeper.

"I'd like to speak to my lord the seneschal."

"My lord the seneschal is not to be seen."

"I met him yesterday in the forest—I daresay he'll see me."

The gatekeeper risked going to tell the seneschal.

"The rogue is lying," said Bistécol. "I don't know him."

The gatekeeper brought this answer back to the broom-maker, who went sadly home to his mother.

"My lord was no doubt in a bad mood," she told him. "Have patience, and try again tomorrow."

They got by that day on credit, and the next day Caracol went to knock again at the castle-gate. At his earnest entreaty, the gatekeeper again agreed to go ask the seneschal.

But Bistécol, in a rage, grabbed a stick, ran to the door, and beat the hunchback so furiously that poor Caracol was left for dead on the threshold.

Some charitable passers-by picked him up and carried him to his house, where he had to stay in bed a fortnight. His mother did her best to take care of him, and sold off the little they owned to get them some food.

IV

Once he was back on his feet, Caracol went to cut some birchwood in the forest. When he got near that unlucky trap, he found himself face to face with a lion. He was astonished, but the lion said to him, "Wait for me here," and was off like a shot.

Caracol recognized him as the one he had drawn out of the trap.

The animal soon came back, holding in its jaws a big sack of gold florins, which he deposited at the feet of his rescuer. He had gone to find it in his cave, where some robbers had hidden it under a pile of dead leaves.

The broom-maker thanked the lion and went back to his hut. With the gold, he paid his debts royally, and, as he and his mother had enough left over to live on, he stopped making brooms.

From then on he could just enjoy himself, go for walks morning to evening, and soon finished, as you might expect, by getting bored.

One day, he was smoking his pipe in the woods, watching the birds building their nests, when he ran into his friend the lion. He got the idea of traveling through the world with him, for amusement.

He proposed this plan to the king of beasts, who accepted, and they planned to get together and start out the next day. The next day, Caracol rose at the same time as th sun, said goodbye to his mother, and rejoined his friend.

They set off, and, on the road, they encountered the bear, who was coming, with his most gracious air, to give a polite greeting to his rescuer. They asked him to accompany them; and, although he was hardly fond of society, the bear was too grateful to give them a box on the ears. A little farther on, they found the hare, too, who did not run away when they drew near, and they enlisted him, as well.

All four went in this way through cities, towns, and villages, earning a living by displaying their talents. The lion and the bear danced the gavotte, while the hare played the tambourine, and Caracol passed the hat.

V

For five years, Caracol traveled through the world, after which he started longing to see Flanders again.

When he got to the forest of Binche, he dismissed his animals, and went to kiss his mother, and then wandered around the town.

He was greatly surprised to find that it was all hung with black crape, like a church where someone important is being buried.

Phirin Simollet, the innkeeper of the Hurtebise, was standing at his door. He caught sight of the hunchback coming and, for the first time in his life, he hadn't the heart to sing:

Caracol,
Wry-neck,
Show us your horns,
Your horns.

"Why is the town all covered in crape?" the traveler asked him.

"What!" said Phirin, "don't you know about the misfortune that's stricken us! Are they that far behind in Waudrez?"

"I was only there in passing—I've been traveling about the world."

"Oh, well! the town, my boy, is given over to grief, because the lovely Eglantine, the baron's daughter, must die tomorrow."

"Is she so dangerously ill?"

"Not at all—she's a delight to see, she's as fresh and rosy as a wild rose , but—alas! she's still going to die."

"But why?"

"Two leagues from here, on the side toward Ath, there's a giant who was born in this town, in the Brantegnies neighborhood. But he grew so big that by the time he was five he couldn't stay here. He couldn't find a house big enough to hold him. People called him Goliath, after the giant who was killed by the shepherd David, but David's Goliath was hardly more than ten feet tall, whereas ours is more than twice that size.

"And he's so prodigiously strong that he pulls up trees by the roots, and he crushes lions and bears between his arms. He goes into towns and sacks them all by himself. He pulls the roofs off houses as easily as his mother pulls the lid off her cooking pot, and he would demolish everything top to bottom, if you don't surrender to him unconditionally.

"We've sent whole regiments out against him, but he goes clad in iron, and the arrows bounce off his breastplate. He pierces through their ranks with an oak for a club, and, as he kills two men with one blow, it doesn't take him long to make the rest scamper. He's forced the whole countryside to bring him cartloads of soil and build him a high mountain, with big trees planted on it. At the summit of this mountain he's made them build him an immense tower. He lives there by hunting and also by the contributions he makes the country give him. Every year, at the feast of our patron saint, he has himself a feast—the flesh of a young woman. This year, the lot fell on the lovely Eglantine, the baron's daughter, so tomorrow she must be led to him in state."

"Hasn't anyone come forward," said Caracol, "to slay him, either by strength or trickery?"

"The baron has declared," said Phirin Simollet, "that he would give his daughter's hand to anyone who would kill the giant. But there's not a knight who's dared to try it."

"They must not have any heart or any spirit," said Caracol.

"I'd like to see you try it yourself! Come to that, you must be a brainy sort of fellow, marked with the letter B as you are! I'd bet on you to make an end of Goliath!"

"Who knows!" said the hunchback, "a little man can cut down a great oak." Paying no heed to Phirin's laughter, he started thinking about it. He wouldn't be sorry to show him that hunchbacks were, in fact, something more than ordinary people.

VI

The following day, Caracol got up as early as the hens and took out his crossbow and his quiver.

"Are you going to shoot a little bird?" said his mother.

"Yes, Mother, and, if I win the prize, you'll be able to take it easy—we'll have had a good day."

He went into the forest and whistled to his animals.

They came running, one by one, and when they were all seated in front of him, with their tails tucked under them, he said, "My friends, we have to make ourselves known by a master-stroke. There's an immense giant near here who eats up all the pretty girls. People are counting on us to rid the land of him. There'll be the devil in it if we four can't—"

"We four!" said the lion. "I can take care of him all by myself!"

"No," said Caracol. "The giant Goliath is all clad in iron, and he's so strong that he crushes lions in his arms. Courage won't be enough—we'll need some tricks,"

"In that case, that's my job," said the hare, "Let's go check out the place. Once we're there, we can decide what do do."

The four of them left together. When they got to the giant's mountain, they separated, and climbed up, creeping stealthily.

When they were in sight of the tower-keep, the hare circled around it, and examined the place carefully. Then he thought it over for a minute, and whispered into the ear of each of his friends that he would lie low behind the trees.

The giant Goliath was getting dressed. He had put on his iron boots, his thigh-pieces, his arm-pieces, his breast-plate, and his neck-guard. All he had left to put on was his helmet and throat-protector.

Suddenly he heard a singular noise. He looked up from his mirror and saw out the window a hare running around the tower-keep. The hare was followed, silently, by a bear, and a lion behind the bear. The giant thought they looked so funny that he burst out laughing. He went on laughing while the animals came gravely round again, passing in single file, always keeping the same distance apart.

Goliath held his sides. He thought he should be able to get some good out of this windfall, so he got up and went to lie in wait behind the door. At the moment when the beasts came round again, he leaned forward to grab them up in an armful—the hare, the bear, and the lion together.

Suddenly, twang! An arrow flew into his right eye and went deep into his head. He lifted his hands up and drew the arrow out, but with one bound the lion leaped at his throat and, holding down his arms, began devouring the giant.

The bear seized the legs, and together the two of them overwhelmed the giant, who was pulled down, clanging as he fell, as loud as a tower collapsing. But in a few moments, leaping like a carp, he was up, raising them from the ground, and he would no doubt have succeeded in freeing himself from their hold, if Caracol had not bravely plunged his knife into the giant's throat.

The giant gave up the ghost with a frightful groan.

VII

Meanwhile, the princess was approaching, with the court of Binche. When they got to the foot of the mountain, weeping, she kissed her father, who himself was melted in tears, and she climbed up toward Goliath's tower-keep.

Then the baron and his court withdrew, for they could not bear to stay and see what was coming. Bistécol alone stayed, looking as if nothing was happening. Secretly, he hated the princess, because she had sometimes laughed at his hump, and he was not sorry to be there to see her torment—from a safe distance.

Poor Eglantine found it hard to walk, and stopped at each tree to rest, for her legs were weak with terror. When she came at last to the summit, she was much astonished at not seeing Goliath standing in front of his tower.

She took a few steps more, and—instead of the giant—it was Caracol who came forward to receive her.

"Beautiful Princess," he said, "don't be afraid! Goliath is dead, and there's his body."

Eglantine, at this sight, was so overcome with joy that she fainted. Caracol soon awakened her.

"So it's you who will be my husband," she said, opening her eyes. Her heart was at peace, and her rescuer was so welcome a sight that she felt there was nothing in the world more beautiful.

She took off her coral necklace, so long it went around her neck six times, and shared it out among the animals. The lion got the part with the gold clasp. Then she gave the broom-maker her cambric handkerchief, with her name embroidered on it.

Caracol then cut off the tip of the giant's tongue, folded it in the handkerchief, and put it carefully in his pocket.

He stayed no longer, and started to lead the princess back to her father, but the lovely Eglantine was worn out with all she had been through.

"I beg you," she said, "let me sleep here a little while—I'm so exhausted."

"Sleep, lovely Princess," said Caracol. "I'll keep watch over you."

Lady Eglantine stretched out on the grass and soon was fast asleep. Caracol sat down beside her, took out his pipe, and began smoking, while he waited for her to wake up.

Unfortunately, he, too, was tired, and, while he sat smoking, he felt sleep coming over him. He called the lion and said to him, "I'm going to sleep a little. Keep watch over us so that nothing comes and takes us by surprise."

And he fell asleep.

The lion stood guard, but he, too, was tired after the battle. He called the bear and said to him, "Stay here, Martin, my friend. I need to nod off for a bit. If something happens, be sure to wake us."

The bear sat down next to the lion, but he was just as weary as the others. He called to the hare and said to him, "Come here. I can't keep my eyes open. If there's any trouble, wake me right away."

Unluckily, in running right under Goliath's nose, the hare had been so scared that he was ten times more worn out than his friends. He fell asleep, and that's why, to this day, when something that was supposed to be watched is badly guarded, we say that the order fell in a hare's ears.

So they were all asleep—the princess, Caracol, the lion, the bear, the hare—and they slept as soundly as judges at a hearing.

VIII

When the giant did not appear, the seneschal wondered if something had happened to him. Little by little, his curiosity won out over his fear, and he decided to risk climbing the mountain.

When he got to the top, he saw Goliath's immense corpse, and, not far away, the princess, Caracol, and the beasts, all fast asleep.

At once a diabolical idea occurred to him. "Ah, my beauty!" he said, "so hunchbacks make you laugh! Well, now!—you'll have a hunchback for your husband, and not the one you're expecting!"

He drew his sword and cut off Caracol's head. Then he managed to cut off the giant's head, too, so that he could take it away with him as proof of his victory. When he'd done that, he took the sleeping girl in his arms, and, holding the head of Goliath in one hand, he went back down the mountain.

But the head was too big, and the seneschal soon found it too much to manage. He dropped it in front of him and rolled it with his foot down to the bottom. When he got there, the princess awoke.

She looked at him with astonishment, and then said, "What are you doing? And my rescuer—where is he?"

"That's me," said Bistécol. "I rescued you."

"No, my lord seneschal," said Eglantine. "The one who rescued me isn't anything like you. Don't think you can take his place."

"As to that—we'll see," said the seneschal, and added, drawing his sword, "You're going to die this instant unless you swear to me, by your hope of a place in Paradise, that you'll let your father believe that I saved you all by myself."

Princess Eglantine knew what the seneschal was capable of. She resigned herself to it for the moment and swore the oath he wanted.

A peddler from Jolimetz came driving by in his cart just then, shouting, "Cherries for old iron!" Bistécol stopped the cart and put the giant's head into it, on the straw at the bottom, then made the princess climb in, climbed in himself, and ordered the trader to take them to the castle of the Baron of Binche.

At the sight of his daughter, safe and sound, the baron was beside himself with joy.

"I have killed the giant and freed the princess," the imposter said then, "so I claim the hand of the lovely Eglantine."

"That's only right," said the count, and no matter what it cost him to accept a son-in-law who was such a lump of a man, he asked the princess to say what was in her heart."

"I have to go along with that," she said, although she could not understand how the seneschal had stolen her from her liberator.

IX

On the mountain, lying next to their dead master, the animals were snoring, almost harmoniously. Just then, a big fly came along to join the party and landed on the hare's nose.

The hare was deeply asleep, even though his eyes were open, and he brushed her away with his paw and went on sleeping. The fly tried again, but the sleeper again shoved her away, and with the drowsy sound of the fly's buzzing, slept more soundly than ever.

The fly tried a third time, and thrust her long needle of a mouth into the hare's nose. The hare sneezed and woke up.

"Devil take it!" he said. "It looks as if I fell asleep just like the others. I'd better hurry and get them up, and not wait for a warning!"

And he quickly woke the bear, who woke the lion.

When the lion saw that Caracol was dead, and the princess vanished, he flew into a fit of rage, and let out such horrible roars that the mountain shook with it.

"Who cut our friend's throat?" he cried. "Bear, why didn't you stay awake?"

And the furious bear said to the hare, "Why didn't you stay awake, you little fool?"

The poor hare didn't know how to reply. His terrible companions were about to fall on him, when he begged them for pity's sake to hear him out.

"Don't hurt me," he said, "and I promise to bring our master back to life."

"How?" asked the lion.

"On the road to Tournai," said the hare, "I know that on Trinity Mountain there's a root that has been gifted with such power that anyone who gets a bit of it in his mouth will be healed of every wound."

"Go this instant," said the lion, "Bring it back to me inside a quarter of an hour."

The hare darted away, and in less time than it takes a poor old man to thread his way through three *Pater Noster* prayers and two *Ave Marias*, he brought back the root.

The lion put their master's head back on his shoulders, and the hare put the root in his mouth. Instantly, his heart started beating, and the color came back into his cheeks. Caracol drew a long breath, sneezed, and opened his eyes.

"Ah! What a good sleep I had!" he said, stretching. Then he looked around and asked the animals, "What about the princess? What have you been doing?"

"We were overcome by slumber," said the lion, "and when we woke up, we couldn't find her."

"She's run away," thought Caracol, "for fear of marrying a hunchback as ugly as I am."

This idea made him so sad that he had not the courage to go to the castle to reclaim the hand of the princess.

He took up his crossbow and quiver, bade farewell to his animals, and returned to his mother's house.

X

He got there just as the cuckoo was singing noon. The soup was steaming in the soup-pot, but the mistress of the house had gone out. As he was very hungry, he sat down at the table, not waiting on ceremony.

At the first spoonful, he was much surprised that he couldn't find his mouth. Then he realized that his head was on backwards, with his face looking out over his back.

Until then, he had been so absorbed by his grief, that he hadn't noticed an extraordinary thing—instead of his hands and feet, it was his hump that was right under his eyes!

"What's going on?" he said to himself. "How could this have happened while I was sleeping?"

To find out, he went back to the forest, and he whistled for the lion. The lion, who was not far off, ran to him at once.

"How did this happen?" said Caracol. "My head's looking backward instead of forward!"

"That accursed slumber!" cried the lion, "That's what's played this trick on us! When I woke up, I found you dead, your head cut from your body. At once I sent off to Trinity Mountain to find the root of life, and I was in such a hurry to get your head back on your shoulders, that I got it on the wrong way round."

"What a nuisance!" said Caracol. "Not to mention that it's not easy to eat a bowl of soup—"

"Oh, don't worry about that!" said the king of beasts.

And without a word of warning, he bit off Caracol's head, stuffed the root between his teeth, and put the head on again, the right way round.

He'd hardly finished, when Caracol's mother came back in, all upset.

She had just been to buy a half-ounce of chicory with suet, and while the soup was getting cold, she had asked, "What's the news?"

"Well!" she said to her son, "it seems the giant is dead now, and he was killed by a knight who brought the princess back."

322

"Oh!" said Caracol, "and who is this knight?"

"They hadn't heard yet at Waudrez, but if you want to find out, all you have to do is pay a visit to Binche."

"I'll go tomorrow," said the hunchback. He was thinking over the sorceress's prediction. Hadn't he just seen his hump under his nose?

He would have gone right away, but, having had his head cut off twice in one day, he had a bit of a migraine.

XI

The next day, he went into the forest, called his animals, and set off with them for Binche.

From one end of town to the other, from the Hurtebise inn to the baron's castle, the town was hung with scarlet.

Caracol went to the inn and asked what was the cause of all these joyous decorations.

"They're celebrating the engagement of the lord's daughter," said Phirin.

"Who's she going to marry?"

"Dear God! It's Bistécol, the seneschal."

"So he was the one who killed the giant?"

"The very one. For proof, he brought back the giant's head."

"She's going to marry Bistécol!" thought the hunchback. "But he's even more misshaped than I am, and she knows perfectly well that he had nothing to do with rescuing her! How can I find out if she's doing this of her own free will or not?"

"You've been touring your hump all round the world—were you showing your beasts in an animal act?" Phirin Simollet asked him.

"Yes, that's right."

"Well, well! You're going to be as welcome as fish in Lent, because we're going to be having magnificent entertainments. Are your beasts well trained?"

"You'll get to judge for yourself," said Caracol. Phirin Simollet's question gave him an idea for finding out what he wanted to know. "I'll have dinner here at your place with my troupe, but I don't want to eat your cooking."

"Whose cooking do you think you want?"

"The baron's cook."

"Bah! Just how do you think you're going to get that?"

"These fine fellows will go get it for me." And Caracol nodded at his animals.

"That's a good one!—but you're joking."

"I'll bet a hundred florins that before the table's set, they'll bring me back a superb roast."

"Done!" said Phirin Simollet.

"Well, then! Loosen your belt-buckle, my boy, because I'm inviting you," said Caracol, and he threw a hundred florins on the table. Then he turned to his animals and said, "Be so kind as to do me the favor of going to ask the princess for a roast like the one the court is eating."

"On my way!" said the hare, and in two jumps and four bounds, he was out of sight. But he hadn't reckoned on the village dogs, who ran after him, barking and baying at the top of their lungs.

When he got to the castle, he slid into the sentry-box, without being spotted by the guard. The pack fell on the sentry-box in a whirlwind of paws and jaws, but they were driven back with blows from a crosse-stick, and they fled, howling.

With the dogs gone, the hare saw his chance, and, Presto! he jumped on into the courtyard of the castle. He looked around for the lovely Eglantine, and saw her leaning on her elbows to look out from a window on the floor above. He hurried up, ran into her room—the door was ajar—and lightly scratched the princess's foot.

"Go away!" said the princess, thinking it was only her little dog.

The hare scratched again, getting the same answer, but at the third try Eglantine looked down and recognized the hare by the collar made from her necklace.

At once, she took him in her arms and said to him, "What do you want, little Hare, dear friend?"

"My master, who killed the giant," said the hare, "has sent me to ask you for some of the roast that the court is getting to eat."

At this moment, the bear and the lion appeared in the hall. They came in very peaceably, and the people weren't afraid of them. They confirmed the hare's request, and the princess's eyes sparkled.

She sent someone to find the cook and tell him to carry to the Hurtebise inn the finest filet of beef the cook had browning on the spit.

She said she also wanted some special mincemeat pies, a fat capon, a quarter of venison, and, for dessert, a basket brim-full with sweet flemish cakes, bar cookies from Lille, and some hidden-toast, as some call it—and some call it french-toast, but here in Condé we call it mud-toast—and some cherries, raspberries, peaches, and oranges. And she ordered the servants to be sure to include six bottles of the best wine to wash down this lordly feast.

"If it isn't too much trouble," said the hare, "could the cook carry me back, so that I don't have to have all the dogs at my heels?"

XII

The master-cook took the hare in his arms and set off for the Hurtebise with his kitchen-boys. They followed after him two by two, carrying the filet of beef, the mincemeat, the fat capon, the quarter of venison, the dessert, and, last of all, the six bottles of wine.

The bear and the lion came at the end of the procession. On the way, it happened that the ion got thirsty. So he grabbed a bottle and took a big gulp, after which he zig-zagged a bit as he walked, to the great amusement of the Binche-folk looking out their windows.

Beside him, the bear—who was as fond of sweets as any man—wanted to be sure the cakes were nice and fresh. So he grabbed a slice of fried mud-toast and boldly crunched into it. This amused the Binche-folk even more, for they like to make fun of people.

"Here, here's for tomorrow's feast," said the bear, "for all the scamps in the window." And he grabbed an orange and threw it at the noisiest mocker.

Suddenly, there was a cry of "Now!" and from all the windows came a hail of oranges falling on his furry coat and landing right in his mouth, or anywhere! But the bear wasn't annoyed—quite the contrary!—he caught them in mid-air and sank his eager teeth into them.

The result was that, in spite of the messenger's greed, the basket reached the inn almost intact. At the sight of such a river of fine dishes, Phirin Simollet was stopped in his tracks with astonishment.

The hare jumped out of the cook's arms into Caracol's, who whispered to him, "Where did you find the princess?"

"In her chamber, Master."

"What did she seem to be feeling?"

"She seemed very sad, but when she recognized me, her eyes sparkled like two stars."

"Good!" said Caracol. Feeling easier about the princess, he told the chief cook to give her his thanks, and then turned to the inn-keeper.

"Here it is," he said, "not only the roast, but an entire dinner fit for a lord. Let's sit down and enjoy it."

Noon had just sounded as they sat down at the table, and ate and drank. And Caracol, happy as could be, gave his beasts a share, too.

When they had finished, Caracol said, "Now that I have drunk and eaten as a lord eats and drinks, I'm going to go to the castle to ask for the hand of the lord's daughter."

"Now you're going too far!" cried Phirin Simollet. "How can you expect that the princess would want to marry an ugly hunchback like you?"

"She's going to marry Bistécol."

"All the more reason she's not going to marry you!"

"I have something here that will change her plans," said Caracol. And he drew from his pocket the embroidered handkerchief that he'd wrapped around Goliath's tongue.

"No handkerchief can manage that," said Phirin Simollet. "People don't put honey in a donkey's mouth, and I'll bet my house that you'll be as welcome in the castle as a dog in church."

"Done—here's my stake," said Caracol, and he dropped on the table a purse that held a thousand gold florins.

XIII

Meanwhile, the engagement feast was going on in the castle. Seated beside the lovely Eglantine, Bistécol looked like a snail next to a rose.

The conversation was flagging, and the baron, unhappy with the match his daughter was going to make, wasn't trying to brighten the mood. His gloom gave the lie to the proverb that says:

> By the seneschal's estate
> You can know the baron's rate.

The baron was a generous soul, and he adored his daughter. During the dessert, he said to her, "What did these animals who came to see you want with you?"

"They came to see me on behalf of their master," said the princess.

"You know their master?"

"Yes, and I'd advise you to get to know him. Invite him to take coffee here—you won't be sorry if you do."

"What animals are you talking about?" asked the seneschal. He hadn't seen them, but the words put a flea in his ear.

"You'll know later," said the lovely Eglantine.

She spoke so gravely that the lord sensed some mystery behind her words and sent a squire hurrying off in a coach.

The squire arrived just when Caracol dropped his purse on the table.

"You see," Caracol said to the inn-keeper, "already, now, the baron has sent me transportation to make a proper entrance."

He climbed into the coach and commanded his animals to follow him.

The lord saw him coming with his escort.

"How must I receive him" he asked his daughter.

"Go show him the way in," said Eglantine. "You won't regret it."

The baron went to lead Caracol up to the foot of the front stairs, where he greeted him with great ceremony, and then brought him into the dining hall, with his animals following him. He invited him to take a seat opposite his daughter, while the animals sat down all around the table.

Bistécol trembled like so many walnut-shells—well, what I mean to say is, his teeth were clacking like castanets. At the first glance, he had recognized Caracol, and he could not understand how the man whose head he had cut off himself and rolled two feet away from the body could be there, alive, before his eyes.

"One might say that you're trembling, my lord seneschal," said the princess.

"Indeed, seneschal, you don't have the air of someone about to get married," the lord added. "Has the sight of these animals given you a fever?"

"Or perhaps rather the sight of their master?" said Eglantine.

"I don't fear the master any more than I do the animals," stammered the master of Malicorne, "and anyhow I don't know any of that lot."

"You have a short memory, my lord seneschal," said Caracol then, "because indeed you found yourself in the company of these beasts, and they are the proof that it was I, myself, in the forest, who drew all four of you out of the ditch where you had fallen."

"Oh? You'd fallen in a ditch?" said the baron.

"I don't remember anything of the sort," mumbled Bistécol.

"Then you probably also don't remember that yesterday you cut off my head," said Caracol dryly.

"The proof that I didn't cut off your head," said the seneschal, with more assurance, "is that it's still here on your shoulders."

"That argument," said the lord, "seems irrefutable to me."

"It can be refuted," said Caracol, "because I'm going to put back what is missing from the giant, if my lord baron will allow me to have it brought in."

"With pleasure," said the baron.

And he gave the order at once for the head of Goliath to be brought in.

XIV

"Well, what's missing from the giant's head?" he said. "Indeed, Seneschal, you must know, since it was you who cut it off."

"It's missing the left eye. I gouged it out," said Bistécol, confidently.

"What else?" said Caracol.

"What else!—why, nothing, that's all!"

"But that's not all. It doesn't have the tip of its tongue. And here it is," And Caracol opened the handkerchief, pulled out the bit of the giant's tongue, and showed that it fit perfectly onto what remained in the giant's mouth.

"So it was you," said the lord, "who cut off the tip of the giant's tongue before the seneschal chopped off his head?"

"No, no, lord Baron!—it was I who killed Goliath. But after that I was weary, and my beasts were, too, and it was while we were asleep that the seneschal chopped off my head and stole Goliath's head. Here's the proof."

He took the root of life and stuffed it in Goliath's mouth. Suddenly the eye gleamed in the giant's head, as the head came to life.

It looked at Bistécol with indifference, but when the eye fell on Caracol, it emitted sparks of lightning, and the mouth, in turn, gnashed its teeth. And it would certainly have gnawed at Caracol's hand, but he took a pair of tweezers and used it to pull the root out again.

"You see," said Caracol, "that I'm the only one this good Goliath was trying to get at. Do you need more proof? Please beg my lady to tell you who she gave this handkerchief to."

"To the giant's vanquisher," said Eglantine.

"And these collars?" added Caracol.

"To the animals who helped win that victory," said the princess.

"You swore by your hope of a share in Paradise to be silent," cried the seneschal, his rage winning out over his prudence.

"But I didn't say who the giant's vanquisher was," said the princess, with the cleverness that we know all women have.

"You yourself," said Caracol, "have now revealed your infamy, by revealing the promise you forced her to make."

"Very well, my daughter," said the baron, "you'll marry the giant's vanquisher, and you will not be any the less able to enter into Paradise. Now all we have to do is find what punishment a man capable of such a crime deserves. Should we have him torn apart by four horses, or plunged into a pot of boiling oil, or sawed in two?"

XV

At this moment, a fairy no bigger than your little finger appeared on the table, although no one understood how she got there.

She rode forward in a sapphire conch-shell drawn by four enormous gold scarab-beetles. Her coachman was a big bumblebee in a black livery relieved by lines of yellow and red. For a whip he had a cricket's bone with a bit of spider-thread, as delicate as the threads the Holy Virgin spins, hanging from the end.

"Don't you recognize me?" she said to Caracol in a sweet little voice. "I am the queen of the fairies, and it was me you saved from that wicked spider. It was the morning when, in accordance with the law by which, one day in the year, we are changed into beasts, and I had hidden myself in the woods in the form of a fly. And that's why you are going to be rewarded now, as greatly as the ingrate will be punished who wanted to rob you of your princess."

She touched him with her wand, which was a slender golden pin. At once his hump melted away, and he became as erect and well made as you and me.

"Look at that! Your promised husband doesn't have his hump anymore!" cried the baron.

"Was he a hunchback?" said Eglantine. "I hadn't noticed."

The fairy struck the lord of Malicorne, and now he had two humps, instead of one, one in back and the other in front.

"Now go and dance, seneschal," said the fairy, and the seneschal fled, in leaps and bounds, followed by the hoots of the servants, mixed with the howls and roars of the animals, who showed their joy in their own fashion.

And it's because of this that, ever since, "making someone dance" is used to mean "a severe punishment."

The marriage was held a few days after. Phirin Simollet was invited, and the Baron of Binche gave his arm to lead Caracol's mother in.

During the dessert, Caracol said to his friend Simollet, "You know that your house is mine now, right?"

"Yes, I know," said Phirin.

"Well, then! I'm giving it back to you as a present, and twelve hundred gold florins into the bargain, on condition that you sing for us:

Caracol,
Wry-neck,
Show us your horns,
Your horns.

To remind people of this curious event that—just as you can go see the Battle with the Lumçon at Mons, or the procession of Gayant at Douai—every year in the village of Ath, on the Sunday of the festival of their patron saint, they hold the Procession of Goliath. And it's not the least gorgeous or the least famous of the three festivals.

It's also in memory of Caracol and Bistécol that the Binche carnival is still the finest carnival in the Low Countries.

On Mardis-Gras, three-fourths of the Binche folk go in costume as hunchbacks, dressed in bright-colored clothes, with fine sabots on their feet, feathered hats on their heads, little bells on their belts, and two humps, one in front and one in back, all decorated with flowers made of lace.

Everywhere, people sing:

Caracol,
Wry-neck,
Show us your horns,
Your horns.

They pelt each other with oranges, and if there are still some bits of glass lying about here and there next day, you can be sure that means that there's not a single keg of beer left unopened in all the good town of Binche.

The Maids of Wheat-Marie

I

In olden times, there was a widow who lived near Valenciennes, in the village of Marly, who had two daughters, both young and beautiful, but with different kinds of beauty.

The older girl was a proud brunette, with rosy-red cheeks; the younger was a gracious blonde, with pale pink cheeks. They were nicknamed Pione and Magrite, which around here means Peony and Daisy.

They were as different in character as they were in face, for Magrite was gentle and hard-working, while people thought Pione was arrogant and lazy. The younger girl did the spinning and took care of the housework, while the older girl would get all dressed up and admire her reflection in the well.

The Count of Flanders in those days held court in Valenciennes, in his palace of the Count's Hall.

His son often went horseback riding to Marly, and, when Pione heard him coming she would run to stand in the doorway—for in her eyes only a prince was worthy to marry her.

One morning, near Christmas, when the ground was all frozen white, and Magrite had gone with her mother to the town market, Pione heard a cracked voice on the other side of the door mumbling prayers.

She opened the door and saw a beggar-woman who wore a covering of wretched burlap. She was bent over a cane and looked as old as time.

"You can go warm yourself at the fire with the dogs—they're making waffles," Pione said spitefully.

And the old pauper went, without saying a word.

II

The next day, there was a thaw, and the air was mild, and the sun shone, and Magrite was sitting on a stone bench by the wall, spinning thread on her distaff.

The beggar-woman came by again and, seeing the distaff full and the girl's hands busy spinning, she said:

The thread is well spun
And the year's well begun

Then she began mumbling her prayers again.

Magrite jumped up, went in the house, and brought out a hunk of brown bread and gave it to the old beggar-woman, saying, "Here's something for you from God, granny."

"God will repay you, my pretty girl," said the beggar. "When someone throws two grains of wheat to a sparrow, the bird takes one of them and God grows an ear of wheat from the other. Since you have showed me a soul so charitable, I grant you as a gift that the first thing you do tomorrow morning, after you've said your prayers, you shall do all day long."

Magrite stared at her in astonishment.

"I am not what you think," the old woman added. "I am Wheat-Marie, the housekeeper up above, and it is my task to cover the earth with the white mantle that keeps it from freezing. You know the proverb:

Snow on the ground is there to bless,
As for the old a warm pelisse.

"Each year, I choose a brave-hearted girl to help me during the snowy season. I've been watching you this winter. I will come back this way on the evening of Epiphany, the Feast of the Kings. Try to have finished spinning all the flax in your attic by then, for Wheat-Mary wants none in her house but maids who really know how to work."

III

The next day, when she got up, Magrite said her prayers, and then, without remembering Wheat-Marie's gift, she spread out on the table some linen that she'd taken out the evening before to cut up for hat-ribbons.

She took the linen and unrolled and unrolled it. To her astonishment, the cloth kept growing longer and longer, and the more she unrolled from it the more there was, and the roll was none the smaller.

She kept unrolling it, and unrolling it, and unrolling it, until the room was full of linen.

Magrite opened the door and called to her mother and sister. They were amazed, and they hurried to roll up the cloth on one side, while Magrite kept unrolling more from the other.

But they couldn't clear the room fast enough, and Magrite backed down the stairs, unrolling all the while, and filled the lower rooms with linen, then covered the front walk and the yard. Finally, they'd heaped up such a lot that by evening the house, from cellar to attic, was full of pieces of linen piled in heaps, one on top of another.

Now, you must know that it was fine Cambric linen, and they sold it for more than a hundred thousand shillings, and so they were able to help themselves by hiring a servant-girl.

The hunk of brown bread had thus been repaid in plenty, and yet Pione was unimpressed.

"What a fool you are!" she said to her sister. "In your place, instead of unrolling linen, I would have been counting shillings, and so by now I'd be rich enough to marry the Count's son. Just give me a chance like yours, and then you'll see!"

Every morning, as soon as she'd fed the cat, Pione sat herself down with her distaff on the doorstep and pretended to spin, but it was in vain that she waited for Wheat-Marie.

However, the evening before Twelfth Night, when she was alone in the house, she saw the old beggar coming.

"Please forgive me, my lady," she cried, as soon as she saw her approaching. "If I gave you a poor welcome the other day, it was because I hadn't really looked at you."

She set the table at once and put on it a side of bacon, some bread, some waffles her mother had made to celebrate the New Year, and then went to draw a pot of beer in the cellar. Wheat-Marie ate and drank, then thanked Pione and took her cane to start on her way again.

"Aren't you going to give me a gift as you did my sister?" said Pione.

"Yes, indeed, my pretty," said Wheat-Marie. "I will give you, too, the gift of doing all the day long whatever you start to do tomorrow when you wake up."

Pione showed the celestial housekeeper out with her most gracious smile, and that night, when she went to bed, she was careful to put a purse full of shillings under her pillow.

IV

The ambitious girl got to sleep very late that night.

She dreamt she was marrying the lord's son, and that her friends were bursting with envy.

Chantecleer's cock-a-doodle-doo awoke her, which wasn't her habit. Soon, without losing time by saying a prayer to God, she looked for the purse under her pillow.

Just then, she felt a flea run along her shoulder. She tried to catch it, but with a single bound the flea escaped her and bit her on the arm. She tried to trap it under her hand.

Suddenly the flea jumped again and was going to fasten on to her behind her ear. Pione impatiently kept after it, caught it, and killed it.

Alas! there were two more, then four, then ten, then twenty, then a hundred, all landing on her, biting her, jabbing her, stinging her feet, her knees, her sides, her arms, her head, in a thousand places.

Pione chased them, caught them, killed them, but still more followed, so many that the unlucky girl lost all hope of getting free of them.

It wasn't enough for her to scratch herself with both hands until the blood ran all down her body—she rolled back and forth on her bed, desperate, panting, foaming with rage, and she scratched—and scratched—and scratched so much that by nightfall all that was left of her, so people said, was a pair of arms scratching a skeleton.

Actually, Wheat-Marie didn't go that far in punishing her, but the naughty girl had to take to her bed for three days following.

V

On the eve of Epiphany, Magrite had been sitting since dawn beside the well, and she was just hurrying to finish off her last distaff-full, when she thought she saw the stranger at the bend in the road.

She was so excited that in her confusion she pierced her hand on the spindle. Her blood ran out and turned the spindle red. Magrite wanted to wash it in the bucket from the well, but, unluckily, it slipped from her grip and fell into the water.

Quickly, she started turning the pulley, to send the bucket down and try to fish the spindle up. Alas! in her hurry, she leaned too far over, lost her balance, and fell headfirst toward the bottom, which was shining like the starry sky.

When Magrite landed among the stars, she fainted. After a few moments, she woke up again—I don't know how soon—and found herself on the edge of a fountain. She looked all around her, surprised and charmed by what she saw. She found herself in a pleasant field, where the wheat was turning yellow. Trees were there, too, and plants and flowers such as spring up on the earth, but the trees that grew there were handsomer, the grass softer, the flowers brighter and all of it gilded by gentle sunlight.

She stood up and saw, flying just overhead, a green bird as beautiful as a bird-of-paradise.

The beautiful bird landed in a tree and sang a marvelous song, then flew away a little farther, as if inviting the girl to follow him.

She followed, and he landed on the roof of a cottage, She went in and found a stove full of bread.

"Pull me out of the oven, pull me out of the oven! I'm done!" said the bread.

She took the bread-shovel and slid the bread out.

The green bird flew a little farther and stopped on an apple tree full of apples as red as the cheeks of a girl of fifteen.

"Shake me, shake me! My apples are so heavy I'm going to break!" said the apple tree.

Magrite shook it, the apples fell, and the bird flew on.

She followed and saw a pretty little white house, covered with vines.

At the door was a lovely lady, dressed like a woman of substance.

Although Wheat-Marie looked some thirty years younger, Magrite recognized her at once,

"Welcome, little one," said the celestial housekeeper, "I was waiting for you."

"I'm at your service, good mother," said the girl, and at once she set to work.

VI

As a diligent maid, she began by scouring the kitchen utensils, and soon the red copper saucepans, big and little, shone like the sun when it bursts through the haze.

Then she washed the house with plenty of water, and, with the hearth-brush, she drew pretty designs in white sand on the threshold. Then she made the bed, and, when she started to shake out the bed-covers, Wheat-Marie said, "Go shake those outside, downstairs, under the poplars, and made sure that the feathers fly and fall into the hole there."

The serving-maid went out and stood over the hole, where she carefully shook out the feather-bed, the quilt, and the pillow.

Soon the little feathers flew through the air, and it seemed to her that they spread out and fell in white flakes that filled the air and hid the light.

And down below the good people watched as this white furry coat fell from the sky to cover the breast of the earth and keep it from freezing, and they said, with joy in their hearts, "It's snowing, it's snowing! Wheat-Marie is making her bed!"

Each morning Magrite went to the hole, and it snowed a lot that year, and the wheat grew tall, and the year was so prosperous that there'd never been one like it, not even in the records in the almanac.

In exchange for these services, Wheat-Marie taught her to make dresses, to embroider, and to make lace. Magrite learned to make lace more skillfully than anyone until then could do. And it's because of her that the lace-makers of Valenciennes have remained the best lace-makers in the world.

VII

When winter started to give way on the earth—not where Wheat-Marie was, because perpetual spring reigns there—Magrite said to her, "The snow is over for the year, and the swallows are going to come back to Marly. Would you let me go back to my mother's house?"

"Yes, my child," said Wheat-Marie.

"How can I get there?"

"Go into the barley-field and pick some of the finest stalks of hemp. You can spin a rope-ladder out of them.

Magrite obeyed, and she went to work at it with such a good will that in six weeks she had spun her ladder.

When she was ready to leave, Wheat-Marie attached one end of the ladder to a poplar tree, threw the other into the well, kissed Magrite on the forehead, and gave her a little sack, saying, "You have served me as a sensible and faithful maid. Here are your wages."

Magrite was discreet enough to wait to open the bag, and she set about bravely climbing down the ladder, and—what a wonder!—the farther she went, the longer the rope grew.

I don't know how long it took her to climb down, but when her feet touched the ground, it was night-time, and all was dark.

She noticed then that she was wearing a magnificent robe made of silk and cloth-of-gold that shone as if the good God had scattered stars over it.

When she got to the yard of the house, Chantecleer was ready to greet the dawn. He clapped his wings together and sang as loud as he could:

Cock-a-doodle-doo! Cock-a-doodle-doo!
Now the day is new! Now the day is new!

Her mother and her sister welcomed her home with great cries of wonder. People in Marly and round-about soon learned that Magrite was back, and that she had brought with her a gold robe, and the people came parading by who wanted to see the marvelous robe.

Word of this came to the Count's Hall, and the lord's daughter longed to see Magrite's robe of gold.

Magrite brought it to the palace, and at the first sight, the Count's daughter was seized with desire for it, so the Count offered to buy it for her from the peasant-girl.

The sensible girl felt that such an outfit was too fancy for her, and agreed to sell it for a thousand schillings, giving the money to her mother.

As she was a little taller than the Count's daughter, the robe was too long, and though they searched from Valenciennes to Mons, they couldn't find a dressmaker skillful enough to shorten it.

Magrite then offered to try, and they were amazed at her skill. They were even better pleased when they saw how she embroidered and made lace. The chief courtiers in the palace became so fond of her that they never wanted to part with the pretty lacemaker.

The honest girl felt she was being rewarded too generously, but when she opened her little sack, she saw there was nothing in it but a handful of grains of wheat. Pione would have scorned such a gift, but Magrite thought that Wheat-Marie no doubt had her reasons, and she took good care of the precious bag.

IX

Meanwhile, the happiness of the younger sister left the older sister unhappy, and pining away.

Although she had distrusted Wheat-Marie, she did want a robe of gold of her own, no matter what it took, and when the snows returned, she pierced her hand on a thorn-bush, let some blood fall on her spindle, then threw the reddened spindle into the well and tumbled in after it.

Like her sister, she woke in a marvelous meadow and followed the green bird. But when the bread said to her, "Pull me out of the oven, pull me out of the oven! I'm done!" she replied, "I'll take you out of the oven when the world turns topsy-turvy and hens need crutches."

And when the apple cried, "Shake me, shake me! My apples are so heavy I'm going to break!" Pione just shook her head without even bothering to reply.

Finally she came to the house of Wheat-Marie, who took her into service.

On the first day, everything went well, but on the next day, the sun had already covered a third of his day's work, when the lazy girl had not yet begun hers.

It was even worse on the days that followed. She didn't scour either the big saucepan or the little one. Wheat-Marie's bed was not made properly, and, when the maid went to the hole to shake out the bedding, she would stay there for hours on end to watch what was going on below.

That's why it snowed so little that year, and as the ground was not covered with its white coat, it froze, and only a quarter of the wheat it would have yielded ordinarily came up.

The idle girl did a little better during her last week, and, thinking that she'd done enough work, she boldly went to ask for her wages.

"Name them," said her mistress.

"Oh, well, I want a gold robe like Magrite's, but I'd rather have something better than a bag of grains of wheat."

"What, then?"

And the maid said brazenly, "I'd like a magic wand that changes everything it touches into gold."

"Here you are," said Wheat-Marie, with a scornful smile. She cut a forked branch off a hazel tree and gave it to her.

X

Pione did not dare to risk the same road back as Magrite. Wheat-Marie opened a door at the end of the yard for her, and the naughty maid suddenly found herself twenty steps from her mother's house.

Her robe didn't light up the darkness—quite the contrary. Instead of white, as it had been, it became as black as soot. It wasn't Chantecleer, but the brown owl that the naughty girl heard. Sitting in the hollow of a dead tree, the brown owl hooted, as if making fun of her:

Tu-whit! Tu-white!

Now it's night! Now it's night!

Pione ran furiously upstairs to her room, and, cursing Wheat-Marie for, as she said, cheating her of her wages, she threw the wand on the table and went to bed.

But the next day, when she woke at the stroke of noon, what was her joy to see, resplendent as the sun, her table changed to a table of pure gold!

"Now, that's as welcome as the rain in May!" she cried. Without remembering the proverb that says, "Give or take, be on your guard against a mistake!" she jumped out of bed, took the wand, and touched the chairs, the bed, and all the furniture in her room. And the chairs, the bed, and all the furniture in her room were turned to gold.

Then she called her mother, who called the neighbors, and the news spread like lightning, and all the people of Marly, Saultain, Curgies, Aulnoy, Etreux, Saint-Saulve, and Valenciennes came running in crowds to see this marvel.

The Count himself came with his courtiers. He offered to buy Pione's wand, but she refused to sell it, thinking that no one could meet the price.

XI

Now, the Count of Flanders was a greedy man, who loved gold better than anything. As he could not take possession of the precious wand, he wanted to at least have the girl it belonged to. And he offered her the hand of his son in marriage.

Pione accepted, and the contract was signed with great ceremony. But the young lord, who was not in such a hurry to get rich, asked that the marriage not take place until a year had gone by.

In awaiting the exchange of engagement rings, it was, contrary to the usual custom, the daughter-in-law-to-be who gave a bride-price to her father-in-law-to-be, and she gave him nothing less than a palace of gold.

From the cellars to the attics, she touched everything with her wand, and changed the beautiful palace of Count's Hall into thirty-two carat gold. And the palace, including its out-buildings, was immense.

The people of Valenciennes, great and small, envied the happiness of the young husband-to-be, but he himself didn't feel happy. Pione could turn everything into gold, but her pride had grown with her good fortune, and she became more and more unendurable.

XII

On the day of the engagement ceremony, while they were going in procession to Our-Lady-of-the-Hall, Pione noticed that the eyes of her future husband were turning sadly toward Magrite.

"What are you looking at?" she said, frowning. "You should be looking at me, not my conceited sister."

And she struck a violent blow on the ground with her wand.

Suddenly, all through Flanders, the ground, and everything that grew from it—grass, trees—turned into gold, and it was a magnificent sight to see.

The Count of Flanders was not annoyed to think of himself as reigning over a land of gold, and the ceremony was held, although a blow of the wand, struck by his future daughter-in-law, was a grave infraction against the laws of etiquette.

The good Flemish folk were enchanted, and considered Pione's gold much superior to the pittance Magrite had given them.

But their happiness did not last long. They soon noticed that apples of gold are much harder to digest than apples of fruit, and a land of gold doesn't have what it takes to feed its inhabitants.

Soon a frightful famine was declared, and people were starving to death from the excess of the very same stuff that people use to get the things that satisfy their appetites.

XIII

Under such circumstances, the Count called his council together, and the councilors came armored in blue goggles, for the color of all that gold was hard on the eyes. They made some fine speeches, and then parted without having found a way to melt the crust of metal.

The Count sent his trumpeters to announce that he would give his daughter's hand in marriage to anyone who could put an end to the sufferings of his subjects.

Nobody came forward, and the Count was already considering fleeing the country, along with all his vassals, when Magrite came forward timidly, and said:

"Would your lordship like to allow me to try to break the spell?"

"Try, my daughter," said the Count, "and see if you can repair the harm your sister has caused us!"

Magrite had been thinking that the little bag Wheat-Marie had given her might be just what was needed now. Perhaps the moment had come to put it to use. She drew it out of her pocket, took out a grain of wheat, and scratched at the ground with her little finger, saying, "Wheat-Marie, take pity on you!"

And something marvelous!—the crust of metal softened, like soil under the plough, and Magrite's finger sank into it without meeting any resistance.

She deposited her grain of wheat and covered it over with soil—I should say, with gold dust. A moment later, a thin blade of grain pierced the ground with its green shaft.

XIV

Soon the gold crust disappeared as if by enchantment, the sap began to rise again in the plants, the earth put on its coat of many colors, the wheat so long overdue began to grow, and, in a quarter of an hour, formed into ears of grain at the top that turned yellow as they ripened. And since then, when the ground becomes fertile each year, no one has seen any kind of gold shining in the fields except the bright yellow of the crops.

The people of Valenciennes fell to their knees, blessing Wheat-Marie, and the Count, cured of his folly, said to Magrite, "Obviously, I cannot give you my daughter, but if you would like to marry my son—take him!"

Magrite, blushing, held out her hand to the young lord, and Pione gave her assent, for she had been hiding herself for fear that the people would grab some of the gold ingots and stone her.

The marriage was held a month later. Wheat-Marie attended, and, thanks to her, that year the harvest was as abundant as it had been barren the summer before.

XV

The memory of the celestial housekeeper and her maids has not been entirely forgotten in the Flemish countryside. Less than fifty years ago, around mid-July, the carters and the ladies from Halle still used to carry Wheat-Marie in procession through the streets of Valenciennes.

For a week, the whole company, dressed in white and rose, would go from door to door. They would dance, and offer the first-fruits of the harvest, displayed on a tin platter. People would eat sweets, and, with the tips earned by the maids of Wheat-Marie, they would empty five or six bottles in the duchy of Marly, which was Magrite's home.

This festival has disappeared, like so many others that used to make good souls glad in bygone days. The world, nowadays, is so sad that it no longer knows how to have fun, and if I have brought these old stories back to mind, it wasn't with any idea of pleasing the notaries or the lawyers, but simply to amuse little kids, out playing with their toys, and their grandmothers.

Pipette's Paradise

I

In olden times, there lived in Condé-sur-l'Escaut, in the Capelette Square, an old shoe-mender. This cobbler was called Pipette, because you never saw him when he wasn't smoking his pipe.

Pipette loved his pipe so much that all through the night he would keep waking up to light it. He was a good, cheerful soul, quite the opposite of his wife, whose rough humor made him devil-may-care.

His sole grief, apart from his household, was that he didn't have enough money to buy something to celebrate Saint Crispin on Mondays, and he had to sit working away with his awl during the days of our patron saint's festival, when people were holding a lovely ball in Green Square.

"I always have to stay open," the poor shoe-mender would murmur to himself then, "and I always have to wrestle with the leather! What a rascal of a life! And to think that if it weren't for that idiot Adam, we'd live in Paradise, with nothing to do but enjoy ourselves!"

II

One summer night as he was finishing his day's work, he was repeating his usual complaint, when he saw someone going by, carrying a basket of beans. It was one of those peddlers who around here are called compénaires. He noticed that there was a hole in the basket, and the beans were falling out all along the road.

"You're losing your merchandise, friend," he said.

The man set down the basket, the cobbler offered to mend it, and the peddler accepted. When the work was done, he said, "I don't have one red cent, and all I can give you is a bean."

"Oh, my boy, it was nothing."

"Bah!—take it all the same. Who knows what might come of it!"

Pipette took the bean, and, as soon as the compénaire's back was turned, he threw it in the chimney. Suddenly, in the middle of the cinders, a green stem sprouted up, and began growing fast enough to see.

Astonished at this marvel, the good fellow ran to the door, but there wasn't anyone still there.

When he turned back to eye the plant again, it had already got into the flue. It climbed and climbed and climbed, so fast that he could no longer make out the top of it.

"That's my supper shooting up," said the cobbler. "All I have to do is go harvest it."

He relit his pipe, left the shoes still waiting to be mended, rolled up his sleeves, put both hands on the stalk, and, without stopping to remember the story of the man who went looking for wool and came back shorn, he climbed up, branch by branch. He didn't find any pods bigger than a perch for a bird, but halfway up to the sky he heard some music that seemed pleasant to him, but very different from the fiddle of Colas Chomy, the Condé violinist. The higher he climbed, the sweeter the music seemed to him, like a caress.

Meanwhile, his ladder was taking him right to the Moon. The planet seen from below looked to him like a nice porkpie in a brass dish.

The Moon grew bigger, little by little, and, when he got there, he was surprised to find it was a hundred times bigger than the town of Condé.

III

He set foot on the ground in an uninhabited spot. He walked for some time without seeing anything of the man who, they say, wanders about the Moon with his dog and his bundle of firewood, but he saw some ways off a bright light.

He drew near and saw that it came from a flaming sword that an angel was holding in his hand.

The angel was standing watch in front of a gate that opened out through a green palisade.

"Where am I, child of God?" asked Pipette.

"At the gate of the Earthly Paradise," said the guardian.

"Oh, bah!—since when was that on the Moon?"

"Since it was no longer of any use on Earth."

"Really!—Can anyone visit it?"

"One can even live there."

"For always?"

"For always—if one knows how to behave."

"Oh, my boy, there's not the least danger that I would touch your apples."

Seeing that the sentry was smiling, he added quickly, "Anyway, I hate apples! They put my teeth on edge, and keep me from smoking."

"No smoking. That's precisely what's forbidden."

"Oh! So there's no smoking? Well, let it be so."

"That doesn't scare you?—Go in, then, but remember the rule."

"Devil take me if I forget it!"

All the same, the guardian took the precaution of searching him. He took away his pipe and his tobacco, after which the good man went in, full of joy.

IV

He turned into a long avenue, bordered on each side by vast fields of hops, and at the end of a quarter of an hour he came to a belfry, with a pear at the tip of its spire.

"Now, wouldn't you just swear that there's the Condé belfry!" cried Pipette. "What a lucky chance it would be if I were to find the Capelette jokers here! Dear Lord, what games of ninepins they play! What rounds of drinks they have! What good luck! This is just what I always dreamed Paradise would be!"

Pipette did not ask himself how such a thing was possible. If the bean had led him to the Moon, he could believe anything.

It was clearly the Condé belfry, and the cobbler's heart beat happily, when he made out the four turrets and the gilded cock, perched on top of the pear, and smiling down on him in a ray of sunlight.

V

He went into the town without being stopped to go through customs or pay an entry fee, for they don't have customs officers or entry fees there. He jumped for joy as he came up to the figures of Samson and his wife that, as everyone knows, keep watch over the Valenciennes gate. He made a deep bow to Saint Roch and his dog, who looked at him solemnly from the depths of their chapel, and he came to the Swing Bridge, where he recognized the fellows who gather at the lock of the Great Canal— Marmin, Béquinet, Guerlot, Camarin—everybody!—and everybody called out a welcome to him.

"Look! Here's Pipette! Hello, Pipette!"

"Hello, my friends, hello. I'm glad to see you all in Paradise."

The town had a festival air. The port was full of barges flying their flags, the streets were well swept, and the houses were freshly white-washed, mopped, and sanded, as they are on the first Sunday of the festival of their patron saint.

The cobbler walked down Escault Street, and it led straight to his shop. At sight of him, his starling clapped its wings and cried, "Hello, Pipette!"

In turning about to reply to this courtesy, Pipette happened to look into the mirror. Oh, joy! Instead of his old wrinkled face, he saw a round, rosy face—the good fellow had grown young, and looked only thirty.

The shop seemed to him to be in order, and the household chores completed. All that was lacking was his wife, and he looked cheerfully around to see if she was there. The neighbors did not whisper a word to him.

Everyone had become young, like himself, and their faces were as open as the full moon that brings joy to your soul.

VI

Arriving there just at Evensong, the happy man went to take a pint at the Gold Broque Inn. He found all the Capelette neighborhood there, the jolliest in Condé: Polydore the tailor, Nanasse, the cabinet-maker, Firmin, the draper, Tuné, the turner, or perhaps I should say the wheel-wright.

They were playing Piquet, and drinking excellent beer, their special recipe, with barley and hops, but no one was smoking at all.

At ten o'clock the bell in the tower rang the curfew, and they stayed put for half an hour, but no one put a nose in at the door.

"Aren't there any town officials?" asked the cobbler.

"They got left down below."

"Really?"

"What use would they be here?"

"That's true—no wife and no officials. Yes, this is definitely Paradise!"

VII

It was called Paradise, a true Paradise for the Flamands, and such as we would evidently have had here below, if not for the gluttony of Mrs. Adam and her husband.

As there was an abundance of good things there, people worked at their leisure, and only as a pastime.

They had their four meals a day, and pie every Sunday, they finished the day's schedule between three and five o'clock, and then they'd go to the green to play ball games.

The bird's perch was always put up on the Quesnoy gate, and they used it as an archery target from morning to evening. They also shot at the mark, and they had long games of many kinds.

They played crosse over the meadows, and Pipette became almost as good at it as the Wheelwright of Coq, who was called the Champion Crosse Player.

Sometimes by the light of the stars, on the parade ground, all the Condé-folk—men and women, girls and boys—would sit down in a circle on the pavement and play kick-boxing, with no intention of doing any harm.

They all mixed together there higgledy piggledy, rich and poor, and the ladies with fancy hats on did not disdain to crouch down side by side with the ladies who had bonnets or caps.

In short, everyone was equal there, as we are not down here, except in the graveyard, and no one bothered to obey the proverb that says that, to have a good time, you have to sort like with like, and the Devil in with the charcoal-burners.

VIII

Pipette in Paradise encountered only one foreign face, that of the new bell-ringer who had just succeeded Grandfather Jacob and who was, besides, a superb krummhorn player in the parish.

He was a man with a crafty air, a suspicious look, a sanctimonious voice, and a big red mottled nose, which kept him from being admitted into Capelette society. He drank a pint every evening at the Gold Broque.

"What fine beer, and how the beads form on the glass!" the krummhorn player said one day, raising his glass to eye-level. "How sweet it would be to smoke a pipe while emptying a pitcher of this nectar!"

"You know very well that's forbidden!" said Pipette.

The good Flamand led a life so enchanted that he had completely forgotten his pipe. This insidious proposal brought it back to his memory, but he chased the thought away by concentrating on the happiness he tasted by the exchange.

The bell-ringer returned to this topic often, and everyone agreed with him. One fine evening, he suddenly stopped making his complaint.

After that, when a drinker was recalling the happy days when you could smoke a pipe, the krummhorn player just shrugged his shoulders and looked at him with pity in his eye.

IX

One Saturday, when he was going to ring the bells for a baptism, he called the cobbler over, who was walking in the marketplace and ogling the pretty peasant girls from Fresne and Macon.

"Come along," he said, "let's walk to the bell-tower. There's a superb view from there."

Pipette followed him and climbed all the way up to the pear on the spire. From there he saw, through a telescope, a ball that was turning, far, far away, in a pale grey cloud.

"What's that ball?" asked the cobbler.

"You don't recognize the Earth?"

"By heaven, so it is!—but what's that smoke around it?"

"That, my boy, is the cloud formed by the pipes of all the inhabitants of the globe."

"Oh! yes—those folks, they're allowed to smoke!" Pipette could not help muttering.

It was with some pain that he tore himself away from this spectacle, and he climbed down with a sigh. Some days later, he climbed up to the pear again and spent a whole hour ascending to the clock just watching the pale cloud.

He went there again, one time and another. It seemed to him that he could smell the tobacco, and, besides, by squinting his eyes, he thought he could make out the people who were smoking down there.

It was his dearest amusement, and, no matter how hard he tried to control himself, his feet invincibly brought him back to the bell-tower.

X

One morning, he found the krummhorn player at the bells, calmly lighting his pipe.

"You poor fool!" cried Pipette, "you're going to get yourself chased out of Paradise!" And he tried to take the pipe out of his mouth.

"Let it be," said the other. "I've been smoking for more than a month, and nothing's happened to me."

"Oh, bah!"

"You must know that they're making fun of us," the bell-ringer went on, blowing great puffs of tobacco in his face. "Who's harmed by it? It would be all right if we were children. But you're a man, aren't you?"

"Yes," said the cobbler, "I'm a man!" And in spite of himself he admired his friend's nerve.

"Then smoke, if you're a man, and you'll enjoy yourself like a god!"

And the krummhorn-player handed him his pipe. The cobbler looked at it out of the corner of his eye, like a cat staring sidelong at a roast chicken. It was an alluring yellow-and-black Nimy pipe. The tobacco smoke crowned his head with a wreath of gold, and Pipette inhaled with delight that exciting perfume that never rises to the nose of a good Flamand without making him reach at once for his pipe.

He was reaching out a hand, when the memory of the angel came back to his mind.

"Get thee behind me, Satan!" he cried, and went tearing down the stairs.

The kurmmhorn-player acknowledged his flight with a sneering laugh, and, when Pipette was down, in Saint-Wanon Square, the bell-ringer sent after him all the way home this mocking refrain:

> I've got some good tobacco in my baccy-box
> I've got some good tobacco, and you can't have any.

For the next six weeks, the cobbler kept up his anger at the krummhorn-player, and, when he came into the Gold Broque, he would turn his back on him so as not to see his teasing smile.

> I've got some good tobacco, worth a pretty penny
> I've got some good tobacco, and you can't have any.

Nevertheless, he soon felt an irresistible urge to go up the bell-tower again. As soon as he heard the bells, he would nudge the door open and creep out onto the stairs, where he held still, breathing in the provoking odor of tobacco.

Night and day, the poor man dreamt of his pipe, and in a town full of delights, in the bosom of the most perfect felicity, he was as sad as the stones.

XI

One day he climbed up to the carillon. The krummhorn-player wasn't there, and he had forgotten his tinder-box, his tobacco-pouch, and his pipe in one corner.

Pipette stared at the pipe a long time, took it with a trembling hand, put it back, took it again, filled it, hesitated a moment, struck a spark from the tinder-box, stopped again—then, as if seized with a frenzy, he put the pipe to his lips and lit it.

He smoked so fast, with such big puffs, that he had finished his first pipe in less time than it takes to say a Hail Mary.

He finished off a second pipeful, and a third, putting the leaves in doubled up, like a man who wants to make up for lost time. He was enveloped in a cloud of smoke, and, at each instant, he expected to see the angel with the flaming sword appear.

The angel did not appear, and Pipette felt bold enough to carry the pipe and tobacco into his house, where he smoked non-stop until the next morning.

In the evening he confided what he'd done to Tuné, who told Firmin, who told Polydore.

Thanks to the krummhorn-player, who provided them all—no one knew how—with pipes and tobacco, they all imitated him, at first secretly, indoors, but then, encouraged by finding that no punishment followed, they started breaking in their pipes in all the inns of Paradise—and it was all Pipette's fault.

Even the women started in and were glad to smoke as much as a Flemish barge-woman.

XII

Pipette gave the lie to the proverb that says that shoemakers wear the worst shoes—to go to the Moon, he had worn shoes with silver buckles and patterned insteps, as well as his nankeen-cotton britches and an

apple-green jacket with turned-up cuffs. Head to foot, he was quite the
dandy, a fine-looking fellow, and well-made, for a cobbler.

One Sunday, leaving the church, he thought he noticed a young lady, the burgomaster's daughter, who blushed as she looked at him.

Miss Jean-Codaque was as lovely as the day, and Pipette found her
very much to his taste. But even though he had become a young man, he
did not dare to lay claim to her hand.

Really, how could a poor devil of a cobbler find a way to marry the
daughter of the worthiest mynheer in Condé? What would Paradise say,
if ever the Codaques came to be connected by marriage to Pipette?

The next day, the burgomaster came to the handsome cobbler's
shop. Pipette, who was amusing himself with doing some work, politely
put away his pipe and stood up to do him honor.

"How can I serve you, Burgomaster?"

"The thing is, my daughter loves you, and, on your side, it seems to
me I've noticed—Would you like to marry her?"

"With pleasure, Mynheer!"

"Well, then, that's agreed! Come tomorrow and have dinner with us.

XIII

Pipette was overjoyed.

"You can see clearly," he told himself, "that we're in Paradise. Never on earth would Mr. Jean-Codaque, a as well off as he is, have asked
for me to marry his young lady."

From then on, he went every evening to chat with Miss Jean-
Codaque on her doorstep. One evening, she said to him, "Fie!—you
smell like a tobacco pipe. If you love me, don't smoke anymore."

Pipette broke his pipe, and what he would not do for the Creator, he
did for the creation. The marriage was going to be celebrated in state at
the end of a month.

Everybody in Condé was invited to attend the wedding, and they
filed into the church, two by two, flowers at their sides, and music in
their heads.

The flower-girls from Neuve Street went ahead of them, strewing
the pavement with leaves and blossoms. The bell in the tower rang out,
the carillon played its tunes, and the porters pulled out the cannon in all
the squares.

For three days and three nights, everyone ate pancake-rats, the kind also called beer-batter crêpes, and everyone drank themselves full of light beer and dark, and they danced everywhere. The most perfect order was observed throughout.

There was a little brawling, here and there, on the second day, when people's heads were getting over-heated, but at least they all agreed that it was brawling by choice, and no one was bothered by it.

On the third evening, more than a hundred barrels of tar were lit up, and the celebration, in the light of the splendid fire, ended in an immense bout of kick-boxing.

XIV

This time, Pipette had truly reached the height of happiness. He was no longer just on the Moon—he was on his honeymoon. Even so, he noticed one day that the star of love would be even sweeter still if he could smoke his pipe.

This idea soon nagged at him ceaselessly, and all the more because everywhere he went he ran into people who—thanks to him!—were strolling along with their pipes in their mouths.

It was an unending torture. One night he could take it no longer. He got up quietly and struck his tinder-box. The smell of tobacco woke his young wife.

"Oh! you bad boy," she said, "you're smoking, even though I asked you not to!"

"I really needed it!"

"Is it so great a pleasure, then?"

"The proof is that everyone on Paradise is smoking—all the men and all the women, except you."

"That's true enough."

"Try it, my angel, and you'll see how delightful it is!"

Adam had succumbed only to please his better half—Pipette, deeper in guilt, urged the evil on his.

He filled a pipe, lit it, and handed it to the young Flemish woman. She took it curiously, and the couple sat smoking together.

Then Pipette saw a strange sight.

The more the puffs of tobacco smoke came out of her pretty mouth, the more her young face yellowed, her lovely eyes grew hollow, her round cheeks wrinkled, and furrows lined her forehead.

"Stop!" he cried, "for the love of God, stop!"

"No, let me be. It seems to me that I'm ten times, a hundred times more alive!"

The unlucky woman had, in fact, lived forty years in a few minutes. Her husband, in the grip of the same intoxication, could not put down his own pipe.

He saw in the mirror his face was shriveling, like an apple drying in the sun, and, in spite of everything, he went on smoking, until he fell exhausted into a deep slumber.

XV

When he woke, instead of his young wife, he found an old woman beside him—his other wife, his first wife, his grumpy wife.

"Get up, you good-for-nothing, and make the coffee," she grumbled.

Pipette obeyed mechanically, still half asleep. He got up, lit the fire, made the coffee, and opened the shutters.

"Hey, aren't you going to get around to cleaning the gutters?" cried a harsh voice.

He recognized Grobohr, the town constable. No doubt of it—he had come back to earth. He set about the chore, with a broken heart and a weary spirit.

By the time the night was getting dark, the old cobbler, sitting on his stool, was again hammering leather into shape, sweating heavily. The peddler came passing by again.

"Well, my boy!" he cried, "now what do you think of that simpleton Adam?"

Pipette lowered his head and hammered away twice as hard. He thought he saw that the bean-peddler vaguely resembled the angel with the flaming sword.

Notes

In his second collection of fairy tales, Deulin structured "Gayant the Bold" as a counterpart to "Green Jeans," providing a supposed origin for Douai's popular festival as "Green Jeans" in the first volume had done for the festival in Mons. (Mons is in Belgium, and although Douai is in France, Deulin, for his long-ago setting, described it as part of Flanders.)

Both use the basic plot, popular in many fairy tales, of the hero who rescues a princess (or princesses) from a monster (or monsters) and whose deed is claimed by an impostor. "Bold Gayant" closely resembles the French tale of "The Story of John-the-Bear," although differing in many details (notably in having an affectionate mother bear rather than a ferocious father bear, and one treacherous comrade, instead of two, who receives forgiveness rather than execution). "The Story of John-the-Bear" was written down and published in 1833 by Léon Vidal and J. Delmart (they also had in their collection "The Story of Cricket," which closely resembles the second half of Deulin's "Manekin Pis."

"The Tailors' Flag" is similar to the Grimms' "The Tailor in Heaven," but adds details of the tailor's lifetime, showing him as an occasionally repentant trickster

"The Devil's Stewpot" is similar to Washington Irving's "Rip Van Winkle" and was probably modeled on it—although Irving's story was modeled on "The Goatherd," a German folktale written down by Johann Karl Christoph Nachtigal, and published in 1800. Deulin might have known this earlier version, but his version is closer to Irving's in such details as spirits in the shape of dwarfs rather than as medieval knights, and in connecting the results of the long sleep not just to the changes in the sleeper's village, but to the wider social effects of a Revolution—for Deulin's sleeper the Industrial Revolution rather than Rip's American Revolution.

"The Twelve Dancing Princesses" is similar to the Grimms' "The Shoes That Were Danced to Pieces." Deulin's cow-herd hero, a dreamer and idler, is a shyer, more wistful figure than the Grimms' pragmatical soldier. (Andrew Lang included "The Twelve Dancing Princesses" as the lead story in *The Red Fairy Book*.) There seems to be a touch of Hans Christian Andersen (whose stories Deulin knew and admired), in the detail of the princesses' delicacy, so great that they would feel a pea even through the mattress.

"The Lady of the Lights" starts as a parallel to the Grimms' "Rapunzel," but it extends the story into the heroine's marriage by adding events parallel to the story of the drowned husband in the Grimms' "The Nixie of the Millpond. The two stories are unified by having a single antagonist, the Lady of the Lights, replacing Rapunzel's witch and the nixie.

"The Nettle Spinner" appeared, somewhat abridged, in Andrew Lang's *The Red Fairy Book*. The plot is perhaps original with Deulin. He may have borrowed the detail of spinning thread from nettles to make a linen-like cloth from Hans Christian Andersen's "The Twelve Wild Swans." In the Grimm Brothers' cognate story, "The Six Wild Swans," the heroine spins thread from the more heavenly-sounding "starwort" (sternenblümen). Although Andersen is usually thought of as more literary, and less authentically folkloristic than the Grimms, in this detail it is probably Andersen who is the more traditional, as thread can actually be spun from nettles. (Starwort is not similarly useful.)

"La Ramée's Sack" parallels the Grimms' "Brother Lustig," although with many differences of detail. Deulin's version gives more attention to La Ramée's feelings, following him home to his native village, where his life, even with the magic sack, but without other resources and without family or friends still there, is not altogether as easy as he might have hoped.

The first part of "The Wolf-Oak" follows the plot of "The Tiger, the Brahman, and the Jackal," an ancient tale from India. Mauritz de Meyer's catalogue of "Les Contes Populaire de la Flandre" (in *FF Commentaires* No, 37, 1921) lists two examples of "La patte du loup dans le fente de l'arbre" ("The wolf's paw in the tree's crevice"), Belgian folktales recorded a little later than Deulin's story, but evidently cognate with it. Deulin's version extends the action with comically shocking cynicism, to reveal the Man as outdoing the Wolf in violence and ingratitude and the Fox in chicanery.

"Caillou qui Biques!" follows closely the plot of the Grimms' "Iron Hans," but expands considerably on the relationship that grows between the disguised prince and the princess, adding the theme of the importance of being sure she loves him for himself.

"The Viol d'Amore" is based mainly on literary rather than folklore sources. The traditional account of Saint Cecilia, the patron saint of music, has it that she was a Roman Christian who had taken a vow of virginity. Forced to marry a pagan, she sang songs to God in her heart. Impressed, her husband converted, and they were martyred by the Emperor Alexander Severus. Deulin, with his fondness for imagining how stories would be transformed if set in Belgium, made her a Flemish noblewoman with a love of music, instead, (For good measure, he included an origin for the sweet-toned viol d'amore, as the invention of Cecile's musical admirer.)

The idea of a romantic attraction between a lovely statue and a human man evidently reflects the legend of the young man who puts a wedding ring on the hand of a statue of Venus and is claimed by her as her bridegroom. According to Theodore Ziolkowski's *Disenchanted Images: A Literary Iconography*, the earliest known version of this legend was recorded in William of Malmesbury's *Chronicles of the Kings of England* (twelfth century). But although the legend presumably was based on a folktale version, by the time folklorists began recording folktales as such some centuries later, this story was not among the ones they found. In the early nineteenth century, writers such as Thomas Moore ("The Ring," 1802) or Prosper Mérimée ("La Venus d'Ille," 1838) revived the legend from the old chroniclers and encyclopedists. Deulin substituted his version of Saint Cecilia for Venus and made it her own promise of a gift that the statue came to life to fulfill, rather than a claim she made on her human admirer.

"Love's Desire" follows the plot of the Italian fairytale, "The Love for Three Oranges," drawing details from both of the best-known versions, the story of "The Three Lemons," by Giambattista Basile (in his collection, the *Pentamerone*, in the seventeenth century) and the play, *The Love for Three Oranges*, by Carlo Gozzi (eighteenth century). Under the title of "The Enchanted Canary," Deulin's version, slightly abridged, was included in Andrew Lang's *The Red Fairy Book*.

"The Champion Crosse-Player" is another of Deulin's variations on the theme of the cheerful rogue who manages to trick his way into Heaven (as with "The Guerliche's Nutmeg-Ball" in *Tales of a Beer Drinker*, or "The Tailors' Flag" and "La Ramée's Sack" in *Tales of King Cambrinus*). It slightly resembles his tale of "Misery's Pear Tree," as well, with the imprisoning pear tree changed to an elm-tree stump. The theme of the rogue who succeeds (or sometimes fails) at tricking his way into Heaven is found in many folktales. As in the Grimms' "Gambling Hansel" or the Norse folktale of "The Master Smith," the magical tree and the Crosse-Player's other two magical gifts are wishes given him as a reward for befriending Saint Peter.

"Caracol Bistécol" is a variation on the plot of the hero whose heroic deed is claimed by an impostor, but who manages to prove his right to the reward with the assistance of his faithful animal friends. The complication of the animals' sleepiness is similar to the Grimms' "The Two Brothers." There are many variations on the plot of the impostor's claim. Deulin himself made use of it in "Gayant the Bold" and "Green-Jeans." The Stith Thompson *The Types of the Folktale* lists a few examples of folktales of a virtuous hunchback whose deformity is magically cured, but making him the monster-slaying hero and the impostor claimant his opposite, an evil hunchback, seems to be original with Deulin. As with "Gayant the Bold" and "Green-Jeans" the story provides an origin for a local festival.

"The Maids of Wheat-Marie" combines two plots, both featuring two sisters, one kind and one unkind, who meet contrasting fates. The first part of Deulin's story follows the plot of "The Wishes" (a story recorded in many folklores). A Belgian version that Deulin may have known from an oral telling, although it was not recorded in written form until somewhat later, is "La Première Action" ("The First Action"), in *Contes Populaires du Pays Wallon* (1891), by Auguste Gittée and Jules Lemoine. The second part of the story follows the plot of the Grimms' "Mother Hölle." (Another version of this plot, not as close to Deulin as "Mother Hölle," is Charles Perrault's "Toads and Diamonds.") Deulin's version stresses Wheat-Marie's role as a nature-spirit governing the crops more strongly than the Grimms' version. Deulin closes the story with an element from the ancient Greek myth of King Midas, the disastrous Golden Touch.

For English-speaking readers, the opening of "Pipette's Paradise" with a magic beanstalk reaching to a magical realm in the sky, inevitably suggests "Jack and the Beanstalk," but such beanstalks occur in a variety of folktales. Deulin might have known an oral version of "Rougedos et son Sifflet" ("Redback and his Whistle"), recorded in in Gittée's and Lemoine's *Contes Populaires du Pays Wallon* (1891), in which Rougedos, like Pipette, climbs up to Paradise on the magic "feuille de Rome" ("Rome-leaf"). The narrative does not specify just what sort of plant that is, but an editorial footnote points out that in similar stories the plant that grows so prodigiously is generally a bean. The rest of the story is not otherwise like "Pipette's Paradise," which seems to be largely original with Deulin, although the basic theme, of the foolish man who boasts that he would have resisted temptation in the Garden of Eden better than Adam did, can be found elsewhere. Deulin would have known Hans Christian Andersen's "The Garden of Paradise." He might also have known an early literary version, the thirteenth of Jacques de Vitry's *Exempla* (1200)—Joseph Jacobs, recording an English version of this plot, "A Son of Adam," in his *More English Fairy Tales* (1894), remarked that a parallel to de Vitry's Exemplum had been collected as an Italian folktale. But their treatments of the basic theme are all quite different.